Since winning the Catherine Cookson Prize for Fiction for her first novel, *The Hungry Tide*, Val Wood has published twenty novels and become one of the most popular authors in the UK.

Born in the mining town of Castleford, Val came to East Yorkshire as a child and has lived in Hull and rural Holderness where many of her novels are set. She now lives in the market town of Beverley.

When she is not writing, Val is busy promoting libraries and supporting many charities.

Val is currently writing her next novel and has no intention of stopping!

Find out more about Val Wood's novels by visiting her website: www.valeriewood.co.uk

www.transworldbooks.co.uk

By Val Wood

THE HUNGRY TIDE
ANNIE
CHILDREN OF THE TIDE
THE GYPSY GIRL
(previously published as THE ROMANY GIRL)
EMILY
GOING HOME
ROSA'S ISLAND
THE DOORSTEP GIRLS
FAR FROM HOME
THE KITCHEN MAID
THE SONGBIRD
NOBODY'S CHILD
FALLEN ANGELS
THE LONG WALK HOME
RICH GIRL, POOR GIRL
HOMECOMING GIRLS
THE HARBOUR GIRL
THE INNKEEPER'S DAUGHTER
HIS BROTHER'S WIFE
EVERY MOTHER'S SON

THE MAID'S SECRET (available as ebook only)

CHILDREN
OF THE TIDE

Val Wood

CORGI BOOKS

TRANSWORLD PUBLISHERS
61–63 Uxbridge Road, London W5 5SA
A Random House Group Company
www.transworldbooks.co.uk

CHILDREN OF THE TIDE
A CORGI BOOK: 9780552171274

First published in Great Britain
in 1996 by Corgi Books
an imprint of Transworld Publishers
Corgi edition reissued 2014

Addresses for Random House Group Ltd companies outside the UK
can be found at: www.randomhouse.co.uk
The Random House Group Ltd Reg. No. 954009

The Random House Group Limited supports the Forest Stewardship
Council® (FSC®), the leading international forest-certification organisation.
Our books carrying the FSC label are printed on FSC®-certified paper. FSC
is the only forest-certification scheme supported by the leading environmental
organisations, including Greenpeace. Our paper procurement policy can be found at
www.randomhouse.co.uk/environment

Typeset in New Baskerville by Kestrel Data, Exeter, Devon.
Printed and bound by CPI Group (UK) Ltd, Croydon, CR0 4YY.

2 4 6 8 10 9 7 5 3 1

For my family with love

Acknowledgements

General sources of information.

A History of Hull, by Edward Gillett & Kenneth A. MacMahon. (Hull University Press 1989)

Ragged London in 1861, by John Hollingshead. (Everyman Classics 1986)

The National Railway Museum, Leeman Road, York.

The Wellcome Institute for the History of Medicine, 183 Euston Road, London.

My thanks to Clive Bowes, Curator, Skidby Mill, East Yorkshire, for his invaluable help into the aspects of milling;

to Chris Ketchell, Local History Unit, Park Street Centre, Hull College, for information on cholera in Hull in the nineteenth century;

and to Peter Burgess for the generous loan of his research material into the opening of Pearson Park and the Music Halls of Hull;

to my daughter Catherine for her assistance once again.

Note

The celebrations and opening of Pearson Park, Hull, in August 1860, was an actual event, and Zachariah Pearson, the benefactor and Mayor of Hull, a real person. The dialogue between him and the fictional characters is imaginary.

1

It was a long walk from Hull to Anlaby. It was also an unknown country as far as the woman was concerned. A country far removed from the mean streets of Hull. She raised her head and sniffed. For a start, there were no foul smells, but for another, the road was lonely and therefore threatening. She shifted her bundle from one arm to the other. The child wasn't heavy, how could it be, being only a few hours old? It was merely unwieldy, a cumbersome parcel that was unwanted. An anger began to envelop her, an anger which displaced the lethargy and dullness that usually swamped her mind. The anger was not directed at the babe, but at life itself for giving her this heartache, a life given an additional sorrow for the daughter she had lost.

The iron gates loomed large in front of her. On one of the pillars which held them, a name was etched into the stone: Humber Villa. This was it. This was the name she had been given when she had asked for directions to the Rayners' house.

As she trudged up the long gravelled drive she kept her eyes straight in front, ignoring the sweep of lawn and the scent of blossom, intent only on mounting the short flight of steps and reaching the panelled front door topped by a coloured fanlight, and ringing the bell before changing her mind and tearing back to Hull, no matter what the consequences.

'Back door if you please!' The housekeeper was terse. It had taken her only a second to know that she wasn't the sort of person to be admitted to the front of the house.

The woman put her foot inside, blocking the door's closure. 'Fetch Mr Rayner – the young 'un. I've got summat here belonging 'him.'

Sammi looked across at her cousin James as he stretched himself and fidgeted in the deeply buttoned chesterfield and adjusted the tapestry cushions behind his back. He gave her a wry grin and she smiled back; he was bored, she could see, and so was she.

Do come, he had said in his letter to her. *It will be the dullest birthday ever if you don't. I wish I was back at school with the other fellows.* So she had come, bringing with her a puppy as a birthday present, which now snored gently on her lap, and she thought that she would be happy to leave in the morning when her father's carriage came to take her back to her home at Monkston, a village in Holderness, which sat at the edge of the sea.

James's mother and his sister Anne were both sitting silently, busy with their sewing, as they waited for his father Isaac and his brother Gilbert to arrive home from the family firm of Masterson and Rayner, the shipping merchants, so that they might begin supper. The chime of the longcase clock in the hall broke the silence, and the sound of the front door bell made them all shuffle and rouse themselves expectantly.

'Gilbert's mislaid his key again,' James remarked, and when Mary knocked and opened the drawing-room door, it was expected that she would announce that Mr Rayner and Gilbert would be down as soon as they had changed.

'Beg pardon, ma-am.' She bobbed her knee. Her face was slightly flushed and she fiddled nervously with the frilled bib on her white apron. 'There's a person at the door – a woman – she wants to see Master James.'

'A person? What kind of a person?' Mildred Rayner

looked up from her tapestry. 'Who is this, James, calling at such an inconvenient hour?'

'I've no idea, Mama. Did she give a name?'

The housekeeper shook her head. 'No, sir, she just said she had something belonging to you.'

'You must have lost something, James, your watch or pocket book.' Anne folded up her sewing and put it on a pedestal table at her side, then glanced at her brother. 'She probably wants a reward for finding it. Does she look the sort who would want a reward, Mary?'

Mary looked uncomfortable. 'I wouldn't like to say, Miss Anne. She's not the usual kind of caller.'

'Whatever do you mean?' Mildred Rayner's voice, which was quite often sharp, had an even icier edge to it. 'Is she at the front door?'

'Yes, ma-am. I'm afraid she is. I told her to go to 'back, but she put her foot inside so that I couldn't shut it.'

Mrs Rayner put down her tapestry and rose to her feet, her purple supper gown rustling.

'It's all right, Mother,' James cautioned her. 'I'll go if it's me she wants to see, though I can't think that I've lost anything.'

The firelight cast a rich glow on Sammi's red hair as she sat beside it in a deep leather chair. 'But you know how absent-minded you are, James.' She gently fondled the puppy's soft ears. 'You put things down and then forget where you have put them. You've probably not missed whatever it is you've lost.'

He gave a rueful grimace, got up and went to the door, then he turned and with an inclination of his head gestured her to follow him. The outer front door was partly open, but not held by the offending foot, and as James opened it wider he saw the woman standing at the top of the steps with her back to him, looking out at the garden.

'Can I help you? I'm James Rayner.'

The woman turned. Mary had given no indication

13

of the woman's image, except in describing her as a *person*, and his eyes widened at the sight of someone in such a ragged, miserable state as the woman staring at him, with such a hopeless, resigned look upon her face.

'You're young Mr Rayner, are you?' Her voice, though coarse, trembled a little.

'Yes. I am.' His brows creased and Sammi, standing behind him, wondered whatever could this poor wretch want with James?

The woman stepped inside uninvited and put out her arms, thrusting a bundle towards him. Instinctively he put out his hands and took it. 'Then I'm returning what belongs to thee.'

'What's this? What are you giving me?'

The sitting-room door opened and his mother's footsteps clicked on the tiled hall floor. 'What is it, James? What's happening?'

Her imperious tones rang out and he turned to look at her in some bewilderment. 'I don't know. She's given me this.'

'It's a baby!' Sammi reached to look over his arm. 'Why is it here?'

'It's here, miss, because this is where it belongs.' The woman gazed stonily at Mildred Rayner, even though it had been Sammi who had asked the question. 'This babby belongs to 'young master here.'

James gave a short nervous laugh and made to hand back the bundle. 'You've made a mistake, I'm afraid. This has nothing to do with me.'

The woman stepped back out of his reach, almost knocking over a pedestal which held a potted palm. 'If tha's young Mr Rayner, then it's thine.' Her voice took on a harsh, rough quality. 'My daughter vowed it.'

'Then your daughter is either very much mistaken or she's a liar,' Mildred Rayner cut in. 'Why isn't she here with her false accusations? If you or she think

14

you'll get money out of us then you're on a wasted errand.'

The woman looked at her with contempt. 'I'm not after money, I'm just bringing 'bairn back where it belongs. Me daughter's dead. She died giving birth. It was her first babby and, God rest her, it was her last.' She inclined her head towards the door. '*He* said that I had to bring 'bairn here, we can't feed 'ones we've got, let alone another.'

James's face had become sheet white. 'I don't understand. Who is *he*, and why should you think it has anything to do with me?'

Sammi went to take the baby from him, and he handed it over, trance-like. She undid the thin blankets which wrapped it and a wisp of her hair from beneath her lace cap touched its face as she bent over. 'Why! It's such a new baby. It shouldn't be out, it should be in a warm crib!'

The woman shook her head, a mocking twist on her lips. 'A warm crib, miss? And what would that be? An old drawer more like, or a bit o' damp straw!' She turned towards James who was staring open-mouthed at her. 'My daughter confessed to me and her da that babby was thine. She'd allus been a truthful lass and there was no need for her to lie. She's not here to take care of it and so I've brought it here.' She reached out for the doorknob, and looked James directly in the eyes. 'Responsibility's thine, sir.' She opened the door and, before anyone could make a move, was gone.

It was Anne who broke the silence. She had been staring at James with her eyes wide and her hands clutched across her mouth. 'You wicked reprobate! How could you? How could you mix with such people?' She started to shriek at him. 'You dirty, filthy creature, you're as dirty as that – that – awful woman.' She half ran towards him, her feet making pattering noises in her neat slippers, her small white fists raised. 'I never want to speak to you again.'

Her mother moved to stop her. 'Don't be so ridiculous, Anne. There's been a terrible mistake.' She glanced round and spotted Mary hovering by the door leading down to the kitchen. 'Quickly, run after her. Make her come back. Tell her she's got the wrong people!'

Mary darted a glance at James and at Sammi, still holding the baby, and then back to her employer. She nodded. 'Yes, ma-am.' Her voice was scared and tearful, and she had a flush on her cheeks as she rushed out of the door.

James ran his fingers through his thick, dark hair and paced the small area of floor between the clutter of furniture in the sitting-room, whilst his mother and sister stared stony-faced into space, and Sammi silently sat holding the baby. Mary had run down the drive and part of the way down the road and come back, breathing heavily, unused to such exercise, and unable to find the woman.

'It's nothing to do with me!' James burst out. 'How can I convince you? I didn't – haven't! I've never—' *How can I possibly speak to them of such things?* How could he tell his female relatives that he had never been with a woman? That he was still in a state of celibacy, even though he had impulsive yearnings to be otherwise.

'Here's your father.' The front door banged and they heard the murmurings of voices as Mary greeted Isaac Rayner. Mildred Rayner's voice trembled and she didn't look at her son as she spoke. 'He'll know what to do.'

James felt sick with apprehension. He and his father had had a long talk just a few days ago, when it was outlined what was expected of him now that he had finished school. James, who was undecided over a career, could take three months to think about it, and if he hadn't decided in that time then he must either join his father and Gilbert in shipping, or join the army. He didn't want to do either, but the

16

problem was that he didn't know what he wanted to do. His drawing master at school in York had said he should become a painter, he had even offered to buy one of his water-colours, but James, embarrassed though flattered, had made him a gift of it.

'Ask Cook to delay supper, Mary. I'll ring the bell when we're ready.' Mildred Rayner stood up as Isaac came into the room. 'And please do not mention this, er, incident to the other staff.'

'No, ma-am.' Mary bobbed her knee and carefully closed the door.

'What incident?' Isaac kissed his wife on her proffered cheek. 'Why can't we eat? We're already late. I waited for Gilbert, and then he decided he would stay over in Hull. There are people he wants to see about the new house.'

'Oh,' Mildred tutted. 'How annoying.' She turned to her daughter, who was sitting at the other side of the room, as far away as it was possible to get from James. 'Anne, you'd better go to your room whilst I speak to your father. You too, Sarah Maria.'

Sammi looked up at her aunt; she was the only one in all the family who called her by her full name. Aunt Mildred had definite views on names as well as most other subjects; a pedant, Sammi's father called her whenever he had a verbal brush with her. 'May I stay, Aunt? The baby is very comfortable.'

'No, you may not. Please go upstairs with Anne until I call you, and take the – the child with you.'

'Wait a minute, wait a minute. What baby? What is this?' Isaac noticed for the first time the wrapped bundle in Sammi's arms.

Anne was hesitating by the door, but on seeing her mother's clenched lips and interpreting her mood, left the room without waiting for her cousin.

'Where has it come from? Why is it here?' Isaac peered down at the baby. 'Of course, it can't be yours, Sammi? It wasn't here this morning!'

'Of course it isn't hers! Don't be so ridiculous,

Isaac.' Mildred put her hand to her head. 'I think I'm feeling unwell.'

Isaac rushed to draw a chair for his wife and Sammi rose to her feet, while James, in a stupor, just stood and stared at them all.

James found his voice. 'A woman brought it. She said it's mine.'

'Yours!' His mild-mannered father's voice thundered out. 'What did she mean, yours?'

The two male members of the Rayner household stared at each other. James, struck dumb with fright and apprehension, and his father speechless with amazement.

Isaac looked at his wife as she leaned forward in the chair, her hands over her eyes. 'Sammi, take your aunt to her room, she'd better lie down, and you stay upstairs until I call you.'

'Yes, Uncle Isaac.' There would be no persuading him otherwise. Her uncle was angrier than she had ever seen him.

'You young dog! How dare you? How dare you upset your mother in such a way?' Isaac raised his voice again once the ladies had gone, his face was pale, but with an angry spot of colour on each cheek. 'Why has the child been brought here? Who is this woman you have got into such trouble? Is she marriageable?'

'Sir – Father. I don't know. I've never – there's been a mistake.' James implored. 'The woman who came said that it was her daughter's child, and that she is dead. She said that her daughter told her it was mine!' He started to sob. 'It can't be mine, sir. It's just not possible.'

Isaac frowned. 'What are you telling me? That you haven't – that you haven't been with a woman?'

James nodded miserably and wiped his eyes. 'I think I would remember, sir.'

'I imagine you would,' Isaac said, his manner calming. 'Are you absolutely sure? You hadn't been

18

drinking and things got out of hand? Think, man! Work back nine months.'

'Nine months, sir?'

'Nine months! That's how long it takes for a baby to grow. Good God, James. Don't you know anything? Surely – the fellows at school . . .'

James shook his head. He'd never really listened to the lewdness or salaciousness of some of his fellow students in York. He and his friends discussed music, the arts and literature, they didn't steal out of the college buildings to meet women, or get drunk and have to climb up a drainpipe to get back into their rooms. They had, of course, to put up with many obscene suggestions from some of their fellows, but as he didn't always understand some of the comments, they didn't really bother him.

I've only been drunk once, he thought. *And that was Gilbert's fault. He was the one who kept plying me with strong ale. It was the night Gilbert had announced his engagement to Harriet Billington. When was that? During last summer before I returned to school. Gilbert insisted that I stay with him in Hull to celebrate.* The colour suddenly drained from his face and he sat down abruptly, even though his father was still standing. There had been a girl. Two girls. Gilbert had met them outside the inn where they were going to stay the night rather than drive back home, and he'd brought them in to join them. 'It might be my last taste of freedom,' he'd whispered in James's ear. 'That's why I didn't want to stay with the Billingtons, even though I was invited.'

'What's the matter with you? Are you ill?' His father's voice came from far away.

'Not ill, sir. I've just remembered something.' He'd been mildly shocked at his elder brother. He thought that he might well have stopped his philandering now that he was to marry the sweet and gentle Harriet, but James was already under the influence of the strong Hull ale and in no state to dissuade his brother. Besides, the girls were pretty, he remembered; one of them very pretty indeed and rather shy. The other was rather worse for drink and had clung on to him as they'd climbed the stairs to the room which he and Gilbert were to share.

The dashed thing was that he couldn't remember anything else. The shy pretty one had sat beside him, but the next thing was that it had been morning and he was still lying cramped on the sofa. His head had felt as if it had had a hammer blow, and his mouth was as thick as a crow's nest. The girls had gone and Gilbert was asleep in the bed.

'Well! Come on, sir. What have you remembered? Is the child yours or not?' His father was standing in front of him, urging him to answer, his face anxious.

Was it possible? he thought. Could he have taken that girl and not remembered? Was she experienced enough to know what to do? He dare not for the life of him ask his father if it was possible. The only person he could ask was Gilbert, and he wasn't here, and if he had been, without a doubt he would have laughed.

'I think, sir, that perhaps it could be.'

His father, with an exclamation, turned from him. 'You young fool! You're going to have to pay these people to take it back, you know that don't you? We can't have any scandal, your mother would be simply furious. And we've Gilbert to think of, we don't want anything stopping his marriage. And then there's Anne, young Mark Tebbitt is hovering.' He turned to James and shook his head more in anguish than anger as he quietly said, 'Totally selfish, James. You should have thought of the consequences before taking your pleasure.'

James nodded dismally. The one time in his life, the anticipated joy of manhood, and he couldn't even remember it.

* * *

'Mary!' Sammi called in a whisper through the kitchen door. 'I think the baby needs a drink. Can you bring some warm milk and an old sheet?'

Mary nodded conspiratorially. 'Yes, miss.'

She can never have known such excitement in all the years she has been here, Sammi thought as she went up to the guest room. It was usually a very dull household unless James was there, and he'd certainly put the cat among the pigeons now. How on earth had the woman got his name? She doubted that the accusations levelled against her cousin were true. *He's such a child himself,* she mused as she laid the infant on the high feather bed. *He probably doesn't even know how babies are made. Although,* she pondered, *that wouldn't actually prevent him from making one.*

Anne knocked and opened the door. 'Is Father very angry?' she whispered. 'Is he turning James out?'

Sammi looked at her in amazement. 'Turn him out? But where would he go?'

'I don't know, nor do I care.' Anne drew herself up to her full height, which wasn't very great, and smoothed her hands down her sprigged muslin gown. 'I only know that I shall never speak to him again in my life.' She gave a dramatic shudder, and a single false ringlet from her upswept fair hair danced about her neck. 'He's despicable.'

'Nonsense.' Sammi started to take off the baby's thin blanket and it moved, stretching its tiny mouth and nose. 'We don't know for sure that this *is* James's child. Poor little mite. Come on, let's have a look at you; see what you are.'

'Sammi! What are you doing? You're not going to undress it?'

'Of course I'm going to undress it. How else will we know if it's a boy or a girl? Anyway, it needs some clean clothes. Is that all right?' she added, suddenly remembering that this wasn't her home and that the rules were different. 'I asked Mary for an old sheet.'

Anne shrugged. 'I suppose so.' She dropped her voice. 'But can you tell? What kind it is, I mean?'

Sammi laughed. Anne was seventeen, not much younger than her. Surely, surely she knew? She had two brothers, after all. 'Have you not seen a baby undressed before?' she asked. 'But you've seen kittens, and puppies like Sam?'

Anne averted her eyes. Her cheeks flushed. 'Of course not. I wouldn't look. It's not the thing to do. It's rude.'

Sammi unwrapped the thin scrap of sheet which swaddled the baby. 'Well, whether it's rude or not, there he is. It's a boy.'

The supper bell still hadn't rung, even though half an hour had elapsed since they had been ordered out of the room by her uncle, so Sammi decided that she would risk going down. She knocked tentatively on the sitting-room door and walked in. She had left the baby in her room, having taken an empty drawer out of the bottom of the wardrobe and placed him in it. She had given him a spoonful of milk and wrapped him in a clean sheet, though not bound so tight as it had been.

'Uncle Isaac!'

Her uncle had his back to her, with one arm leaning on the mantelshelf and studiously watching the fire burning in the grate. On the shelf, a collection of coloured glass was reflected in a gilt-edged mantel mirror, and in the flickering firelight and the glow from a table lamp and tall candles, the dark mahogany furniture gleamed.

'Uncle Isaac. If you haven't yet decided what to do, I have a suggestion.' She glanced at James. He looked terrible. His face was pale and his hair awry.

'I have decided.' He turned to her and he had, she thought, such a sorrowful look about him. 'But you mustn't bother your head, my dear. This is not a suitable subject for you to be worrying about, and I'm only sorry that you have become involved.'

'Oh, I'm not worrying, Uncle. I only want to help James. I just thought that if we went to try and find the woman, we might persuade her to take the baby back. We might find out also why she thinks he belongs to James.'

'My dear, that is what I intend. We're waiting now for Spence to bring round the carriage. We shall try to find the woman, she can't have got far down the road, if indeed she is making her way to Hull, as I suspect she might be.'

'I'll get my cape then.' Sammi turned for the door.

'What? But you can't come. Good heavens, no.' Isaac pulled down his grey waistcoat and then fiddled with his watch chain. 'What are you thinking of, Sammi? I wouldn't dream . . .'

'But you are taking the child with you? So who is going to hold him?' she asked quietly. 'You, or James?'

He coughed and humphed. 'Well, I er, I was wondering about that. I did think of asking Mildred,' he muttered as if to himself, 'but no, perhaps not.'

'Aunt Mildred has gone to bed, and Anne doesn't want to talk to James. So there's only me, unless you ask one of the servants.'

'Oh no. Out of the question. We mustn't let this get out, James's mother would be most upset. Mary wouldn't mention it, I'm sure, but the others! Well – very well. Go and get your things.'

As she turned to go upstairs, she wondered what had been said which had turned her uncle's demeanour from anger to such obvious distress.

2

The woman kept in the shadow of the trees and bushes. She had known that someone would come looking for her to fetch her back, to offer her money or some inducement to keep the child. She saw the maid run down the drive and out into the lane, whilst she watched from the safety of the garden. When she saw her return and enter the house, she felt it safe to leave and make her way back down the long, lonely Anlaby Road, towards Hull.

'He'll be all right there,' she muttered. 'If they'll keep him.' She fantasized about this mansion that he would live in, the food he would eat, the warm bed he would sleep upon, how he would play and tumble in the garden. *If they keep him. If they don't take him to the workhouse.* That worried her a lot, and she knew that she would have to check; she would have to call at the hospitals and charity homes which housed the unwanted and the very poor. 'For, God forbid,' she muttered, 'I couldn't do that to him; not to my own.'

She moved back into the shadows as a carriage drove towards the hamlet of Anlaby. Some nob going home to a good supper, she surmised, and ran her hand over her own swollen, empty belly.

The young girl looked kind, she reflected, *young Rayner's sister perhaps? She seemed to know how to handle bairns. Perhaps she would persuade 'lady that they should keep him, though I have my doubts about that; and 'young man — why, I would never have guessed it, little more than a bairn himself, an innocent, I would have thought, but there, there's no telling what can happen when passion's aroused, it makes no difference if tha's fifteen or fifty.*

As she approached the outskirts of the town, several carriages and gigs passed her by, and again she kept to the shadows; she mingled with the crowds who were making their way to the inns and hostelries, and slipped unnoticed into the maze of alleyways and dark courts which clustered about the river, and opened the unlocked door to her home.

Her body felt heavy and bloated as she slumped onto the bed; her feet and ankles were swollen from the unaccustomed long walk, and the veins in her legs stood out, purple and knotted. Two children lay awake in the bed, and another was asleep under the thin blanket. She gazed fixedly at her husband, his mouth open as he slept in the only chair, and wondered what had happened to the passion that they had once shared.

He was so handsome, so strong, full of hope and optimism. We used to sing and dance, be happy. Now he's bitter and melancholic and all we have is despair. A tear trickled down her cheek. *At least Silvi had been young and lovely, she'll never grow old and ugly like her ma, and I hope, oh how I hope, that 'bairn was born of love and not abuse.*

Her husband stirred in the chair, then he opened his eyes and saw her watching him. 'Well? Is it done? Did tha tek him?'

She nodded wearily. Who, she wondered, would take care of her children when she had gone?

'How much did they give thee?'

'What?' She gazed at him through glazed eyes.

'Did they give thee owt? Money!'

Perplexed, she shook her head.

'Daft bitch! Didn't tha ask?' He sat forward in the chair, staring at her with hatred in his eyes.

'Ask? Ask? Would I ask for money when his ma is only just dead?' Her voice sank to a whisper and she put her head in her hands and started to sob. 'I've not yet sunk so low that I'd sell my own grandson.'

He got up from his chair and she thought that he was going to strike her as he came near, but he sank down beside her on the narrow bed and put his arms around her, his head against hers, and held her close, and joined her in her weeping.

The brougham rattled along the turnpike road towards Hull, and James and his father peered out of each side of the carriage windows in an attempt to see anyone who might be walking along the road. Spence stopped once, as he had been instructed to do, should he see anyone, but it was only a vagrant with a pack on his back, who asked them if he could ride alongside the coachie. He was refused, and they continued on slowly, stopping occasionally when James or Isaac called out that they thought something had moved in the hedge.

As they approached Hull they passed the redbrick workhouse, and Sammi gave a small shudder and held the child closer. If they couldn't find the woman who had brought him, she didn't want to contemplate the fate which awaited him. 'Where will you start to look, Uncle? Who will you ask?'

Isaac gave a deep sigh. 'I'm not sure; I suppose I'll try the clergy. We'll try the Holy Trinity first, they'll no doubt know if any of their congregation has gone astray. A child is hardly something that can be hidden.' He stopped abruptly as if he had said too much and Sammi knew that, had she been able to see him, his face would have been red with embarrassment.

'They may not be church-goers, Uncle.' More than likely not, she thought. The poor ragged woman wouldn't have been welcome among the estimable congregation. She probably did her praying at home, if she had one.

'Chapel, you mean? You think that she might be chapel?'

'No, Uncle. Having seen her, I think she wouldn't

have the energy or inclination for either. Why not try some of the inns? They are more likely to know the people who live in the town.'

'Sir!' James had hardly spoken on the journey, and had mostly kept his eyes glued to the carriage windows. Now he turned towards his father. 'Perhaps we could try The Cross Keys. The landlord might remember.'

His father drew in a sharp breath. James had told him that the only occasion when something might have happened was when he had stayed the night in town with Gilbert, though he was careful not to implicate his brother.

The Cross Keys Inn was a busy coaching inn and stood opposite the golden statue of King William in Hull's Market Place. It was also the departure point for the coaches to York and London, whose services were still flourishing while the North Eastern Railway board of governors and the town aldermen wrangled over where the next railway line should run. There was an arrow-straight railway track between Hull and Selby, and others not so straight to Bridlington and Withernsea on the coast, which had opened up the possibility of day excursions to see the sea.

But the crowds of people who were passing the carriage as Sammi waited for James and his father to come out of the inn were not the kind who would be travelling by rail or coach. They teemed by on their way home from work, if they were lucky enough to be employed, from the oil or flax mills in Wincomlee, from the shipyards or the docks, and they spent their money and sought relaxation and entertainment in the streets of Hull.

And if they were not employed, they still came out of their overcrowded, dismal houses which were squeezed together in the squalid streets and courts in the heart of the old town, searching for simple pleasures: dogfights or prize-fights made them forget their misery and poverty, and gave them their only

27

taste of excitement, or if that failed, they pursued oblivion in drink.

Sammi crouched into a corner of the carriage so that she wouldn't be seen, and felt the occasional thud on the carriage door when someone banged it as they went by. There was some coarse bantering as well-dressed visitors arriving at the inn mingled in the street with the ill-fed and ragged poor, with beggars and thieves.

A face pressed against the window and leered in at her; she heard Spence shout to get away and a minute later she jumped in fright as the door handle rattled and then opened, but it was only James and his father come back from a fruitless errand.

'We've drawn a blank there, I'm afraid. The fellow's not talking, even if he knows anything.' Isaac sat down beside her and took off his top hat and tapped it thoughtfully. 'We could get out and walk and ask a few people. They might talk if persuaded by a copper or two, but I don't like to leave you here with only Spence.'

'I'd rather come with you, Uncle Isaac. If we find the woman and she sees the child, she might have second thoughts about abandoning him.'

'Very well. We'll walk a little way, although I fear we must be alert constantly.'

Sammi realized that her uncle would know of the dangers. His office was not far from the Market Place, in the old High Street which ran alongside the River Hull. It was an area which, though safe enough during the day, at night the inns and taverns would be overflowing with seamen and travellers, and others who might be on the lookout for easy money, and who would not be too particular or discriminating about delivering violence in order to get it.

She wrapped the infant inside her cape, and James and his father came on either side of her. She was glad that she was dressed in her plain cape and bonnet, but wished that she had changed from her

28

flounced silk gown which she had dressed in for the ill-fated supper, and which peeped from below her cape. Her uncle, though, was conspicuous in his greatcoat and top hat and with his silver-topped cane clutched firmly in his hand. James, though hatless, was wearing a velvet coat and a cravat at his neck, and both men, she thought, summed up the epitome of wealth.

They moved away from the inn, following the crowd down from the northern end of the Market Place towards St Mary's Church where there were several inns and grocery shops and all manner of business premises, and which led ultimately to the Queen's Dock, the first dock to be built in this town of shipping, whaling and fishing. Here, too, in this crowded area were banks and brothels, alms-houses and pawnbrokers, temperance houses and sailors' mission homes.

'I think we must go back,' Isaac said nervously. 'The crowd is too great. We'll turn around and knock on someone's door. It will be a start at least.'

The first door on which they knocked was in Vicar Lane, a quiet street near the ancient Holy Trinity church.

'A respectable place,' Isaac said. But it was so respectable a place that the residents of the house wouldn't open the door to their knock. A twitch of curtain was the only indication of anyone's presence within, and although they all thought they had seen a glow of candle flame as they approached, the house was now in darkness.

'Here's someone coming, Father. Should we ask?' James's voice was husky as he whispered.

Isaac nodded and called out to a man approaching them. The man stood back, he appeared as nervous as they were. 'I'm looking for the family of an infant. The child has been abandoned or lost, it needs immediate attention if it is to survive.'

The man came closer and stared curiously at them.

'If it's been abandoned, then whoever abandoned it didn't intend it to survive. Where did tha find it?'

'Oh, er, out in the country.' Isaac pulled up his coat collar and adjusted his scarf so that it hid the lower half of his face.

The man grunted and started to move away. 'Then I don't know why tha's bringing it here, sir. If it's a country bairn tha'd better look elsewhere. There's enough starving infants round here without bringing 'em in from out of town.' He walked away down the dark street and then turned back. 'Tha could try workhouse, but I doubt if they'd tek it. They're all full up and they'll onny tek bairns from Hull.'

They moved out of that street and down others, and once more knocked on other doors, but again there was no answer except from the bark of a dog. They heard a cough and rattle of someone clearing his throat and saw the movement of a dark bundle huddled in a doorway, and they quickly turned away. Then came the sound of loud voices and a crowd of people turned the corner.

Women were laughing and Sammi determined that this time she would speak. 'Uncle, please may I ask this time? They may tell me something, being another female.'

Her uncle nodded wearily. He was tired. He had had a busy day at the company. He was hungry and it seemed that he might have missed his supper. He was also angry with James, who was in such a stupor that he said hardly a word over this damnable affair. What was worse, he had to face Mildred when he got home and he didn't know how he could.

'I beg your pardon for intruding,' Sammi began. 'We're looking for a woman – grandmother to this infant. The child has been abandoned and we wish to return him.'

'Like a parcel!' one of the men guffawed. 'Lost and found.'

Sammi ignored him and turned to one of three

women. 'We understand that the baby's mother has died, but he needs a nurse or he'll die.'

'Then it's a pity he didn't die with her.' One of the women spoke up coarsely. 'Death can't be worse than 'workhouse.'

Another of the women came across to Sammi and undid the blanket wrapped around the child, and peered at him. She smelt of gin and Sammi turned her head away. 'He's not one of mine. And none of my mother's have died this week, though I lost two a month ago. This is a new bairn, no more than a day old. Have a look, Ginny. See what tha thinks.'

The third woman moved forward slowly, and reluctantly, Sammi thought. She, too, looked down at the child, who was beginning to stir. She ran a rough finger across the child's cheek and he moved his open mouth towards it. She glanced at Sammi and then back at the baby. 'He'll last a bit longer on milk and water, then tha must feed him on pobs if a nurse can't be found.'

'But we must find his family, he needs love as well as food,' Sammi implored.

'Maybe they can't afford to love him, miss. It costs money to love a bairn, but maybe tha's too young to know that. Too young and not poor enough.' She was dressed shabbily, but her eyes were honest and she looked directly at Sammi and then at James and Isaac. 'If there's nobody to take care of him, then tha'll have to take him to Charity Hall. They'll take him. They'll allus take them that nobody else wants.'

James's mother was waiting for them on their return; she was wearing her bedgown and robe, and her eyes were red as if she had been weeping. She was angry and ashamed, she said, at the disgrace that James had brought on the family. 'What will people think?' she cried, as they told her that they had not been able to find the woman. 'How can I possibly meet people if this scandal gets out?'

31

'It won't be the first time,' Isaac said patiently. 'I'm not diminishing what has happened, my dear, but I imagine that there are very few people whose lives could bear scrutiny.' He put his hand out towards her. 'There's many a young woman slipped up!'

Mildred ignored his gesture. 'James must go away for a while so that no-one hears of it.' Her voice was hushed, but as Sammi watched her she thought that there was fear in her eyes. 'If he wants to support the child out of his allowance, then that is up to him.'

'But where will the child go, Aunt?' Sammi appealed in vain to her aunt. 'There's only the workhouse or charity!'

Her aunt didn't answer, but simply sat straight backed and stared in front of her. There was a clatter of wheels on the drive and Isaac shook his head impatiently. 'I'm forever telling Gilbert not to come so fast up the drive. The gravel gets knocked all over the flower beds, but I can talk till I'm blue in the face for all the notice he takes!'

Gilbert was whistling cheerfully in the hall and he put his head around the door. 'Hello! Still up at this hour?'

'You're very late, Gilbert. We expected you earlier!' His mother spoke sharply.

'But I told Father I wouldn't be home; you didn't wait supper? I've been to the house, I wanted to speak to the builder about some alterations that Harriet wants, and then I went on for a game of billiards.' He bent to kiss his mother on the top of her head and as he did, he looked across at Sammi and winked.

He could get away with murder, Sammi thought. His mother's favourite, whilst poor James— The two brothers were quite different in temperament as well as in physical attributes. Gilbert was self-assured, sociable, arrogant even sometimes. He was tall and athletic, and his side whiskers and his hair, which he hated, were red, like his father's. James, on the other hand, was short and dark, like his mother, quiet and dreamy unlike her, and absent-minded to an irritating degree.

'So what's happening? I gather you're not having a party.' Gilbert looked quizzically round at them as they sat still and silent. 'Sammi! You've been letting that young pup tear up Father's newspapers?'

She shook her head and rose to leave the room. 'If you will excuse me, Aunt Mildred, Uncle Isaac, I'm rather tired. I think I shall go to bed.'

'I shall go too.' Her aunt rose from her chair. 'It has been a very tiring evening. No doubt you gentlemen will find plenty to discuss.' She ignored James, sitting hunched in a chair, and swept out of the room.

Sammi gave a sympathetic nod to James, said goodnight to her uncle and Gilbert, and left them. She wanted to weep. The thought of the innocent baby, whoever he belonged to, spending the rest of its infant days unwanted in an institution, filled her with dread and pity. The lamp had been left lit in her bedroom and a fire burnt brightly, making the room, with its dark heavy furniture, look quite cosy. Mary had left a covered jug of water at the side of the bed, and a small silver cup and spoon which must have once belonged to the Rayner children.

Sammi leant over the makeshift crib at the side of her bed and thought of the woman who had brought him. 'How desperate she must have been to leave you,' she murmured. 'And how sad to have lost her daughter.' She suddenly wanted to see her own mother, to feel the comfort of her loving arms and to tell her of the great sadness which filled her whole being.

'Something momentous has happened, Gilbert, so you'd better sit down. James here has got into a spot of bother.' Isaac outlined the evening's events, starting with the woman coming to the house as it had been told to him, and finishing with their visit to Hull.

'You never went searching for her, Father? Why,

she'd be hidden away deep down some alleyway where you'd never find her. It's some trick. Some mischief. It can never be true!'

'I must go to bed.' Isaac got up and put his hand across his eyes. 'I am so weary and sick of the whole business. And I have an important meeting in the morning. You won't forget, Gilbert, will you? I need you there.'

Both his sons rose. 'I'm sorry, Father,' James began, 'so very sorry.' His eyes filled with tears. He wouldn't have upset his father for anything.

Isaac nodded, embarrassed at the show of emotion. 'It's your mother I'm sorry for. But you must find somewhere or somebody to take the child first thing tomorrow. I don't know where,' he said vaguely. 'I wouldn't know where to start. Perhaps one of the hospitals. Ask Sammi if she'll go with you. Then we'll talk in the evening about what you shall do, where you shall go. Your mother's fixed on that, I fear.' He cast a glance at James's look of misery. 'We'll see what we can do.'

'You blithering idiot, Jim,' Gilbert remonstrated when their father had gone. 'How did you get into such a scrape?'

'I don't know. The woman just said, "Are you young Rayner?" and when I said yes, she thrust the child at me.' He started to pace the room. 'The worst thing is that I can't even remember it happening.'

'Then it can't be yours,' his brother insisted. 'It must be a prank. Somebody has given your name out instead of their own. But who would do such a dishonourable thing?'

'No.' James shook his head. 'Father said I had to work back nine months, and when I did, I remembered.'

'But you just said that you couldn't remember!'

James blushed to his hair roots. 'No, what I meant was that I couldn't remember the er, the er, you know, *it*, happening with the girl. I can remember going up to the room; you remember, Gilbert? It was the night your engagement was announced and we stayed at The Cross Keys. That's the only time that I've been drunk or out with a woman, so that must have been the time.' He sat down again and sank his chin into his hands. 'What a mess! I've ruined everything for everybody. And I can't even remember what she looked like! She was pretty, I know that; but I can't bring to mind a single feature or even the colour of her eyes.'

They were blue, Gilbert deliberated with alarm. *The deepest, loveliest blue eyes I have ever seen, and her lashes were long and dark and thick and swept her cheeks when she closed her eyes. And now they're saying she is dead!*

'Can you remember her, Gilbert? There were two girls, but one fell asleep on the floor and they had both gone when I awoke the next morning.'

Gilbert cleared his throat. 'Like you say, she was pretty. Dark hair – not very tall, and slim, not much plumpness on her at all.' *She was so slender and fragile I could have picked her up with one hand, and her breasts were small and round. She was probably ill-fed, for when I brought her in . . .* He recalled seeing her begging outside the inn. She had extended her hand as he'd passed, asking for a copper or two, and in fun he had grabbed it and held on to it. It was small and cold and she'd tried to pull it away.

There was something appealing in her eyes as she'd looked up at him, and impulsively he had invited her in for supper. 'Bring your companion too,' he'd said, for she'd looked questioningly at the shabby girl at her side.

I swear I never meant her any harm, he pledged silently as he stared at his ashen-faced brother. *It was only meant as fun to begin with. I never meant to go so far.*

She had been hungry, both girls were, but whereas her companion had torn into the bread and cheese and slices of beef, and drank thirstily of the ale that had been brought up to the room, she had eaten slowly, as if she was savouring the taste, but had no great appetite. And as she ate, she watched him warily from her great, luminous, shadowed eyes.

By the time she had finished eating, the other girl, with a loud belch, had curled up on the floor by the fire and closed her eyes. 'Thanks, mister,' she'd said. 'Wake me up if tha wants owt,' and James, who was having difficulty in staying awake, had succumbed to the effects of the strong Hull ale, and fallen asleep on the sofa.

He had stretched out his hands to the girl and drawn her towards him; her shawl was thin and her dress shabby and mended, but her face and hands were clean. 'What's your name?' he'd asked gently, for she suddenly seemed afraid.

'Sylvia, sir. But my friends call me Silvi.' Her voice had been low, and she trembled.

'Don't be afraid, Silvi. I'm not going to hurt you. You can go home now if you want to.' He'd felt some kind of shame when he saw the relief on her face. She obviously thought that she would have to pay for her supper. But he was always careful. True, he had visited brothels, but only those which were well-run establishments. He had never taken a street girl; there was too much at stake, he couldn't risk his health or reputation, or his forthcoming marriage.

But there was a waif-like charm about her which had appealed to him, a naïve freshness in her eyes which surely, he had thought, couldn't stem from innocence. He had kissed her then, just a small, tender kiss on her cheek, but it had raised a yearning response in him, and when she lifted her bowed head to look at him, he had kissed her again, this time on her mouth.

'I didn't even know her name,' James said gloomily. 'The mother of my child, and I don't even know what she was called.'

'Oh, don't be so dramatic, James,' Gilbert said irritably. 'What does it matter now?' But it had mattered then, when he had whispered her name again and again as he kissed her moist lips and ran his fingers through her long hair and down her slender throat.

'What's your name, sir?' she'd asked softly as she'd lain beside him on the bed and he'd fumbled with the buttons of her bodice.

He had been hypnotized by her, struck by a melting, terrible need to possess her; and yet he hadn't forced her. It was as if she willingly, yet timidly, acquiesced to a need stronger than either of them could ignore.

'Rayner,' he'd breathed in answer as his eyes feasted on her nakedness.

She'd touched his lips with her fingertips and gently traced around his eyes. Then she'd closed her eyes as he bore down on her and he saw the long lashes brushing her cheek. 'Is that – what I should call you, sir?' Her words fluttered, she drew in small gasping breaths and he thought that he had hurt her, though she assured him that he hadn't.

He'd cradled her in his arms and given her gentle kisses on the top of her head; he'd felt loving and protective towards her and, as sleep overcame him, he knew most surely that he must see her again.

He was awakened early the next morning by the street sounds outside the window of the room, and found that she and her friend had slipped away. He'd thrown back the crumpled covers and stared at the dark red patch staining the white sheets and remembered now with shame; the relief, yet joy, that he had felt on discovering that she had been a virgin.

3

Isaac had left for the firm, Aunt Mildred and Anne were still in bed, and Gilbert was nowhere to be seen when James and Sammi, who had breakfasted together in almost complete silence, finally boarded the carriage which had come to collect Sammi.

'Mother seems to have washed her hands of me,' James said bitterly. 'I knocked on her door but she wouldn't see me.'

He looked down at the baby in her arms. 'I feel nothing for it. Should I?'

'No tenderness for something small and helpless?' she asked, embarrassed that James had admitted that the child might after all be his.

'Well, I feel sorry for it, but, well, it doesn't feel like mine. Not like Sam that you gave me.' He fondled the pup's ears as it sat beneath his seat. 'I'm so sorry that you have to take the pup back, Sammi, but Mother couldn't possibly let him stay, not now, if I'm going away.'

'It's so unkind,' Sammi said hotly. 'How could your mother send you away? Or the child?'

'Oh, she'll never accept the child, and I don't think she knew what to do with me in any case, now that I've finished school. She says that I moon about.' He stared moodily out of the window. 'I suppose I do. I never quite know what to do with myself. I miss the other fellows, you know. We used to have such grand talks.'

The carriage rattled on through the hamlet towards the turnpike road, and Sammi looked out of the window at the surrounding countryside and the neat cottages and handsome mansions. It was a desirable place to live, she thought; near enough to the River Humber to feel the breezes from its waters, and good air coming down from the Wolds. A prettier place than her own Holderness countryside.

'But not the place for you, James.' She spoke her thoughts out loud. 'It's perhaps as well that you have to go away.'

'What?' James, locked in his own thoughts, looked perplexed.

'Why don't you get in touch with your master from school? You know, the one who said you should paint. Ask his advice.'

'It's odd that you should say that. Peacock. I was just thinking of him.'

The carriage slowed in front of the redbrick workhouse just outside the town, and came to a stop. James pulled down the window and put his head out.

'Is this the place, sir?' Johnson called down from his box.

'Tell him no, James,' Sammi said impulsively. 'We'll try the charity homes first and ask them, this looks so gloomy.' She was thoughtful as they drove on into the town, and then suddenly said, 'Let's walk. We'll ask Johnson to wait for us. If the guardians see us in a carriage they might not be inclined to take him.' She looked down at the sleeping child. He was so still. He had cried during the night and she had given him water to pacify him, but she knew that, like the baby lambs on her father's estate which she hand fed when their mothers had died, he needed more sustenance now.

Gilbert had heard the child cry, he'd knocked softly on her bedroom door and asked if he could come in. He said that he couldn't sleep and offered to go down to the kitchen to warm some milk. He watched her as she tried to spoon it into the baby's tiny mouth and then, surprisingly for Gilbert, she thought, he stroked the child's cheek with his finger.

Johnson drove the carriage into Masterson and Rayner's yard, and Sammi asked him to wait for them there. 'You won't be long, Miss Sammi?' he queried. 'Your mother needs 'carriage this afternoon.'

She promised that they wouldn't be, and James held one arm as they walked across the High Street and she crooked the baby into the other. They retraced their steps from the previous evening and made their way down Silver Street, the street of jewellers and pawnbrokers, and into the ancient street named Land of Green Ginger, looking for charity homes and hospitals.

The old town of Hull was expanding rapidly as the increasing population demanded more space. The crumbled medieval walls had come down long ago, and the land was built upon to accommodate the migrant settlers who came seeking employment: labourers and craftsmen, fishermen, railway workers, merchants and manufacturers, all vied for space; and, crushed in between and behind the impressive business premises in the main streets of the town, the heaving and crowded slum dwellings were homes for the poor and the destitute.

'There can't be one down here, James.' Sammi put her hand across her nose and mouth. 'We've come the wrong way!'

They had turned a corner and found themselves in a stinking alley. An overflowing cesspit had spewed its contents towards the dilapidated and decayed houses, and the stench was intolerable. They hurried back the way they had come, back to the crowded Whitefriargate, where shoppers strolled past the parade of shops, and fashionable ladies inclined their heads to bankers in top hats and stovepipe trousers, and brushed shoulders with fishwives in shawls and clogs.

They found a hospital, tucked away off the main street, a neat but dark house with a locked and barred gate and iron railings around its front area. James rattled on the gate to attract attention, but no-one came.

'Tha must wait till eleven,' a passing woman shouted to them, 'they don't admit bairns till then.'

'We can't wait, James. I have to get home.' Sammi was tense. 'We'll try somewhere else.' She called to the retreating back of the woman. 'Excuse me. Is there another home? This child has been abandoned.'

The woman came back. 'Is it a pauper's child? They'll not tek it here if it isn't.'

They both remained silent. The word pauper had filled them with dread.

'Try 'Morris Hospital,' she indicated with her head back the way they had come. 'They might tek it, but—' she seemed to be assessing them, casting her eyes at their appearance, at Sammi's fine wool buttoned jacket, at her velvet pork-pie hat with feathers and trailing ribbon which perched neatly on her head, at James's cut-away coat and checked trousers – 'on 'other hand they might not.' The woman pulled herself upright and stared accusingly at them. 'What's a fine young couple doing giving away a poor bairn?'

'No, you don't understand,' James began, but Sammi pulled him away.

'Come, James. We must go.' She took his arm. 'Hurry.'

The door was open to the Morris Hospital, and they walked into a small dark hall. The building was old, the paint on the windows and doors peeling, but there was a strong smell of disinfectant as if there was a battle going on against dirt and disease.

'Is there anyone there?' James called out. 'Hello!'

A small face peered round a doorway and a pair of round blue eyes looked up at them. There were tear streaks down the cheeks of the small girl, and her nose was running; her brown hair was cut short above her ears and plastered down with some greasy

41

substance. 'Matron's through in 'kitchen,' she sniffled. 'She's telling Cook about us dinner.' She motioned to a door down the hall and then disappeared again behind the doorway.

James knocked on the kitchen door and opened it. The room was full of steam, and there was a strong smell of cabbage. A woman encased in a long white apron was standing by a blackened iron cooking range, beating furiously at the contents of a pan, while on the fire bars a range of cauldrons stood spitting and steaming. A young girl of about seven years was standing on a stool at a long wooden table, up to her reddened elbows in a bucket of water. She looked up as they entered, but made no comment, nor did her face change expression. Her hair, too, was cut short and spiky, and she was scrubbing potatoes for all her worth with a stiff-bristled brush. Another child, a boy, was on his hands and knees washing the stone-flagged floor.

A woman was standing at the other end of the table slicing up chunks of bread, and she shouted as the door creaked on its hinges, 'I don't allow anybody in this kitchen! Didn't tha see 'notice on 'door?'

'Oh! No. Sorry,' said James. 'I was looking for, er, there doesn't seem to be anybody about.'

She looked up and wiped her hands on her apron as she heard him speak. 'Beg pardon, sir. Can I do anything for you?' Her voice and manner changed from rough and hostile to fawning servility. 'Come this way.' She beckoned them back down the hall, but turned as she left the kitchen and bellowed to the child, making Sammi jump and waking the baby who started to cry. 'Look sharp with them spuds! We haven't got all day.'

She led them into a small, stuffy room which had a coal fire burning in a grate, above the mantelpiece a crude coronation portrait of Queen Victoria gazed down. She placed herself behind a desk and indicated for them to be seated.

Sammi perched on the edge of one of the chairs and was glad she was wearing a cage beneath her moiré skirt, for the prickly horsehair stuffing would have been very uncomfortable. James declined the offer and remained standing.

'So what can I do for you, sir, madam?' The matron gazed at them.

James swallowed and looked at Sammi. 'We need your advice if you would be so kind,' he began. 'This child—' he waved his hand vaguely to the child in Sammi's arms; he was still crying, a plaintive wailing, like cats, James thought, suddenly becoming irritated by the sound. Why was it crying?

'Does it want feeding?' the woman asked. 'Sounds to me as if it's hungry.'

'Yes.' Sammi rocked him gently to quieten him. 'He's only a day old and has only had a few spoons of milk.'

'Why not? Hasn't your milk come through?'

'Oh! He's not my child!' Sammi blushed scarlet. 'He's been abandoned – his mother is dead and his grandmother brought him and left him with us, and we don't know where to take him.'

Matron's mouth narrowed. 'Why would she do that, pray?' She glanced at James. 'Who's the father?'

Now James blushed and he fingered his high collar nervously. 'She said it was mine.' He cleared his throat as his statement came out high-pitched and squeaky.

The matron spoke patronizingly. 'And you thought to bring him here, did you, sir? You thought that somebody else could look after 'little fellow?'

Sammi felt tears gathering in her eyes. She was imagining this baby left behind, with no-one to rock him or comfort him as she was doing now. She thought of him with his hair cropped short, scrubbing the floor of the kitchens.

'Governors will only take him if he was born in Hull,' the matron rasped. 'I'd have to make a request out, giving 'details of where he was found, 'name of his mother and father, things like that.' She stared hard at James, her small eyes piercing into him accusingly. 'Are you sure you want that, sir? How will your parents feel?'

'You don't understand.' Frustration engulfed him. 'I've only the woman's word that it is mine. I can't remember—' He saw the curl of the woman's lip as he haltingly tried to explain. *Now she's going to think I'm a decadent young buck with bastards all over the place.*

Sammi shivered, then rose to her feet. 'We've changed our minds.' A tear trickled down her cheek. 'We won't leave him after all.'

'But Sammi!' James spluttered. 'What will I do with him?'

'Good day to you.' Sammi made towards the door. 'We're sorry to have troubled you.'

'Wait, miss.' The matron hesitated. 'If 'bairn really has been abandoned, with no-one who'll claim him, then governors might take him. But it's not much of a life; there's no comfort here, nobody to hold your hand when you're feeling sorry for yourself. I know,' she said grimly. 'I've been here twenty years. It's a life sentence, and it makes thee hard.'

Sammi shook her head. 'Thank you, but no. We'll not leave him.'

As they returned to the hall, a bell rang with ear-shattering intensity. Doors opened upstairs and down, and there was a great clattering of feet and shuffling of bodies as children and old people appeared from every corner of the building and descended into the hall and lined up in an orderly fashion against the wall.

They all looked clean, the children especially were red and shiny as if they had just been scrubbed, and their clothes, though thin and patched, were not untidy.

Sammi looked at them, her eyes searching each face in front of her. She was looking for some gaiety, a joyous spirit, an animation that would show there was a kind of hope living in this place. But there was none. Each child's face stared back at her, unseeing, only waiting for the next meal, the next order, the next job of work to be done, while the old people, in submissive resignation, were simply waiting.

She turned again to the matron. 'Thank you, but no.'

James chased after her as she hurried away down the narrow street. 'But Sammi! What can I do?' Wild ideas of leaving the child in a doorway flashed into his mind, but he shook his head to dispel them. Sammi would be horrified if she knew he had even thought it. 'Sammi! Help me!'

She stopped and turned towards him. 'What we are going to do, James, is—' Her face was set and determined. '*You* are going to see your master in York. You must tell him that you need to earn your living, and you will send me money for the child as soon as you have some. And *I*, I am taking him home with me.'

Gilbert waited in a corner of the stables behind the house until he heard the rattle of the carriage moving off. He harnessed up Caesar and Brutus, climbed into his gig, and in response to an imperceptible flick of the reins the pair moved off. The horses started to lengthen their stride into a lively trot as they entered the lane outside the gates, but he checked them, holding them on an unaccustomed short rein and keeping well back from the carriage in front.

He pulled in beneath the shade of trees when they stopped at the workhouse, and heaved a sigh of relief as they moved off again. He followed them as they drove towards High Street and saw them coming out on foot from the company yard.

''Morning, Master Gilbert,' his father's senior clerk called to him from across the narrow street. He had a thick wad of papers in his hand. 'Mr Rayner's been looking for you. He's gone on to the meeting. He said to tell you to come as quick as you can. I was taking these to him.' He lifted up the papers in his hand. 'But if you're going . . .'

'Erm, take them down for me, will you, Hardwick? I've an urgent call to make. If my father should ask, tell him I've been delayed, would you?'

Hardwick raised his eyebrows. 'Very good, sir.'

Damn. Father's going to be furious. Gilbert drove into the yard at the back of the office and jumped down from the gig. *But I must see where they are taking him.* He called to a stable lad and threw him the reins, then dashed out of the yard in pursuit of his brother and Sammi. He followed them as they walked down Whitefriargate, and waited in a doorway until they came scurrying out of an old part of the town, and saw them hesitate before hurrying on again.

Oh, God! He rubbed his whiskers hard as he thought. *They're looking for a hospital. What can I do? They're terrible places. He'll not survive. But if I go after them and tell them that the child is mine, Harriet won't marry me. The wedding will be called off!*

He was already racked with guilt at letting James take the blame, and he had spent a sleepless night worrying what to do. He had heard the infant cry during the early hours and, trusting that no-one else would hear him, he'd knocked on Sammi's door. His mother would have had apoplexy if she had known he was in his cousin's room, but he gave no regard to that, and Sammi had let him in. He had been surprised at her maternal instinct as she held the child in her arms, trying to soothe it.

'I'm used to babies,' she'd whispered. 'When the village women have them, I always go to see them and ask if I can hold them. And we have puppies and kittens at home, and baby lambs, and they're all the same really.'

But they're not the same, he thought, as he followed them again and watched them turn towards another

46

hospital. *Dogs can be trained and mastered. Cats can fend for themselves. Infants grow into people.* He could only just remember James being born, and more clearly his sister Anne, but he remembered how he wasn't allowed to touch them in case he hurt them. This child he'd touched. He'd stroked his soft cheek and marvelled at his tiny hands and nails, and had seen as Sammi took off his covering blanket, his downy head of pale hair.

He drew out his pocket watch. He didn't know what excuse he would make to his father. The meeting was an important one. The local shipping and whaling merchants were meeting to discuss the ever-declining whaling industry.

Sammi appeared suddenly from the end of a street. She was still holding the child, and looked as if she had been crying, then James came running after her. He, too, looked upset.

This is no good. Gilbert suddenly made a decision. *I'll have to tell them. They're so young, they can't take on my responsibilities.*

'Good morning, young Rayner! What are you doing mooching about at this time of day? No work to do?'

Gilbert looked stupefied as Austin Billington, his future father-in-law, stopped in front of him. He lifted his top hat. 'Good morning, sir. I, er, I'm just about a spot of business, just, er, wondering which call to do first.'

'Mm. I see.' Austin Billington was wearing a dark, formal frock coat with a brightly patterned waistcoat beneath it. In his lapel he wore a rose which he bought every day from the flower seller before he went into his bank. 'We were only talking about you at breakfast. Most of the arrangements have been made for the wedding. We only want your final list of guests.'

'Yes, I, er, I haven't forgotten, sir. I'll let you have it by this weekend.'

'Yes, I was only saying to Mrs Billington that

47

perhaps it is as well that we had to delay the marriage because of her ill health, though I know you young people wouldn't agree,' he chortled and winked and stroked his pointed greying beard. 'But I do believe we are going to have some very good weather in the next few weeks, and there's nothing quite like a June wedding. But there we are, I always was a sentimental old fool.'

Gilbert laughed heartily, though inwardly disagreeing. There was nothing sentimental about this hard-hearted banker, except where his daughter was concerned, and Gilbert knew with a sinking heart that, if word should get out about the child, he would be finished completely in this town. Billington would make sure of it. He walked with him to the steps of his bank and then turned to go back to the High Street. James and Sammi had gone. He was sunk in misery. Perhaps, he thought, they had been turned away from the hospital, and it seemed to him now that the only solution would be to find a foster home for the child, and for that, someone would have to pay.

As he walked into the yard, Sammi was stepping into the carriage. She was empty-handed. 'Hello, Gilbert. I can't stop, I'm afraid. I'm already in trouble with Johnson for being late.'

He gave her a small smile. 'I'm in trouble too, Sammi. It's not a very good start to the day, is it?'

She got down from the carriage steps. 'Oh, I'm sorry, Gilbert, everybody's got such troubles, and poor James more than anybody.'

He nodded, hesitating. 'Where's the child, Sammi? What's happening to him? Has James taken him somewhere?'

She looked up at him solemnly, her brown eyes appealing to him. 'You won't tell anyone just yet?'

He swallowed hard, he was hardly likely to. 'No. I won't, Sammi. Trust me.'

She took his arm and showed him inside the

48

carriage. There, tucked up in a corner of the upholstered seat, was a small wrapped bundle. 'I'm taking him home to Garston Hall.'

He felt such a tremendous lightening of spirit, a great sense of relief flooding over him. Aunt Ellen! Of course! She wouldn't turn the child away. He wasn't so sure that Uncle William would approve, but he was convinced that Sammi's warm-hearted mother would come up with a solution.

Perhaps I won't have to confess after all – not yet, anyway. His mind flickered to his wedding: perhaps afterwards he could tell? And it wasn't unusual, he thought, as his conscience eased, for families to look after each other's children. The poorer working classes did it all the time.

'Oh, Sammi. What an angel you are.' He put his arms around her and gave her a great smacking kiss on her cheek. 'I love you.'

She pushed him away. 'Get off, Gilbert! You're as bad as James. That's just what he said.'

He watched the carriage as it lumbered away, then Sammi put her head out of the window. 'Will you give my love to Billy? Tell him I can't stop.'

He nodded. Her brother would be beavering away, anxious to be doing well at his first week's work with Masterson and Rayner.

'I'm sorry, Gilbert,' she called again, just before the carriage pulled out into the street. 'I forgot to ask. What did you say your trouble was?'

'It's nothing. Nothing at all.' He waved a good-bye to her. 'It's only that I'm late.'

4

As the carriage approached the village of Tillington, Sammi put her forehead against the window and looked out. The mill beyond the church showed black against the wide sky, and the white canvas sails were sweeping square to the north-east wind, their shades partly closed to spill the gusty breeze.

Her father's cousin Thomas and his three sons Tom, Mark and George would be working hard in the heart of the mill, harnessing the power of the wind which drove three pairs of millstones to grind the raw grain. She thought of them running nimbly up and down the steep and narrow access ladders to the five floors, while their sister Betsy would perhaps be indoors, going about the womanly tasks which she had reluctantly undertaken four years ago at the age of fourteen, when the housekeeper, who had looked after them all since their mother's death, had also died.

The pair of greys pulling the carriage turned instinctively down the winding road towards her home village of Monkston, even before Johnson gave the signal. Sammi was thankful that the weather was dry, for the old road often became a quagmire after rain, when the potholes and ridges made by the wheels of carriages and carts filled with rainwater and mud, and made it almost impassable.

She looked up at the high banks on either side of the narrow road: yellowhammers were nesting in the hedgerow, and early bluebells were emitting their glorious heady perfume. Sammi pulled down the window and then picked up the baby. 'Look,' she said, holding him up, 'Your first flowers. If you'd been a girl we could have named you Flora.' The baby puckered up his mouth and started to cry. 'Well, that sounds healthy enough.' Sammi rocked him. 'I was beginning to get quite worried about you. But you're not a girl,' she mused. 'So what name shall you be given, I wonder?' She felt a small chill as the thought struck her that her parents would be angry with her for bringing him home, but she brushed it aside and refused to think about it.

Her home, Garston Hall, was nearly a hundred years old and had been built on the site of an old castle. It was designed to follow the Gothic architecture so admired at the time, and was embellished with round towers, turrets and battlements, and in the autumn its south face was covered in red creeper. To the east, by the round tower, a cascade of winter jasmine straggled and tumbled over the stone walls, and facing north, a glossy-leaved ivy battled against the elements. It was also very close to the sea, with only an orchard and rose walk between it and the house, and a fifty-foot drop over the cliffs to the sands below.

Her mother was waiting at the door, fully dressed in her warm cloak and hood. She came out as the carriage approached, the wind catching hold of her skirts and whipping away the shawl which she had draped around her shoulders.

'I'll get it.' Sammi jumped from the carriage and chased after the fluttering shawl.

'Leave it. Leave it, Sammi!' Her mother called after her. 'I must go. You are *so* late. I particularly told Johnson that I wanted you home early. You are too bad!'

'I'm sorry, Mama.' Sammi kissed her mother. 'Johnson did say. It's all my fault. Well, not completely. I—'

'Oh, hush now, Sammi. I must drive into Tillington. Richard has taken the gig, otherwise I would have borrowed that rather than this great lumbering thing. I'm sorry, Johnson. You're going to have to go back into Tillington again.'

Johnson touched his top hat and murmured something and glanced at Sammi.

'Mama! Before you go! I have something to tell you.'

'Not now, Sammi. I have a call to make and I'm already late.'

Johnson opened the carriage door, his eyes averted to the sky.

'Victoria has gone to bed with a headache, she's not well, so don't disturb her, there's a dear. There's cold meat in the larder if you're hungry. Help yourself. Don't bother Cook if she's busy.'

Sammi waited with baited breath as her mother put her foot on the step.

'What's this? You've left something. Sammi!'

The baby stirred as an icy blast from the open door filled the carriage, and he opened his mouth and wailed. Hunger and thirst cramped his stomach and he screwed up his face and screeched.

'Sammi! For heaven's sake. What's this?'

'It's a baby, Mama.'

'I can see it's a baby, foolish girl! But what's it doing in our carriage?'

Ellen Rayner leaned in and lifted him out. 'Whose child is it? Is it hungry? Why, it's such a young baby!' She looked at her daughter in alarm, her large blue eyes widening. 'Sammi! You have some explaining to do.'

'Can we go inside, Mama? He's cold and hungry. I'll need to warm some milk.'

'Milk!' Sammi's mother swept inside with the child in her arms. 'He needs the breast, not warm milk! Where's his mother?'

Sammi cast a glance at Johnson waiting resignedly by the carriage. He raised his eyebrows at her as she closed the door. 'Sorry,' she mouthed. ''Fraid you're going to have to wait again.'

* * *

Cook hovered with a basin of warm milk, and the two kitchen maids gaped open-mouthed as Sammi's mother sat on a kitchen stool and spooned the milk into the baby's lips from a tiny silver teaspoon. Martha, the elderly housekeeper, had gone off to delve into her linen cupboard to find something more suitable to wrap around the baby.

'These are clean sheets,' Sammi explained, but Martha only humphed in displeasure.

'They're onny fit for rags, these bits; not suitable for a new bairn, and he wants summat warm, especially for round here.'

'He won't be staying,' Ellen Rayner said matter-of-factly. 'So don't anyone get too excited. As soon as I find out where this daughter of mine found him, he's going back where he belongs.'

'Mama. Can I explain?' Sammi sank down onto a chaise longue in the drawing-room, and watched as her mother deftly unwrapped the child and dressed him in a sweet-smelling cotton carrying gown, the bodice tucked and threaded with ribbon.

'This was Richard's and then Billy's,' she said, ignoring Sammi's question. 'And then we got new ones for you and Victoria. I can't think where Martha has been hiding it all this time.' She wrapped him in a square of white blanket which Martha had cut from a larger one, and fitting the child comfortably into the crook of her arm, she turned a resigned face to her daughter. 'Yes, Sammi,' she said calmly, settling herself back into her chair. She had removed her cloak and undone the broad ribbons on her capulet hood which covered her fair, smooth chignon. 'I think you had better start at the beginning.'

She sat listening, without questioning, until Sammi had finished, then she looked down at the contented sleeping baby. 'And you are telling me that James is the father of this child?'

Sammi shook her head. 'No. What I said was, that the woman claimed that he belonged to James.'

'That boy?' She removed the blanket from the baby's head and gently fingered the pale pulsating down. 'And his mother, was she dark or fair, do you know?'

Again Sammi shook her head. 'James can't really remember, but he said that Gilbert said she was dark.'

'I see!' Her mother pursed her lips. 'And what did his mother have to say about all of this? Mildred would be delighted to be presented with a grandson no doubt?'

'She's furious with James, Mama, and says that he must go away so that no-one finds out; and Anne is being beastly towards him and refuses to speak to him,' she added heatedly. 'I don't think he's totally convinced that it is his child, but he is so confused.'

'Well, quite rightly everyone will be shocked and angry; and it could be his child, Sammi, though I have to say I am very surprised,' her mother mused. 'But we only see our friends and family as we believe them to be. Everyone shows a different face for different people or circumstances, and the cousin James that we perceive might well be cast in a different mould.' She rose to her feet and reached to press the bell on the wall. They heard its faint ringing in the kitchen. 'But you still haven't explained why you brought him here. He can't stay here, you know that?' She instinctively rocked him. 'He will have to go back to Anlaby. He's their responsibility, whether they like it or not.'

'They'll send him to a charity home.' Sammi started to weep. 'They're awful places. I've been. I went with James. The children have to work in the kitchens; they can't play and there's no-one to love them. Please, Mama. Please don't send him there.'

'He's not a puppy or kitten, Sammi, that we can put in a box in the stables,' her mother said sharply, 'and I see that you've brought Sam back too. Wouldn't Mildred let James keep him either?'

Sammi wiped her eyes and took a deep shuddering breath. 'James said that if he had to go away, he wouldn't be able to look after him, so I said I'd bring him back here until he could.'

A frown wrinkled her mother's smooth forehead. 'So Mildred really means James to go?'

'She means it.' Sammi gave her nose a huge blow on a handkerchief. 'He was going off to York to see his drawing master, to ask if he could recommend what he should do.' She cast a beseeching look at her mother. 'Mrs Bishop in Tillington has just had another child, she always says she has enough milk for a houseful of babies. I thought we could ask her if she would nurse him? I'll pay her out of my allowance, just until James finds a position, and then he'll pay me back. He promised he would!'

'You little minx! I can read you like a book. You've been planning this all the way home, haven't you? This is what you had in mind the whole time!' Ellen turned to the housemaid who had knocked and entered. 'Ask Johnson to bring the carriage round again, please.' She stood deliberating for a moment after the maid had left the room, and then pulled a cynical face. 'I just hope you didn't speak to your Aunt Mildred and Cousin Anne of Mrs Bishop and her ample milk supply. How very shocked they would be!'

Mrs Bishop was pleased to nurse the baby. 'Bless thee, Mrs Rayner,' she said, 'tha's saved my life. This little lass of mine is a right poor feeder; try as I might she won't tek 'milk and I'm fair beside myself to be rid of it.'

Ellen Rayner hastily stood up and indicated to Sammi, who was hovering over Mrs Bishop's large white breasts as the baby hungrily searched for her nipple, that they should go. *We're known to be liberal, I know,* she thought, *but this, I think, has gone far enough.* 'It won't be for long, Mrs Bishop. The baby won't be staying; he's not our responsibility – but if you could nurse him until other arrangements are made?'

'It's not wise to give him more than one nurse, ma-am,' Mrs Bishop settled back in her chair. 'It unsettles 'em. Still, it's up to thee, I'm onny 'milk nurse.'

Sammi sat beside her mother in the carriage and looked anxiously at her as Ellen put her head against the lace headrest and said quietly, 'You know that your father will be angry with you?'

Sammi gave a little shrug and pressed her lips together. 'He doesn't stay cross for long, Mama. His humour soon returns.' She knew that her father's temper, as fiery as his greying red hair had once been, could always be turned to laughter and her advantage.

'Not this time.' Her mother gazed frankly at Sammi. 'This time you've really gone too far. This latest escapade is just not acceptable.'

Her father was angry. Very angry indeed. But not just with her. He was angry with his brother Isaac, his sister-in-law Mildred, and with James for allowing Sammi to bring the child out to Garston Hall.

Sammi stood in front of him in the drawing-room with her eyes lowered and her hands behind her back as he spoke in bitter tones of his family shedding their responsibilities onto someone else.

'Uncle Isaac and Aunt Mildred don't actually know that he is here, Pa,' she ventured when he finally paused for breath. 'Uncle Isaac told James to find somewhere that would take him, and Aunt Mildred wouldn't discuss it. Only James and Gilbert know he is here.'

'So why did you bring him here?' he roared, and she flinched.

'I couldn't bear to leave him,' she whispered. 'If he belongs to our family, he deserves more than those dreadful places.'

'So James has been playing in the dirt and we're left to pick up the pieces!'

'William! William! That's enough,' Ellen chided her husband. 'We don't know what happened. The child's mother is dead. There are things here that we might never know of, nor wish to know.'

'Ring the bell, Ellen,' he commanded, 'and ask them to tell Johnson to bring the carriage round.'

'But where are you going? Supper will be ready.' Ellen gazed up at her husband in some alarm.

'I'm going to drive to Anlaby to see my brother and his precious wife, and find out just what is going on!'

She placed her hand on his arm to stay him. 'Not tonight, William, it's late. Wait until tomorrow. Don't go when you're feeling angry. You'll say something that you'll be sorry for. You know how Mildred always irritates you. Have supper and we'll talk about it, and then – and then, in the morning, perhaps I could go instead?'

He looked down at her. 'You're trying to twist me around your finger, Ellen. And as for you, young woman,' he turned to Sammi and shook a finger at her, 'this time you have gone too far. No. I mean it. Don't smile at me like that, you're as bad as your mother. We cannot keep this child. We have problems enough of our own, without taking on other people's, even if they are family. Like it or not, he has to go back.'

Ellen dropped Sammi off at the mill house the next morning as she had requested, and told her that she would collect her later in the day when she returned from her visit to Mildred.

That lady isn't going to be pleased to see me without an arrangement, she thought grimly as the carriage rocked along the Hull road. She and Mildred had very little in common, save that they had married two brothers. *Poor Isaac*, she mused. *We all thought that Mildred would be good for him; she seemed loving and kind, and he needed*

57

*someone strong to give him a push. But we didn't realize
what a tartar she would turn out to be.*

She wasn't looking forward to this confrontation.
For no doubt, that is what it will be, she pondered. *And
the whole atmosphere in that house makes me feel creepy.*

Being a farmer's daughter brought up on the
Wolds, and marrying William who farmed on the
plain of Holderness at the edge of the sea, she was
used to open spaces and an abundance of brisk fresh
air, and Garston Hall, which had been her well-loved
home for nearly twenty-five years, since William's
parents had welcomed her as a young bride, with its
spacious rooms and muslin drapes enhancing rather
than obscuring the view of the garden and cliffs
below, suited her very well.

Mildred was a banker's daughter who had been
brought up in a town house. She had an aversion to
draughts, and kept her windows draped with nets and
laces and heavy hangings to keep them out, but
excluding also any natural light, so that the rooms
were gloomy and dark even during the day.

It was noon before Ellen left the suburbs of
Hull and the horses began their swift trot towards
Anlaby. Such a pretty village. She echoed uncon-
sciously Sammi's thoughts from the previous day as
they passed the grand mansions and large country
houses which had been built, some on the common
land where once sheep had grazed.

But she sighed and a sadness descended on her as
she observed the progress and development of the
land, here to the sheltered west of Hull. Not a sadness
such as Sammi had experienced in her concern
for the child, nor even for Victoria, her youngest
daughter who was so frail, and certainly not for her
merry son, Billy; but for her husband William. For
William and her eldest son Richard, who were losing
their livelihood, day by day, week by week, as the sea
took its toll on the land which they all loved.

*   *   *

'Please be seated, Ellen, and I'll ring for refreshment. You are very fortunate to find me at home. I was expected at Mrs Beadle's of Hessle this afternoon, but she has just this half hour ago sent a message to say that she is unwell and cannot receive me.' Mildred fussed and prattled, plumping up cushions, straightening the numerous pictures on the walls, rearranging the bric-a-brac and ornaments which decorated the tables and what-not, and moving infinitesimally the glass dome which held an arrangement of waxed flowers to the exact centre of the table.

Ellen waited patiently. Mildred always went through this ritual whenever she called, even when she was expected. 'Well, Mildred,' she said, as her sister-in-law finally ceased her flutterings and sat down opposite her, 'you have no doubt been expecting me?'

'Why no!' A pale flush suffused Mildred's thin neck above her narrow white collar. Her hair, coiled in a low chignon, was covered by a crocheted net, and she patted it nervously. 'As I just said, I was expected at . . .' Her voice trailed away as Ellen looked directly into her eyes.

'But you knew I would be coming sooner or later?' Ellen persisted. 'Surely, neither you nor Isaac expected William or me to accept the situation as it stands?'

'I really don't know what you are talking about, Ellen.' Mildred's round and once-pretty face shuttered, and she primped her lips firmly.

'Oh, for heaven's sake, Mildred.' Ellen spoke impatiently. 'Of course you know what I'm talking about. Don't pretend. I'm referring to James and his child, the child that Sammi has brought home to us because you refuse to acknowledge it.'

'The woman was lying!' Mildred's voice became shrill and she rose to her feet. 'It has nothing whatever to do with us. We are a respectable family. The very idea is totally abhorrent.'

'Then why are you sending James away?' Ellen

spoke more quietly, she wanted this matter settling as quickly as possible and she had obviously touched a raw nerve with Mildred's sensibilities. 'Why can't he stay, find the woman and give the child back? Explain – if there really has been a mistake?'

'James is going away to avoid embarrassment, and I don't wish to discuss it any further. As far as I am concerned the incident is closed.' Mildred sat down again breathing heavily, the ruches on her bodice rising and falling rhythmically.

'The incident! The incident!' This time Ellen rose from her chair, her passions aroused. 'You can't call a child an incident! You can call what leads up to its conception an incident if that is how you see it, but we are talking about a human life.'

Mildred got to her feet once more and the two women faced each other, both their faces were flushed, their hands clenched. 'How dare you speak so!' Mildred's voice was low and scathing. 'I never thought to hear such things in my own home, especially from someone who is kin.' She put her hand to her chest and breathed heavily. 'Thank goodness Isaac isn't here to witness this, or my daughter.'

'A child who is reputed to be *your* grandson is at present under *my* daughter's care and protection, and you worry over how Anne would feel?' Ellen fastened her cloak and prepared to leave. 'I just don't understand you, Mildred. Where is your compassion? Would you leave it to a young and inexperienced girl to accept what should be your responsibility?'

Mildred's face drained of colour and she seemed to be fighting for self-control. 'I will say once more, and only once, this has nothing to do with us.' She took a deep breath. 'If Sarah Maria wishes to indulge herself over a child, then she should marry and have some of her own instead of collecting others' waifs and strays. Good day to you, Ellen. You must excuse me, I have a busy afternoon ahead of me.'

Ellen didn't answer. She picked up her reticule and whirled out of the door, the feathers on her small hat bobbing and bouncing, and it wasn't until she was back in her carriage and heading back down the drive, her mouth clenched in anger and her eyes filled with tears of fury, did she realize that, although Mildred had offered her refreshment, she hadn't actually given her any, and she faced the long drive home without the prospect of food or drink.

I shall visit the company, she decided. *I will speak to Isaac, he surely will come to some arrangement; and if he is not there, then at least I shall see Billy and he will give me tea.*

Their younger son, Billy, had joined Masterson and Rayner as a very junior clerk who would learn the company business from the bottom up, and in time, if he proved adaptable, would become a director. William, Isaac and their brother Arthur had shares in the company, with Isaac in control as managing director, for he was seen to be the one with the most interest and expertise in the whaling industry.

William wanted only to continue farming at Garston Hall as he had always done, whilst Arthur, whose business was the railways, lived with his wife and three daughters in York, the northern base of railway operations. He had seen the fall from grace of the great George Hudson and assumed a complacent satisfaction, which he never failed to talk about, at his business acumen in having moved his shares from the Railway King's company at just the right time.

Johnson negotiated the clumsy old carriage through the busy High Street, and Ellen looked up at the name above the company building: Masterson and Rayner. A name well thought of in the shipping industry. *And the name of Foster is still perpetuated,* she thought as the carriage pulled into the yard. Sarah Foster, her mother-in-law, who had married John Rayner, had been proud of her background, telling in her gentle manner to anyone who was interested, that she was the first Foster to be born in Monkston and that her father Will, who had been an ordinary whaling seaman from Hull, was the bravest man who had ever lived. And in his memory, as well as Sarah's, the Foster name was continued through their children and grandchildren.

'Mr Rayner is not in the office at present, ma-am,' said the clerk who greeted her. 'Perhaps I can assist you? Or young Mr Rayner is here – Mr Gilbert.'

She stared at him for a moment and then blinked. 'Oh, er, no. Perhaps I could see my son for a moment – Mr Billy Rayner? I won't keep him long.'

'I beg your pardon, Mrs Rayner, I didn't recognize you.'

'No reason why you should.' She smiled faintly at the embarrassed clerk, and pressed her fingers to her temple; she was starting a headache and his words had triggered a train of thought which was muddling through her mind.

'Hello, Ma! What brings you here?' Billy kissed her warmly on both cheeks. 'Come upstairs into Uncle Isaac's office, he won't mind. He's out at a meeting somewhere, but he'll be back soon.'

'Will you be home this weekend, Billy?' He didn't come home every weekend and she missed his exuberant chatter.

'Perhaps not. One of the fellows here has asked me if I want to join him and a party to visit the theatre, and afterwards there's a glee.'

She surveyed him anxiously. He was very handsome, everyone said so, it wasn't just a mother's pride. At nineteen he was tall, slim and willowy as a reed, and with a shock of hair as fair as hers, unlike his siblings who all had a tendency towards shades of red. She was understandably anxious: living in Hull, he was no longer under her influence. He was bound to be attractive to women, she thought affectionately, and vulnerable too – look what happened to James!

'A glee?'

'Yes. You know, music and singing and such.' He smiled down at her teasingly.

'Yes, I know what a glee is, Billy, but you won't take strong drink, will you? Just drink a little wine, it's safer.'

He pulled out a leather chair for her to be seated. 'All right,' he said, amused. 'I will. Don't worry. Let me send for some tea for you, you look tired.' He opened the door and called out to someone below.

She looked around the room, she hadn't been in it for a long time. The large desk which her late father-in-law, John Rayner, had once used, was still set near to the window with a view onto the river below; a wooden filing cabinet on the opposite wall held private papers. Two embroidered texts sat side by side on the window wall, which she guessed were Mildred's work, and opposite the desk were two portraits, one of John Rayner as a child and another as he had been in his capacity as chairman of the board of directors. Between the two was a smaller picture set in an oval gilt frame. It showed an older man, his wrinkled hands clasping a cane, this was Isaac Masterson, uncle of John Rayner and founder of the company.

'Will you excuse me for a moment, Ma? I must just see Hardwick about the accounts I'm working on. They're bringing you some tea.'

'I don't want to keep you from your work, Billy. Tea would be lovely. Off you go, I'll rest for a while and, if Isaac hasn't returned, I'll go home. You know how your father worries if I'm late.'

'You didn't say why you were here.' Billy paused with his hand on the door. 'Shopping, I expect?' He gave her a quick merry smile as she nodded her head in response.

No point in discussing the issue of the child with him yet, not until it was resolved. He obviously hadn't heard or he would have mentioned it. There were no secrets between this branch of the Rayner family. Open discussions were always the order. *Mildred would be most uncomfortable to listen in to our conversations. A respectable family!* She mused over Mildred's statement. *She will think that we are morally decadent and quite irresponsible, bringing up our children to see animals being born, to know about babies and how they are conceived. And her children were not allowed to play games as ours were! They were shut up in the nursery with their nurses or taken for decorous walks in their fashionable little suits and gowns. They never knew what dirt was!*

Such ignorance. She leaned back in the chair and closed her eyes, and meditated; yet it was one of Mildred's own sons who had committed the unpardonable sin of bedding some poor girl and had given her a child!

The door opened and she opened her eyes, expecting the maid with the tea.

'Aunt Ellen!' Gilbert's face flushed, he'd pushed open the door into his father's office, totally oblivious of her presence. 'I, er, how nice to see you!' He stammered out a greeting and dropped the papers he was carrying.

'Hello, Gilbert. I've been to see your mother, and thought as I was passing through Hull, I would call in to see your father.'

'My father?' He rubbed his chin nervously.

Strange, she thought as she watched him. *He is the one who appears so debonair, such a sport, such a very merry young gentleman, yet here he is acting like a schoolboy.*

The maid brought in the tea and Ellen drank it gratefully. 'I didn't see James while I was at Anlaby; I was hoping to,' she added.

Gilbert shuffled amongst the pile of papers which he had retrieved from the floor and heaped onto the desk. 'He – er, left me a note to say he has gone to York.'

'Oh?' You'd know a Rayner anywhere with that red hair, she thought and watched him as he stared out

64

of the window. No, she corrected herself. The red hair came from Grandmother Sarah, and before that, *her* father, Will Foster. Yet the Foster cousins in Tillington were all as dark as gipsies, their colouring coming from a different stock.

'James has gone back to his old school, Aunt Ellen, to see his drawing master,' he said quietly. 'He's gone to ask him if he can recommend him to a tutor who can improve him in his artistic abilities and gain him employment.' He turned and gazed at her from his dark brown eyes; she couldn't tell, as he had his back turned to the light, what expression to read from them. 'Mother says he must leave home over this – this catastrophe. She says if it gets out it will be the ruination of our respectability and position in society.'

'Indeed! And what of the child?' Her eyes flashed. 'Is he simply to be abandoned? Does no-one care what becomes of him?'

She saw him draw breath, and briefly and swiftly he put his hand to his eyes, then withdrawing it said falteringly, 'It is so regrettable. I will speak to my father on – on James's behalf and that of the child's. Provision will be made, Aunt Ellen. We were wrong to let Sammi take him, I realize now, but she was so taken with him that it seemed the obvious answer at the time.'

She nodded, pacified for the moment, and put down her cup and saucer. 'I'll wait to hear from you then, Gilbert. You or your father.' She looked at him frankly. 'I trust that you will make the right decision and soon.'

He escorted her down to where Johnson was waiting in the yard, puffing on a smouldering wet pipe as he sat on a mounting stool.

'Ready then, ma-am?' Johnson stood up and knocked out the pipe. 'We'd best be off then. 'Master worries if you're late. He allus thinks I've turned this cumbrous old carriage over and you're lying dead in

65

a ditch.' He flicked an imaginary speck from his frock-coat and adjusted his top hat. He gave her a small bow and extended his hand to help her in.

'Good-bye, Gilbert.' She leaned from the carriage window. 'Tell Billy I'll see him soon.'

Gilbert almost collided with Billy as he turned to run up the stairs.

'Oh! Has my mother gone already?'

'Yes,' Gilbert answered shortly.

Billy watched the carriage pull out of the yard and lifted his hand in a wave. 'I say, Gilbert—'

'Not now, Billy.' Gilbert took the stairs two at a time. 'Can it keep?' He closed the door behind him without waiting for an answer, and turned the key. He stood for a moment leaning against the door and stared unseeing, his mind only dwelling on the face of a girl, a girl with a cloud of dark hair who had shared her love with him for such a brief time, and who had died giving birth to his son. *His* son, whose tiny hand he had held. His son whom he had denied. He sat down at his father's desk and looked up at the portrait of his grandfather. He seemed to gaze down, admonishing him. Gilbert clenched his fist and banged on the desk. 'I'm sorry! I didn't mean this to happen.'

Tears gathered in his eyes and a lump came into his throat. He put his head in his hands and started to weep.

5

When James had delivered Sammi and the child safely into Johnson's care, he'd crossed the High Street and entered The Black Boy Inn. He'd ordered a meat pie and a small glass of ale and contemplated what he should do next. Sammi had suggested that he should go to see his former drawing master and, on reflection, that seemed to be the only recourse. He didn't want to go home and face his parents, particularly his mother, and although he wasn't too perturbed about Anne's opinion of his behaviour, he didn't want to be in the house if there was any kind of hostile atmosphere.

The landlord brought his food and ale and placed it on the table in front of him. The aroma rose from the crust and he licked his lips. He had the normal appetite of a young male and now that the immediate problem had been driven away with Sammi, he felt quite hungry. He enjoyed the pie, mopping up the gravy with a chunk of bread, drank to the bottom of the glass and scribbled a note to Gilbert, explaining that he was going to York and why. Crossing the High Street once more, he gave the letter to one of the clerks in the office.

He pulled out his pocket watch and immediately broke into a run. He was familiar with the coaches to York and realized that he had just time to catch the two o'clock diligence before it moved off. James had often wished that the railway companies would make up their minds about a direct line to York, rather than having to take the route via Selby and changing trains at Milford Junction to get there.

For the moment, the regular coach service was the most efficient and reliable, and for several years as he'd travelled the journey to and from his school, he'd watched with his artistic eye the changing vista from the flatlands of Hull through to the gently rolling meadows which skirted the foothills of the Wolds.

In the summer months, the fields of Dunnington on the north-eastern fringe of York were covered with the pale blue flowers of chicory and which, at the end of autumn, swarmed with itinerant workers brought in to gather and harvest the root and transport it to York for drying.

He bought a ticket and climbed aboard, and by early evening the coach was dropping down into the Vale of York towards his destination.

He weaved his way through the warren of familiar dog-leg lanes and narrow passages, which cut a way through half-timbered buildings of merchant houses and ancient dwellings. Some of these lanes were medieval pathways with room for only one pedestrian to traverse, and which, he recalled, could be very awkward if a person of the opposite sex was met up with half-way through. He was reminded of the rules given out by the school housemasters that if this should happen, then no matter what the female's class, be she rich or poor, the young gentlemen should immediately raise their hats and turn around and go back the way they had come, giving the lady free passage to continue.

A small smile touched his lips as he remembered the additional ruder names which he and his friends had invented for the snickets and alleys which threaded a hidden path through the centre of York. Names to confuse new pupils who were not familiar even with the strange-sounding hidden courts such as Mad Alice, Cheats Court, or the Hole in the Wall, which lay at the foot of the majestic Minster.

He hurried on, anxious to see Peacock before he

went in to supper. He pushed open the iron gates set in the high stone walls which surrounded the old school, and walked up the path to the thick oak doors.

'Mr Rayner, sir.' The porter greeted him cordially. 'Didn't expect to see you back so soon!'

'I didn't expect to be back, Lawson. But life is full of surprises.'

'You've discovered that already, sir? Then your education is continuing.'

James waited in an anteroom while Lawson went to look for Peacock, and as he paced the floor he reflected on the change of attitude in Lawson's demeanour towards him now that he was no longer a student. Then, he would watch all the young gentlemen, diligently noting what time they went out and came back, whether they were suitably and tidily dressed and reminding them at all times that their behaviour reflected the school's reputation. Not one note of jollity ever passed his lips, yet now he had a positive twinkle in his eyes.

James had often wondered why his parents had sent him to this school in York, when there were equally good schools nearer to home. Gilbert had attended the Grammar School in Hull which had a fine reputation, but when, at eight, James had questioned his father as to why he should have to go to York, he was told that it was for the best.

He stood up as Henry Peacock came into the room and extended a hand towards him in greeting.

'Rayner! How good to see you. What brings you back so soon?'

James shook his hand and gently retrieved it. Peacock had a habit of holding on to a boy's arm or shoulder when discussing or admiring a work of art, and there was much contemplation in the dormitories after the lamps were dimmed as to whether or not he was effeminate with unmanly traits, or an aesthete. James had always hotly defended the master, stating that Peacock had only eyes for beauty of line and

69

form, and was quite above such commonplace qualities as they were suggesting.

Peacock had opened his eyes to the sculpture and architecture which lay all around them in this ancient city. He had taught him to observe the stark beauty of winter-bare branches in the city parks, and the delicate veil of green as spring unfolded and divulged her presence. So, too, had he shown him the richness of the medieval stained glass in the Minster; made him run his hands over the texture of the stone that he might sense the throbbing of ancient chanting voices still held within the fabric; and told him of the time, twenty years before, when, as a young man, he had wept unashamedly after a fire had destroyed the carved bosses and central vault of the nave.

'I need your advice, sir. I couldn't think who else to ask. I trust you don't mind?' He looked frankly at him. Their eyes were almost on the same level. Peacock was a small man, a little shorter than James himself, but his extravagant mode of dress, his velvet jacket and braided trousers, his long greying hair and clean-shaven chin, caused others to notice his appearance rather than his lack of height.

'Mind! My dear fellow, I am flattered to say the least. Come, we will take a walk. It is a pleasant evening and besides, I have no stomach for the food which is being prepared. I have smelt it and my juices have dried up in apprehension.' He went to fetch his outdoor clothes: a faded cape which once was black but had now a hint of green, and a battered felt hat which he angled carefully onto his head. He drew on to his pale hands a pair of woollen mittens, and they stepped outside.

They walked by the white-painted cottages and redbrick residences which lined the banks of the river Ouse, and James haltingly explained his predicament while Peacock listened without comment.

'Come,' he said, when James had ground to a halt. 'We will take some refreshment. I know of a coffee house if you have any money, for I have only a little. My salary . . . !' He gave a meaningful gesture towards his pockets.

'I have a little money, sir.' James felt for his pocket-book. 'Enough at least for a small supper.'

There were few people in the coffee house, which they reached by turning down a narrow passage and into a small court. It was warm and dark, with only a single candle set on each round table.

'Well, my dear fellow, this is what I suggest you must do. And I must say that the circumstances which have befallen you, whether of your own creation or not, will perhaps prove to be the emergence of you.' He removed his mittens and, dropping them with a flourish onto the table, he leaned back on the spell-backed chair in a reflective manner. 'You have the makings of a lazy fellow, I regret to say, who, if you had ample means at your disposal and were not in such a precarious and impecunious state as I, would sit around waiting for some opportunity to present itself. As it is,' he continued, 'you have no alternative, if you are to help support this child, but to go out and find your living.'

He stretched his long fingers and joined them, tip to tip, into an arch, and with one eye closed, peered through it, framing James's face. 'Your parents will naturally think that they could be ruined socially by such a misdemeanour. The bourgeois classes set much store by convention, and the mediocre opinions of others towards them matters greatly. You should be thankful, James, that you are not a female in such a predicament, for you would, without any doubt, be packed off to an asylum to end your days.'

James felt a great joy unfolding inside him. This, he realized, was what he had missed since leaving school; the conversation, the ideology and sometimes heated exchange of words with his peers. He had had no conversation since going home, and his intellect was starved.

Peacock took out a pencil and scrap of paper from a pocket hidden in the depths of his cape and, pushing aside the cream jug and coffee pot, he leaned on the wobbly table and started to write in an elegant hand, a name and address in London, which he handed to James. 'This is where you must go.' He raised an eyebrow. 'I assume your father will assist you financially until you can earn a living.'

James nodded tentatively. He would be in a predicament if he didn't, but his father had said, 'We'll see what we can do.'

'I will write to Batsford immediately I get back to my room, and he will have the letter the day after tomorrow,' Peacock continued. 'The fellow is an excellent tutor and a painter in his own right. For a small fee, he takes students in order to eke out a living while he paints. He has not, like so many of us, sold his soul in exchange for a little comfort and a regular, if meagre, salary.'

It was almost dark when they finally left the coffee house and, although Peacock suggested that a bed could be found in the school, James declined with thanks.

'I have relatives in York, sir. I can stay there. I used to stay with them on my holidays if the weather was bad and I couldn't get home.'

'Does your uncle keep a good cellar? It is of no comfort whatsoever if the bed is warm and the wine poor.' Peacock once again drew on his mittens and wrapped his cape around him. A fresh breeze had sprung up and he shivered.

'I believe he does,' James smiled, 'although I am no expert on the matter, but he does have an excellent cook.'

'I will leave you, then, in the anticipation that you might eat another supper, and I will return to the aroma of overcooked cabbage, and compose a letter to Batsford.' Peacock hesitated slightly and then, tapping his mittened fingers against his chin, said, 'It is perhaps only fair to warn you, James, that the bohemian classes are unconventional. You may find their attitudes and behaviour a little strange or even disturbing, especially as you have been brought up with middle-class standards of morality. Be circumspect at first, choose your companions cautiously until you are sure of them. But accept them for what they are and do not put a judgement on them too hastily.'

James was intrigued. He walked swiftly through the sweet-smelling city of cocoa beans, chocolate and confectionery, avoiding now the alleys and courts which, after dark, were the hunting ground of prostitutes and thieves, and made his way to his uncle's house near the Knavesmire racecourse. He realized, with a strong grip of excitement which filled him to the core, that he couldn't wait to get away. That a very different life was waiting for him in London.

His uncle and aunt and their three daughters were at supper. They were seated around the dark polished dining table arranged with a shallow crystal flower bowl, silver cruets and bread baskets, and glass candle holders which gave out a soft flame from the wax candles inside them.

His aunt, Henrietta, brushed aside his apologies for disturbing them. 'Do not think anything of it, James. You are most welcome.' She raised a finger to the waiting butler. 'Bring a chair, Summers, and another setting. You must eat of course, James, and will you stay the night? I fear you have missed the train.'

'Please, Aunt, if I may. If it doesn't inconvenience you too much.' Since he was a small boy, he had admired his aunt. In her early forties, she was much younger than her husband, and retained the beauty and style of her youth.

Their daughters, as fair as their mother, but plain and with a tendency towards being slender like their father, rather than inheriting their mother's pretty plumpness, were considered to be highly marriageable, with expectations of handsome dowries.

'So, James,' his uncle boomed, 'what do you intend doing with your life now that you have finished your education? Not going into whaling I trust? That's finished, I keep telling your father. Shipping is all right if you are in the right commodity.'

'No, sir. I'm – erm – I'm going to London, sir. I have a letter of recommendation, which is why I am here in York. I, er—'

'Splendid! Splendid!' His uncle cut in. 'Breaking out of the mould, hey? I'm glad to hear it.' He refilled James's wine glass. 'It was in my mind to suggest you might like to join me. I'm fond of you, you know, and there's money to be made in railway companies, take my word for it.' He patted his nose. 'You have to learn to sniff out the good ones of course, but it can be done.' He leaned forward, his face expectant. 'So what is it to be, eh? Law? Banking? Yes, I could see you in banking, James. It's safe, and you're using other people's money and not your own.'

He paused again, and James felt all five pairs of eyes lingering on him. His voice broke as he started to speak, and he hastily cleared his throat. 'No. None of those things, Uncle. My former drawing master seems to think,' he blushed modestly, 'he seems to think that I have a little talent which, with tutoring, could be improved enough for me to become a painter – an artist!'

There was a silence in the room. One of the candles guttered as it burned low, and the butler standing stiffly by the serving table moved forward and replaced it, returning immediately to his station.

'An artist?' His uncle glanced up at the walls which held several large oil paintings and water-colours, as well as miniatures and tapestries on its background of red-flocked wallpaper. 'As a living!'

'Oh, no, James!' His aunt was startled. 'We are, as you know, patrons of the arts. We attend all the exhibitions and concerts; we have even entertained artists in our home, but it is not a suitable career for a young man of your background.'

'Of course it isn't!' his uncle barked, a touch of laughter softening the harshness. 'Whatever are you thinking of? What does your father say of it?'

'He, er, he doesn't know, sir. I haven't yet discussed it with him. I've only just decided.'

'Ah. Then it's just a whim!' His uncle visibly relaxed. 'Take my advice, James. Find yourself a worthwhile career and do your bit of dabbling as a hobby.'

James felt so let down. He had thought that this aunt and uncle would have understood, even if his parents did not. They visited the theatre, though not the music halls. He had attended concerts with them, though declined their musical soirées. They had even taken him to hear Mr Charles Dickens give a reading from *A Christmas Carol*, and had joined with him in the rapturous applause of the audience.

He had thought wrongly, he now surmised, that they were forward-thinking people with a wide social circle which embraced flamboyant artistic and literary figures. He realized now that their involvement was merely a veneer; it was considered fashionable and reactionary to be seen in the company of actors and artists, to read racy novels and discuss them, or to give a considered opinion on a water-colour. But to suggest that one of their relatives should become such an artisan, then the idea was rejected with typical, traditional prudishness.

Bourgeois! Frustration and anger provoked him. *Bourgeois!*

6

As Sammi waved good-bye to her mother and walked across the yard to the millhouse, she could hear the sound of raised voices. Uncle Thomas was railing against someone, and another voice was wailing – Sammi recognized it as Betsy's, her very best friend as well as her second cousin – and then came yet another, a conciliatory deep voice of a male which, she thought, could only belong to Tom, Betsy's brother.

She knocked on the half-open door and called through. 'Is it safe to come in or shall I walk back to Monkston?'

'Sammi! You're just in time to sort out my da and Betsy.' Tom greeted her with a smile. 'Come on in.'

'I hope you've had breakfast,' Uncle Thomas growled and sat down in his chair and started to unfasten his boots. ' 'Cos there's none here. Not for anybody.'

'I'm cooking it now, Da. Don't keep going on. It won't take long.' Betsy glared at her father as she slipped a white apron over her shirt and long woollen skirt. Her dark hair was tousled and her deep blue eyes sleepy. 'I slept in,' she carped, 'and I'll never hear the last of it.'

'We've been working half the night,' her father started complaining again. ''Least we can expect is a pan of gruel waiting when we come down.'

'All right Da, leave it now. Betsy said she'll do it.' Tom patted his father on the shoulder and signalled to Betsy to hurry up. 'Sorry, Sammi. The wind has been blowing all night and we're dead tired. Da especially, he's been doubled up in the cap for the last half hour, chocking up the brake wheel and greasing the bearings.'

'Aye well, I like to do it missen and I know it's done,' his father grunted as he heaved off his boots.

'Let me help you then, Betsy. I'll cut the bread and get the dishes out.' Sammi took off her jacket. 'I'll just wash my hands.'

'I haven't brought the water in,' Betsy said sullenly and glanced at her father. 'You'll have to use the pump.'

Sammi went back out into the yard and Tom followed her, rolling up the sleeves of his flannel shirt. He started to work the handle of the pump and a stream of crystal clear water gushed out. Sammi held her hands beneath it and then rubbed them briskly together.

'Now let me do it for you, Tom.' The skirt of her gown dipped into a puddle of water but she put her hand to the handle to work it for him.

He shook his head and with a laugh he brushed her aside. 'You're not cut out for hard graft, Sammi, neither are you dressed for it. I'll fill the pail and bring it inside.'

She watched him as, with a few swift strokes, he filled the wooden pail. His shoulders were broad and his arms were brown and strong. She had admired Tom since she was a small girl, and she had often watched him in the mill as he effortlessly lifted sack after sack of corn, hanging them on to the hoist chain on their journey up through the trap doors to the top of the mill; she had seen him run nimbly up the access ladders, or chop a pile of wood in the yard. She had seen him, too, with his strong gentle hands, easing a sticky baby lamb from a birthing ewe.

'What's happening, Tom? Why are Uncle Thomas and Betsy arguing again?'

He pulled his shirt over his head and handed it to her to hold, then worked the pump handle again.

When the water gushed out he put his head under it and came up spluttering. He shook his head, showering her with water, and ran his fingers through his wet black hair. 'Same old thing. Betsy can't get up in a morning, and if she does get up, then she either lets the fire out or she burns the porridge. She just can't seem to get the hang of things.'

'You should get another girl in to help her. It's too much to expect Betsy to do everything.'

'We do have someone to do the rough work, but Betsy always seems to rub them up the wrong way, and they don't stay.' He took his shirt from her and vigorously rubbed his hair and face on it. 'Come on,' he said, taking her cold hand into his. 'Let's see if breakfast is cooking and if there's a clean shirt for me to wear. We don't often have company for breakfast.'

'So what brings thee out so early, Sammi? Was that your ma in 'carriage?' Uncle Thomas seemed to have recovered his humour as he sat hunched over his porridge.

'Yes, she's driving into Anlaby to see Aunt Mildred.'

'Humph. I shouldn't have thought your ma would have much to jaw about with that dowly woman.'

'There was something in particular that she wanted to discuss with her.' Sammi dipped her spoon reluctantly into the lumpy gruel.

'Did you enjoy James's birthday, Sammi? Was there a party?' Betsy sat at the table and tucked her chin in her hands and gazed at Sammi.

Mark and George, Tom's younger brothers, had both come in for breakfast. George tucked into his porridge, but Mark spoke cuttingly. 'A party? We didn't get an invitation, did we, Da? Not good enough for that lot of Rayner folk.'

Sammi started to protest, to explain that there wasn't a party, but her uncle raised his voice to his middle son. 'That's enough of that sort of talk. I'll not have bickering between family.' He lifted his

78

spoon to his mouth and looked across at Betsy who was sulkily staring at the table. 'Besides,' he said, 'we none of us like Mildred, so it would be hypocritical to go and eat at their table.'

'Well, I would have put up with her just for once,' Betsy pouted, 'if it meant wearing something nice and meeting company.'

'But there wasn't a party!' Sammi thrust in when she could. 'Far from it. You would have hated it, Betsy.'

'Aye, well, lass, even if there had been tha wouldn't have been invited, so it's no use chewing it ower.' Her father with a sigh put his spoon into his dish and pushed it away. He put his elbows on the table. 'Tha's burnt porridge again, Betsy! Pass me a hunk o' bread.'

'I'm so miserable, Sammi. I'm no better than a servant. I'm like a wife or a mother to those four, and I have no life of my own. I'm at everybody's beck and call day after day and it's not fair!'

They had cleared away the breakfast dishes and left the kitchen tidy. Sammi had fuelled the fire and put a pan of water over it, so that there would be hot water ready to make the men a drink when they came in again later in the morning.

'You need to be more organized, Betsy, but you also need more help. I'll get Mama to speak to your father, shall I?'

Betsy nodded. 'Please,' and picked up her shawl. 'Where did you say you wanted to go?'

'I've something to show you. But we'll have to walk into the village to see Mrs Bishop.'

'Mrs Bishop? But why?'

'Wait and see.' Sammi refused to be drawn further and, linking arms, they set off down the lane where the horse chestnut trees threw a leafy, pale green canopy over their heads. Sammi paused by the wooden gate which led into the churchyard. 'May I

79

pick some flowers from your garden later, Betsy, to put on Grandmama's grave?'

Betsy squeezed her arm. 'Of course. You miss her, don't you? But then, we all do; she always listened to me when I had a grumble or a grouse.'

Sammi nodded and felt a lump in her throat with the sad, sweet memory of her grandmother, Sarah Rayner. Sarah *Foster* Rayner, she corrected herself: *Grandmama said we must never ever forget that we were from plain working stock.*

They walked down the main street of the village, a village that was growing now that some of the Monkston villagers were being re-housed there, and those who had come were, it was said, quite satisfied with their move, for this village had a church and two inns, The Raven and The Ship, as well as the mill where they could buy their flour. Monkston had none of these, for its ancient church and inn had succumbed to the sea many years before.

Mrs Bishop was sitting outside the door of her cottage with a child at each breast. ''Mornin', Miss Rayner, Miss Betsy. Fine day. Thy da will be pleased with this breeze, though it seems to be freshening too much for my liking.'

Betsy looked down at the two babies, one contentedly feeding, the other wriggling and squirming. She compressed her lips together. 'I didn't know you had two babies, Mrs Bishop.'

'Bless thee, haven't I got half a dozen to my name? But these are not both mine. No, one of 'em belongs to Miss Rayner here.'

Sammi laughed at the astonished look on Betsy's face, and lightly admonished Mrs Bishop. 'He's not mine, Mrs Bishop, as you very well know. I'm simply looking after him until arrangements can be made for him.'

'Aye, so tha said, miss.' Mrs Bishop took each child away from her nipples and swapped them over to alternate breasts. She squinted up at Sammi. 'But mind out, 'cos folks'll start to talk, and mind as well that tha doesn't get over-fond on him, 'cos if tha does, tha won't want to give him back.'

'Whatever have you been up to, Sammi? Whose child is it?'

Betsy plied her with questions, but Sammi refused to answer until they were well out of earshot of Mrs Bishop.

'That's why Mama has gone to see Aunt Mildred,' she said as she finished the explanations. 'Pa is furious! With James and Uncle Isaac and Aunt Mildred; but especially with me for bringing him home.'

'James!' Betsy breathed, her eyes wide. 'I don't believe it! He's such a child! He doesn't know anything. Did I ever tell you that I once took him behind one of the barns when we were about fourteen, and made him kiss me?' She giggled. 'He was *so* embarrassed!'

'You are bad, Betsy.' Sammi gave Betsy's arm a shake. 'You're such a tease.'

Betsy fell silent, then said petulantly, 'I know. But there are few men to tease around here, Sammi. I want to go to parties and meet some nice young men, not farm lads like the ones around here. I want their hands to be smooth, not rough. I want them to smell of spice and cologne, like Gilbert and James, and not of pigs and sheep or grain. And I want them to coax me and compliment me, not just want to tumble me in the hay.'

Sammi stopped in her tracks and stared at Betsy. 'Betsy! You haven't done that, have you? Say that you haven't!'

Betsy shrugged her shoulders and brushed off the question. 'How could I? I can't get out to meet anyone. I've got three brothers and a father to keep an eye on me. The chance to keep a tryst would be remarkable, I can tell you.'

They continued their walk up the lane towards the

mill, and then Betsy pulled on Sammi's arm. 'Don't let's go back in yet. Let's just take a walk in the meadow. Just for another ten minutes. I don't want to go back to the chores.'

Poor Betsy, Sammi thought. *She should have been the daughter of a landowner and not a miller, instead of me. She was made for wearing pretty clothes and partying. I hope Aunt Mildred invites her to Gilbert's wedding. Perhaps she would meet someone there.*

But she thought it highly unlikely that Aunt Mildred would invite the Fosters to the wedding. She didn't care for Uncle Thomas's blunt manner, and as she didn't consider that they were proper relations, even though Isaac and Thomas were cousins, she made sure that they had little social contact now that all the sons and daughters were grown up.

The wind was brisk, blowing in from the sea. They both put their heads down and huddled into their shawls.

'Let's walk as far as the new copse, Sammi, then we'll turn back for home.'

The young saplings were bending in the stiff breeze, but they would hold, their young slender trunks were resilient and they had been planted in and around a clump of mature trees which gave them shelter and some protection.

'There's someone in there.' Sammi slowed her steps.

'Poachers probably. Somebody after a pheasant, or maybe they're rabbiting. No. It's not.' Betsy smoothed her windswept hair. 'It's Luke Reedbarrow.'

A youth of about twenty came out of hiding and walked boldly towards the two girls. 'I'm glad it's only you, Betsy. I'd have been in right trouble if Redshaw had caught me in 'copse. He'd have said I was up to no good.' He touched his cap. ''Morning, Miss Rayner.'

'You probably are up to no good, if I know you, Luke Reedbarrow.' Betsy arched her eyebrows. 'And

I'll thank you to address me as Miss Foster and not by my first name.'

He looked astonished for a moment, then his mouth twitched in a wry grin. 'Beggin' tha pardon, Miss Foster. I was forgetting meself. I was thinking we were friends. I quite forgot tha was miller's daughter.'

Sammi watched them as they sparred and she couldn't decide if Betsy was serious and meant what she was saying, or indeed if he was apologizing. *It doesn't seem like an apology,* she thought. *In fact, he appears to be very familiar.*

His deep blue eyes seemed to be appraising Betsy, sweeping down from her face to her neck, from her shawled bodice and down to her booted toes. He caught Sammi's eye and touched his cap again. 'Haven't seen thee about much, miss. Not till just yesterday when I saw thee with Mrs Rayner in 'carriage.' He gave her an engaging smile. 'I thought I was seeing things at first when I saw thee wi' a babby. Why, I thought, it can't be Miss Rayner's, I was sure I'd have heard tell if she'd got wed.'

'I'm sure you would indeed have heard if I'd got married,' she interrupted his flow. 'But I haven't, you may be assured. We'd better get back, Betsy.' She turned away from him. 'Your father will be wondering where we have got to.'

'I'll walk back with thee.' Luke Reedbarrow shortened his long stride to walk alongside them. 'Ma will have me dinner on 'table and she doesn't like me to be late.'

There was a gap in the flowering blackthorn hedge which bordered the back of the mill house's garden, and Sammi looked through as they passed. The vegetable garden which Tom and his father worked between them was dug over and planted out with potatoes and onions, and early peas and beans were spiralling green tendrils over a trellis of canes. A dozen sheep were grazing in a small paddock where hens were also scratching, and on the other side of the house, nearer to the mill, was a granary, a stable and a barn with a dilapidated roof where they kept the bedding and fodder for the animals. Sitting astride the roof with tiles in his hand she saw Mark; he looked up as they went by and she waved.

'I'll be off then.' Luke walked with them to the mill gate. He nodded to Sammi and as he raised his hand, he turned to Betsy, lingering for a moment as if he was about to say something. 'I'll be off then,' he repeated.

'So you said,' Betsy said pertly. 'Well go on, then. You'll be late for your dinner.'

'I can't make him out,' Sammi said as she took off her shawl in the parlour. 'But then I never could, not even when we were at school.'

Sammi, with Betsy and George, had attended the village school in Tillington until she was ten, and had then had a governess at home in company with her sister Victoria, who was considered too delicate for the rough and tumble of the village children.

'Is he dimwitted or not?'

'No! He's not!' Betsy answered sharply. 'He puts on an act. He says that everybody thinks that all the Reedbarrows are stupid because of one of his relations who wasn't quite right in the head. He's handsome.' Her voice became softer. 'Don't you think, Sammi?'

Sammi shrugged, she hadn't thought of Luke Reedbarrow as being handsome; he was big and fair and he reminded her of a young bullock, and he disturbed her by his manner. His eyes were hypnotic: there was a challenge in them, as if he was compelling any woman to be aware of him. There was an animal magnetism about him which she found both fascinating and yet repulsive. She glanced at Betsy who was gazing meditatively into space, and guessed that she felt it too.

*   *   *

'Have you told Uncle Thomas about James, Sammi?'
Ellen Rayner sat down in a chair in the Fosters'
kitchen and accepted a cup of tea and slice of fruit
cake from Betsy.

'No Mama. I've only told Betsy. I wasn't sure
whether I should.'

'It will come out sooner or later, seeing as the child
is here in Tillington, so better from us than a garbled
story from the village gossips.'

'Don't be telling me anything about that family
unless I need to know, Ellen. You know I've no time
for that woman, though Isaac was always all right,
leastways he was when he was a lad.' Thomas stretched
his stockinged feet out towards the fire. He was
scrubbed clean from the dust of the mill, which
accumulated under his finger-nails and on his eye-
lashes and beard, making him look greyer than he
was. He was ready now for his supper, but quite
prepared to have to go out again, should the wind
rise and set the sails turning.

'You needn't have known anything at all if it
hadn't been for my impetuous daughter taking it
upon herself to interfere in something which didn't
concern her.'

Sammi started to protest at the harsh words, but
she was silenced by her mother's raised finger.

'James has apparently fathered a child, and Sammi
has brought it home,' Ellen began.

Uncle Thomas sat up in his chair. Tom flushed and
stared first at his aunt and then at Sammi. George
from behind his hand suppressed a laugh, and Mark
sneered. 'That fop! He wouldn't know how!'

His father rose from his chair. 'Outside!' he roared,
pointing his finger to the door. 'Go on. Out! I'll not
have you speaking in that manner in front of ladies.'

Mark bit his lip but defiantly stood his ground. 'It's
true and you know it, Da, he's nowt but a daft lass.'

'Out!' His father took a step towards him. 'Get tha
head under that pump and wash tha mouth out. And

don't come back until tha's ready to apologize!' he shouted at Mark's retreating back.

'Sorry, Ellen.' He breathed heavily as he sat down again. 'I don't know what I'm going to do with that lad; he gets worse.'

Ellen nodded. Mark had never been an easy child. He was only six when his mother had died, and he had fretted over the loss of her. George and Betsy had been only babies and didn't remember her, and Tom at eight years old was already a sensible, steady child who comforted his father and helped him and the housekeeper who came to live in, to look after the other children.

Mark seems always to have a grudge against the world, she thought, *whereas Tom, who must have missed his mother, too, is calm and patient and always tolerant.*

She sketched the final details and concluded by saying, 'If Sammi hadn't decided to interfere, we shouldn't be involved, but she did, and so we are.'

'But Mama!' Sammi burst out. 'We took him to a charity home, James and I. But I couldn't leave him. I couldn't pretend that he didn't exist! You taught us to think of others – to be considerate. How could I leave that poor child, especially if he's family?'

Hot tears streamed down her cheeks, and she put her hands to her face. Ellen compressed her lips into a determined line. Betsy and George both looked embarrassed, whilst Tom, looking quite miserable, stared down at his feet.

'Come, come.' Uncle Thomas spoke gruffly into his beard. 'Something will be sorted out; don't worry m'dears. It'll come right at 'end. It always does.'

Tom, George and Betsy stood by the yard gate to wave good-bye as the carriage pulled away, and Tom closed the gate after them. Mark stood back from them all and turned away as they came towards him. His dark hair was damp from pump water: he knew better than to defy his father.

'You'll be for it now, Mark,' Betsy laughingly confronted her brother. 'Da will have something to say about you being so rude in front of Aunt Ellen and Sammi.'

'You mind your own business, Betsy Busybody,' Mark snapped. 'Or otherwise I won't mind mine, and I'll tell him about thee seeing Reedbarrow.' He grinned as, startled, she began to protest. 'Don't think I don't know,' he sneered. 'I saw thee this morning. Didn't see me, did tha? No! Well, I was up on 'barn roof and *I* saw thee.'

'So what if you did!' She pushed her face towards his. 'I was with Sammi, he just happened to be passing by at the same time. Anyway,' her voice rose shrilly, 'I'm sick of you three always watching me, seeing who I'm with or talking to. I can't even go to the privy on my own but there's somebody following me.'

'That's enough, Betsy,' Tom admonished her. 'You'll get the same treatment as Mark if you talk in that way. Stop it, both of you. Mark, go and make your peace with Da, I know you apologized to Aunt Ellen, but Da will expect the same. George, go and lock up the pig pen; look sharp, 'cos there's a wind getting up, and we'll be needed aloft.'

His brothers went off, Mark sullenly kicking a pebble which was in his path, and George with his hands in his breeches pockets whistling a tune.

'Is it true what Mark says, Betsy?' Tom caught her arm as she turned to go into the house. 'Have you been seeing Luke Reedbarrow?'

She shrugged. 'What if it is? I can see who I like, it's nothing to do with Mark – or you,' she added defiantly.

'Da wouldn't like it, you know that perfectly well.' He stood with his feet apart and arms folded, barring her path.

'Well, *I* like it! So there's an end to it. It doesn't mean anything, Tom,' she added pleadingly. 'He's just somebody else to talk to, to flirt with. I never see anybody, I don't go anywhere. Don't tell Da. Don't spoil my only bit of fun.'

'Betsy, you don't understand!' He took hold of her by the shoulders. 'Luke will think you're egging him on. He'll read more into it than you intend. Men are like that. Don't be such a little fool. Look, if even James can get a girl into trouble—' He stopped, embarrassed by having to talk this way to his sister. 'I'll get Aunt Ellen to talk to you.'

'Aunt Ellen!' She burst out laughing. 'What makes you think that Aunt Ellen can tell me anything I don't already know? Oh, Tom, you're as green as the rest. I haven't lived all of my life in the country not to know how things are! But you needn't be concerned. I won't tie myself to someone like Luke Reedbarrow for the rest of my days. Credit me with a little sense. No, he's purely for my amusement until someone better comes along.'

Laughingly, she left him staring after her, shocked by her outspokenness. They had always, brothers and sister, been treated as equals by their father, until the day when Betsy was about thirteen; then he had brought the boys together and told them that their sister had come into womanhood, and was therefore to be protected. They'd understood immediately, and each in their own way had kept a watchful eye on her. She was escorted to any village function, and any predatory male was given a silent warning by their presence.

He was bewildered by her attitude. She wasn't grateful for their concern, rather she was irritated by it. Betsy, it seemed, was going to live her life the way she wanted to.

How strange women are, he thought, then reflected that he hadn't known enough women to be able to judge. Even Sammi, who, as a high-spirited child, would usually listen to reason, had behaved in a manner which had surprised him. She had defied the adults in the family and made her own decision about bringing James's child to Holderness. He breathed out a sigh. He had been so startled by Aunt Ellen's words in their kitchen, not an hour ago. 'James has fathered a child and Sammi has brought it home.'

He had stared in confusion as he saw a very different Sammi from the young cousin he had always known. Sammi, with tears streaming down her face and wisps of red hair escaping from her ribbons had, by defying her elders, become an adult, and for a brief, tormented second only, he had misunderstood and thought that the child was hers.

7

Billy dampened his fair hair in an attempt to hold it down, and vowed, as he looked in the bedroom mirror of his lodging house, that he would have it cut shorter, as most of the young men in Hull appeared to be doing. The house where he lodged was situated in a small court just off The Land of Green Ginger, a street so called because of its association with spice merchants many centuries before, and where, on warm muggy evenings, the residents would lift their heads and declare that they could still smell the aroma of nutmeg and ginger drifting about them.

Mace's Court had houses with railings around their small front yards, and polished brass knobs and knockers on their doors. Thick lace curtains and half-drawn blinds allowed but a glimpse of the numerous ornaments and potted plants set upon the wide window-sills and the gleam of dark, polished furniture in the neat interiors.

Yet not one hundred yards beyond this desirable neighbourhood were overcrowded courts and alleys, packed so close with dwellings that the sun never filtered through to warm the damp and festering walls. The residents of these abodes would sometimes wander out of their own area and hang untidily over the respectable iron railings, until someone fetched the uniformed constable to flush them out and send them back where they belonged.

Billy ran down the stairs. 'I'm off, Mrs Parker,' he called. 'I might be late, but don't worry about supper, and I have a key.'

His landlady came out of the parlour. 'Oh, I shall

worry, Mr Rayner. I've always worried about my young men, but there we are, it's my nature you see, and I can do nothing at all about that.' She nodded at him, the ribbons on her cap bobbing around her chubby chins. 'I'll dampen down 'fire and leave 'kettle on 'hob so's you can make a drink if you want it. But if you can't manage that, for I know what you young men are,' she dimpled with an entreating girlish laugh, 'then just knock on my door and I'll come and make it. I won't be sleeping. I never sleep!'

He thanked her and said that he would, even though he had no intention of doing so. He had been brought up with a cook and kitchen maids and a bevy of housemaids in his home, but he still knew how to cook a simple supper for himself. His mother had sent both him and Sammi down to the kitchens when they were very young, telling them that if they didn't learn how things were done, then they would never appreciate those who did for them.

He walked briskly down Posterngate and Lowgate to the Cross Keys Inn. Roger Beresford-Brown was already there and waiting for him, with brimming tankards which slopped their contents onto the small round table. Billy pushed his way through the crowd and waved his hand to another companion, Henry Woolrich, who was also battling his way across to them.

'There you are, old fellow.' Roger pulled out a chair for him. 'Sit down and put that inside you. I've ordered a jug, but this will do for the time being.'

'I'm not used to strong ale,' Billy began, mindful of his mother's warning. 'I only usually drink wine at supper.'

Roger and Henry both guffawed. 'We'll have to take you in hand, Rayner. You need to oil the wheels, and all the other bits and pieces, eh?' Roger winked and nudged him in the ribs.

Billy shrank away from the offending elbow. 'I thought we were going to the theatre?'

'Music hall, old fellow. There's only boring old Shakespeare playing at the Queen's, so I thought we'd go and have a laugh and a bit of a singsong at the Mechanics. The one and only Herr Dobler is opening his Palace of Illusions for our entertainment!'

'Shakespeare isn't boring!' Billy protested, annoyed at the thought of having to spend the evening watching a magician, even though it was one who was billed as having appeared before the Queen.

'He's right, old boy.' Henry took the jug of ale from a barmaid and slipped a coin down the front of her bodice. 'There's lots of dirty bits if you listen; you know, by the minor characters, the plebeians and such. Don't you remember how we used to pick them out to read when we were at school?'

Billy looked from one to the other and wondered why he had ever thought that they were sensible, well-bred fellows.

'Come on, then,' Henry Woolrich hiccupped at last. Their third jug of ale was down to the dregs, he and Beresford-Brown shaking out the last drops after Billy had refused once again to take more, having already drunk more than he had intended.

'Let's call for a chair, like the fine ladies do.' Roger looked down at the debris on the road, blown over from the Market Place, and then at his shiny shoes and neat pin-striped trousers.

'Good idea!' Henry swayed unsteadily and had difficulty putting one foot in front of the other. 'Call for a double, there's a good fellow. I say – I say! A double, do you get my meaning? Mine's a double!' He bent over, his hands on his knees, creased into paroxysms of laughter at his own wit and crashed down, his chin hitting the ground and his top hat rolling into the gutter.

Billy retrieved the hat and, seeing a sedan on the other side of the road, whistled across.

'Where to, sir?' The two carriers looked down at

Henry still sprawled on the floor, his chin bleeding and convulsed with tittering inane giggles.

'Take these two gentlemen to the Grand Saloon at the Mechanics Institute.' Billy felt in his pocket and gave them money enough for the journey and helped push Henry and Roger inside. 'I'll see you there.' He put his head inside the curtain of the two-seater sedan. 'I'd rather walk, if you don't mind.' *And with a bit of luck*, he thought, *I might lose you*.

The night air had grown damp and chill, a few drops of rain falling, causing him to hunch into his jacket and turn up his collar. A slight breeze was getting up, blowing in off the estuary and bringing with it a sharp smell of the sea. He took a short cut to the theatre, passing through narrow streets where lighted windows showed the presence of gin shops.

A woman with bleached hair and reddened thin cheeks confronted him. 'Hello, darling! How are you? Were you looking for me?' Her voice was a crude imitation of sensuality and seduction.

'I'm sorry,' he stammered, taken aback by her approach. 'You're mistaken. You don't know me.'

'I'd like to get to know you, dearie. I've got 'time, if you have.' She sidled up to him and linked her arm in his. She was wearing a thin satin dress, the cleavage low, showing the shape of her breasts. She ran her fingers down her throat and towards her neckline, easing the buttons undone. 'Want to see a bit more, darling?' she crooned softly. 'I don't charge a lot. Leastways, not for a fine young fellow like you. Why, I'd get as much pleasure as you. What do you say?'

Too polite to push her away, he eased himself from her grip. 'Sorry. I can't. I have an urgent appointment.'

'Give us a tanner then, love.' She dropped her extravagant air. 'Go on. I've had nowt to eat all day. Just enough for a bit o' bread or a drop o' gin.'

He fished again into his pocket and mused that this

appeared to be a night of philanthropy, and reasoned that perhaps the woman was more deserving than his drunken companions, who were being transported to an evening of revelry.

'Bless thee. Tha's an angel.' Her voice became husky and grateful. She shivered and buttoned up her dress and put her hands across her chest. 'It's that bleeding cold out here.' She tapped him briefly on his arm. 'I'll just go and get summat to warm me up. Cheerio, darling. Tha knows where to find me if tha wants owt.'

'Wait! Why do you do this?' he asked in concern. 'Can you not earn money some other way?'

She gave a short sharp laugh. 'Why, I like it, don't I, darling?' Her voice became affected again. 'There's nobody would do this job if they didn't like it, now would they?' She folded her arms in front of her and put her head on one side. 'Why, Queen Vicky herself asked if I would go and live at 'Palace and be one of her ladies in waiting, but I said, no, I couldn't possibly. Not when I've got a job like this one. She was ever so disappointed as you can imagine.' She started to walk away. 'Go on home, darling. Go back to thy ma. Tha wants no truck wi' likes o' me.'

He turned and watched her disappear into a lighted doorway and guessed that the money would be pressed into the warm hand of a publican and in return she would savour a fleeting gulp of pleasure, warming her blood temporarily before returning to her vigil in the darkened streets.

He could hear the sound of music as he walked along George Street and approached the Mechanics Institute. Street musicians were entertaining the waiting crowd. A fiddler was playing a jig and a young girl was dancing to it, her bare feet pattering on the flagstones, her dingy skirt and petticoats flying, and the crowd clapping their hands in time to the music. A few yards from them, a tumbler was somersaulting in front of the queue, throwing his rubber-like body over and over, going into splits and contortions so that some of the wags in the crowd called, '*Ow*', and shouted that he would do a mischief to his person if he wasn't careful.

Billy heard a commotion outside the building and saw Beresford-Brown and Woolrich arguing with the doorman, who was refusing to let them in until they had quietened down.

Inside the Music Hall, he saw them up in the gallery. They were in the company of two women, and they all leaned precariously over the balcony, waving and calling to the audience below. Billy couldn't help but grin and, relieved that they hadn't spotted him, for he was concealed from them by a pillar, he sat back to view the entertainment which was about to unfold. It was not quite the third-rate review he had expected, but there was some singing and low jokes which set the audience laughing and responding, and sentimental monologues which brought them to tears. Herr Dobler performed his magic with his Enchanted Flowers and Enchanted Butterflies which filled the stage. A sweet young singer, dressed in a ragged costume of white, stood in the middle of the stage and sang of her mother dying in poverty and the crowd openly wept in sympathy. Then the final act, which sent them home happy and jolly again, was a military band which marched back and forth on the small stage, playing popular songs to which the audience joined in with enthusiasm, and the curtain fell to tumultuous applause.

Billy fought his way to the door and had just reached it when his name was called from the crowd.

'There you are, Rayner, old fellow. We'd lost you. We'd lost him, hadn't we, Woolywich – Woollich – Woolly – Woolly Whatsit?!'

Beresford-Brown beamed at Billy, he had a bottle of spirits in one hand and the other around the waist of a woman. Henry Woolrich was leaning heavily in the arms of another woman, who appeared to be also leaning on him, and together they held each other up.

'Come on, we're going to the King's Arms, we're going to have another drink.' Beresford-Brown leaned confidentially towards Billy. 'This lady here. This one, I mean, that's standing next to me. This lady here. She's a beautiful shinger – singer. She's going to give us a song, aren't you?'

The woman gazed at Billy through glazed eyes, she was older by far than Beresford-Brown. 'If you like,' she said, through loose red lips.

'You go on.' Billy made his excuses. 'I'll maybe catch up with you later.'

Beresford-Brown waved an admonishing finger. 'You've got somebody lined up! I knew you were a dark horse, Billy Rayner. Well, bring her along and we'll have a party, all of us.' He waved his arm to include the crowd flocking out of the building into the street. '*Everybody* can come.'

Outside the theatre a small group of Methodists stood together in the middle of the road. One of them, a minister by his dress, held up a placard which read, 'Damnation awaits you in the House of Sin'. 'Give up your evil ways!' he called to the theatre crowd. 'Give up your sins and come to the Lord.'

He received much barracking and jeering, but the crowd were merry, not antagonistic; they had had a jolly evening and there was no ill humour, and eventually the Methodists moved into the crowd, cajoling all who would listen, to come and join them.

Billy looked down the street as he heard another sound. A drum was beating, loudly, insistently and enthusiastically. A small boy, almost hidden by the size of the drum he was banging, was leading a long stream of children, some tall, some small, some only toddlers who were being carried by others not much bigger than themselves. A young girl, waif-like, with a thin face and long wispy hair, walked at the front of the line next to the drummer and held out her hand to the crowd who were leaving the theatre. 'Give to 'poor,' she called. 'Spare a copper, sir.' She spotted Billy watching and came towards him. 'Has tha a penny to spare, sir, with nowt wanted in return?'

Billy stared. Whatever did she mean? Whatever could this child give him in return for his money? The image of the whore who had accosted him came to mind. Surely, surely, this young girl didn't mean . . . ? He put his hand in his pocket once more and brought out sixpence. The girl reached out eagerly. 'Wait,' he said, drawing his hand back. 'Where are you children from? Why are you out so late?'

The girl eyed him and then gave a cynical grin. 'Does tha mean we should be tucked up in our warm cots at this hour, sir?'

'Are you from the workhouse? Do your parents know you are here?'

He had, he knew, a lot to learn about life, he had had a sheltered existence, cocooned by the comfort and security of his family. But something was surely wrong here? It was eleven o'clock at night, these children must be in danger, with no adult to watch over them.

'If we were from 'workhouse, we wouldn't be allowed out at night, and some of us haven't got any parents.' She started to turn away, as if sensing that she wasn't going to get the money still clasped in his hand.

'Here, take it.' He held out his hand and she snatched the coin. 'I was curious, that's all. I wondered where you were from – where you lived.'

Distrust veiled her face. 'We're from nowhere and belong to nobody,' she said. 'And where we live is nowt to do with anybody else. We mind our own business and look after ourselves. Big 'uns look after little 'uns.' She gave a piercing whistle which brought the others back from the theatre crowd where they had been begging, caps in hand. She held out a cotton drawstring bag which was tied around her wrist and they emptied the contents of their caps into it.

She rattled it confidently and spoke in a forced cheerful manner. 'Come on then, let's be off and get our supper. Cheerio, mister,' she said to Billy. 'Be seeing thee.'

8

Sammi sat carefully on the edge of Victoria's bed. *How pretty she is*, she thought as she looked down at her sister, *so delicate and fragile, as if a breath of wind would blow her away*. Victoria's pale face was framed by her fine red gold hair. *Even her hair is pale compared to mine*. Sammi fingered it gently so as not to wake her, but the slight movement made Victoria stir, and she slowly opened her eyes.

'Hello, Sammi,' she said drowsily. 'I didn't know you were here.'

'Hello, Tori. Sorry, I didn't mean to wake you. Are you feeling better?'

'I'm fine, thank you. I shall get up soon.' Victoria winced as she eased herself up onto the pillows, and Sammi got up to plump them up for her.

'I've had the most frightful headache for the last few days, but it's almost gone now,' she said breathlessly. 'I need to get out for some air.'

'You get too much air. You spend too much time wandering on the cliff top. It's a wonder you don't get blown away.' Sammi moved across to the open window and closed it against the buffeting breeze. 'Stay tucked up in bed where it's warm, there's a good girl. That sunshine is very deceptive, the wind cuts like a knife.'

'No, I shall come down for supper,' Victoria said with all the determination of a fourteen-year-old. 'I feel as if I'm missing something when I'm up here. What's been happening anyway? Mama has been preoccupied over something, and so has Papa, and I've hardly seen you since you came back from visiting James.'

Sammi sighed. 'It will take for ever to tell, but I'm in trouble again as usual.' She gave such a wit-less grimace that Victoria broke into a laugh. 'It's true, Tori. I don't know why I can't be good like you.'

'I'm not good,' Victoria protested. 'I only seem to be because I spend so much time ill in bed.'

Sammi patted her hand. 'I know. All right. Sit back and I'll tell you what's been happening. It all started while we were waiting for supper at James's house, and the doorbell rang.' As she related the events leading up to her bringing the child home, she felt a wave of depression flooding over her. Her mother had said she would discuss the issue of the child later when Sammi's father was there.

She rang the bell for one of the maids to come and help Victoria to dress, and went downstairs. She had already changed for supper into a grass-green silk dress with a broderie anglaise collar and wide pagoda sleeves. She caught sight of herself in the oval mirror at the foot of the stairs and patted her hair which had been plaited around her ears, then she went across the hall into the drawing-room, where her brother Richard was reading a newspaper.

He partly rose to his feet as she entered the room, but sat down again as she plumped down beside him. 'We're having a family conference, I gather.' He folded up the paper and put it beside him and slightly loosened his narrow tie which he wore beneath his brown wool jacket. 'What's it about?'

'About me, I expect,' she said gloomily. 'And James's baby.'

'James's baby! James who?'

'Our James,' she whispered. 'Cousin James Rayner. Hush, Mama's coming downstairs. You'll hear about it soon enough.'

Their mother looked solemn as she stood looking out of the long window into the rose garden. Dusk had gathered, and pockets of shadows from the timbered rose walk hid the pale shoots of clematis which intertwined with the tight buds of white and yellow roses, but in the misty half light, blue and white forget-me-nots glowed in massed profusion. The scent of wallflowers and woodbine drifted towards the house and mingled with the perfume of lavender which grew in shrubby bushes beneath the window.

Victoria came into the room and stood next to her mother, putting her hand into hers. She had dressed in an ankle-length, pale blue muslin dress which showed the edges of her white petticoats and the frill of her drawers; on her white stockinged feet she wore dainty black velvet slippers. Unlike her mother or Sammi, she did not wear a hoop beneath her gown, but layers of petticoats beneath her skirt rustled as she walked.

'Isn't it beautiful, Mama? I do so love spring. I think I prefer it to any other season, it's such a special time.'

Her mother squeezed her hand. 'And I remember you saying the same thing last autumn, when the leaves started to change colour. Every season has its own beauty, Victoria, even the winter, when the snow is on the ground.'

'You wouldn't say that if you were out working in it, Ma,' Richard cut in. 'Try digging out a sheep from a snowdrift or bringing a beast up from the cliff when it's fallen over. Or,' he emphasized, 'being up to your knees in mud when you're ploughing. Any sort of weather is all right when you're inside looking out at it.'

They none of them believed a word he was saying. Richard of all people was always the first up to sample the morning air and usually the last to come home. He was a true countryman, indifferent to the weather unless it affected his livestock, his sowing, reaping or harvesting.

Their father came in as they were talking. William

Rayner had changed for supper into dark trousers and a formal black jacket, and around the neck of his high shirt collar he wore a bow-tied cravat.

'I must tell you, Pa, before it slips my mind,' Richard said. 'We'll have to move the fence near the old barn, it's teetering on the edge. It's good fencing, we don't want to lose it.'

His father sat down in his chair and gazed into the fire. He suddenly looked older and tired. 'Put someone on to it tomorrow. There seems to be no end to it,' he said wearily. 'Back and back.'

'Yes, the sea will be at the front door before we're finished,' Richard commented. 'There's some land coming up for auction at Tillington, Pa. I think we should take a look at it.'

'Yes, I heard. Well, the sea won't reach Tillington. At least, not for generations. But this village is finished.' His voice had a bitter edge. 'Monkston will one day be no more, nor Garston Hall, it will be just a distant memory, like so many other villages along this coastline.'

'Your mother always used to say that one day we would have to move back.' Ellen gazed sadly at her husband.

William nodded. 'It's inevitable that we lose. We can't fight the sea. In my father's day there was a constant battle, the sea versus the land. But we have worked so hard, and we haven't had the workforce, not like in the old days when there were village men available to work the land; though my father must have worked hard too,' he added, 'running the estate and the shipping company.'

'Don't forget your mother,' Ellen chipped in. 'This place was her whole life, he couldn't have done it without her.' She went across to her husband and kissed his cheek. 'But that is all in the past, we must look forward to the future, wherever it is.'

Martha tapped on the door. 'Supper in ten minutes, ma-am?'

Ellen nodded her thanks and turned to her husband. 'Shall we discuss the child after supper?'

'What is there to discuss, Ellen?' William frowned. 'There can be only one decision. The child is not our responsibility. He has to go back to Anlaby.' He looked across at Sammi knitting her fingers together as she watched their faces. 'There will be a rift within the family because of this, Sammi. Isaac and Mildred will be too embarrassed to visit us. Things will not be the same.'

'They will stop coming anyway, William, now that your mother is no longer here,' Ellen said softly. 'She was the thread that kept us all together. Isaac likes to come, but Mildred and Anne hate the weather out here, they complain of the cold even in the summer. They only ever came under sufferance. You can't blame Sammi!'

'I wasn't apportioning blame,' he reasoned. 'But you must understand, Sammi. The child can't stay here.'

'I *don't* understand.' She rose to her feet and burst out impetuously, 'I don't understand! They will put him in one of those terrible places. He'll have no identity, no name, no-one he can call his own.' She burst into tears.

'Sammi! Sammi! Be still a moment and listen.' Her mother came across to her and put her arm around her. 'He won't be sent to a charity home. I've spoken to Gilbert and he promised me he would speak to his father and to James; he said that something would be done; that they were wrong to let you assume the child's care.' She lifted her daughter's chin so that she would have to look at her. 'He is not your responsibility, Sammi,' she said firmly. 'You cannot become involved.'

Sammi wiped her eyes as she followed her parents into the dining-room. Victoria gave her a look of sympathy, but Sammi put her head down lest she start to cry again. Victoria hadn't seen the baby, therefore she couldn't understand how vulnerable, how dependent, how beautiful he was, with his soft transparent skin and dark eyes. She gave a deep trembling breath. *Mama and Pa are afraid for me. They think I will spoil my chances of marriage, that people will say the child is mine.* She sat down at the table and stared at the soup dish in front of her. *What can I do?*

She had always been the scapegrace of the family. Bold and impulsive, she had always drawn the others into her improbable schemes when they were children. Now, her parents were expecting her to behave in an adult manner. Her mother was constantly encouraging her to attend parties and dances where there were eligible young men attending, yet anxious, she knew, that she would make a love match, and not a marriage of convenience.

But I'm not ready for that. I'm not ready to tie myself to a stranger. She stopped in mid-thought. *The baby is a stranger, but I am involved. I feel bound to him, because no-one else seems to care. James won't know what to do,* she fretted. *The baby will have to go to a charity home if Uncle Isaac refuses to help. He won't want to cross Aunt Mildred. And why is she being so stubborn, refusing even to discuss the child? Refusing almost, his very existence! She will, I feel sure, abandon him.*

She finished her soup and waited for the next course: mackerel, freshly caught only this morning by one of the fishermen in the village and baked in a herbed crust of pastry with flour milled by her cousins at Tillington.

I'll go to Tillington and stay with Uncle Thomas. She was suddenly inspired. *I will ask his advice. He said everything would turn out all right. That's what I'll do! I'll ask if I can stay with them until I hear from James; they won't be embarrassed by gossip or angry like Pa is, and while I'm there I'll search for a good home for the baby myself.*

She looked up and gave such a sweet smile to her

mother across the table, that it was answered by a crease of misgiving across her parent's forehead.

It won't be as if I'm running away, she reasoned, as the idea took hold. *They'll know I'm perfectly safe with Uncle Thomas and Tom and the others. That's what I shall do. I'll go to Tillington.*

9

Betsy eased back the bolt on the door and slipped
out, closing it quietly behind her. It was five o'clock,
and the dawn had already broken. Slender streaks of
white and rose fingered the wide skies, and a chorus
of blackbirds were calling in the elms behind the mill.
There was a flurry of tiny wings as a wren flew busily
in and out of a hawthorn hedge along one side of the
yard, and from a neighbouring farm she could hear
the barking of dogs.

She had heard her father and brothers come to bed
not an hour ago, when the breeze which had been
blowing steadily all through the night, finally stilled.
The sails ceased their gyrating, the creaks and groans
of the rotating cap settled and the spin of the
wallower bevel gear which drove the cast-iron shaft
and the great spur wheel ceased, as the massive brake
wheel was wedged securely to stop the sails; and the
millers could dust themselves down and tumble into
bed to sleep like dead men until she roused them
again at six o'clock.

She slipped into the garden behind the house and
through the gap in the hedge onto the footpath
which bordered the field behind. She glanced quickly
behind her to make sure that there was no-one about,
and then walked swiftly towards Redshaw copse.

Will he be there, or was he only baiting me? She felt
breathless with barely concealed excitement. *Anyway,
I don't care if he isn't.* She was trying to convince
herself, in case he didn't come, in case Luke Reedbarrow was merely having fun with the miller's
daughter, as he so often called her. She had met him

on the previous day in the village, where she had gone on a message for her father to the wheelwright. He was leaning on a gate, looking into a grassy paddock where sheep were grazing. He'd turned towards her as she passed and gave her a lazy smile, removing the grass stalk that he was chewing from his mouth. He was dressed as if for work with leather leggings and heavy boots, and he had a battered felt hat tipped on the back of his head. She'd merely given him a superior nod and looked away as she passed, but he'd put out his hand to detain her.

'What's tha hurry, Miss Betsy? No time to talk? Is tha frightened tha brothers might catch thee talking to common folk?'

She'd stopped then and protested that she did as she pleased and would talk to whomsoever she wished. 'I'd even talk to somebody like you, if I had a mind,' she'd said in what she imagined a cutting manner. 'But I haven't.'

He'd simply grinned back at her and chewed again on the piece of grass. 'It's a bit public here, Miss Betsy, half of 'village would have us married off if they should see us jawing.'

She'd tossed her head and looked at him through lowered lashes. 'Don't act the village half-wit, Luke Reedbarrow,' she'd said derisively. 'You don't fool anyone talking the way you do.' He'd stood up straight when she spoke, and looked down on her. He was huge, bigger than any of her brothers. The top buttons on his flannel shirt were undone and she could see his muscular neck and the dark hair curling on his chest.

She swallowed and felt herself blushing as he looked at her. He had a head of thick fair hair and she found that she was surprised that his chest hair wasn't the same colour, nonplussed at the realization that she found the sight of it so pleasurable. He asked her to meet him, so that they could just have a little talk, he said. But she had, of course, refused. He'd persisted, and when she lamely said she was busy all through the day and couldn't get away, he challengingly suggested meeting at dawn.

'You said you could do whatever you wanted,' he said, dropping the broad country accent which he always adopted when talking to her. 'Go on. Just this once. If you dare.'

The challenge was rashly accepted. She wasn't going to be dared by such as him. Who did he think he was? She cared not a jot, but she would show him that she could do whatever she wished and meet whomsoever she wanted.

She pulled her shawl around her. The morning was still cold, the sun had not yet any warmth, and she shivered. *You're a fool, Betsy Foster. What are you doing out here at this time of the morning? He won't come. He's been having a joke with you.*

The pathway down to the copse and beyond was deserted. Few people came down here unless it was to sow or reap the harvest, and now the fields were greening with young crops which were being garnered by flocks of partridge and pigeon. A low whistle attracted her; she glanced about her, her gaze going back towards the mill in fear that her brothers or father were up and about. It came again and someone signalled from the copse. It was Luke. So he had come.

'You came then!' Again he gave her that lazy smile, which turned up the corners of his mouth and crinkled his eyelids in an amused manner.

'I was awake,' she said carelessly.

'Aye, so was I.' He gazed intently at her from deep blue eyes, his smile disappearing. 'I haven't slept all night for wondering if you'd come.' He glanced over his shoulder into the shadow of the copse. 'Come back in here if you like. Nobody will see us in here.'

Her heart started to pound. 'I'd better not,' she whispered. 'I'm only out for a walk.'

'Aye, so am I.' He took hold of her hand and drew

her into the shelter of the trees. 'But nobody would believe that if they should see us. Better not tek 'risk. We can talk just as well in here as in middle of 'footpath.'

She allowed herself to be led a little way in. It was only a young copse, but already an under storey of shrubs was growing thickly between the young saplings.

He took off his jacket and laid it on the ground. 'Would you like to sit down a minute, Betsy?'

She shook her head. She felt so strange, an excitement welling up inside her, tightening her throat, her pulses throbbing and making her feel quite lightheaded. 'No,' she said. 'I'm not tired, why should I want to sit down?'

'Well, folks often do sit down to have a bit of a jaw,' he said patiently. 'Still, if you'd rather stand.' He stood looking at her for a moment and she could almost swear that a laugh was playing around his lips. She looked up at him defiantly and was about to say something cutting when he took hold of her, crushing her into his arms and kissing her forcefully on the mouth.

'Stop that, Luke Reedbarrow. I didn't come here for that sort of thing.' She wriggled in his arms and tried to push him off.

'What did you come for then, Betsy?' Now he was openly laughing at her, but still held her fast. 'You didn't really come just to have a bit of a chat?'

'Get off me, Luke. I have to get back. Stop fooling around.'

He lowered his hands and put them around her waist, he spanned it easily with his large hands, and with his thumbs he stroked her abdomen. 'I'm not fooling, Betsy. I wanted to kiss you. I've wanted to for long enough.'

She stopped her struggling and lowered her eyes and inwardly smiled. *I knew it*, she thought triumphantly. *I knew he'd always been sweet on me, hanging around the mill yard, casting sheep's eyes at me.* She felt a sense of power, a need to tantalize and invite, to provoke him with fire and then to spurn him. She lifted her head and gazed at him with what she thought was a look of allurement, but she hesitated as she saw an ardent eagerness in his eyes and wondered if she had, after all, made a mistake.

'Don't tease, Betsy.' He licked his lips, the smile had gone. 'You don't know what happens to a man when a woman leads him on.'

Again she felt the sense of control. This, then, was how to bring a man to his knees, to have him begging for just a kiss. She leaned against him ever so slightly, so that he would feel just the brush of her body, nothing more, and reached to fasten the top button on his shirt.

'You're not decently dressed, Luke Reedbarrow,' she said softly, and was cut short as he stopped her hand with his and once more drew her close, his lips hard on hers and holding her face fast between his hands.

She didn't stop him. She couldn't have stopped him even if she'd wanted to, which she didn't, for kissing was, she decided, as she swam willingly into a haze of pleasure and desire and put her arms around his neck, a most delightful sensation. She didn't stop him as he undid her bodice and cupped her breasts into his mouth, devouring and sucking each nipple in turn until she was gasping with pleasure.

But she cried, 'No,' when his hand crept beneath her skirt and she felt the strength of his fingers pressing on her bare thighs.

'No. Stop. Stop.' She gasped and tried to sit up. They were lying on his coat and she had barely been aware of them gently sinking down on to it.

He pushed her down again and strode across her, pinning her with his muscular legs. 'Don't say that, Betsy,' he groaned. 'Please, not now. I want thee. Please!'

She licked her dry lips and closed her eyes. She felt as if she had been running, her breath was so short. *I want you? What does he mean, he wants me? I'm here now; he's kissing me, holding me, doing things which surely are wrong, but which are so wonderful, I don't want him to stop. But I must say stop. I must go home, Father will be up and looking for me.*

'My father will be awake soon,' she whispered. 'I can't stay.'

He bent again to kiss her, his lips demanding against hers, and he forced them open with his tongue. When he released her he was breathing heavily and he held the lower part of his body as if he was in pain.

'Come back later, Betsy,' he begged. 'When your da and the lads are in 'mill. Meet me later, *please.*'

'All right,' she said breathlessly, and sat up as he released her and started to fasten up her bodice. He bent once more and kissed her breasts and she thought she would explode with joy. Yes, she would come back. If she had known how wonderful the sensation of being kissed and fondled was, then she might have thought of tempting him before. She stood up and looked down on him and smiled. He was so very handsome. His face was weather brown, and his fair hair streaked blond.

He smiled back at her and lay on his back. 'Are you glad you came, Betsy?' He reached out a hand and she stepped towards him and put out hers.

'Yes,' she admitted, feeling suddenly shy.

'Come here, then. A bit closer.'

She stepped closer, thinking that she might kiss him once more and stood nearer to him. He sat up and once more put his hands beneath her skirt and petticoat, sliding them over her nakedness towards her buttocks and hidden places and burying his head in her skirts.

She took in several gasping breaths, and pressed her hands to her skirts to stop his exploring hands.

111

'I'm not going to hurt thee, Betsy. I just want to hold thee.' He gazed up at her, his lips parted and his eyes glazed. 'Tha's so beautiful. I want to kiss thee everywhere.'

She could scarcely breathe, her throat and ears were hammering, her heart thundering, her whole body trembling and pulsating.

He dropped her skirts and stretched out again, putting his hands behind his head. He smiled and she saw that one of his front teeth had a small chip in it. 'Off you go, then, if you must. Back to your da.'

She was taken aback, her passion brought to an abrupt halt. 'Shall I – when shall I come back?' she breathed. 'Today, did you mean?'

He looked up at her through his fair lashes. 'Does tha want to, Miss Betsy?'

She swallowed and pressed her lips together. Damn him! Yes. Yes. She did want to. She had an ache inside her body that told her that she did. And a confusion in her mind that told her that she shouldn't. 'I can do,' she whispered. 'If I can get out. Maybe this afternoon?'

He sprang to his feet and stood in front of her, his legs wide apart and his arms folded across his chest. He nodded. 'This afternoon then.'

She wanted him to hold her again, but he made no move towards her. 'Yes. I'll try. I won't promise.'

He didn't answer, but just stood looking at her. Impulsively she stood on tiptoe and offered her mouth to him. He bent his head and touched her lips with his, not hard or passionate like before, but softly and tenderly, then gently he kissed her neck and throat and ran his fingertips down her breasts and waist and around her hips. 'Go on, then,' he said huskily and pushed her away.

Betsy didn't know whether to run with joy or slink with shame at her scandalous behaviour. *I should never have gone. I won't go back. Never. I only said I would to get away. Oh, but I want to. Oh, please,* please *let the wind blow so that Da and the lads have to go into the mill.* She clasped her hands together and thought of the strength of him, his big body holding her so close. *He's so strong, yet he's so tender too. He makes me feel – he makes me feel so, so . . . !*

Never before had she felt as she did now, never before felt desire or sensual craving. She had kissed boys often, stolen kisses for a dare or a tease, but had never been so aware of her body as she was now. She walked briskly along the path, ignoring the gap in the hedge, not wanting to sneak through in case Tom or anyone was in the garden, and skipped into the lane and towards the mill gate. There she stopped abruptly and flushed in confusion as she was confronted by Sammi, who was struggling to open the gate and at the same time keep hold of the bridle of her horse. On the floor of the trap was a large carpet bag.

'Betsy! Betsy! What are you up to, girl?' Her father, washed and dressed, called from the doorway, and she and Sammi came running from the paddock where they had turned out Sammi's mare.

'Sammi? What's tha doing here so early? There's no breakfast of course – unless we make it for ourselves.'

'Good morning, Uncle Thomas. Betsy and I will make breakfast in no time at all. She's been helping me with Boreas.'

Betsy heaved a sigh of relief as her father grunted and went inside. He would have asked some awkward questions if Sammi hadn't been there, questions as to where she had been so early in the morning, which she wouldn't easily have been able to answer.

But coupled with her relief at reprieve was frustration, for if Sammi was going to stay as she had requested, then she wouldn't be able to slip away to meet Luke as they had arranged.

And he'll think I don't want to, she thought miserably. *And I do. Oh, how I do!*

10

Ellen Rayner lay wide awake at the side of her sleeping husband. It always amazed her that, no matter what his worries, he fell asleep as soon as his head touched the pillow. *Unlike me,* she thought, gazing up at the ceiling and watching the first dawn-painted fingers of rose and gold streak across it. She could hear the sigh of the sea as it washed on to the shore. *It's gentle today. Perhaps today we won't lose any more land.*

She felt so sad as she thought of William's words last night: that Monkston was finished and one day would be no more. She felt so sad and sorry, for she knew how much he wanted to leave the estate to his sons, as his own father had done. Perpetuity. Eternal. For ever and ever. Amen. A tear trickled down her cheek. *I must be getting old,* she thought. *I'm becoming wise. When did I become aware that nothing lasts for ever? Not the land that we love, not the people that we love.*

Her mind fluctuated to Victoria, her beautiful, fragile daughter who needed such care, yet didn't complain and who wouldn't outlive her parents. *So I needn't ever worry that one day we might leave her.* She thought then of Richard and his cheerfulness; he'd not let a landslip deter him from his farming, he'd simply move back the fence and continue as usual; and Billy, he too would survive; they came from good strong stock, her sons.

She sighed and turned over in bed. *But Sammi! What am I to do with Sammi? She has such a capacity to love.* Her parents, sister and brothers, cousins, all had a share of her bounteous affection. Dogs and cats, horses, lambs and now James's child. *But is he?*

I have a lingering doubt that I can't quite put my finger on.

She heard a rustle outside her door and as she lifted her head from the pillow, she saw a white envelope being pushed beneath the door. She waited for a moment, then threw back the sheets and padded to the door and picked it up. '*MAMA and PA*' was printed on the outside, and it was securely sealed. It had to be from Sammi, she was probably going off for a morning ride. She glanced at the French clock ticking on the mantelpiece. She blinked and looked again. It was only five o'clock! Not even the servants would be up yet.

She sat on the edge of the bed and, brushing her long hair back over her shoulder, carefully tore the envelope open.

'*Dear Mama and Pa,*' it read. '*Please don't be cross with me, but I have decided to stay with Uncle Thomas and Betsy for a little while, if they will have me. If James's baby has to go away, then I would like to choose a place for him myself, somewhere kind where they like children. I promised James, you see, that I would be responsible for him as he isn't able to. I'm taking Boreas and my trap so that I can get about.*'

Ellen turned over the page.

'*I'm not running away. Please do not think that I am, for I love you all too much to do that, but I am so concerned about the baby's welfare and cannot bear to think that he will be rejected again. From your ever loving daughter, Sarah Maria Foster Rayner (Sammi).*'

Ellen put her hand to her face. She wanted to cry. It was so typical of Sammi to take matters into her own hands, yet she felt also a warmth in her heart, that her daughter's compassionate and tender nature had enfolded to encompass a small and defenceless infant. No thought that the child might affect her own future, but only concern for the plight of the child. She walked across to the window and, still grasping the letter, she looked out. The wide skies were lightening across the sea, bringing an unfledged day, and the sun tipped its brightness into the sea, casting its strong light into the grey water and turning it to silver.

I should fetch her back. She'll barely have harnessed up yet. I should bring her in and reason with her, explain that she might regret her action, that people are bound to talk, that she has her own future to think of, a life of her own, a husband, children.

On the distant horizon, the sea and sky fused together in a strong pencil line of aquamarine. She considered it for some time until the chill of the morning roused her. 'It's a long way off,' she murmured. 'Too far to see.'

She slipped the letter under her pillow and, climbing back into bed, she put her arm across William, gathering up his warmth. He turned towards her and sleepily opening his eyes he mumbled, 'Is everything all right?'

'Yes,' she whispered. 'Go back to sleep. Everything is fine.'

In one of the front bedrooms in Humber Villa in Anlaby, Isaac Rayner lay awake, thinking about his youngest son. James had come home from York and told them boldly that he wanted to go to London. 'I want to train to be an artist,' he'd announced, lifting his chin defiantly. 'I hope eventually to be able to earn my own living and become independent.'

He'd looked at his mother as he spoke, hoping, Isaac was sure, for some response from her, perhaps implore him not to go, that she would, after all, prefer him to stay in spite of his alleged misdemeanour. But there was no acknowledgement, no signal even that he should take care amongst strangers and in a strange city. Only a tightening of her lips and a hard swallow in her throat when he said that he was going to paint, and a paleness in her cheeks which only Isaac appeared to notice.

Isaac looked at his bedside clock: five o'clock. Another hour and he would get up. He'd told James that he would go with him to Hull to catch the London train. James had demurred, saying that he would walk into Anlaby and get a lift with the carrier.

At this, Mildred found her voice. 'You cannot possibly ride in the carrier's cart. Your father has offered to go with you. Do not be so churlish as to refuse him.' It was then that Isaac saw anger in his son's eyes as he stormed upstairs to pack a case, and knew that he would never return.

He heard a sound from the adjoining bedroom. *Mildred must be awake too. I wonder if she has slept, or like me, lain awake half the night?*

He got out of bed and, putting on his dressing robe and velvet slippers, he padded to the door and listened. There was a sound of snuffling, of indrawn breaths, and he quietly opened the door. Mildred was sitting on a chair by the window. She must have been there for some time, for she had a blanket wrapped around her. Her bedgown was buttoned high up to her neck, and on her neatly curled head she wore a cotton bedcap.

'Can you not sleep, my dear?'

She turned reddened eyes towards him. 'You know I hardly ever sleep, Isaac. Why should today be any different?'

He nodded. She said she never slept, but often he had looked in on her during the early hours, and she was usually sleeping soundly. But her insomnia, as she called it, was one of the reasons for their separate bedrooms, and had kept him from her bed since their last infant had died.

'I'm sorry, Mildred,' he began. 'So sorry that you can't find it in your heart to forgive James.' He had

117

his own doubts about the child's parentage. James still had the aura of innocence. 'But we must support him financially, even though I know that in view of the scandal you would prefer him to go away. He is so young,' he appealed. 'We all make mistakes when we are young.'

Her face started to crumple at his words and she turned away towards the window. He moved towards her and put his hand on her shoulder.

'Don't touch me!' she cried. 'You know I can't bear it.' She bent her head. 'I'm sorry. But I just can't bear it.' Not since she had given birth to James had she wanted him near her, and only twice since, when he had appealed in despair to her, had she agreed. Anne and the unfortunate babe had been the result, giving her the perfect excuse that as she was so fertile and their family was complete, there was now no necessity for them to share the marital bed. He had not looked for consolation elsewhere, but instead had thrown himself wholeheartedly into the shipping company, working late hours for the last sixteen years, and only now when he thought that passion was finally spent, did he allow himself a little leisure time.

He looked down on her with compassion. She had been such a pretty little thing when he had first met her. Small and dark, and very vivacious, full of energy and vigour, totally unlike the woman she had since become. A woman of frustrated passions, wedded to the wrong man. And now the wheel had turned full circle.

'It is time, I think, for us to talk, Milly.'

She looked up at the sound of her almost forgotten pet name and her eyes filled with tears. 'You haven't called me that in a long time, Isaac.'

'You never wanted me to, my dear,' he said softly. 'You said it reminded you too much of your lost youth.'

'So it did,' she whispered. 'But it doesn't seem to matter any more.'

'No,' he said, looking down at her. 'And soon the last reminder will be gone.'

She looked up at him suddenly, fear showing in her face.

'James won't come back,' he said quietly. 'You realize that, don't you?'

'What do you mean?' Her voice was a strangled whisper.

'I mean that once he gets away, he won't return. He thinks that he is unwanted. I believe that he has always thought that.'

'No.' She stared up at him. Her face was pale and pinched. 'I meant – when you said about the last reminder.'

He said nothing, but sat down in the basket chair opposite her and took hold of both her hands.

'Isaac!' she whispered. 'What was it that you meant?' She swallowed hard and withdrew one of her hands and pressed it against her lips. Her eyes were opened wide. 'Isaac?' Her voice cracked and trembled, but still he didn't answer. After all these years, after all the misery he had suffered, why should he make it any easier for her?

But he wasn't a hard man, rather he was full of compassion for his unhappy wife, warm-hearted, but with no place for his tenderness to fall.

'You know?' she whispered. 'You've always known?'

He nodded. His eyes now filled with tears and he bent his head and kissed her hand. 'I knew from the start,' he mumbled, and reached into his pocket for a handkerchief. 'It was so transparent, and if I hadn't realized at the time, I would have known when James was born. Everyone said how much like you he was. But I knew. I knew from the moment he was born, that he was just like him.'

Isaac stood with James at the door of the carriage. 'Now you're sure you've got all you need for the journey, James? You've got enough money for buying luncheon, and for your lodgings?'

'Yes, Father, you've been more than generous with my allowance. I can't thank you enough for being so understanding, especially about the child, even though I'm not—'

The guard waved his flag and he hastily put out his hand, but his father reached out with both his arms and hugged him. 'You'll write, James, won't you? And you'll try to come for Gilbert's wedding? We'll miss you. I'll miss you. And don't worry about your mother and Anne, they'll come round eventually, and – and as for the child – yes, yes, something must be decided. We must do what we can.'

James nodded, but ignored the questions. 'I'll miss you too, Father, more than I can say.' He looked very young and scared, but there was a bright look of excitement in his eyes. 'You'll be proud of me one day when I'm famous, and everyone is clamouring for me to paint their portraits. You'll be able to say, that's my famous son!'

Isaac gave him a trembling smile. 'I'm proud of you now, James. Don't ever think that I'm not.'

It was still quite early and a bright morning, so Isaac sent the carriage on, telling Spence that he would walk to the office from the railway station.

He wanted to walk in order that he could think. A brisk walk, a look at the ships in the docks or in the Old Harbour, would clear his head and put his problems into perspective. And he wanted to think of James, and of the child, and of Mildred. He had felt an ache in his heart as the train drew away in a great cloud of steam, and James, with his curly black hair blowing, reached out of the carriage window to wave good-bye. He had never thought of James as being anyone but his own son, even though he had always known that he belonged to another man. James had always had a special place in his affections, perhaps because Mildred had spurned him. Spurned him, not because she didn't love him, but because he reminded her of her lost love.

'Do you ever think of him?' he had asked her this morning, as they sat by the window watching the dawn rise.

'Not a day passes,' she said, looking at him with such sorrow that he could have wept, 'that I wonder where he is and if he ever thinks of me.'

And as he watched her he saw, not the middle-aged woman with the lines of age around her eyes, but the beauty of the woman who had once been his and whom someone else had stolen from him.

He stood now on the staith side outside his company building, looking down at the muddy water and the ships moored there, and wondered how passion could last so long. Yet when he had first seen them together, when they had first met, he knew that it was the meeting of twin souls. He suddenly felt very tired, so he rested against a bollard and watched as a Liverpool steamer was being loaded with goods. His hands were cold and he thrust them deep into his greatcoat pocket, and felt the slip of paper which James had given him with the address where he could be contacted.

'Excuse me, sir.'

The voice came from behind him and Isaac turned round. When he turned he grimaced as a pain tore across his shoulders and down his arm.

'Mr Rayner, sir?'

'Yes.'

The man was unknown to him. He wasn't one of their regular workers, nor, he thought, one of the casual men, though he didn't know them all by sight. But then, this man didn't look like a labouring man; his face was too pale, as if he spent a deal of time indoors, and his clothes were thin and though mended with even thinner patches, were not at all suitable for outdoor work. Isaac glanced down at the man's boots, they were stuffed with paper, the toecaps had been cut away to accommodate his feet, and they had no laces.

He put his hand into his waistcoat pocket to take out a coin, one of two which he always kept for beggars, should he be asked.

'Is there any work, sir? I'll do owt. Cleaning out 'holds or privies. I'm not fussy.'

He wasn't pleading, nor being servile as sometimes those who searched for work were. It was as if he didn't really expect anything; yet his eyes scrutinized Isaac's face intently as he waited for his answer.

'You'll have to go to the yard and ask. See the foreman, he deals out the casual work.' His words came out brusquely as he strove to release the tightness of his breath, but he felt uncomfortable under the man's enquiring gaze.

'I went there yesterday, they said there wasn't owt, that's why I waited to see thee, sir.'

'I don't hire the men, you'll have to see the foreman,' he repeated. 'Now, if you'll excuse me.' He rose to go and again fingered the coin. The man hadn't asked for money; should he offer it?

The man shrugged and turned away, and then as if he'd bethought of something, turned back. 'My wife was wondering about 'babby. How he's fairing?'

Isaac stared at him, still clutching the coin between his fingers. 'I'm sorry. What did you say?'

'Our lass's babby that thy son fathered. Missus has been bothered about him, forever moithering; she was wondering if tha kept him or sent him to 'workhouse?'

There was a blackness descending on him. It was gathering around him, sweeping over his eyes and ears like a thick black cloak, covering his mouth so that he couldn't breathe and someone was pulling it tight, tighter and tighter around his chest. 'My son!' he gasped in a barely audible groan.

'Aye. Thy son! I thought it was thee she meant at first, when she said Rayner, but on that morning that she died I realized that it was thy lad that she meant. 'Young Rayner.' He gave a harsh laugh. 'She said that she could have loved him. She said she used to go and wait in a doorway, watching for him at 'yard in hope of seeing him. Love!' He scorned. 'What does anybody know of love.'

Love, Isaac thought, as he bent double in pain. Love is patience. It's waiting and hoping and praying that it will come your way again.

'Is tha poorly, sir? Mr Rayner!'

'Yes.' Isaac sank to his knees on the wharf side. He feared he was going to be sick. 'Get help! Get my son. Gilbert!'

Gilbert after all. Not James. James had gone. Sent away because his mother couldn't bear to watch him grow in his father's likeness.

As he fell, the coin slipped from his fingers and started to roll away towards a stack of packing cases. The man watched it in its convolutions. There was a loaf of bread and a pinch of tea. Or a jar of ale in which to drown your sorrows. He looked down at Isaac Rayner as he lay sprawled on the ground. Money makes no odds at 'end, he thought. No odds at all. He put his fingers to his lips to whistle and a porter at the other end of the staith looked up.

'Fetch help!' he shouted. ''Mayster here is sick.'

When he looked down again the coin had disappeared. He peered between the wooden crates. He could see it. Too far inside for him to stretch his fingers and retrieve it. He grimaced and pulled up his coat collar as he walked away. Somebody would find it. He hoped it was somebody worse off than he was. But he doubted it. It was an unfair world.

When Gilbert arrived at the company in his usual haste, he was given the news that his father was very ill and had been taken to the Infirmary. He looked down at his unconscious father in the hospital bed, and knew that there was little hope of a full recovery.

If, in fact, there was hope at all, for the doctor had pursed his lips and shaken his head, said that he couldn't guarantee anything, and that Mrs Rayner should be sent for immediately. He raced to Anlaby and found that his mother was still in bed and his sister preparing to go out.

'You must cancel your arrangements,' he told Anne. 'Mother will need you. As soon as she is up I will take you both to the hospital.'

Anne started to cry. 'But I can't bear it when anyone is ill, you know I can't, Gilbert. Can't I stay here?'

'No. You can't. You're a selfish little miss and it's about time you thought of others for a change instead of yourself.'

He left her in a sulk and climbed the stairs to his mother's room and knocked on the door. She wasn't sleeping but lay propped on her pillows, a tray with untouched breakfast on the side table.

'Mother. I have to ask you to get up and come with me. Father is ill and in hospital.'

She turned to look at him, her eyes were bright as if she had been crying and there were deep shadows beneath them, and yet as he looked at her, he thought how different she looked. Her face had lost its customary sternness and she had loosened her hair from her cap so that it flowed around her shoulders. In her hand was a tortoiseshell mirror.

'Ill? What do you mean?'

'Seemingly he collapsed at the riverside. Mother, will you get dressed? We must go immediately. Spence is waiting now with the carriage.'

She reached for her robe and put it around her and then threw back the quilted bedspread. 'Then it is my fault. I have brought him to this.'

'What nonsense are you talking, Mother? You were not there. And had you been, there wasn't anything you could have done. Now, get dressed. I'll send Mary up to help you and we'll go as soon as you are ready.'

His mother's words, though he didn't understand

them, had increased his own sense of guilt, for once again he had been late to the office after spending a late evening playing billiards and losing money at cards. He had also fully intended seeing James off on his journey. Instead, having spent an uncomfortable night on a truckle bed in his empty house in Charlotte Street, he had fallen fast asleep at six a.m., and not woken again until nine.

His mother came down within half an hour to where he and Anne were waiting in the hall. 'We must send for James,' he said as he handed them into the carriage. 'He will have to come straight back.'

His mother stared at him and clung to his arm when the carriage jerked as it turned into the road. 'James?' she said vaguely. 'Oh, yes. I suppose that he must.' She looked away out of the window. 'He won't arrive in London until this evening.'

Gilbert was preoccupied with what he must do. His father took on so much of the responsibility of running the company, and Gilbert, unlike his father, had never been to the Arctic, had never sailed further than Holland, and therefore didn't understand the needs of the whaling men who sailed in their ships.

'You must give me his address, Mother, and I'll get a telegram off straight away.'

His mother clutched her fingers together in a tight knot. 'But I don't have an address. I don't know where he is staying.'

'You don't know?' Gilbert stared at his mother. 'But does Father know? You know how woolly-minded James is, he'll forget to write!'

She hung her head and bit her lips together. 'I don't know,' she repeated. 'Your father said that he wouldn't return, and I fear he may be right.' Tears started to trickle down her face, and Gilbert and Anne looked at her in dismay. 'The only person who could bring him back is your father.'

Gilbert shook his head in disbelief. 'And Father is

unable to. If James doesn't hear from him, then we may never see him again!'

Anne fainted at the sight of her father lying so white and still, and had to be taken to an anteroom to lie down. Gilbert stayed a little while with his mother as she sat at Isaac's bedside, and then left her to go to the office, to send messages to those who would be concerned.

Mildred looked down at Isaac. 'I'm sorry, Isaac,' she whispered. 'So very sorry that I have brought you to this. How I have wasted our life together, how very cruel I have been.'

She ran her fingers over her cheekbones and around her mouth. 'I looked in the mirror this morning after you and James had gone, and I saw myself as I was. Not someone still young and beautiful as *he* would remember me, but a middle-aged, bitter woman who has wasted away any chance of happiness with the man who really loved me – by waiting for someone to come back for me.' She took hold of his still, pale hand. 'And because of me we have lost a son; a son who loved you and hated me.' She stroked his hand with her fingers. 'But, please. If you will only get better, I will try to make it up to you. I'll try to salvage some kind of happiness for you, for us both, before it is finally too late.'

11

When James emerged from the train at King's Cross station he was nervous with pent-up excitement. He picked up his bag, said good-bye to the other occupants who had shared the long journey from Leeds Central station and walked out of the station concourse.

There was a bustle here which was different from both Hull and York. There appeared to be thousands of people milling outside the station, but there was also a mêlée of hackney carriages, omnibuses crowded with passengers, cabriolets and costermongers' carts; adding to the confusion were teams of drovers and their barking dogs who were bringing in flocks of sheep from the country districts on their way to market.

Many of the women in the crowd were fashionably dressed. Some in dome-shaped crinolines and velvet jackets trimmed with fur, others, though they wore cages beneath their gowns, had the fullness of their skirts pushed back, making the front flatter and the bustle enormous. Their headwear, he noticed, as he watched and admired for a few moments, was small and neat; toques and spoon-shaped bonnets placed precariously on high-set chignons and ringlets, as well as on neat smooth coils. But he noticed, too, that amongst the affluent crowd, and mingling between the hurrying top-hatted men of business were small boys in threadbare coats and caps too big for them, and labouring men who appeared to have no labour at that time of day, and were listlessly watching the scene with no enthusiasm whatsoever.

He hailed a hansom cab and asked the driver to take him to the riverside village of Chelsea, and sat in the low-slung cabriolet gazing with bright eyes at the prospect of the new life in front of him as he was bowled along the streets of London.

Red brick and grey Portland stone dominated the scene, and pillared porticos fronted some of the more elegant buildings. He glimpsed small squares with cobblestones and plane trees within the railed gardens, and black-and-white timbered houses with overhanging gables which reminded him of the Tudor houses in York. Cool courtyards with marble and stone statues were glimpsed behind low walls, with the flickering shadow of tall trees dappling enclosed circles of grass. The cab driver took him along the tree-lined road by the Thames. Steamers, yachts and pleasure boats plied along the choppy water, and there was a village atmosphere as they approached Chelsea, with its pretty houses and flowering gardens.

Batsford's lodgings were in a tall Georgian house in Cheyne Walk, overlooking the Thames. James opened the high iron gate which led into the small square of grassed garden, mounted the three steps to the front door and rang the bell.

A man's felt hat appeared from the basement steps and beneath it a woman's face, upturned to look at him; as she walked up the steps the rest of her appeared. A large apron covered her black dress and she carried a pail in one hand and a broom in the other. 'There ain't nobody in, my dear, but Mr Batsford or Miss Gregory will be back soon if you want to wait.'

'Mr Batsford will be expecting me, I think. I've come from Yorkshire.'

'I dare say, sir,' she agreed. 'But that wouldn't stop him going out for his walk along the bank. I can't let you in. He wouldn't like that. He don't like folk seeing his things. Not without him being there. You can sit on the steps or across on the seat by the river.' She pointed over her shoulder towards the river and then threw the contents of the pail into the garden and once more disappeared below into the basement.

James put down his bag and sank down onto the steps. He was stiff with travelling and also hungry. There was no food available once he had left Leeds and he had eaten his parcel of food before the train had gathered steam and left the station. He sat for half an hour on the cold step and was beginning to feel chilled. Dusk was drawing in and a damp mist from the river was thickening about him; leaving his bag behind, he got up and crossed over the road and stood looking at the river, at the busy traffic of steamers and barges which were travelling up and down the Thames, and at the donkeys and carts, farmers and country folk, who were passing over the old bridge which ran over the water towards Battersea. He glanced down the road; there were a few people strolling in groups of three or four, hansom cabs and gigs were bowling along with their jaunty high-stepping pairs or single horses, and striding along in the middle of the road was a short figure with a swirling cloak and a large black hat.

He watched the man as he approached and saw him turn into the gate and stop as he saw James's bag on the steps. He stooped to look at it and then turned back towards the river.

James lifted his hand in greeting and hurried across. 'Mr Batsford? I'm James Foster Rayner. I believe Clive Peacock has written to you about me.'

Batsford rubbed his clean-shaven chin. His hair was long and dark, and beneath the rim of his hat, a greying fringe on his forehead was curling in the damp air. 'Did he? Perhaps he did. You're right, I'm sure he did write about somebody.' He fished around in his waistcoat pocket, brought out a key and put it in the door. 'You'd better come in while I try to remember what it was that Peacock said about you.'

James picked up his bag and followed him in to the small hallway.

'Did he say you were a poet or a plumber? My memory is not what it was. I get so engrossed, you know, when I'm busy with a work that I don't absorb what anyone is saying or doing. In fact, if it were not for Miss Gregory reminding me to eat or drink and sending me out for my constitutional walk, I would stay locked in my room for weeks.'

He was a man of about forty, with a gaunt face and myopic grey eyes. He peered at James through round spectacles which perched half-way down his nose.

'No, sir.' James grinned at him. 'I am in neither of those occupations. Peacock suggested that I might become an artist.'

'*Might* become an artist?' Batsford frowned. 'You either are an artist or you are not! You cannot become one by a mere suggestion. Come. We cannot talk out here.' He led the way up the stairs until, at the third and final floor, he opened up another door which led into his rooms. 'I make no apology for the state of housekeeping. If you can find a free chair you may sit down.'

James glanced around the room. An unmade bed was beneath the window. Unfinished sketches and paintings leant against the walls. Empty picture frames were stacked in untidy piles in the corners of the room, and in two of the three chairs, an assortment of velvet and lace drapes and shawls, fruit and vegetables, bread, bowls and jugs were heaped in a colourful confusion. In the third chair, a young woman lay fast asleep.

'That's Miss Gregory.' Batsford flicked his hand towards her by way of explanation.

'Oh,' James whispered.

'No need to whisper.' Batsford unfastened his cloak and let it fall in a heap on to the floor. 'She won't wake up for hours.'

James gazed at Miss Gregory. She was full-lipped,

with long lashes on her heavy sleeping eyelids, and her thick reddish hair floated across her face and shoulders like a shawl. She wasn't what he considered beautiful, he contemplated, but she had an interesting face. He viewed her with all the astute experience of his eighteen years, safe in the knowledge that he could observe her without her awareness; he wondered if she was Batsford's model.

'Is this where you paint, sir?'

'What?' Batsford was searching amongst a pile of papers, books and unwashed dinner plates which were littering an oval table. 'Oh, no. Not at all. Ah, here it is.' He pulled out a sheet of writing paper from beneath the jumble. 'I knew it was around somewhere. No. I'll show you.'

He waved a finger at him and opened a door to what James had thought must be a cupboard. Inside the door were steps leading up to another room within the roof space of the building.

'This is magnificent,' James breathed. Though the room was now dim, he could imagine it as it would be during daylight hours with the light flooding in. It was a long room, painted white, spreading the length of the building. A skylight was set in the roof and a large window overlooking the river had been added. Unlike the living-room, this studio was bare: uncluttered but for an easel with a virgin canvas; a table, with neatly arranged boxes of water-colours and tubes of oil paints, a jug holding various brushes, and a chaise longue draped with a heavy shawl.

'Magnificent,' he repeated, 'to have a room such as this with no distractions, no discord or ornament to sidetrack one's concentration. Nothing to interrupt the inner thought or inspiration.'

Batsford's face broke into a smile. 'So! Perhaps you are an artist, after all?'

'I'd like to be, sir; if I'm good enough. But I need to be good enough to earn my living. I want to be independent from my parents.'

'Peacock says that you have talent, but that it needs to be brought out. Well, I trust his judgement, but I don't take many pupils. We will talk. Do you have any money?' he asked abruptly.

'Erm, a little, sir. I took the precaution of not bringing much with me, in case of pickpockets, you know. My father will transfer a sum to a bank as soon as I am settled.'

'Good.' Batsford swept out of the studio and down the steps. 'In that case we will eat.' He picked up his cloak from the floor and swung it around his shoulders. 'I know of a place where we can eat a good meat pie and drink a glass of wine and meet some friends you might be glad to know.' He banged the door behind them, mindless of the sleeping Miss Gregory, and marched along out of Cheyne Walk and around the corner into the King's Road, with James hurrying beside him.

'You have heard of Rossetti, of course, and Ruskin? You may perhaps meet them in due course. If I decide to take you, I mean. Rossetti is in Paris just now, he has at last married dear Elizabeth and taken her on honeymoon. He is working more and more in oils, but alas, her illness distracts him.'

James was speechless. To hear the revered names dropped so casually from Batsford's lips stunned him so much that he couldn't even bring himself to question him about them. They entered an inn and Batsford made his way to a rear room where several people were seated at a long table. He introduced James as a friend of Peacock's from Yorkshire, and dropped random names so quickly that he couldn't immediately match names with faces. But there were several young men there, two whose names he caught as William Morris and Burne-Jones, who were maybe only six or seven years older than himself, which he found encouraging as he had expected to meet only older persons such as Batsford and Peacock. Two young women were in the company, one a poet and the other, Eve, a model for Burne-Jones.

He bought supper for Batsford and himself and looked in some dismay at his thin pocket-book when he had paid the bill, but he ceased to worry over finances as he became engrossed in such conversations as he had never dreamed of: of literature and poetry, of architecture and art, of music and symbolic beauty, and his head swam with the wonder of it all. He drank his fourth glass of red wine and leaned his elbow on the table, cradling his head in his hand. He smiled blearily at Eve, who was sitting opposite him, and thought that she must be the most beautiful woman he had ever seen. He tried to ask her if one day she would model for him, but each time he opened his mouth, nothing but a jumble of muttered words fell from his loose tongue. He was desperately tired and he put his head on the table and closed his eyes.

When he awoke, daylight was streaming in above the bed where he was lying in Batsford's living-room. There was no sign of Batsford or Miss Gregory, but on the table which had had some of the objects swept aside, was a jug of milk and a fresh loaf of bread. He poured himself a glass of milk and cut a thick slice of bread and as he sat on the edge of the bed, eating and drinking, he wondered how he had got back to Batsford's rooms, for he could remember nothing. But he had no headache or tiredness. He was simply filled with a joyous expectation of happiness and fulfilment.

I am going to be a painter, he exulted. *I shall meet Rossetti and talk to him and perhaps ask him his opinions of my work. I might even go abroad to study. Maybe to Paris or Florence or Venice, where I will observe the paintings of the great Masters, and meet with the contemporary painters of today. I shall one day be renowned for my mastery in the techniques of realism or – perhaps – mysticism.* All this he would do, just as soon as he had persuaded Batsford that he must take him as a pupil, and had found himself a room and bought paint and canvas.

He listened. A faint sound, a creak of a board or a window opening, and he surmised that there was someone in the upstairs studio. He put down his empty glass and brushed crumbs from his shirt and wondered what had happened to his shoes. He opened the door and mounted the steps to the studio, unwilling to intrude if Batsford was working. Which he was. He had his back to James and was completely absorbed with his subject which he was portraying on the canvas.

James drew in a sudden silent breath and his jaw dropped at the sight of Miss Gregory lying languidly on the chaise longue, her eyes closed as they had been yesterday evening. One plump arm was behind her head, her glorious hair covering one abundant breast, whilst the rest of her was completely naked. Once more he gazed at the sleeping woman, but this time he was open-mouthed, as he had never before seen a real woman in nakedness. When painting in school they had only ever used wooden manikins, and Peacock had often bemoaned the loss of real flesh and form, to the amusement and regret of his students.

As he silently observed her, he was in some way reminded of his cousin, Sammi. Not in a lascivious manner, for it wasn't the woman's body which reminded him, but the sweep of her hair which was thick and luxuriant as Sammi's was, and in the complete, innocent repose which surrounded her. At the thought of Sammi, his mind immediately linked with the child, and the reason for him being here, so far from home. *How in heaven's name? How could I have been with a woman? How could I have been with a woman and known such beauty, and not remember? It cannot be possible!*

As he pursued these silent questions, Miss Gregory opened her eyes. They were large and dark, with huge pupils which stared right back at him. Her eyebrows raised, and in a single swift movement she drew a muslin shawl, which was lying beside her, around her body, and in doing so portrayed herself, not as a human form, but as a sensual physical woman.

'I beg your pardon.' James flushed to his hair roots. 'I didn't mean to intrude.'

Batsford turned, a paintbrush held in his hand. 'Come in, Rayner, come in. I trust you slept well? Miss Gregory and I have been working for hours, ever since sun-up. We'll take a break now and a bit of a stretch.'

Miss Gregory slipped on a robe and walked up and down the room. She was perhaps in her middle or late twenties, and James wondered what compelled her to such an occupation. She must be very poor, he thought, to submit to displaying her body; allying in his naïvety the art of modelling with that of prostitution.

'Well, now, Rayner. Could you paint such a subject as Miss Gregory? And how would you portray her? She is one of the best models in London, so if you should want to paint her you will have to speak very nicely to her.'

James swallowed hard, but took heart when Miss Gregory smiled at him. 'I, er, I think I would portray her as a country girl with flowers in her hair, or perhaps sitting in a meadow or walking by the sea.'

Batsford pursed his lips and then nodded. 'Yes, she could have that quality, perhaps. What do you think, Miss Gregory, could you see yourself as a country maid and not a siren or Muse as some do?'

Miss Gregory shrugged. 'Right now,' she said, 'all I can think of is a nice cup o' tea and a biscuit.'

'Alas, it is merely a job to her,' Batsford sighed as she disappeared down the stairs. 'She has no higher feelings than wondering what is for her lunch or supper.' He looked James over appraisingly and then nodded. 'We'll see what you can do. Have you materials with you?'

'I have my drawing pad and pencils in my bag, sir.'

'Good. Then you can start now. Go off and do a sketch and come back in an hour. By the way, Rayner, don't keep calling me sir, there's a good fellow. You're no longer at school. Batsford will do.'

'Yes, sir – Batsford, I mean. Thank you. Thank you very much.'

With his pad beneath his arm and his pencil bag clutched in his hand, he ran down the steps and across the road to the river. The morning was warm and he had left his jacket inside. He put down his pad and pencils on a seat and rolled up his shirt sleeves; he was beginning to feel such freedom, even with such a simple act as being out of doors without his coat.

He put his hand to his forehead and with narrowed eyes looked at the bright rippling water as it flowed beneath the bridge. He knew what he would sketch. He would sketch his first memorable view of London. He would draw, and then later paint, a picture of Battersea Bridge crossing the Thames. He sat down on the seat and closed one eye and, aligning his pencil against the outline of the bridge, he sought the proportions and started to draw. Thoughts of home, his parents, his reason for being here, were gone. He was totally absorbed. *I am going to be an artist. I am an artist. I shall hyphen my name as Burne-Jones does, and sign myself Foster-Rayner; and all the world will know me.*

12

Sammi was puzzled by her cousins' demeanour when she asked if she might stay for a little while. Betsy, whilst proclaiming that she was overjoyed to have Sammi visit, appeared nervous and ill at ease, and kept looking through the window or wandering to the door and looking out across the yard.

Tom seemed stunned at her request to stay, and hardly said a word to her, and Mark was positively aggressive, muttering under his breath something about a Rayner brat, and she wasn't sure if he was referring to her or to James's child. Uncle Thomas said he didn't mind so long as her mother agreed, and George seemed pleased about the arrangement, although she suspected that he thought they might get their supper on time if she was around to organize it. She was surprised, too, and just a little hurt that her mother or father hadn't come hurtling over to Tillington the same day, to try to take her back or to ask for further explanations, which she had rehearsed over and over again.

At least Mrs Bishop was pleased to see her when she visited her the next day, especially when she said that she would take the child off her hands for part of the day.

'What name has this bairn been given, Miss Rayner? I can't keep calling him, *him*.'

'He hasn't got a name yet, Mrs Bishop. At least, not so far as I know. What should I do?' she asked anxiously. 'No-one has thought about it.'

'What? Tha's not saying poor bairn hasn't been baptized? That's a sin! Tha must see to it straight away. Tha'll not be able to tek him into anybody's house till tha does.'

'But you have him in your house, Mrs Bishop.' Sammi looked at her in alarm. What if she refused to feed him any more?

'Oh, aye. But there's not so many heathen such as me. Most of good Christian folk round here wouldn't have him inside of 'house door. Besides,' she added, 'I put a screw o' salt in his crib to keep 'Devil away.' She unbuttoned her dress and started to suckle her own child. 'So, I'm telling thee, miss. Go and see 'parson now whilst 'bairn is sleeping, and see if he'll do him straight away.'

Sammi took the child in her arms and wrapped him in a blanket. He was warm and smelt of milk and she hugged him and put her face next to his.

'Tek care, miss. Tha'll 'come over fond on him like I keep telling, and won't want to let go.' She called Sammi back from her door. 'Bring him back when he's hungry – and Miss Rayner?'

'Yes?' Sammi turned to her and smiled. Mrs Bishop looked the picture of contentment as she sat by her low fire. The room was clean though sparsely furnished, another child slept in a cot in a corner and two more were by her feet on the floor. She had a glass of ale by her side which she kept sipping as she fed her baby.

'Think on how tha names him. It's with him all of his life, and think too how tha names his parents.'

I know what she is telling me. What a good woman she is. The villagers will think he is mine if I say that his name is Rayner.

She passed a group of women standing outside their cottages, some of them dipped their knee as she passed, but she felt all eyes upon her and their curiosity.

They all knew her, she worshipped at Tillington church where the family had their pew; she visited those in need with her mother, and she was known as a member of the Rayner family who had lived all of their lives at Monkston. But what were they thinking now, and what would be the gossip when she was out of hearing? She lifted her chin and walked on. They could think what they liked. ·

The vicarage was opposite the church just down the hill from the mill, but she hesitated at the entrance to the large redbrick house, and on impulse turned back, crossed the lane and went through the lych-gate into the churchyard. She cut across the winding path and made her way up the sloping grassy area to the highest point where her grandparents' grave was laid. Here was the spot which her grandmother, Sarah Foster Rayner, had chosen when her husband John had died. She had chosen it especially, knowing that one day she would lie here with him, and that together they would be within the sight and sound of the German Ocean which washed the cliffs below their beloved home. How they loved the sea, Sammi thought, though they loved the land more; Grandmama, especially, was devastated each time the sea claimed more land. What an appetite it has, she used to say. What hunger.

Sammi looked down at the grave, neatly kept and garlanded now with flowers from the Fosters' garden. *What would you do, Grandmama? What would you do about this child?*

She heard the creak of the church gate and glanced up to see Luke Reedbarrow coming across to her. He touched his hat. 'How do, Miss Rayner. Grand morning.'

'Yes.' She prepared to move away, down to the gate, her reverie disturbed. 'It's very pleasant indeed.'

'Taking 'bairn for a walk, is tha?' He opened the gate for her and stood back as she went through.

'Did you want something, Luke? You didn't come into the churchyard to chat about the weather?'

'By, tha's that sharp, Miss Rayner.' He glanced at her sheepishly from beneath his long lashes and she wondered why she had the impression that he was mocking her. 'How did tha guess?'

'What is it then?' she said. 'I must be going.'

He took off his hat, and his fair hair ruffled in the breeze, and she mused that Betsy was right, he was quite handsome, not in a gentlemanly way with fine chiselled features, but with broad, strong cheekbones and a winning smile on his wide mouth.

'Will you give Miss Betsy a message for me?' he asked. 'Will you tell her I waited? And I'll do 'same again.'

Sammi stared. What was this? A tryst between Betsy and Luke Reedbarrow? Uncle Thomas would be furious if he knew.

'Please.' His blue eyes were appealing. 'I'd be grateful.'

She swallowed. Would it do any harm? Betsy never had any fun. A mild flirtation wouldn't go amiss, surely? 'I'll try,' she said. 'But I won't promise.'

He grinned and put on his hat again. 'Thanks, Miss Rayner. I knew I could rely on thee. I'm much obliged.'

She watched him go back down the lane. *What an infuriating fellow*, she thought. *I'm sure he was laughing at me.*

The bell on the vicarage door jangled and she asked the maid who answered if she could speak to Mr Collinson. Mrs Collinson crossed the hall as she waited and invited her into her husband's study.

'What have we here, my dear? Whose child is this?'

Sammi felt some reluctance to discuss the baby with her. She had always found the vicar's wife an overbearing, condescending woman who habitually lectured her husband as well as his parishioners.

'His mother is dead, Mrs Collinson.' She gave scanty explanation. 'She died giving birth to him.'

'And so the Rayners have shown compassion on the little one!' Mrs Collinson clasped her hands together in praise. 'How commendable. But it is of course our Christian duty to assist others in their need.'

Sammi heaved a sigh of relief as the door opened and Mr Collinson entered and greeted her. He looked dour, his thin face hiding a benevolent nature.

'Would you baptize this child, Mr Collinson? His mother is dead and I—'

'You mean he hasn't yet been baptized and you have brought him here?' Mrs Collinson threw up her hands. 'Take him out. Take him out at once. He is unclean until he has been blessed at the font!'

'Come, come, Mrs Collinson,' Mr Collinson protested. 'We don't believe in that superstitious nonsense. God blesses all of His children.' He put his hand out to Sammi and she followed him, turning her head to see the indignant horror on Mrs Collinson's face.

'I don't understand.' She hurried beside the vicar across the lane to the church. 'How can innocent babes be unclean?'

He opened the heavy church door and ushered her inside. 'There are many who believe that children are conceived in sin, Miss Rayner, and therefore with their mothers must be cleansed before being accepted back into society.'

'You don't believe that, Mr Collinson?' she asked as she watched him pour water into the font.

'No.' His face lit with a radiant smile. 'I don't. I believe that God accepts all of His children, sinners and all, without question. But,' he raised his eyebrows, 'don't tell my bishop or my wife that I said so.' He took the child from her and unwrapped his head. 'We should also have witnesses to this baptism, Godfather and Godmother to guarantee his Christian upbringing. Is there no-one who will stand for him?'

She shook her head. 'Only me. Can't I be his Godmother? There is no-one else who cares.'

He looked at her for a moment, a candid question

in his eyes, and then nodded. 'I will join you then as a second witness. Together we will take care of his spiritual upbringing. How do you name this child, Miss Rayner?'

Sammi hesitated. *It isn't really up to me,* she thought. *But then no-one else seems inclined to trouble themselves. So what name shall I give him?*

Her mind turned again to her grandmother. She wouldn't have turned this child away. She would have shown compassion. *As James's child, he would have been her great grandson, as much a part of her family as I am and my family and cousins are. How wide the ripples spread.*

And, she realized, he was the first. She gazed at him sleeping contentedly in the vicar's arms. The first of the next generation.

'Adam,' she said. 'Adam Foster Rayner.'

'Can tha be sure he's a Rayner?' her uncle asked when she told them that evening. 'There's no proof.'

'Why should the woman lie, Uncle? There's no reason why she should walk all the way to Anlaby if she didn't know; she could so easily have taken him to any other family with sons in Hull.'

'Why did she walk all that way?' Betsy wondered. 'Why didn't she just take him into Masterson and Rayner's office?'

'She'd have been turned away,' her father said, lighting up his pipe and stretching out in his chair. 'She'd never have got past 'door.'

'Perhaps she was hoping to see a woman there,' Sammi said thoughtfully. 'Someone who would show compassion.'

Her uncle gazed at her as he sucked on his pipe. 'Just as well tha was still there, then. She'd have been sent off wi' a flea in her ear if it had just been James's ma.'

Tom had been sitting silently, just listening to the conversation, and Mark had turned his back, whittling furiously on a thin sliver of wood.

'God's teeth.' Mark dropped the wood and threw the knife on the table. Blood gushed from his hand.

'Watch thy language!' his father barked. 'I'll not have blasphemy in front of thy sister and Sammi.'

Mark put his hand to his mouth and sucked the blood. 'Tha'll not have blasphemy. But tha'll have a bastard child in 'house!' He pointed a bloody, accusing finger, first at Sammi and then at his brothers and then at his own chest. 'Just wait. Afore long there'll be rumours all round Holderness that 'child belongs to one of us. Why else would it be here? And if *she* stays here,' he pointed again at Sammi, 'everybody will think it's hers and that she's been turned out by her ma and da.'

For a second, no-one spoke. Sammi felt sick with dismay. She had had no intention of embroiling her uncle and cousins into any controversy over the child, and the fact that Mark had suggested that she had, horrified her. 'No-one would think such a thing,' she began, but Mark interrupted her.

'Everybody *will* think it.' He stared her in the face and she shrank back from the anger she saw there. 'Tha knows there's every reason why. Women can hide a babby under their skirts 'till it's time to drop.' His lip curled. 'We've onny thy word that it isn't thine.'

'*Enough!*'

Tom and his father rose to their feet at the same instant, and Sammi didn't know who it was who had roared out. Uncle Thomas's face was flushed and furious, while Tom's was ashen.

'Outside!' Tom spat through clenched teeth. He pointed to the door. 'Go on. Out!' He moved towards his brother and helped him on his way with a prod to his ribs. '*Out*, I say!' His voice grew to a roar and he started to unfasten his shirt buttons.

Without a backward glance, Mark reached for the brass door knob, leaving a smear of blood on it, and charged outside.

'They'll have a scrap now, Da.' George rose to his feet and made for the door. 'I'm going to watch.'

'Sit down!' his father bellowed. 'This isn't a game. Tom will give him 'hiding he deserves, and if he doesn't I will, and thee as well if tha doesn't watch thaself.'

Sammi sat frozen-faced and trembling. She wasn't used to violence. Her father, Richard or Billy settled their differences by talking them through, and her father's temper, which often simmered below the surface, was usually kept well in control.

But Mark had always been hot-headed and quick-tempered, yet she was amazed and not a little confused to find that his anger had been directed at her and the child.

'Get your coat off.' Tom rolled up his sleeves.

'I've no quarrel with thee.' Mark kicked the dust with his boot.

'Shall I send Sammi out to fight with you then? Is that what you want?' Tom pushed his brother on his chest and Mark turned away angrily. 'Is that why you picked on her? A woman who can't fight back?'

'I didn't pick on her. I'm onny saying what's true; folks will think 'bairn belongs to one of us.' Mark laughed mockingly. 'Maybe tha won't mind, tha's allus been sweet on her.'

Tom aimed a fist at Mark's jaw and he staggered back, holding his chin.

'Truth hurts, does it?' Mark undid his waistcoat. 'All right, if tha wants to fight, so be it.'

They both unfastened their shirts and pulled them over their heads and dropped them. The night was warm and it was still light; a moon had risen over the sea and was shedding its brightness over Tillington, and the church and the mill stood out in silhouette against the sky.

Sammi came to the door and Tom heard her gasp as she saw them half-naked, preparing to fight.

'Go back inside,' he ordered. 'We don't need spectators. This is our fight.'

'Aye.' Mark gave a short laugh. 'Go inside. Tha won't want to see our Tom bleeding all over 'yard. 'Sight would sicken a lady like thee.'

She picked up her skirts and ran towards them and hammered blows at Mark with her fists. 'Don't you dare!' she threatened. 'Don't you dare!'

Mark doubled over with laughter then swiftly picked Sammi up and swung her out of the way and, aiming a swift blow at Tom, hit him squarely on his nose.

'Leave them.' Betsy had followed Sammi outside and pulled her away, as she helplessly watched the two brothers punching each other with their bare fists. 'They've been building up to this for weeks. Don't think it's just about you,' she said calmly. 'Mark's been asking for a hiding and now he's getting one.'

'But they're killing each other!' Sammi with her hand over her mouth watched from the doorway. 'I'm going to fetch Uncle Thomas.'

'Aye, all right, little lass. I'll go and stop them if it upsets thee.' Her uncle knocked out his pipe and rose reluctantly from his chair at her plea to come at once. 'But it doesn't mean owt. They'll not be sworn enemies 'cos of this, though Mark spoke out of turn; and it'll not happen again.' He went out into the yard and stood for a few minutes watching his sons as they grappled together on the rough ground. Then with a sigh, he walked across to them and with a heave of his brawny arms he took hold of both of them by their hair like a pair of young pups and hauled them to their feet.

'Pump!' he roared and both Betsy and George dashed forward to the water pump. George got there first and with a grin of delight started to work the handle. Sammi watched with her mouth agape as Uncle Thomas shoved both his sons beneath the rushing water and held them there though they spluttered and cursed, until he finally let them go.

Then turning to the grinning George, who was having great enjoyment as he watched his two older brothers in such an exhausted bloody state, he grabbed him too and pushed him under the flowing water.

'That's not fair!' he gasped as he came up. 'I didn't do owt. I never said a word.'

'No?' said his father. 'Then I do apologize. But perhaps it'll do for 'times when tha did and I didn't catch thee.'

'Sorry, Tom.'

The two brothers were upstairs changing out of their wet trousers.

'It's Sammi you should be apologizing to.' Tom's voice was bitter. 'That was a terrible thing to say.'

'I know.' Mark sat on the edge of the bed and peeled off his socks. 'I'll tell her I'm sorry.' He grinned slyly. 'It's true though, what I said about tha being sweet on her. Tha allus had a soft spot for her, even when we were bairns.'

Tom didn't answer him, but sat tenderly touching his swollen nose. Mark, too, ran his fingers over his jaw, and with his tongue felt a chipped tooth.

'It's not really her or 'babby that's irritating me,' he confessed. 'I just feel – I just feel that life's moving on without me. I'm stuck here, day in, day out, shifting sacks of grain and flour, and I can see myself still doing it when I'm Da's age.' He shook his head despondently. 'There's got to be more.'

'Well, what do you want to do?' Tom was sharp. Mark's words had hit a nerve. 'You could go somewhere else and be a miller. You could go to Beverley to Uncle Joe's, he'd take you on.'

Mark reached into a cupboard for another pair of breeches. 'Look at these,' he said, throwing them on the floor. 'They've not been washed! Betsy should get herself organized.' He rooted around for another pair. 'No. I don't want to go to Beverley. That would be just 'same as being here.' He pulled on an old pair of cord breeches and buttoned them. 'You know, when I'm up on 'top of barn mending 'roof, I can see right across to Monkston. I can see 'ocean, and ships sailing across it, and I just thought – I've lived within 'sight of German Ocean for twenty-four years and never once been across it. All I've ever done is fished from a coggy boat within sight of 'land.'

'You should have been a sailor then,' Tom said grimly. 'You didn't have to be a miller, nobody forced you.'

'It was expected though, wasn't it?' his brother replied resentfully. 'Carrying on family tradition. Well, I'd like to do something for my own sake and not because Da and his da did it. Aye, maybe one day I'll up and go, 'cos I want more than being rooted here and maybe bedding and wedding some village lass. There's got to be more to life than that.'

'Betsy? Are you asleep?'

'No. I'm wide awake.'

Sammi sat up in bed and, leaning on her elbow, looked across the room at Betsy in the other bed. 'Do you think I should go home? I don't want to be a trouble. I didn't think. I'm really sorry about what happened tonight.'

Betsy turned over to face her. 'No. Don't go, Sammi. I like it when you're here. There's no-one to talk to otherwise, only Nancy when she comes in of a morning, and she doesn't have any conversation.'

'I should think she doesn't have the time to talk, and anyway she comes to work, not to be a companion. You need more help, Betsy. It's not right that you have to do so much. Can your father afford more help, do you think?' she whispered into the shadows.

'Yes, of course he can, he just doesn't think of it,

that's all. I've asked him, but he never gets round to doing anything about it.' Betsy yawned. 'And I'm too lazy to keep pressing him.'

'I'll ask Mama, shall I?' Sammi lay down in bed again and stared at the square of light from the window. 'When she eventually comes. She'll know what to do.' She was missing her family more than she thought she would. It was different here, fewer comforts, no servants to bring tea or cook or make the beds. She realized how sheltered and cushioned she had been in her own home. 'By the way. I almost forgot. I saw Luke Reedbarrow today. He gave me a message for you.'

'What? Oh, Sammi – what?' Betsy was out of bed and sitting almost on top of Sammi in her eagerness. 'Tell me!'

'All right, all right. Erm, he said that he'd waited, and would do the same again.'

'Yes – anything else?' Betsy shook her arm. 'Anything else?'

'No,' Sammi said. 'Should there have been?'

Betsy folded her arms around herself and Sammi saw her in the half light, smiling triumphantly. 'No,' she said. 'Not really.'

'You'll be careful, Betsy? If your father should find out you were meeting someone!'

'Oh, it's nothing, Sammi.' Betsy climbed back into bed. 'Don't worry. I probably won't go.'

As the dawn broke its light through the square window in their room, and the insistent call of a cuckoo echoed from the copse behind the mill, Sammi turned over and opened one eye. She forgot for a moment where she was and looked hazily at the empty bed next to hers. Then she remembered and closed her eyes again. Betsy had obviously turned over a new leaf and had gone to prepare breakfast for her father and brothers before they started in the mill. She gave a deep sigh and snuggled beneath the covers. *Just a few more minutes and I'll get up and help her.*

Betsy buttoned her boots onto her bare feet and threw a shawl over her dress and crept out of the door. She slipped through the hedge onto the path and gasped when Luke stepped out in front of her.

'You came then?' he said softly.

'Yes.' Her voice was low and tremulous.

He reached out his hand for hers. 'Come on, then.'

Timidly she gave him her hand and then as he gave it a gentle squeeze, she smiled at him. They locked their fingers together and broke into a run, down the path and towards the copse.

13

'Billy! Billy! Can you come into the office for a moment?'

Gilbert sat behind his father's desk and pondered. So much to do. He really didn't know where to start first. There was a pile of correspondence on the desk waiting for attention, and he didn't know the answers to most of the queries which were contained in them. *I wasn't cut out for business*, he thought, looking gloomily at the letters. *I'd much rather be out riding or playing cards.*

That thought reminded him that he was in debt for a considerable amount of money, money that he hadn't got until his salary was due. The furniture for the house was costing a fortune, he mused. Yet Harriet would have it. Or her mother would, he considered. It was her doing, he was convinced. The house in Charlotte Street, where he and Harriet would live, was only a short walk from the Billingtons' home in Albion Street, an imposing town house of four floors, where the Billingtons liked to entertain, when Mrs Billington was well enough. And if she wasn't well, which was usually the case, then Harriet was called upon to be hostess to her father's friends and business associates.

That will have to stop, he determined. *Harriet is marrying me. I will not have her hurrying home at her mother's or father's every whim.*

'Yes, Gilbert?' Billy put his willowy frame around the door. 'What can I do for you?'

'Will you deliver some messages for me, and then if you'd go out to see your father? Tell him what's happened to my father, and say I would really appreciate it if he could come straight away.'

'It's really bad, is it – about Uncle Isaac?' Billy's face creased in sympathy. 'I'm so sorry, Gilbert. Of course I'll go. But I've no transport, no horse. I'll have to borrow a mount or trap.'

'Take my gig. I won't need it. I'll stay in Hull tonight.' Wearily he rubbed his hands across his eyes. 'I might well be needed at the hospital. They said they'd send for me if there was any news.'

'Aunt Mildred? Where is she?'

'Still at the hospital. She wouldn't leave. I've arranged for her to spend tonight at the Billingtons'. She's worn out. It's only a step across from the Infirmary, so she's agreed.'

'Right. I'll just clear my desk and then go. They'll come, my parents, be sure of that, Gilbert. They'll be here first thing in the morning.'

Billy went down into the yard and asked one of the stable lads to prepare Caesar and Brutus for the journey, then he went back inside to clear his desk and tell Hardwick that he would not be available until the following day.

''Polar Star Two will be leaving early tomorrow, Mr Billy. Will you be here?'

Billy shook his head. 'I can't get back in time. Remind Mr Gilbert, will you? He's got a lot on at the moment, with Mr Rayner being so ill, but I'm sure he'll be there.'

Tradition had it that a senior member of Masterson and Rayner was always at the dock side to see their ships depart for the Arctic, and the *Polar Star Two* was leaving at dawn for the Greenland fishing grounds after a major refit and strengthening.

Billy clicked his tongue, shook the reins and moved off out of the yard. *They're beautiful animals,* he thought, *but I don't know if they'll care for the rough roads out at Holderness. Such elegant creatures, they're only suited for high-stepping over flagstones and cantering down*

151

turnpikes. The horses which he rode on his father's estate were sturdy mounts, used to the muddy, rutted roads of the country.

He drove first into Lowgate to deliver one of Gilbert's messages and then turned the gig down the side of Holy Trinity Church to deliver another. He whistled a boy to hold the reins while he went into the office of a chandler, and when he came out he saw that there were now three children standing by the gig. He reached into his pocket to give the lad a coin and climbed back into the gig.

'Hello, sir.' One of the children, a girl, spoke up. 'These is a nice pair of hosses.'

He nodded and smiled. 'Yes, aren't they!'

'Wish I could have a ride!'

'Not today, I'm in rather a hurry.' He looked down at her. Her face was sooty and her hair knotted and disarrayed, but she had an appealing grin and a free and easy manner.

'Tha doesn't remember us, does tha?' she said as he prepared to move off. 'From that night – outside theatre?'

'Oh! Yes, of course.' He tightened the reins to hold the horses. 'I do remember.'

She nodded. 'We didn't make much that night, not when we counted up. Onny enough for a bit o' bread.'

'Do you live around here?' He'd asked her before and she had refused to say. This time, though her face shuttered, she cast a thumb over her shoulder and vaguely waved it down the street.

'Over yonder.'

He glanced down the street. There were mainly offices and business rooms clustered around the church, with courts and alleyways running off, and a warehouse on North Church Side, which had burnt almost to the ground, stood derelict and abandoned with its roof open to the skies.

'Come on, Jenny.' One of the boys tugged at her skirt. 'We'll get nowt else here.'

'All right, I'm coming.' She seemed reluctant to leave. 'Where 'you going, mister?'

'I'm going home, to the country. To see the sea,' he added.

'What does tha mean?' she laughed. 'See what?'

'To see the sea,' he grinned. 'The ocean!'

The girl looked uncomprehendingly at him. 'I don't know what tha means. What ocean?'

He leaned towards her and saw a questioning, responsive longing in her face. 'The ocean that the River Humber runs into. It's like a big pond, Jenny. Bigger than any of the docks where the ships are. And the ships, when they sail down the River Humber, sail into the German Ocean and across to other lands.'

'Like 'Arctic?' she said eagerly.

'That's right,' he smiled. 'Good girl.' He shook the reins. 'I have to go now. Good-bye, Jenny.'

She slowly raised her hand. 'Be seeing you, sir.'

He turned to look back as he reached the main street again. The children had gone. There was no sign of them. He frowned, how could they have disappeared so quickly? He shrugged and turned the gig towards the North Bridge and the long road to Holderness.

The familiar hummocky landscape seemed to stretch for ever in front of him. A vast, unfolding plain of green and brown, with a twisting, meandering road leading on as if to the edge of the world. Within the boundary of hawthorn hedges, an occasional small white cottage or dwelling house hid, with red-roofed wagon shed or cow house; or beside a thicket of trees, clusters of farm buildings sheltered, their red pantiles and grey slate tiles standing out against the brick buildings and the leafy green shelter belt; vast wide skies unfurled a moving panorama of drifting white clouds, swooping seabirds, lapwings and sparrow-hawks.

Billy deliberated as he let the pair have their heads along the empty road. *Gilbert will take over the firm now that Uncle Isaac is ill. He won't come back now, not even if he recovers. Gilbert will be in charge,* he mused, *and I don't think he will function very well. And as for me, well, I can't see myself forever in shipping; but what else is there? I don't want to waste my life.* His thoughts turned to the beggar children, to the eager upturned face of the young Jenny.

What a waste of life that is, he pondered. *She seemed so eager for knowledge when I was telling her about the sea, and yet she's doomed to spend her life begging, or else –* he gave a small shudder as he thought of the whore who had accosted him *– or else a life of prostitution. If only there was something I could do. How I wish I could help her.*

14

'I mustn't be long, Luke,' Betsy breathed as they ran towards the copse. 'I'm afraid of being missed.'

'Oh, Betsy. Nobody will be up yet. They'll all be sleeping.'

The cuckoo echoed above them, and they both looked up as the big brown bird flew from the woods over their heads.

'Sammi will miss me, she'll wonder where I am.'

He drew her towards him as they entered the copse. 'It'll be all right,' he insisted. 'Don't worry. Come here.'

He kissed her on her mouth and she pulled away and hung her head. 'It's not right, is it?' she whispered. 'I ought not to be here with you.'

He ran his hands along her face and neck and across her shoulders. 'Who should you be here with then, Betsy, if not with me? Is there somebody else tha'd rather be with?'

'Oh, no! I didn't mean that.' She looked up at him, longing for him to kiss her again. 'You know I didn't. It's just that I'm scared—'

'Don't be.' He started to unfasten the buttons on her bodice, but his fingers were clumsy and she put her hand up to his to help him.

She wanted him to hold her the way he had before, when he'd cupped her breasts into his mouth and teased her nipples with his tongue. A pulse started to throb in her throat and she felt her heart pounding. Her body throbbed in so many places, places that were becoming soft and yielding.

This time she didn't object when he placed his

jacket on the ground, and she sat on it whilst he lay on the ground beside her, crushing the white flowers of Jack-in-the-woods beneath him and releasing its pungent aroma. He pulled her bodice from her shoulders and gently pulled her down, holding and stroking her naked breasts and bending to kiss each in turn. She licked her lips and held his head between her hands, her breathing becoming faster.

'Do you like that, Betsy?' he asked softly as he lifted his head to look at her.

'Yes,' she whispered. 'Yes.'

His hand stole beneath her skirt and she knew that this time she wouldn't stop him. Didn't want to stop him as his fingers explored every sinuous curve and valley of her rounded buttocks and arching belly which she thrust towards him.

She closed her eyes and then opened them as he pushed aside her skirt and with his muscular legs straddled her and held her fast. 'Wait, Luke.' She was trembling. 'No. We mustn't.'

He didn't answer. Though he looked at her, his blue eyes were glazed as if hypnotized, and his lips parted as he ran his tongue over them.

'Luke! You're hurting me.' Tears stung her eyes. She didn't think that it would be like this. He was breaking her in two. Why didn't he stop? 'Luke. Please. Please stop.'

'I can't,' he gasped as he bore down upon her. 'It's too late!' His fingers gripped her arms with powerful bruising strength as he shuddered and then lay still. 'I'm sorry.'

She cried as he held her close and whispered that he was sorry. 'I thought you wanted it too, Betsy. You seemed as if you did.'

'I didn't know. I didn't know that it would hurt,' she sobbed quietly. She hadn't known, hadn't guessed that he would be so big. It wasn't like when she had seen her brothers run naked around the yard after washing under the pump. She hadn't known that he would enter her with such vigour and strength.

'It hurt me too, Betsy,' he murmured into her hair.

'Did it?' she gulped, and wondered then why he had done it, or perhaps like her he hadn't known.

He nodded and wiped away her tears with his fingers. 'You see, it's 'cos you were a virgin. It's a bit like coming across a locked door. If you haven't got a key then you've got to use a bit of force to open it. But now that 'door's open, it won't hurt so much next time.'

Her lip pouted. 'There'll be no next time. I shan't let it happen again.'

He smiled lazily at her and ran his fingers around her nipples. 'Is tha sure about that, Miss Betsy?'

She pulled away from him and started to fasten up her bodice, he was making her tingle and throb again in spite of feeling sore and bruised. Then she turned again towards him and once more undid the buttons at her breast. 'Just kiss me, Luke,' she whispered. 'Like you did before, that's what I like best.'

He laughed softly and shook his head at her. 'Tha can't have one without 'other, Miss Betsy. It drives a fellow wild.'

'Docs it?' she said huskily, as he fastened his mouth around her breast. 'But you said that it hurt.'

'Aye, it does, but it's worth it.' He breathed heavily. 'And you'd better get dressed or else I shan't be able to stop myself again. I'll see you again tomorrow morning, shall I?'

'I don't know,' she answered. 'I said, didn't I, that I wouldn't let it happen again.'

He lay on his back and watched her through half-closed eyes. 'Well, I allus knew that it would happen, sooner or later.' He grinned at her. 'I allus knew I'd have 'miller's daughter.'

'What do you mean?' she demanded. 'How could you know?'

He pulled up a stalk of red campion and teased her cheek with it. 'I allus used to say to 'village lads, I'll be first wi' Miss Betsy.' His eyes teased hers. 'I had a bet on it.'

Horror-struck, she stared at him. 'You don't mean that?' Her eyes filled with tears. 'Say you don't mean it?' She shook his arm. 'Please, Luke. If my father heard – or my brothers—'

He pulled her down again towards him, his mouth against her ear. 'If you'll come again tomorrow, then I won't claim my bet.'

'Promise?' she whispered, feeling herself melting once more.

'Aye, I promise, Miss Betsy. I'll not tell 'other lads. It'll be our secret.'

Sammi woke again and saw the sun streaming through the window. She sat up abruptly. *I'd better get up and give Betsy a hand, and then I can go and see Adam.* She felt a warm glow when she thought of the child; how he was filling out with the abundance of milk that Mrs Bishop was so lavishly providing. His little belly was becoming rounded and he was stretching and reaching with his tiny fingers and toes.

I must be careful, she thought, *as Mrs Bishop would say, of becoming* over-fond *on him. But how can you become over-fond of a child, surely they all deserve love?*

There was only a little water in the jug on the wash-stand, and she poured it into the china bowl and dabbed her face and arms, neither was there a clean towel, the wooden towel stand was empty; Betsy had obviously forgotten to get them out of the press, so she briskly rubbed her face and arms with her petti-coat until she was dry. She dressed and quietly went downstairs and opened the kitchen door.

It was empty, and, puzzled, she went to look for Betsy outside in the yard. There was no sign of her. She returned to the kitchen and put some dry kindling which was lying in the hearth, onto the low, banked-down fire, and then filled the kettle with water and placed it on the hook.

Now what do I do? she thought. If she had ever thought to consider it, she would have imagined herself perfectly capable of doing housewifely things; yet she had no practical experience, but only a smattering of knowledge of what happened in a kitchen. *I have been cosseted,* she mused, *brought up to be a lady, while Betsy—*

There was a creaking of boards overhead as someone put their feet out of bed and the sound of someone yawning loudly, and then another thump as another body got out of bed. She could hear the muffled sound of voices as the men upstairs called to each other through the bedroom walls. But where was Betsy? She was beginning to get anxious, knowing that the day would get off to a bad start if there was no breakfast for the men.

The outer door quietly opened and Betsy slid in. 'Where have you been?' Sammi began, but Betsy urged silence with her finger against her lips. Her cheeks were pink and her hair tousled and she reached above the mantelshelf for a hairbrush and ran it through her hair. She perfunctorily straightened her dress, put on an apron and, taking some oats from a crock, she put them into a pan with water and placed it on the fire.

'Tha's never up, Betsy? 'Sky'll fall in today.' Mark was the first to come downstairs, fully dressed, followed by Tom, who had on his breeches but was without his shirt, his muscular chest dark with hair.

'You'll have to excuse me, Sammi,' he muttered. 'I didn't think you'd be up yet.'

She blushed, she didn't know why, and she bent her head as she lamely said that it didn't matter. As the two men went out into the yard to wash, she caught a twisted grin from Mark to Tom whose response was to give his brother a sharp shove, and she wondered what Mark found so funny.

'Betsy!' At last she could ask her where she had been. The men had breakfasted and gone across to the mill. Again Betsy put her fingers to her lips and shook her head. She listened, her head on one side.

'George!' she whispered. 'He's still pottering about outside and he's got ears like an elephant.'

'He wouldn't know what we were talking about. Where have you been?'

Betsy collapsed into a chair by the fire and clasped her hands beneath her chin and closed her eyes. When she opened them they were tender and misty with emotion. 'Don't tell, will you, Sammi?'

Bewildered, Sammi shook her head. 'Of course not, but . . .'

'I went to meet Luke.'

Sammi caught her breath. 'So early? But why?'

'Because I can't get away at any other time. If Da knew, he would stop me. Oh, Sammi!' She put her hands to her mouth as if to stop herself from saying more.

'But, Betsy, it isn't wise,' Sammi said earnestly. 'You mustn't go alone! Luke might get the wrong impression. If you really want to meet him, I'll go with you, so you can walk and talk together.'

Betsy smiled and stretched her arms above her head. 'Thank you, Sammi. You're a dear. I'll remember that another time.'

It was just striking eight o'clock as Nancy, the girl who came to help, knocked on the door and entered the kitchen. ' 'Morning, Miss Betsy. 'Morning, Miss Rayner.' She flopped down on a stool by the kitchen table and wearily put her elbows on the table and cradled her chin in her hands. 'I'm that tired this morning, I've not got a ha'porth of energy.'

Sammi looked at Betsy. This was no way for a servant to behave, but Betsy simply gazed into the fire. Sammi swallowed. It wasn't her place, she knew, but surely! 'Betsy? Weren't you going to ask Nancy to clean the bedrooms this morning?' She had noticed the layer of dust on the chest of drawers and around the skirting boards.

'Was I?' Betsy looked up vacantly. 'Oh, that's a good idea. Yes, if you would please.'

Nancy got up sullenly from the table and went towards the stairs.

'You'll need a duster and a broom,' Sammi called her back, 'and the water jugs need washing and refilling.'

'Yes, miss,' she muttered. 'I'll see to it.'

'Betsy!' Sammi said in hushed tones after the girl had gone upstairs. 'She's useless! You must be firm with her.'

'I don't know how to be,' Betsy said. 'No-one ever showed me how to treat servants; they always take advantage of me. I'm too soft with them.'

'You are,' Sammi agreed, 'but they do like to know their duties, at least ours do, and if you don't tell them what they have to do, how are they to know? Betsy! I know that I am only a guest, but shall we light a fire in the parlour? It's such a pleasant room and you hardly ever use it.'

Betsy looked at her in astonishment. 'We only use it at Christmas. Why should we use it now?'

'It would be nice if you and I could go in there after supper, just to talk, or Uncle Thomas could go in and read his papers in peace.' She smiled cheekily. 'Or you could take a beau in there, if one came calling!'

Betsy laughed out loud. 'There would be no likelihood of that. If Luke came calling, he would be shown the door, and there's no-one else around here.' Her face melted and looked wistful. 'There's nobody else.'

'Why don't they like Luke? He's not so bad, and he works hard, doesn't he? He's not lazy?'

'I don't know if they like him or not. The subject has never cropped up. His father has a smallholding and Luke works with him, but I don't think there's much money.' She sighed. 'They probably only grow enough for themselves, so he's hardly a good catch.'

Sammi made Betsy call Nancy down to light the fire

in the parlour, which she did with poor grace, and after a few minutes they heard her shouting and coughing, and calling them to come. The parlour was choked with thick smoke which swirled around the room covering the furniture with soot.

''Chimney's blocked, miss. It must be,' she spluttered.

'Open the window,' Sammi cried, 'and the door, and dampen down the fire.'

Nancy rushed past them, coughing and spluttering, into the kitchen and dashed back with a pan of water which she threw with great force onto the flames in the hearth before either of them could stop her.

'You silly girl!' Sammi shrieked at her as soot and smoke gushed into the room. 'I said *dampen* it, not flood it.'

They all dashed for the door and stood in the yard gasping for breath and then looked up as they heard the rattle of carriage wheels and Sammi saw her mother and father step down from their carriage, and her brother Billy driving Gilbert's gig drawing up behind them.

Ellen Rayner stared at her daughter standing in front of her with her face spattered with soot and streaks of grime down her dress. 'Is there a fire?' She stared from Sammi to Betsy and to the crying maid behind them.

'No, Mama. But there should be.' Tears started to run down Sammi's cheeks. 'Oh, Mama, Pa. I thought you were never coming to see me. Are you very angry with me?'

Ellen held Sammi at arm's length and gingerly kissed her cheeks. 'Angry? No. We thought that this was what you wanted! I didn't realize that you were playing at kitchen maids!'

'I say, Sammi, what have you been up to?' Billy grinned at her. 'You do look a mess!'

Sammi pushed her hair back from her face. 'We were trying to light a fire in the parlour, but the chimney is blocked.' Her lip trembled. 'Mama, there's so much to do here, you must speak to Uncle Thomas about getting some proper help for Betsy.'

Ellen peered into the parlour. 'It is in a mess. You'd better send for the sweep, Betsy.'

They all adjourned outside again away from the smell of smoke, and William went into the mill to tell Betsy's father of Isaac. 'I'll do what I can, Betsy,' Ellen said. 'After we have seen Uncle Isaac, I'll speak to your father. And Sammi,' she turned towards her, 'then I will speak to you.'

15

Isaac had recovered consciousness, and although he was feeble and his speech was slow, he was able to talk to Mildred and Gilbert, and insisted that if he was going to die, then he would rather go home and die in his own bed.

William and Ellen had arrived at the Infirmary when this possibility was being discussed, and although William ruled out the sensibility of removing Isaac at such an early stage of his illness, he realized that sense wasn't an issue, but that the requirements of longing and desire for one's own four walls were. After consulting with the doctor, he arranged that if Isaac would be patient and stay where he was for one more day, he would come back the following morning and take him home himself. Leaving Ellen with Mildred, he then set off to meet Gilbert.

'I'm so glad that you came, Uncle William.' Gilbert ran his fingers distractedly through his crop of red hair, and invited his uncle to be seated in the office which he had now commandeered. 'I don't know which way to turn. There's so much to do. Father took such a lot on himself.'

Billy knocked on the door. 'Sorry, Gilbert, but I thought you ought to know, the men are most unhappy that the *Polar Star Two* went off without acknowledgement this morning. The other seamen are saying it's a bad omen; you know how superstitious they are!'

Gilbert pushed his chair back with a crash. 'What

'in God's name am I supposed to do? My father is in hospital. I'm trying to run a business, and I can't be in two places at the same time!'

'I know.' Billy nodded. 'I just thought you ought to know.'

'Is it too late?' William asked. 'Could you get a tug boat to take you out? Or what about a telegraph to Spurn?'

Gilbert took out his watch from his waistcoat pocket. He shook his head. 'No. She'll have rounded the Point by now.'

'You could send a message with one of the ships from another company,' Billy suggested. 'The *Lara* will be sailing tomorrow. They could give a message to *Star Two* in the Shetlands when they reach there.'

Gilbert gave a relieved exclamation. 'Yes. Brilliant idea, Billy. Draft something out straight away, will you, and I'll sign it and send it over.'

'I'll take it if you like and give it to the *Lara*'s captain. It'll look better.'

William stayed an hour, going over various aspects which were causing Gilbert problems and advising as best he could and after he left, Gilbert sat pondering. How he hated making decisions. He toyed with the idea of asking Billington, his future father-in-law, for advice, and mused that Austin Billington had intimated to him on several occasions that Masterson and Rayner could do better with his bank than with Salters whom he described as old hat and not forward-looking. He had mentioned this to his father, but Isaac had insisted that Salters may not be very ambitious, but that they were safe.

He slipped on his coat and picked up his topper and ran down the stairs towards the door. He would go across to see the Billingtons. Austin Billington occasionally went home for a nap, and if he wasn't there, at least he would see Harriet. He persuaded himself that he needed to see Harriet anyway, to discuss the furniture and drapery which was arriving daily at their future home, and to make final plans for their wedding day, and he pondered that perhaps, in view of his father's illness, it might be more proper to delay it.

Yet he was anxious that the plans should go ahead. If the wedding was delayed and news of the child should get out – and he had been on tenterhooks all morning that Uncle William would mention it – then he was very much afraid that it would be cancelled for good.

He was so engrossed in his thoughts as he went out of the door that he failed to see Billy look up from his desk where he was busily writing a message for the *Polar Star Two*. Billy grimaced and bit on the end of his pen. Then putting his head down again, he finished the message, signed it *Gilbert Foster Rayner*, blotted and sealed it, and put it in his pocket, telling Hardwick that he wouldn't be long.

Harriet and her mother were at home though her father wasn't. 'He said that he has a very busy day today, Gilbert, and couldn't get home,' Mrs Billington gushed, which was her usual manner, unless she was unwell, in which case she spoke only in languid, monosyllabic tones. Today she was well. 'Quite well,' she replied to his query. 'But so concerned about your poor father. The shock of his illness gave me such a turn that I had to retire to my bed.'

Gilbert murmured his thanks for her concern, and Mrs Billington then broached the subject of the forthcoming wedding. Harriet turned a regretful glance towards him, but her mother immediately determined that under no circumstances should it be cancelled.

'I was speaking to your dear mother on the very subject only last evening,' she advised. 'And *we* decided, both of us, that the last thing your father would want would be for you two dear young people to cancel your marriage. Of course,' she added in a low voice, 'if anything should happen, if things got worse,' she nodded her head in gloomy anticipation, 'then of course we would have to postpone.' She clasped her hands together. 'I have my black ready at all times in case of such tragedies.'

Gilbert glanced at Harriet, who raised her eyebrows, and then swiftly lowered her lashes before her mother could see her apologetic expression.

It's all very well, he thought, as he ran down the stone steps and hurried back down Albion Street and across the town towards the High Street. *We had to postpone the marriage when she was ill with some paltry thing, yet my poor father is going to miss the ceremony. He won't be well enough to attend, not in the least;* and he quite forgot the relief he'd felt when hearing that the marriage should go ahead. He cut through a narrow passageway which made a short cut from the banking area of Parliament Street and led into the thoroughfare of Lowgate. There were numerous courts and entrances in this part of town, some of which were not safe to walk through because of vagrants or pickpockets, but most were well used by the business people and residents of the town, and some of the buildings within them were used as residential establishments as well as business premises.

The houses within the court he was passing through now were clean, their front steps well scrubbed, and some had thick lace curtains at the windows to deter the glances of passers-by who regularly used this area, and because Gilbert was one of these self-same wayfarers, he very rarely gave them a second glance. Today as he hurried through, conscious of having been away a long time and not having told anyone where he was going, he had his gaze fixed firmly in front and saw coming down the steps from one of the houses, the stout figure of Austin Billington.

His first thought was to call him, but there was something about the man's demeanour which made him hesitate. Austin Billington pulled his top hat firmly down on his head and with his shoulders hunched and his head down, walked swiftly out of the passageway. Gilbert looked up at the house as he passed. There was no brass plate by the door to indicate what business was behind its red door, and Gilbert couldn't think of a solicitor or merchant house which occupied an address in this court. A pot of red geraniums sat on the top step and an iron footscraper in the shape of a sleeping cat stood by the door.

As he turned the corner he looked along the street, wondering if he could catch up with Billington, and failed to notice a man coming towards him who caught hold of his arm as he passed.

'Hold on, Rayner! Don't you wish a fellow good day? Where are you off to in such a hurry?' The fellow winked and tossed his head in the direction towards the passageway. 'Or perhaps I should say, where have you *been*?'

'Sorry, Craddock. I didn't see you.' *And if I had,* he thought, *I might have gone the other way.* 'I was rushing – got to get back to the firm.'

'Ah! Business calls.' Craddock perused him from down his fleshy nose. 'Sorry to hear about your father, by the way. Bad luck. You'll be running things now, I expect?'

'Er, yes. Yes, I am.' As he spoke, he was immediately cast down. He knew what was coming next.

'You'll be all right for paying off that little debt then, won't you?' Craddock gave him a friendly smile which didn't quite reach his eyes.

'Er, could you give me a little more time? As I explained before, my salary—'

'Oh, come come, old fellow. Surely now, now that you're in charge?'

'It doesn't make any difference,' Gilbert protested.

'Nothing in the till?' Craddock kept his gaze on Gilbert. 'Or surely you could write a cheque?'

'I don't handle cash, and I can't use company funds for personal matters.' Gilbert was beginning to sweat. He should never have agreed to play cards with the fellow. He was known all over the town as a sharper. It was only because of his foolish belief in his own ability, fostered by imbibing too much wine, that he had accepted Craddock's challenge to a rubber of cribbage.

'I hear you're getting married shortly.' Craddock abruptly changed the subject. 'Going to be a big affair, is it? Billington's daughter!' He pursed his generous lips and nodded thoughtfully. 'Well, you'll have plenty of ready money then, I expect. I suppose I could wait.'

'I'd be grateful—' Gilbert began.

'Tell you what, old fellow. I'd love to come, to the wedding I mean. Bound to be some good contacts there, bankers and all. Arrange it, can you?'

'I, I – the invitations have gone out, I believe.' Gilbert sought for an excuse.

Craddock smiled heartily, his small eyes disappearing into a fleshy crease, and patted him on the shoulder. 'Well, you'll be able to arrange an extra one, I expect. Or two rather – I'd like to bring a lady along.'

Gilbert wilted. 'I'll see what I can do.' To have Craddock as a guest at his marriage was the last thing he wanted, but if he wasn't invited, he knew very well just how much trouble he could cause – and if Billington should find out that his daughter's future husband was in debt . . . ! The notion was too terrible to comprehend. He crossed the road towards the High Street and saw a familiar figure looking in a shop window. He groaned. Aunt Ellen!

Aunt Ellen had tried several times to catch his eye when they had been visiting his father in hospital, but he had successfully avoided her glance. It had not been an easy situation, for his mother and Aunt Ellen, though outwardly polite, had barely spoken to one another.

I have every intention of searching out a suitable foster home for the child, he deliberated, my *child, though she doesn't know it, I just haven't got round to it.* Now she was sure to ask him if any arrangements had been made. He turned on his heel to cut down Scale Lane, a narrow street which would take him through to the High Street.

'Gilbert!'

She had seen him. He gave a huge sigh and clenched his lips together, turning to greet her with a ready smile.

'Gilbert! I've been wanting to ask you something.' There was a determined look upon her face.

'Yes, Aunt?'

'I know how difficult it is for you at the moment, and of course you cannot consult your father, but you won't forget your promise to make arrangements about the child?' She looked at him steadily, her eyes keen.

He swallowed. 'I haven't forgotten, Aunt Ellen. It's just that, with Father . . .' His voice trailed away.

She nodded. 'Another thing.'

He held his breath and waited.

'About the wedding. Will you be an absolute dear and invite Betsy? You may have done so already, of course, in which case there is no need for me to mention it; but if you haven't, then will you? She's such a sweet girl and she gets so few outings.' She smiled and he exhaled. 'And she might meet a nice young man!'

'Oh, but of course, Aunt Ellen.' He beamed at her. 'Of course she will be invited. Her name is on the list, but I shall deliver it in person!'

The following Saturday he prepared to do just that. The groom polished up his gig so that the leather was soft and shiny, the brasswork gleaming, and harnessed up Caesar and Brutus. Billy had warned him that the state of the roads in Holderness was quite bad, indeed, he would have known without telling when he saw the muddy state that his gig was in after Billy had borrowed it.

This morning, though, the sun was shining and the roads dry, and he hoped that the weather was now settled, for his wedding to Harriet was only three weeks away. He had the invitation for Betsy in his pocket, an open invitation, because he wasn't sure if the rest of the Foster family would come, for someone would have to stay behind at the mill. He intended, too, as well as his visit to Tillington, to call on Aunt Ellen in Monkston and discuss the future of the child as he'd promised. *There has to be something settled,* he worried as he rattled along. *I have this guilt hanging over me, but I don't want Harriet to find out.* For guilt he felt, not only for the child, but also for the unjustified charge against James, who still hadn't written to give his address. His father had asked him if there was word of him, but he had evaded the question, not wanting to upset his father by admitting that he didn't know where he was.

Mark was in the mill yard as he arrived, loading sacks of animal foodstuff into a cart for a farmer who was waiting. Mark nodded, but barely spoke. *Surly beggar, he never did have much to say,* Gilbert thought contemptuously. Gilbert and Mark were near in age, but they never seemed to have the same common interests as he did with his cousins at Monkston.

There was a horse and trap in the yard, and Gilbert manoeuvred his gig close by in order to leave room for the farmer's cart to turn around. 'At home day!' he commented wryly as he passed Mark. 'Is the lady of the house receiving?' Mark simply looked past him and Gilbert shrugged and knocked and entered. From the small hallway he could hear voices from within the parlour. The kitchen door was open and he saw Betsy there with a young servant girl who was placing a kettle on the fire.

Betsy turned a merry face towards Gilbert. 'How lovely to see you, Gilbert. It's been such a long time.'

'I know, and I'm sorry, Betsy. Time is so pressing these days, not like when we were young and had all the time in the world.' He kissed her cheek and then held her at arm's length. 'How well you look – and so pretty!'

She laughed and returned his kiss. 'When we were young, Gilbert? Are you such an old man now that you are about to be married?'

He put a mockingly weary hand to his brow and sighed deeply. 'Such responsibility, Betsy, the thought of having a wife to protect and maintain.' Then he clasped her hand and whispered, 'And no more flirtations with my pretty cousins!'

She laughingly gave him a push. 'Away with you. Come, come through into the parlour.'

'First let me give you this,' he said as they returned to the hall, and he brought out the invitation from his pocket. 'I drove over especially, Betsy, just to make sure that you would come.'

What pleasure I have brought her, he thought as she opened the envelope and smiled with delight at the contents. *So why did I have to be prompted by Aunt Ellen? I should have thought of it myself. It cost me so little and yet means so much.*

'Oh, Gilbert. Thank you so much.' She opened the door into the parlour which had a bright fire burning and a scent of daffodils from the vase on the window-sill. 'Oh, Da, Aunt Ellen – Sammi! Look what Gilbert has brought. An invitation to his wedding!'

'How de do, Gilbert,' Uncle Thomas greeted him jovially. 'Haven't seen thee in a long time. But tha'll be a busy young fellow now that Isaac is laid up poorly. I was just thinking,' he said in mock gloom, 'that tha'd called in 'nick of time to save me from a great expense that Ellen is planning for me; but it looks as if there'll be more money to be spent if there's a wedding on 'cards. It'll be new gowns and bonnets and fal-de-rals, I'll be bound.'

'You can afford it, Thomas, don't pretend that you can't! Hello, Gilbert.' His aunt extended her hand and, though caught off-guard by finding her here, he hoped his surprise didn't show as he bent to greet her.

His face flushed as he turned to greet Sammi who was sitting by the window in an old wooden rocking chair. The sun was shining through the window, glinting on her thick red hair, which was the same colour as his. He hated the colour yet it looked so well on her, and was absent from the dark heads of these Foster cousins at Tillington and that of his brother James. He felt himself flush, though it wasn't Sammi's appearance which attracted his attention, but the child in her lap which she gently rocked. He greeted her awkwardly and looked down at the babe, a suitable remark on his lips. A remark which faded as he gazed at the child in his long white gown and bonnet.

Sammi loosened the ribbons on the bonnet. 'I took it upon myself to name him Adam, Gilbert. Do you think that James would agree with that? I couldn't ask because I don't know where he is, I haven't yet heard from him.'

'Yes. I mean – I don't know.' Gilbert was lost for words as he saw, peeping from below the child's bonnet, the fine wisps of golden hair. He cleared his throat. 'No-one has heard. But I'm sure it's most suitable.'

He looked up. Uncle Thomas and Betsy were examining the invitation card, but Aunt Ellen was looking at him. Her eyes were wide and her lips parted and a perceptive awareness was etched upon her face. His eyes were drawn to hers. No point in veiling them in deception. She knew! He was discovered. With the utmost certainty, he recognized that she knew the child was his.

16

The basement room which James had rented was in a terraced house just around the corner from Batsford's rooms in Cheyne Walk. It was small and dark and of no use for painting because the light was so poor, but it was cheap and warm, and Batsford was willing to let him use his studio provided he didn't get in his way. He tried to be as unobtrusive as possible when Batsford was working, simply watching and observing his techniques, and trying to apply them to his own work. His sketch of Battersea bridge was finished, but he had decided after all, not to paint the scene, when Batsford had told him that it was a favourite subject of Turner.

I can't compete with Turner, he'd said, and besides, I want to be noted for my own genre, not as a copyist. Batsford had rebuked him, telling him that the subject matter wasn't important but that the interpretation was.

'You could never copy an artist such as Turner; the difference in style and impression would be quite apparent, but you can learn from his technique. *You* must paint what you see through your own eyes, you cannot see through anyone else's.'

Nevertheless, James abandoned the idea and wandered around Chelsea and the river bank looking for inspiration, or taking the long walk into London to visit the National Gallery and admire the portraits of Reynolds, the entertaining and provocative Hogarth, and the classical 'Englishness' of Gainsborough's landscapes. He wandered around the Georgian squares and watched the creation of Gothic public buildings and monuments as they rose in terracotta, Devon limestone, Cornish granite, iron and glass, for, as the railways developed, they carried in the heavy loads of formerly unattainable materials which were now changing the face of London.

By mistake, one day on his wanderings, he ventured into the squalor of the London rookeries, and observing the wretched residents of these habitations who, seeking to escape from the horrors that lay within their doors, sat on their doorsteps with shoeless feet soaking in the filth of overflowing cesspools, he formed opinions, found his voice, and absorbed and contributed to the enlightening conversation of the company who joined them at their supper either in Batsford's untidy living room or at The Six Bells Inn.

Batsford asked Miss Gregory if she would sit for James and she agreed. 'She's good, you see, Rayner. She knows how to sit and she doesn't move her pose as some models do, to scratch an itch or stretch a foot.'

James thought he would be embarrassed, but after an initial flushing of his cheeks when he returned to the studio and found her waiting, already disrobed and in position on the sofa, he found he was viewing her dispassionately as Batsford pointed out the errors on his drawing pad.

'See here,' said Batsford, pointing with a pencil. 'See how the left breast flattens beneath the arm as she has it raised. And here,' he tapped the sketch, 'you have missed the indentation of the calf where the leg is crossed.'

James looked up at Miss Gregory to determine his faults and discovered that she was fast asleep and oblivious of their comments.

'She's quite beautiful, isn't she?' Batsford commented. 'A visual image to be appreciated as much as the painting of a flower or landscape. We're very lucky to have her.'

Later, when she was dressed and ready to leave and

175

Batsford had slipped out for his daily walk, James thanked her for sitting.

'That's all right,' she said. 'Batsford'll give me extra.'

'Why do you do this?' James asked curiously. 'Is there no other work you would rather do?'

She stared at him, then shrugged her shoulders. 'How else could I earn money for sitting around all day? It's better than working in a sweat shop or a kitchen. Besides, I've got a good body and face, and I've been painted by some of the best artists in London. One day I might be famous.' A slight smile touched her lips. 'You think I'm Batsford's mistress, don't you?'

James was flustered, not knowing how to answer, but why else would she sit, in spite of what she had said?

'Well, I'm not, though I know that some of the artists paint their wives or mistresses. But I've never been an artist's doxy and don't intend to be, and if you want to paint me then you'd better look on me as a piece of furniture and nothing more. Don't get any ideas that I might share your bed.'

James gasped. 'I had no—'

'No? Well, some of the young artists that Batsford teaches think that I come with breakfast, but I'll tell you now, once and for all, that I don't.'

James had paid two weeks rent for his room, which had left him with little money, and he had vaguely wondered why his father hadn't sent him an allowance as he'd promised; and it wasn't until his rent was again due that he remembered he had told his father he would send him an address as soon as he was settled. *But I'm sure I gave him Batsford's address,* he thought. *Or perhaps I didn't. I must write.* A twinge of conscience smote him that he hadn't written to Sammi either, or sent her any money for the child, and he vowed that he would write to her too, but then

176

he forgot and it wasn't until his landlady came down to remind him his rent was now overdue, that he realized that perhaps his father might be worrying about him and wondering if he had safely arrived at his destination.

He promptly sat down to write, to tell him that he was now a pupil of Batsford's and that he had found lodgings.

'*I shall be forever grateful to Peacock,*' he wrote. '*My life has opened up anew, and I know that I was destined to be an artist. I can feel it in my blood, in my veins, and although I realize that it is not perhaps what you would have planned for me, Father, circumstances have decreed my true vocation.*

'*I cannot say that I am missing home, as my life is filled to such capacity that I do not have time to think of what I left behind, but I do miss you, and remain your ever loving son. James.*'

He wrote another letter to Peacock, thanking him for the opportunity given to him, sealed them both and posted them. It wasn't until later that he remembered he hadn't asked his father about money, and he hoped that he wouldn't need prompting.

'We have been invited out for supper this evening, Rayner,' Batsford greeted him one morning. 'Jonathon Walker – he is a great patron of the arts. It would be good for you to meet him. He's very influential and has helped many young painters.'

'But I haven't anything to show,' James said in some dismay. 'Only my sketches of Battersea Bridge and Miss Gregory.'

'It doesn't matter. If he likes you, then he will wait for you to produce something.' He looked James over and rubbed his chin. 'Just one thing . . .'

'What?'

'Oh, nothing. It's of no consequence.'

Whatever it was, Batsford obviously had second

thoughts about it, and James dismissed it from his mind as he changed for supper. He combed his hair, which was now long and curling into his collar in the manner of some of the other young men he had met, and tied a silk scarf around his neck in a loose knot.

There was already a crowd of people in Jonathon Walker's home in Bloomsbury when he and Batsford arrived. He could hear piano music, the clink of wine glasses and a hum of conversation and laughter.

Jonathon Walker, a tall slim man with white hair, came over to greet them. 'So nice to see you, Batsford, and this is your protégé?' He extended a warm and flaccid hand towards James. 'I have heard all about you.'

'Really, sir?' said James, feeling uncomfortable with his hand still clasped by Walker's soft flesh.

'Yes, indeed. There is little goes on in the art world that I don't know about.'

James preened. To be included and mentioned in the art world was something he had never envisaged, and with a great passion about to take over his senses, he allowed himself to be drawn, with Walker's arm around his shoulder, to be introduced to other members of the ensemble. Some of the ladies were dressed in extravagant gowns and inclined their heads as he was introduced, and gentlemen in three-piece suits or velvet jackets and narrow trousers nodded and made polite noises; others, shabby in well-worn shirts and down-at-heel shoes, were tucking in to the food which was laid on the white-clothed table in an anteroom – they looked up and spoke briefly, then resumed eating.

'Naughty boy,' Walker said to one, tapping him on his hand. 'This is merely *hors d'oeuvres*! Do not stuff yourself. There is more. This is what you can expect, Rayner, if you become an artist or writer.' Walker took two glasses of wine from a tray which a maid brought at his signal, and handed one to him. 'For half of your existence you will be in a state of delirium because you are close to starvation and long to be invited out so that you can eat; and the other half you will be in the depths of despair because no-one will buy your work.'

'So what is the answer, sir, if a person only has the passion to create and not to earn?'

Walker smiled and, to James's discomfort, once more put his arm about his shoulder. 'We must find someone to take care of you. A patron. Someone who recognizes talent – if you have it.'

As James was silently debating whether it would appear rude if he moved in order to escape Walker's clasp, a woman appeared in front of them. 'Jonathon!' she said. 'You haven't introduced me.' She offered James her hand. She carried no gloves, but held a black feather fan in her left hand; on three fingers she wore diamond rings and around her wrist, several pearl bracelets. Her hair was very dark and sleek and piled into a high chignon with a white flower pinned above her ear.

'I beg your pardon, my dear. Rayner, may I introduce Madame Mariabella Sinclair.'

'James Foster-Rayner, ma-am.' James bowed. He was beginning to feel overwhelmed by the undue attention from Jonathon Walker and now by the intense scrutiny of this most attractive woman who held his gaze with such beguiling amusement in her dark eyes.

'Jonathon! I have just left Raymond.' She rolled her *r*'s slightly, and there was just a trace of foreign accent to her tongue. 'He is becoming cross with you. I think he feels terribly neglected.'

Walker looked across the room. A young man in velvet jacket and narrow trousers was leaning against the wall, his arms folded across his chest and dark hair falling over his lowered eyes, ignoring the conversation going on around him.

Walker gave a deep sigh. 'I'd better go, he'll sulk for days otherwise.' He clasped James's hand. 'Don't go away, my dear. I'll be back.'

James stared after him. Was this what Peacock had meant, when he said – what was it he had said?

Madame Sinclair smiled at him. 'Mr Rayner.' The name rolled off her tongue softly and sensuously. 'Will you find me a seat, and then we can talk?' She gently trembled her fan. 'And then you can tell me how grateful you are for my rescuing you.' Her silk crinolined gown rustled as she sank into a gilt chair. 'Tell me about yourself.' She looked at him from over the rim of the glass of wine which he had brought her. Her eyes were dark, such a dark brown as to be almost black, and he thought that she missed being perfectly beautiful by the fractional – but barely, merely minuscule – by her nose being a shade too long.

'I would rather know about you,' he said shyly. 'I have done nothing as yet with my life. I am just about to start.'

And oh, Madame, how I would love to have you in my life. She was, he guessed, older than him, perhaps six or seven years, or even only four or five, he considered, for it is so difficult to know when ladies are got up so well. *But what does it matter? I do not believe that it matters one jot in the affairs of the heart.*

'James? I may call you James?'

'Oh, please. Please do. I would be delighted.'

'And when we know each other better, then you may call me Mariabella. But not yet; you see, there are people here who know my husband, and I must be discreet.'

She gave him a tender smile which he felt was so special for him and which almost, but not quite, lessened the dismay he felt when she said that she had a husband.

He swallowed and tried not to let his disappointment show. 'Is he not here this evening, your husband?'

'No. We do not attend the same functions.' She flicked her fan to her mouth and looked at him from over the top. 'Neither do we share the same house,' she said softly. 'We live separate lives.'

'How can he bear that?' James whispered back. 'How can he suffer to live apart from you?'

'Our marriage was arranged.' She lowered her fan and her eyes. 'He needed a wife in order to claim his father's estate, though he didn't require a wife in any other sense.'

James felt himself grow hot and he fingered his collar. This life he was entering was undoubtedly quite different from the one he had previously known.

'And I wanted to be married to an Englishman,' she continued. 'An Englishman who would give me his name and take care of me. Italian men are excellent lovers but don't take care of their wives as well as they might.'

'So – you are Italian, Madame?'

She laughed. 'Can you not tell?' She ran her finger provocatively down the length of her slender nose. 'My nose!'

'It is a most appealing nose.' James suddenly became bold. 'The most beautiful nose I have ever seen.'

'Why, James! I believe you are flirting with me!' She leaned closer and he could smell her perfume, feel the warmth of her skin. 'I wonder? I think perhaps you have foreign blood? You have not the manner of an Englishman.'

'English through and through, Madame. Yorkshire born and bred.' He felt a quickening of his pulses. *I do believe I am falling in love with her.*

'I do not know your Yorkshire, I have never been there. Perhaps you will call on me one day? We will have tea and you can tell me about it.'

'Oh, yes. I'd be delighted,' he began, and then glanced up in annoyance as his host appeared beside them.

'James. Would you be an angel and get me another

glass of wine?' She handed him her empty wine glass and her fingers brushed his.

He took it, feeling heady, though he had had only one glass himself, and he drank another swiftly at the wine table before taking two more. She was laughing merrily as he returned, and Walker gave her a small bow and left them.

'Do you know why I laugh, James?' She tapped him playfully on the face with her folded fan, and he felt the whisper softness of the feathers on his cheek.

He shook his head. 'Walker said something funny?'

'Yes.' She took the glass from him and clinked glasses with his. 'Jonathon Walker said of you, "Who is to have him, Madame, you or I?" And I said that I was.'

'To have me?' He felt hot and cold with embarrassment. He was not an item for sale, and for Walker to make the suggestion made it sound very improper indeed. 'To have me?' he repeated. 'I don't understand, Madame.'

She raised her eyebrows. 'Why, to be your patron, of course! What else could we possibly mean?'

'She has not so much influence as Walker,' Batsford commented when James told him later. 'Though she is rich. Still, she will not drop you as easily as Walker might. Walker gets consumed with jealousy if his protégés as much as look elsewhere.'

'I am not of Walker's, er, persuasion,' James said stiffly.

Batsford shrugged. 'It wouldn't matter. If he liked you and your work, then he would see that you met the right people. But there,' he dismissed the subject, 'if you have made the choice, that is all there is to it.'

James called on Madame Sinclair a few days later as she had requested. She, too, lived in Chelsea, in an elegant Georgian house overlooking the Thames, with a small garden at the front and a glass conservatory at the rear which, she said, she had added in order to sit in on hot summer days, amid the ferns and greenery, and pretend that she was in Italy.

'Do you miss your country, Madame, or your family?' James sweated under the domed glass and drank a cup of coffee, while she sat looking cool in her white dress and large summer hat, gently fanning herself with a bamboo fan.

'Sometimes I do,' she admitted. 'When they have visited me, I get homesick, though I would not like to return to Italy to live.' She looked at him from her dark eyes. 'There is so much more here that I like. And also I must stay, because of my husband. It must not look as if I have abandoned him. But enough of me, James. Tell me of your life in Yorkshire and your family; you miss them too, yes?'

'Not so much as I thought I would. The same as you, I find there is more here that I like, although I miss my father—'

'Not your mama?' she asked in surprise. 'I thought all Englishmen loved their mamas better than anyone else?'

'No,' he said adamantly. 'We do not get along. I – I don't think she likes me very much. She much prefers my brother to me. But it is of no consequence.' He brushed away the inference that he was concerned. 'We are better apart. But there is someone I quite miss,' he added. And, he thought, *I must write, as I promised.*

'You have a lover, yes?' Madame Sinclair put her head to one side. 'I should have known.'

'Oh no! No, not at all – my cousin – Sammi.'

'Sammi? A boy, yes?'

'No. Not a boy. She's called Sarah Maria, really. Only everyone calls her Sammi. Everybody loves her, including me. She's my best friend. But my lover! No. Not Sammi!'

The very notion that Madame Sinclair assumed he would have a lover astonished him. *But I recognize that foreigners have a different view of things, especially Italians.*

They are not hide-bound by convention as the English are
with their prudish upbringing. They are warm-blooded and
emotional. And I shall, he determined, *throw aside all*
my preconceived judgements and beliefs. From now on I shall
dare to say what I feel, and do what feels right!

'Madame!' His voice became husky as a question
trembled on his lips. 'I know that the request that I
am about to ask may be a terrible imposition. But,
but – would you sit for me? It is not considered
derogatory for ladies to do so,' he added hastily,
mindful of the lecture he had been given by Miss
Gregory, and despite his new-found liberation. 'It is
quite a proper thing to do.'

A smile flickered over her lips. 'Yes, James, I am
aware of that. Do you wish me to sit naked?'

James was dumbstruck. He shook his head.

'For I could not do that.' Her eyes looked into his.
'My husband – you understand?'

'Of course,' he croaked. 'I had forgotten!'

That night he lay on his bed in his basement room
and through the uncurtained window looked up at
the steps leading to the street, and thought of how,
one day, he would paint Madame Mariabella Sinclair,
if ever she would allow him. He would paint her in
her conservatory with the pale and dark green foliage
surrounding her, and a veil of transparent tulle
draped around her.

'Mariabella.' He rolled the name around his
tongue. 'Mariabella! My beautiful Mary.'

17

'So how much is all this going to cost me? I'm not made of brass!'

'Oh, rubbish, Thomas. You haven't spent anything on this place in years.'

Ellen stood her ground. She was half-way to winning. Thomas was the most generous of men, but it just didn't occur to him that life could be made more pleasant with just a little effort and a minor investment of capital. 'Think how much satisfaction Betsy would have with a new cooking range and a separate room for bathing. And you and the boys wouldn't have to bathe under the pump or fetch water in if it was piped inside.'

'Tha'll have me going soft in my old age, being pampered.' He glowered at her from under his bushy eyebrows. 'Go on then – how much?'

'An extension to the kitchen and another room above, a bathroom and a new kitchen range – how much do you think?' she hedged.

'Good heavens! You'll have me bankrupt, woman!' He hesitated, then said firmly, 'I'll not spend more'n a thousand.'

'A thousand pounds!' She had hoped for only half that amount. If he was willing to spend that much, then they could even build on another small room for a maid, and buy some more furnishings.

'A thousand! Well, all right. I'll make it eleven hundred, and not a penny more! There'll be nowt left to bury me when I dee.'

'Your sons and daughter might as well enjoy the benefits now, Thomas, as spend it on your funeral.

But don't worry,' she added with a wry twist of her lips, 'when you die, I assure you we'll not leave your bones on top.'

Betsy was overjoyed to hear that they were to have a proper bathroom, and although the water would still have to be carried upstairs, the water would be hot from the kitchen range; they wouldn't have to boil kettles and pans when they wanted a bath.

'And we'll see if we can persuade your father to have a live-in maid. Someone young and lively; but you must train her properly,' Ellen added, 'or I will.'

Betsy looked downcast. 'There's no-one in the village that I would want to ask. Most of the young girls have gone into service in Hull. There's only the older women, and they wouldn't live in, and anyway, they don't listen to what I say, but do things the way they want to.'

Poor Betsy, Ellen thought. *She just muddles through.* She felt a pang of guilt. *I could have done more, but would I have done better? My own daughter is rebelling against my advice.* 'We'll find someone, Betsy,' she persuaded. 'We'll find someone that you like, someone who'll be glad to come to this fine place, once you've got a bigger kitchen and a new range, and we've put on a lick or two of fresh paint.'

Betsy got up and gave her a kiss. 'Thank you, Aunt Ellen. I'm so grateful.' She gave a deep sigh. 'Now all I want is a new dress for Gilbert's wedding. Do you think we can squeeze a little more money out of Da?'

Ellen smiled. 'Go out to the trap and fetch me in the parcel that's on the seat. When I went into Hull last, I went shopping at the draper's. I bought a rose silk for you and a pale green silk for Sammi. It's a present. Go on, go and fetch it in.

'Will you come home?' she asked Sammi when Betsy was out of the room. 'We want you to come back so that we can discuss the child. Things are not what they seem, Sammi – and people will be talking.'

Sammi set her mouth stubbornly, then relented, her mother looked unhappy. 'Soon, Mama. I have something in mind,' she said before Betsy burst back into the room with the parcel.

They spent the next hour choosing the designs they would like, for Ellen had also brought a catalogue of the latest fashions. Betsy finally decided on a wide crinoline with an off-the-shoulder neckline and a contrasting darker rose basque and overskirt in muslin. On her head she would wear a small toque with a rose in the centre.

'I can't decide. I can't decide,' Sammi wailed. 'Oh, which shall I have?'

'This!' said her mother. 'This would suit you perfectly.'

The design was of a simple crinoline and over it, a lace mantle with a matching cape and full sleeves.

'Yes,' Betsy agreed. 'And a spoon bonnet in the same green silk and an insert of the lace to frame your face and hair. Oh,' she clasped her hands together, 'I just can't wait.'

And I am dreading the day, Ellen thought. *Gilbert will be too embarrassed to speak to me, afraid I will give him away, and Mildred has completely closed up and won't even discuss the child or James.*

Later, after supper, Uncle Thomas said that he wouldn't go to the wedding; someone had to stay at home to work the sails, and George said that he hadn't a mind to go either. 'I'm not one for weddings and such-like fancy parties,' he said. 'So I'll stay behind with Da.'

'You're just like Richard,' Sammi complained. 'He's made the excuse that one of the cows will be ready to calf.'

'Well, count me out.' Mark had come in in the middle of the discussion. 'I don't fancy hobnobbing with all them toffs.'

'But someone will have to escort Sammi and me,' Betsy wailed. 'Uncle William has ordered a chaise because there won't be room for all of us in theirs, not without crushing our gowns.'

'Riding in a carriage now, are we?' Mark mocked. 'Not content with having 'house pulled apart, eh? By – folk's 'll think Fosters are made of brass!'

Tom remained silent, though he glanced at Sammi and then at his father.

'Tha'll be willing to go, Tom? We can't disappoint Betsy and Sammi,' his father asked. 'If not, then I shall. I'll not have 'young ladies going alone.'

'No, I'll go, Da,' he said quietly, 'I don't mind.'

Sammi smiled across at him, she had been hoping that it would be Tom who would accompany them. He was much better company than Mark, who was such a cross-patch, though Tom had been rather quiet lately, not at all his usual self, and she wondered why, when she had smiled her gratitude, he turned away and didn't give her an answering smile.

Betsy crept from her bed at five o'clock, tiptoed downstairs and out of the door. She slipped through the hedge and onto the path. Luke was there again as he'd said he would be; he took her hand and they sped towards the copse.

She had returned to him the last time as he had asked her to, and she'd realized that, even without the threat of exposure which she only half believed he meant, she would still have wanted to come to him. Their love-making, as he had so tenderly reassured her, was not painful at all, and though she had cried, it wasn't with pain, but because her body had throbbed so much with wanting him so badly.

This morning the sky was overcast and as she lay with her head cradled beneath his arm, their desire fulfilled, they felt a few drops of rain pattering through the trees and she whispered that she had to go.

'Not yet, Betsy.' He gazed at her with sensual demanding eyes. 'Not yet.' He ran his big hands over her smooth bare legs. 'Don't go. Wait a few more minutes. Please.' He groaned and pulled her towards him, his strong legs around her hips. 'Betsy Foster, I hadn't planned for this. You're driving me crazy.'

Sammi lay awake, staring at the empty bed. Betsy had gone again and there was only one reason why she would go out of the house at this early hour. Luke Reedbarrow. *I can do nothing*, she fretted. *I cannot advise her of her foolishness, for it is probably too late for that, and if I tell Tom or Uncle Thomas, then I lose Betsy's trust and friendship. And I couldn't, anyway. I would be too embarrassed to speak of it, especially to Tom, for he doesn't seem to have the same regard for me as he once had.* She wept a few tears, for Betsy and the trouble she might bring, for Tom who seemed always to avoid her, for James who, apart from a brief note to say he was going to London, still hadn't written to ask about Adam or send her money for him, and a few tears of self-pity.

I'll speak to Mrs Bishop today and put forward my proposition, and then after Gilbert's wedding I think I shall go home. It will appease Mama and Pa, and Betsy will probably prefer it now she has Luke to think about. She looked up at the window and saw a few drops of rain spattering down the glass. *She'll be back soon*, she thought drowsily, *now that it's raining.* She snuggled down between the sheets. *Well, you can make your own excuses this time, Betsy Foster, if anyone should catch you. I'm going back to sleep.*

Mark heard the sound of the rain on the window and thought of the barn where the carts and harnesses were kept and where, on a higher level, fodder and grain were stored. He looked across at George who shared the room, fast asleep and gently snoring. 'Damn it,' he breathed, 'I'd better get up. If those tiles have slipped again the rain will pour in.'

He pulled on a shirt and pair of breeches and went downstairs. The outside door was unlocked and he frowned. Who was last to bed? It was Da, and he never forgot. He wondered if Tom had heard the rain, too, and had gone out to check the barn roof, but the door to Tom's room had been firmly closed as usual, and he would surely have left it open had he come out, in case of waking anyone? Dismissing the query, he ran across the yard towards the barn. The rain wasn't heavy, though the sky was grey with the promise of more, and going inside the building he looked up and saw daylight seeping through the roof. He got out a ladder and propped it up against the wall, put the roof ladder over his shoulder and, climbing up, he placed it on the roof and climbed up to the ridge.

Two tiles had slipped at the top of the roof, so he sat astride the ridge and leaned across and pushed them back into position, noting as he did so that the nails had perished. *I'll have to come back up when 'rain has stopped and put in some new nails,* he decided. *That should fix them.*

He looked around before he prepared to climb down. He couldn't see the sea today. Sea and sky merged together in a dank grey mist which obliterated the horizon and hovered over the farmland of Monkston, dispersing into drifting vaporous strands over Tillington. He turned to look the other way across the fields: the corn was ripening nicely, this drop of rain wouldn't do any harm. *'Farmers'll have a good crop, though I expect they'll grumble as usual, and we'll have our noses to 'grindstone.*

He stopped his ruminating. Someone – two people – were coming down the path from the copse. He narrowed his eyes. Luke Reedbarrow, his huge frame was unmistakable, and a girl with him, tucked almost under his arm. *Randy beggar, I can guess where he's been! But what lass would meet him at this time of 'morning?*

He drew in a sharp breath. Betsy! Not Betsy! Anger consumed him as they drew nearer, oblivious of him, so absorbed were they in each other. His breath hissed between his teeth as he saw them stop, and Luke bent his head to kiss her and ran wandering hands across her breasts and around her hips and buttocks.

He slid down the roof ladder and left it there and ran down the other ladder to the ground. 'I'll show her, little bitch,' he seethed as he ran across the yard to the house. He went inside and locked the door and bolted it and stood waiting inside.

She lifted the sneck, rattling it gently when it wouldn't open. He heard the soft thump as she put her shoulder to it and heard with malevolent satisfaction the hiss of rain as it came down faster. Gently he eased back the bolt and turned the key and as she once more put her weight behind the door, he opened it and she fell into the threshold.

'What do you think you're doing?' she demanded. 'Did you lock the door?'

'What do I think *I'm* doing? More like what have *you* been doing? As if anybody couldn't guess. Just look at thee, tha dirty little whore.'

She caught her breath and as she jumped to her feet she lashed out at him, hitting him across the face. 'Don't you dare talk to me like that. What right have you to say such things to your own sister?'

'Sister!' He clenched his fist as if to return the blow. 'It's no sister of mine who goes out at this hour to meet some village lecher. I saw thee – like last time, on 'footpath.'

Betsy's face blanched. 'Luke's no lecher. I love him.'

'Love him!' Mark sneered. 'Half of lasses in 'village love him. Tha doesn't think he'll ask thee to marry him?'

She slumped down into a chair and put her head in her hands. 'Yes.' Tears were overflowing and running down her cheeks. 'If I want him to, then he will.'

He came across to her and put his hand under her

191

chin, forcing her head back so that she had to look at him. 'He won't marry thee if tha gets caught wi' a babby.' His voice suddenly changed from anger to appeal. 'Stop seeing him afore it's too late.'

She knocked his hand away. 'What would you know about anything,' she retorted. 'You're just a country yokel! You don't even try to speak properly.'

'That's what I am. A yokel. And that's what Luke Reedbarrow is! I'm surprised at thee, Betsy. I thought that tha wanted more from life than being wedded to a village peazan. Where are 'dreams that tha used to have, of a rich husband and fine house and carriage? Like Sammi will have one day!' He turned away from her, his face filled with anger and disappointment. 'We're trapped here, thee and me, and if we don't make an effort we'll never do owt.' He leaned on the table, his head bowed, biting his lip. 'It might be too late for thee,' he muttered, straightening up, 'but there's still time for me.'

She stared at him, her cheeks wet with tears and a sob in her throat, her hair was wet from the rain and hung in ringlets on her shoulders.

He looked her up and down, then inclined his head towards the stairs. 'Get thissen upstairs and cleaned up before our da sees thee. He'll know tha's been rolling in 'meadow as soon as he sees thee. Go on, and then get 'breakfast on, they'll all be up afore long.'

She tossed her head and hissed at him. 'Get thine own breakfast, peazan. I'm not thy servant.' She stumbled towards the stairs, her tears running unchecked. 'You talk of houses and carriages and yet still expect me to run after you.'

'I don't want owt,' he replied bitterly. 'Not from thee. I'm leaving. I've had enough. If tha gets pregnant, life won't be worth a candle wi' two squalling bastards in 'house.'

He rushed upstairs after her and barged into his room, waking George who looked at him through one eye and muttered, 'Is 'wind up?'

'Aye, and so should thou be. Rouse thaself.' He opened the cupboard door and rooted around on the top shelf and pulled down a canvas rucksack. He jerked open a drawer in the chest and searched for a woollen jersey, a clean shirt and a pair of cord breeches which he pushed into the rucksack. Then he looked under the bed and pulled out a pair of grey woollen stockings which joined the other garments in the bag.

'What's tha doing, Mark?' George grumbled. 'And can tha do it a bit quieter?'

'Leaving!' he snapped. 'So if tha wants to say good-bye, tha'd better get out of bed.'

'But why, son? Why does tha want to go now?' Thomas rolled up his shirt sleeves to his elbows. His arms were brown and muscular, belying his fifty-two years. 'We're just spending money on 'place and tha's wanting to leave!'

'I've been thinking about it for some time, Da.' Mark looked down at his feet. 'Now seemed as good a time as any.'

His father's brow furrowed, then cleared as he said appeasingly, 'I've been thinking about getting steam in 'mill, – getting an engine in!' He scratched the back of his neck. 'I know I keep talking about it, but this time we will, seeing as builders are coming in. I thought that we could talk about having an engine house tacked on, get modernized like some of 'other millers have.'

Mark shook his head. 'It's not that, Da. I just feel as if I want to see something of life, to see other bits of 'country. I don't want to be stuck here till I dee and know I've never tried to do owt else.'

'Why, son, tha'll find that life goes on just 'same in other places as it does here. Folks get up in a morning and go to bed at night, and do what suits them in between. I can tell thee that, without thee having to stir a foot out of Tillington.' He gave Mark a wistful glance from under his beetling brows and sighed. 'But I know full well that tha'd rather find out for thissen.'

Sammi had been sitting quietly in a corner trying not to intrude, but she stood up at this juncture and spoke to her uncle.

'It's because of me being here, I think, Uncle. That's why Mark wants to leave, because of me, and James's baby. But I won't be staying, Mark, I'll be going home soon.'

'No, it's not.' Betsy had come quietly down the stairs. Her dark hair was brushed and shiny, but her eyes were red-rimmed with crying. 'It's because of me. He said so.'

'Now then! What's this?' Thomas looked from one to another. 'Quarrelling? I'll not have that. If Mark feels he has to leave, then I'd like to think there was no animosity. No anger.'

'It's nothing to do with thee, believe that, Sammi.' Mark looked across at her with something like an apology in his voice. 'And it's only partly to do with Betsy. She onny set off 'spark to light 'tinder, in 'manner of speaking.'

'Set off 'spark!' His father grew impatient. 'What's been going on?'

'Nowt, Da. Just a disagreement we had. It's over with. Betsy shall do as she pleases, just as I want to do.' Mark picked up his sack and avoided Betsy's eye.

'Wait!' his father demanded. 'I'll get to 'bottom of this. Tom! Do you know owt of this?'

Tom was leaning on the door jamb, his arms folded in front of him. His mouth was set in a tight line. 'No, Da. I only know that Mark has wanted to go for some time. He's had enough of milling.'

'Even with promise of a steam engine?' his father asked. 'There'll allus be work here, Mark. Most men'd give their right arm for a mill like we've got.'

'Aye, Da. But one day it'll be Tom's. Oh, I don't mind that. I know that that is how it has to be. Same as you having this mill from thy da, and thy brother having to set up in Beverley. No. Tom is a good miller and there's everything he wants here in Holderness.' He glanced across at his brother and a flicker of a smile touched his lips. 'And I don't mean just 'mill. But I want to be my own master and that's why I'm going.'

'Tha'll go to sea! That's where tha'll end up. A seaman like some of thy forebears.' His father's eyes grew bright and moist. 'Well, so be it, if it's in 'blood.' He put out his hand to Mark who grasped it, and then putting down his bag put both arms around his father and hugged him.

'What about money, son?' His father's voice broke. 'I'll just get thee some out of coffer.'

Mark swallowed. 'I've enough, Da. I aim to go to Liverpool or London, and I've enough to get me there with what I've saved. Then I'll earn whatever else I need.'

He came across to Sammi and bent to kiss her cheek; then first shaking hands with George, who, upset from the suddenness of events, wiped away the tears which were trickling from his eyes, then put his arms around him, and tapped him comfortingly on his shoulder.

He stood in front of Betsy. 'Think on what I've said, Betsy, and be careful.'

She put her chin up and stared at him defiantly. 'You're wrong,' she reviled him. 'You'll see.' She turned her face away as he bent to kiss her cheek and he started back as if she had struck him again.

'Aye,' he said grimly. 'We'll see.'

Lastly he turned to Tom who stood by the door and who opened it to let him through. 'I'll walk with you to 'bottom of the lane,' Tom said quietly. 'You'll be walking to Aldbrough to catch the carrier?'

Mark nodded, then turned to his father who came to stand in the doorway. He lifted his hand. 'Don't worry, Da. I'll write as soon as I can. Wish me luck!'

His father nodded but didn't speak and as Mark closed the mill gate behind him, he saw his father was still standing there watching him as if to etch him into his memory.

'Will Da be all right? He won't worry too much?'

'Fat lot you care,' Tom said viciously. 'What's got into you? Why now? This is coming up to our busiest time!'

'I know, and I'm sorry, but tha'll manage.'

Their long steps were evenly matched as they strode out side by side under the young chestnut trees that lined the lane, spreading their fan-shaped leaves in a canopy above them, the brilliant candles of white blossom glowing, brightening the grey morning.

'It's just – if I don't go now, then I won't go at all.'

'And what of Betsy? What had you been arguing about?' Tom stopped. They'd come to the bottom of the lane. It was time now for Mark to take the road alone.

'I can't tell thee, Tom. Just keep an eye on her, that's all. She's being led astray.' He put out his hand to his brother, who took it, gripping it strongly.

'Take care, Mark,' Tom said gruffly. 'And don't feel you can't come back if things don't work out. You know that you can and you'll be welcome.'

Mark nodded, and then gave a wavering smile. 'I meant what I said about there being everything here that tha wanted. Tha's a good miller, Tom – as good as Da, if not better. I'm not, I haven't got 'thumb for it. And as for 'other—' He grinned and slapped Tom on the shoulder. 'Well, I doubt that she'd have thee, a peazan such as thee, but tha could try!' He strode away whistling and headed off towards the dip in the road which would hide his view of the village until half a mile onwards, when, if he turned, he would see the grey stones and cobbles of the steepled church, the red roof of the vicarage and the mill with its white sails standing pictorially against the wide sky.

He stopped suddenly and turned. 'Tom!' he yelled. 'Tom!'

Tom turned around expectantly and put his hand to his ear.

'I forgot to tell thee.' Mark cupped his hands to his mouth. ''Barn roof needs fixing!'

After Mark had left, Betsy's father had beckoned to her. 'Come here, young woman. I want to talk to thee.'

With a nervous glance at Sammi, she'd followed him into the parlour and Sammi went into the kitchen. Once more Nancy was late, but today, Sammi reflected, it was just as well. It wouldn't have done for servants to hear family quarrels, and it was now that the difference between Sammi's own home and the separating divisions between her family and their servants, and the Fosters' home where the maid could hear all that was happening in the household, became apparent.

George went out to the mill and a few minutes later a subdued Tom returned from seeing Mark off on his journey.

'He's gone, has he?' she said lamely, for something to say.

He nodded. 'Aye. I set him to the bottom of the lane.' He sat down and stared vacantly at the bubbling cauldron on the fire. 'He's had his heart set on going for some time.'

'So it wasn't anything to do with me – or Betsy?' she asked anxiously.

He glanced up at her and frowned. 'Nothing to do with you, no. He was rude to you, I know, but he was sorry about that. But Betsy – I'm not so sure. He's worried about her. He says she's being led astray.'

Sammi felt herself blushing. Perhaps she should have mentioned something about Luke Reedbarrow earlier. Perhaps all this bad feeling could have been avoided. *I've made a mistake*, she thought. *Several mistakes, in fact.* 'I'm sorry, Tom, I should have told you that Betsy was meeting Luke Reedbarrow. But she is so fond of him that it would have seemed like breaking a trust, I—'

He rose to his feet and towered over her, his dark eyes were intense, his voice taut. 'What do you mean? Meeting Luke Reedbarrow! When has she been meeting him?'

Her eyes widened and she put her fingers to her lips as if to silence them. 'I – I thought you knew, I thought that was what Mark—'

Tom shook his head. 'Mark only said to keep an eye on her, that she's being led astray.' Sammi turned away and made to lift the cauldron off the fire. He closed his hand over hers. 'Leave that, Sammi. When has she been meeting Luke Reedbarrow?'

She raised her eyes to his and saw the anger there and was immediately stung by annoyance herself. She shook off his staying hand. 'Don't question *me*, Tom. Betsy isn't answerable to me, or to you! To her father, yes, but not to us. She's nineteen, older than me. She's a woman. She is perfectly able to make her own decisions.'

'She's a child!' he retorted. 'Where men are concerned, she knows nothing. She has to be protected.'

'From Luke?' she said angrily. 'Is he not good enough for the Fosters?'

He put his hands to his head and clenched his black hair. His lips were set in a tight grimace, then he turned to her and grasped her by both shoulders. 'Listen to me, Sammi!'

She looked up into his face and was surprised at the passion etched there. He was usually so patient, so forbearing. She felt the pressure of his hands on her shoulders, not hurting or forceful, but strong and supportive.

'It's not a question of whether or not he's good enough. She has to be protected from men's emotions. Sometimes – sometimes they can just get carried away. Sometimes – women give out meanings without realizing. And not all men are—' He stopped. 'And – they don't – they're not aware . . .' He seemed to be consciously searching for an answer in her face, as if she held the key to what he had to say. He had lost his anger. This was the gentle Tom she knew, yet there was something different about him. He had become unsure and diffident. He dropped his hands and looked away; she wondered why he didn't finish what he was going to say. He didn't speak but stared at the floor. Again she reached for the cauldron, a thick cloth in her hand, and he turned towards her and taking the cloth from her he lifted the heavy iron utensil from the fire.

'You shouldn't be doing these jobs, Sammi. You're a guest here, even though you are family. What would your mother think? Or your father?'

'I'm only trying to help, Tom. Nancy never gets here on time, and my parents wouldn't expect me to stay and be waited upon, especially when I came without invitation.'

'You know you are always welcome,' he said brusquely. 'I didn't mean—'

The outer door crashed open and Nancy came rushing in. 'I'm sorry I'm late, miss,' she began and then stopped as she saw Sammi and Tom. 'Miss Betsy – isn't she here?'

'Yes,' Tom said sharply. 'She is here, and tired of waiting for you. This is the last time you'll be late. You will arrive here at six o'clock every morning except Sunday and the days you are given off, and if you are as much as five minutes late, you will be given notice.'

'Yes, sir,' she replied petulantly. 'But Miss Betsy – she doesn't mind if I'm a few minutes late.'

He leaned towards her. 'Well, I mind, and as I'm the one who has to work to pay your wages, I'm telling you that you will be on time.'

'Yes, sir.' She bobbed her knee and picked up the

empty coal bucket and the water pail and hurried towards the door. 'I will.'

Betsy called Sammi into the parlour after her father had gone outside. 'Sammi! What am I to do? Da wanted to know why Mark and I had quarrelled, and I had to tell him that it was because of Luke, and now he says that Luke must call and see him. He says he's agreeable to my meeting him if you will be with me, but he says that there has to be a proper understanding.'

'Oh, I'm so pleased, Betsy.' Sammi was delighted for her. 'Of course I will go with you.'

'But Sammi! You don't understand. I don't want anyone with me! I want to be alone with Luke. How can I bear it if there is anyone else there?'

Sammi heard Tom's warning ringing in her ears. Betsy was giving out meanings to Luke and she was sure that he would understand very well. She was besotted by him, but was he by her? 'But Betsy,' she replied, 'Luke will surely be very pleased that your father has no objections, and that he can call on you?'

'I'm not sure,' Betsy said slowly. 'I'm not at all sure.'

Luke wasn't very pleased. 'I don't know, Betsy,' he said, fingering the red scarf around his neck. 'I don't know if I want to come calling. I'm not ready for that. I've no money or prospects to offer, even if I'd a mind to.'

'I thought you loved me, Luke,' Betsy whispered. The breeze that morning was brisk and sharp, and she shivered.

He looked down at his boots, shamefaced. 'I'm not sure if I know 'difference.'

'Difference?' She clasped his arm. 'Difference between what?'

He gathered her into his arms. ''Difference between wanting thee, and wanting to wed thee and spending 'rest of our lives together.'

She felt the warmth of his body pressed against hers

and rubbed her face against his chest, then she lifted up her face for him to kiss her. 'I do know how you feel, Luke,' she said softly. 'I do understand. I think we must be very wicked, you and me. We have the devil in us.' A tear trickled down her cheek and he kissed it away. 'But I'm more wicked than you, for you're a man and can't help it, but I'm a woman and shouldn't have such feelings.'

'Mrs Bishop, may I talk to you?' Sammi stepped inside the open cottage door.

'Bless thee, course tha can.' Mrs Bishop motioned her to sit down. 'Summat's troubling thee, Miss Rayner; has been for a day or two, I could tell. Bairn's all right, tha needn't worry about him.'

'No, I can see that.' She smiled; Adam was round-cheeked and thriving. 'Mrs Bishop,' she paused, 'if you should become ill or die and not be able to look after your children, what would happen to them?'

'Why, Mr Bishop'd put older ones out to work and young uns'd muddle along, I expect, but babbies . . .' She had three who were under four. 'Well, I don't rightly know.' A frown wrinkled her brow. 'My sister Dora would take Minnie, I expect, and maybe our Jack and his wife'd take Ben, but this bairn,' she looked down at the sleeping child in her cot. 'She's not thriving well, she wouldn't tek to another nurse. I doubt she'd survive.' She sighed. 'It's what happens, Miss Rayner, to folks like us who haven't 'money to make other arrangements.'

'I'm sorry.' Sammi was penitent. 'I didn't mean to upset you.'

'Nay, I'm not upset. I've thought about it often.' Then she gave a big smile. 'But I'm not going to dee. I'll have more babbies yet unless I can get shot of my old man. But tha's got a reason for asking, Miss Rayner?'

Sammi took a deep breath. 'Adam's mother is dead.

She died in childbirth. His father is one of my cousins.' Mrs Bishop nodded but remained silent. 'I feel very strongly that he should be taken care of by our family, as yours would be,' she added, 'if anything happened to you. But my cousin is very young and immature, and has been sent away to avoid scandal. *His* family,' she said, 'seem loathe to do anything about the situation.'

'So tha's asking me to tek him, Miss Rayner? To bring him up?'

'Yes. I will pay towards his keep until the matter is resolved, or until my cousin is able to. I must tell you, however, that my father is most displeased with me for bringing him here, and that might have a bearing on your decision.'

'Aye, it might. Seeing as Mr Bishop works for thy father.'

They sat for a while, not speaking, and then Mrs Bishop said, 'Folks will talk, miss. They are doing already – and if there's a family likeness . . .'

'It will be a nine-day wonder, Mrs Bishop, and I know you will be discreet.'

Mrs Bishop surveyed Sammi from candid eyes, then she said softly, 'It wouldn't be fair to thee, miss. Gossip would be contained in Holderness, it wouldn't reach Hull and thy cousin's friends; but what about friends of thy parents and their sons and daughters? They'll cut thee dead.'

'Then so be it. I can't throw this child on the scrap-heap because I'm afraid of what people might say. Please, Mrs Bishop,' she pleaded. 'I don't know who else to ask or what to do.'

'I can't, miss.' Mrs Bishop spoke compassionately. 'Not to a young woman like thee. It'd ruin thy chances of being wed. But what I'll do,' she reached over and patted Sammi's hand, 'I'll tek him for six months. Set him up good and proper, and maybe by then thy cousin's family will have come round and will tek to little fellow.' She nodded her head and smiled.

'When they see him, they'll want him, mark my words. Will that do?'

Sammi got up to leave, she tried to smile her thanks but her mouth trembled. 'Thank you, Mrs Bishop. I suppose it will have to.'

18

'There's a letter from James, Gilbert.'

'At last! What does he say? Has he found somewhere to live?'

'I don't know.' His mother averted her eyes. 'I haven't read it.'

She looks very pale, Gilbert observed. *She still hasn't recovered from the shock of Father's sudden seizure.* 'Why haven't you read it, Mother?' he asked gently. 'You want to know what he's doing, don't you?'

'It's addressed to your father,' she whispered. 'You know I don't open his letters.'

He took the envelope from her. James's extravagant handwriting was unmistakable. 'Under the circumstances, Mother, we have to open Father's correspondence, and as it's patently from James, it's obviously meant for both of you!'

'Read it then,' she said, and sat down in her chair by the window, folding her hands in her lap. 'And then you can take it upstairs and read it to your father and put his mind at rest.'

He walked up and down the room as he read it aloud, and smiled as he read out that James knew that he was destined to be an artist! '*I can feel it in my blood!*' he read, '*in my veins!*' He looked up, a glimmer of amusement on his face which faded when he saw his mother's paleness.

'Are you not well, Mother? Would you like your smelling salts?'

She shook her head. 'No. I'll be all right. Just a headache dear, nothing more. Give me the letter. I'll read it to your father. He's been very anxious.'

Gilbert followed her upstairs to his father's room, where he lay propped up on pillows. His countenance was grey and even his hair seemed to have lost much of its colour.

Mildred read the letter aloud but, Gilbert noticed, missing out some parts of it, noticeably the words where James enthused about becoming an artist.

'He seems to be settling, Father,' Gilbert said heartily. 'We don't have to worry about him, he's having a fine time in the capital.'

Isaac nodded. 'Yes,' he said breathlessly. 'I trust he will do well. He has talent. Peacock always said so in his reports.' He stopped for breath and held his chest. He looked bleakly at his wife. 'It requires to be nurtured and encouraged, that's what he used to say. It can't be stopped, my dear. It has to be.'

Gilbert looked from one parent to the other. He didn't understand what his father was talking about, and his mother was staring blankly at a point above his father's head.

'Gilbert. You must send James some money. He doesn't ask for any, I notice, nevertheless . . .' He put his head back onto the pillows. 'Fetch paper, pen and ink, and you can draft out an authority and I'll sign it.' He took a faltering breath. 'And I'll do another for Collins at the bank. My lawyer is coming this afternoon. You'll have to have power of attorney to sign for the firm's accounts. Hardwick will guide you. He's a good man.'

Gilbert wrote in a neat hand the instructions as his father told him, that Gilbert Foster Rayner had the authority to pay on all promissory notes and for monies owing by Masterson and Rayner.

'I must rest now, Gilbert. I'm very tired. Take that to Collins; explain what's happened, if he doesn't already know, and send that money off to James.'

Gilbert nodded. The bank already knew the circumstances and had paid small accounts on their behalf, but there were bigger amounts to pay, insurance cover for two of their ships was due, and the bank wouldn't pay without his father's authority. 'I regret to say, Mr Gilbert,' Collins had said previously, his sombre, joyless manner leaving Gilbert sunk into depression, 'but management is often easier after a death. The authority would have automatically come to you had your father died, he had already arranged that. A company account is much more difficult to administer in circumstances such as this, when a senior partner is merely incapacitated.' Gilbert had almost felt that he should apologize to the banker for his father's lack of consideration in surviving; but he had been too down-hearted and worried to do or say what he really felt.

If only Father would agree to changing banks, he thought as he flicked the reins and moved down the drive. He turned to look back and saw his mother standing by the bedroom window, as still as stone, without a wave of her hand or a nod of her head.

There was a smart gig waiting in the yard when he arrived, which was causing some inconvenience to the porters and labourers who were manouvring their wooden sleds around it, and with a sense of impending disaster he realized that the vehicle belonged to Craddock and that he must be waiting for him inside.

Billy came out to greet him. 'Hardwick wants to see you as soon as you have a minute, and Charles Craddock is waiting. I put him up in your office. I hope that was all right.'

'Yes, but Billy – if he should come again, fob him off, will you? The fellow is a perfect nuisance.' He ran upstairs to the office. *My office,* he thought. *I didn't expect to lay claim to it quite so soon.*

Craddock was sprawled in a chair opposite Gilbert's desk. He wasn't dressed for work, Gilbert mused, in his fancy waistcoat and embroidered braces which he had both his thumbs through; he was obviously off racing or to some gaming party.

'Ah, Rayner. I hadn't realized that you came in to

the office so late. Had a late night, eh?' He nudged Gilbert with his elbow as he stood up to greet him. 'Making the most of bachelorhood before it's too late!'

'You forget, Craddock, that my father is very ill.' Gilbert was abrupt. 'There are other things to be seen to. I don't sit at my desk all day long.'

'Quite. Quite. I do understand. I remember when my father died what a lot of organizing there was to do.'

And what a lot of money there was to be spent, Gilbert reflected grimly, *and from what I hear, most of it has been.*

'Anyway, old chap. I know that I said I would wait a while longer for what you owed me, but the fact is, I'm in a bit of a hole. I need some ready money pretty quickly if I'm to survive; so I was wondering – could you let me have a little on account, say fifty pounds?' He fixed his gaze on Gilbert. 'You know I wouldn't press you unless it was really necessary, but I do need it straight away. Say in an hour.'

Gilbert sat down at his desk and hoped that the dismay he felt didn't show in his expression as he returned his stare. He owed him two hundred pounds. *I must have been mad, gambling with a man like him. What on earth possessed me?*

'Come back then,' he said unblinkingly, 'in an hour. I'll have it for you then.'

Craddock looked surprised, as if he hadn't expected it to be quite so easy. 'Well, there we are then. I knew you wouldn't let me down.' He picked up his shiny top hat. 'Everything going well with the wedding plans? Little lady getting excited? I'm really looking forward to it, as is my, er, friend.'

Gilbert felt a fleeting stab of panic. Who was the blighter bringing with him? Too late now to lay down any stipulation. The invitation had been sent. 'I'll see you in an hour.' He rose from his seat. 'The money will be waiting.'

He sank down again as Craddock left, and put his chin in his hands. *Where am I going to get the money from?* He stared down at the desk and the two envelopes which contained the authority from his father. *I should have asked Father for a loan. He would have given me one. But I don't want to upset him.*

He shuddered as the remark which Collins at the bank had made, about it being easier if his father had died, came back to him. And shuddered again at the realization that he, too, would have been far richer had his father not recovered. *What sort of man am I to even think of such things? Contemptuous. Worse even than Craddock. No. I would rather be in this fix and have Father alive and well, than have his wealth and him gone from us. But what can I do?*

He knew what he could do. He was merely putting up a fight with his conscience that he shouldn't do it. That he shouldn't draw money from the firm's account to pay his debts. As he pondered, he thought of James and the money he was to send him from his father's personal account. Fifty pounds, his father had at first stipulated, and then reconsidered. 'Make it a hundred, Gilbert.' He'd called Gilbert back as he was leaving. 'London is more expensive than here, and he'll need to buy materials for his work.'

Fifty pounds would probably be as much as James will need, he persuaded himself. *I could borrow the other fifty and then give it back when I receive my salary. It won't be for long.*

He started up from his desk. An hour. That was all the time he had. He gathered up the envelopes and rushed downstairs.

'Billy!' he called. 'Hold the fort, will you? Tell Hardwick I'll see him when I get back. I'm just going to the bank.'

Billy was curious about young Jenny and the band of children. He'd noticed them several times since the last encounter by the Holy Trinity Church and thought it odd that he hadn't seen them previously. *They've been here all the time*, he thought, *yet I wasn't aware of them.*

So after supper one evening, he slipped out of his lodgings and walked briskly across towards the old church and the area where Jenny had said they lived. There was a smell of wood smoke, almost like autumn at home, he thought, and not at all like early summer; but there was also a strong smell of soot still lingering from the burnt-out warehouse. None of the children were about, just an occasional figure wending his way home, and a few stray dogs sniffing in the gutters. He sat on the churchyard wall and pondered why he had come. *Nothing to do with me how others choose to live, but it seems wrong, somehow; and do these children actually have a choice?*

The moon slid out from behind a cloud and shone its bright light through the open roof of the warehouse, illuminating the glassless broken windows with lustrous silver curtains. For a moment he forgot the children as he watched the scene, as if waiting for a theatre performance to begin, then suddenly he became aware of a movement, shadows merely, as one by one children appeared, it seemed, like rats from a hole in the ground.

He kept perfectly still; he didn't know if they had seen him, but a moment later knew that they had, as Jenny and the boy she called Tim appeared at his side.

'Hello, Mr Rayner.' She grinned at him. 'What's tha doing here?'

'How do you know my name?' The moonlight cast a glow on her, making her hair silver and casting a shadow on her thin cheeks.

'Not much we don't know about round here,' she said. 'But I saw thee one day and followed thee down 'High Street.'

'Ah! But why did you do that?'

'I wanted to see them fine hosses again, just to stroke 'em,' she nodded.

'They're not mine,' he smiled. 'They belong to my cousin, Gilbert Rayner.'

'Aye. I know,' she admitted. 'I've seen him driving 'em. He's a bit of a toff, isn't he – not like thee.'

He felt vaguely complimented, but before he could think of a suitable reply, she said, 'Got to be off. There's a show on at 'Queens and we want to catch folks while they're in a good mood, otherwise there's nowt for us to eat.' She moved away, then came back. 'Why hast tha been waiting? We've been watching thee for ages. Some of 'bairns wouldn't come up, they thought tha was from 'law, but I said tha wasn't.'

'Come up?' When she didn't answer his query, he said quite honestly, 'I was curious. I wondered where you all lived. You told me that you belonged to no-one, but I can't believe that. If you have no parents, you could live in a children's hospital where you wouldn't have to beg.'

'Huh.' She gave him a look of contempt. 'Tha's been to them places has tha, Mr Rayner? Know all about 'em?'

No, he didn't. He hadn't seen them, though Sammi had, and that was why she was making such a fuss over James's baby.

'Well, some of us have been there and we didn't like it,' she continued defiantly, 'so we decided to take our chance out here on 'streets.'

He jumped down from the wall. 'I'll walk with you to the theatre,' he said. 'If you don't mind.'

She laughed, screwing her nose up, and he thought how young and innocent she looked. She was young, he mused, maybe thirteen or so, but was she innocent? 'I don't mind,' she said. 'But what if some of thy fine friends see thee with us? What will they think?'

'I don't know, Jenny.' He smiled down at her. 'But I don't really care.'

*   *   *

They didn't collect much money. The people outside the theatre and the music hall where they later went were not in a generous mood, but some of the children had scavenged fruit that had been left behind to rot in the Market Place, and Billy watched them as they sat on the plinth beneath the King Billy statue, and saw how they shared it out. He wanted to help. He saw how dirty they were, how shabby their clothes. *It's not a lot to ask for,* he thought. *Clean water and clean clothes. It's hardly riches.* He thought of the good supper that he had eaten at his lodgings and how much there had been left that would be wasted, and felt a sense of shame. 'You've enough money to buy bread and some milk.' He cast his eye over the small pile of coins. 'Would you like me to go to the baker for you, Jenny?' He had the idea that he would buy extra out of his own pocket.

'No thanks, Mr Rayner. I'll go and get it,' she said. ''Baker'll charge thee over 'odds.' She grinned. 'He knows me, we have an arrangement and he lets me have it cheap if I go in later on. He'll be baking at this hour; he doesn't like being troubled when he's busy with his ovens.'

Billy nodded, then pursed his lips. 'What did you say, Jenny?'

She looked baffled. 'What about? I said 'baker would be busy.'

'About you going in later?'

'Oh, aye.' She grinned. 'Don't worry. I know how to look after myself. He just likes a bit of a cuddle, that's all. Nowt else. His wife is upstairs so he daren't try owt, and anyway all 'other bairns wait outside. They'd kick up such a din if they thought I was in 'trouble.'

He was shocked. Shocked to think that a seemingly respectable tradesman would try to take advantage of a child, for that was all she was, and appalled too that the girl was already sufficiently hardened to the manners of such men to know and expect treatment of this kind; and yet she was prepared to condone their behaviour in order to put a crust of bread into her mouth. He felt anger gnawing his insides. *There's something wrong with our society if we allow such hypocrisy in our midst. I swear I will not live by such rules.*

'Jenny! What is your other name? Your surname?'

'Tomlinson.' She gazed at him curiously. 'Nobody's ever asked me that afore.'

He stood up and gave her a short bow and offered his arm. 'Miss Tomlinson. I wish to accompany you to the baker. We are about to buy you some bread.'

The baker would be only too pleased; he bowed and scraped as Billy introduced himself as William Foster Rayner of Masterson and Rayner, shipping merchants. Only too pleased to supply any leftover bread to the children at a reduced price.

'I am calling on as many traders as I think will be kind enough to be accommodating on this worthwhile mission, for it is a terrible indictment on our good citizenship, is it not, sir, that these *children*,' and he emphasized the word, 'should have to beg for their supper?'

Jenny caught his mood and stood with her head bowed as he spoke and then glanced up appealingly at the baker with her saucer eyes.

'And can I take your name, sir, to give us a regular subscription? No, no, not now,' he objected as the baker fished under his apron for his purse. 'It must be done through the proper channels. I might well be a rogue or a charlatan, out to exploit you or these innocent children.'

The baker protested. 'Not you, Mr Rayner. Why the name of Rayner has been well known in this town for years, aye, and Foster too, I've heard tell.' He leaned a floury arm across towards him. 'Here. Take a shilling now,' he said with great philanthropy. 'Tha can get a meat pie with that for 'little lady.' He picked up a loaf, still hot from the oven, 'and have that with

my compliments. Tha'll not get better bread anywhere in 'town.'

The children gathered round Billy outside the
shop, their mouths drooling at the sight and smell of
the warm bread. He gave Jenny the shilling and the
loaf. 'There you are, Miss Tomlinson, I'm sure you
know better than I how to share it out. Tonight
you have earned your supper. Tomorrow is another
day; and it will be better. It has to be. I *swear* it will be.'

19

'It will be a grand wedding, I expect?' The seamstress had eased the waist and shortened the hem on Betsy's gown and put the finishing touches to Sammi's cape.

It would indeed be a grand wedding, according to the guest list. Bankers of the town had been invited, and the Mayor and civic dignitaries, as well as ship owners and merchants. Austin Billington was determined to make his daughter's wedding the talking point of the town.

Sammi and Betsy were to spend the eve of wedding night at Garston Hall and get ready there, as the builders had already moved into the mill, and the house was full of dust as they started to enlarge the kitchen. The cast-iron kitchen range ordered from York had arrived and lay in the yard in its wooden crate. It had a large side oven and a tap for drawing off hot water, as well as the usual accoutrements for hanging a kettle or roasting a joint.

'We'll collect you tomorrow, Tom. Be ready, won't you?' Betsy called to him as she climbed into the trap. He waved his hand in answer and went back inside the mill. The yard was filled with piles of sand and sacks of lime, bricks and pantiles, and the builder's men were mixing mortar, for they had also started on the new building which would house the new steam engine.

'Tom seems preoccupied, Betsy. Is he missing Mark, do you think?'

Betsy shrugged. 'Well, I'm not. Life is a lot more comfortable without him constantly bickering, but I suppose there is more work for them now that he's gone. Still, the new engine should make things a lot easier, especially for Da. Milling is such hard work, and he gets very tired.'

Sammi shook the reins and Boreas picked up into a brisk trot as they turned down the lane to Monkston.

'Are you glad to be going home, Sammi?'

Sammi's face lit into a slow smile. 'Yes. I do miss everyone, and Mama and Pa have agreed a truce, though they're still displeased with me; but I shall miss not seeing Adam for a day or two. I think he knows me now, you know. I'm sure he smiles at me.'

Betsy turned a wry glance at Sammi. 'Mrs Bishop said you would get over fond of him, didn't she? Well, she was right.'

'I hope James is at the wedding. And I wonder if he'll want to know about Adam?' Sammi frowned. 'I've not heard from him. Do you think that he thinks of him at all?'

There was a stiff breeze blowing off the sea as they emerged onto the steps of Garston Hall at ten o'clock the next morning. But the sun was bright and they knew that once they had moved inland the day would be warmer.

'Oh, you do all look lovely, ma-am.' Martha and some of the other maids came out to see them off, and Cook and the kitchen maid peeped from behind the kitchen wall.

William smiled at his wife as he handed her into the carriage. 'You do indeed look lovely, my dear.'

Ellen had chosen a crinoline gown in silver grey, with white muslin sleeves and a matching sleeveless jacket, and a large white hat with a spotted veil.

'May I travel with Sammi and Betsy as far as Tillington, Papa?' Victoria hopped from one foot to another in excitement. She wore a blue-and-white hooped muslin gown with a tucked and pleated embroidered bodice which her mother had painstakingly stitched for her. Over the top she wore a darker blue cloak with a hood, for her mother was afraid of her taking a chill, and on her head, a circlet of blue and white silk flowers.

Her father agreed and escorted her to the chaise where Sammi and Betsy were already seated.

'Uncle William! How very handsome you look,' Betsy said admiringly. 'Oh, how lovely if we could dress like this every day!'

'Then you must try to catch yourself a rich husband, my dear,' her uncle said wryly. 'For you will need a fortune.' He walked back to the Rayner carriage, swinging his silver-topped cane. He flipped up the tails of his frock-coat as he sat down next to his wife, and tapped on the roof to tell Johnson to move off.

'There he is. There's Tom!' Victoria squealed and hung out of the window as their chaise approached the mill. 'Tom! I wouldn't have known you. How very grand you look.'

Sammi shushed her. 'Victoria! Do behave! You'll embarrass Tom,' she whispered as Tom opened the door and helped Victoria out and into her father's carriage, and she felt suddenly shy as he stepped inside their chaise and sat beside her, for Tom was quite transformed. His dark hair was brushed and shiny without a trace of flour which often coated it, and cut so that it curled around his ears, and his grey frock-coat, hired for the occasion, fitted him perfectly, showing off his broad shoulders and slim hips, and beneath his pin-striped trousers he wore shiny black shoes.

'Whew, Tom!' Betsy gazed at him. 'You'll have all the ladies chasing after you. You look so elegant and wealthy. Even Aunt Mildred will be impressed. No-one would guess that you're only a poor miller's son.'

He sat back and crossed his legs and nonchalantly tapped his fingers on his top hat. 'And everyone will know that you are not a lady if you give the game away, Betsy,' he said dryly. 'So shall we have a pact that neither of us will tell?' As he eased back into the seat he brushed against Sammi's hand. 'I beg your pardon, Sammi. Good morning to you.' He smiled at her, his eyes lingering on her face. 'How lucky I am to be in such fine company.'

Uncle Thomas and George came to the gate to wave good-bye. 'Are you sure you can manage, Da?' Tom asked anxiously. 'Don't try and do too much today. We'll catch up tomorrow when I get back.'

His father scratched his chin and shook his head. 'I'm not sure as we can manage wi'out thee, Tom. Maybe tha'd better get out of them fancy clothes after all and I'll go in thy place.' He nodded at Victoria and her mother leaning out of their carriage window. 'If I'd have known there were going to be such beauties around I would have accepted 'invitation.'

Sammi stretched across Tom to speak to George, her skirt rustling against his knee. 'Richard said he would call in to see you later in the day. He has to come to Tillington. Oh! We're off! Good-bye. Good-bye.'

They all leaned out, waving their hands towards Uncle Thomas and George, who stood with raised arms to send them off to the wedding.

20

It was two days before the wedding that Gilbert realized that, when writing to James, he'd forgotten to tell him the date of his marriage. *It's too late now,* he thought in dismay. *What is Father going to say?*

His father was still confined to bed, and spent most of his time sleeping or dozing, comatose from the effects of opium. On occasions when he refused the medication and got out of bed to stagger to the window and stare dazedly out into the garden, he was seized by pains in his chest and very little breath to enable him to crawl back to bed again. And it was out of the question that he would be able to attend Gilbert's wedding.

But there were times when he was rested, and when Gilbert came home, he would send for him to come upstairs and give him the news of the day; in particular, to tell of what was happening at the various shipping companies; to ask if there was any news of missing ships and what was happening generally in the shipping fraternity of which he had been a very active member.

'*The Arctic Star* has sailed,' Gilbert reported. 'I saw her off. Oh, yes, and I saw Pearson the other day and he sent his very best wishes to you; he told me he's going ahead with his plans for a public park. I'll take you when it's opened,' he said heartily. 'And,' he added more soberly, 'I also met Norwood. He's very concerned about safety standards on board the ships, particularly the steam vessels. There have been so many losses that he says if the ship owners don't devise better standards for themselves then the government may step in. He, too, sends his regards to you for a full recovery.'

Isaac nodded. They both knew that the possibility was highly unlikely.

Gilbert reluctantly decided that he would have to confess to his father about the omission of the wedding details to James. He was also worried that James might write and thank his father for the fifty pounds sent to him, and Isaac might well remember that he had asked Gilbert to send a hundred.

I'm walking on eggs here, he pondered. *But I'll straighten everything out just as soon as the wedding is over. I'll sort out the money problem. I'll find a home for the child and relieve Sammi; but there's the rub – if Aunt Ellen has told Uncle William what she suspects, he might mention it to Father, and then I shall be in a scrape!*

He had been tempted many times to confess all to his father: that he was the father of the infant and not James, and that he had been in debt to Craddock. In fact, there were times when he wondered if his father was anticipating some admission or disclosure as he compassionately asked if there was anything worrying him.

'You didn't ask your brother to come?' he now whispered incredulously. 'And did you also forget to tell him about me? Did that slip your mind also?'

'No, no, Father. That's why I forgot to tell him the date of the wedding. I was so intent on telling about your illness that it quite slipped my mind.'

'Don't tell Harriet that you forgot to mention the marriage,' his father said wearily. 'She won't be very impressed. I am very disappointed, Gilbert. Very disappointed indeed. I had hoped he would come. And did you remember to send him some money?'

'Yes, Father.' Gilbert grew hot with shame. 'I didn't forget that.'

'Oh! Here she comes. Let me see, let me see.' Betsy stood on tiptoe, steadying herself on Tom's arm.

'How lovely she is, Sammi – I had no idea – so beautiful!'

The crowd of guests awaiting the bride's arrival twittered and jostled as the carriage, pulled by four greys, their manes adorned by blue ribbons, drew up outside the raised arches of St John's Church.

'She looks charming, doesn't she! How proud Gilbert must be,' Sammi agreed. She took hold of Tom's other arm as she strove to peer over the heads of the other guests.

Harriet was wearing a gown of deep blue velvet with a crinoline so wide that she had difficulty getting out of the carriage door, and on her head she wore a flowered coronet. Her father, Austin Billington, not to be outdone by the occasion, wore a dark grey frock-coat and a silk embroidered waistcoat, light grey knee breeches of the old style, with white stockings and black buckled shoes.

Tom smiled at the enthusiasm of Betsy and Sammi, and offered his arms to them both. 'Come, ladies. Give me the pleasure of escorting you to your pew.'

Betsy ignored him and went on watching as Harriet's train was adjusted before she made her entrance into the church, but Sammi took Tom's arm and looked up at him, bright-eyed in anticipation of the happy occasion, and then lowered her eyes and blushed as he impulsively bent towards her and whispered, 'Forgive me, Sammi, if you think me impertinent, but you are lovelier than any other here.'

She gently squeezed his arm. 'Thank you, Cousin Tom,' she said softly, her head down. 'It's very sweet of you to say so.'

Inwardly he groaned. *Cousin Tom. That's what I am. No more than that.*

Some of the guests waited after the ceremony for their carriages to take them to the Station Hotel, where the reception was being held, whilst others who lived in the town took either a sedan chair or decided to walk the short distance across the town, following the trail of the carriage which now held Gilbert and his new bride.

Sammi and her parents stood in the sunshine and chatted with her Uncle Arthur and Aunt Henrietta who had come from York with their daughters.

'James isn't here, I see.' Arthur looked around at the mingling guests. 'I trust he didn't go off to London on that foolish whim of his?'

'He did go to London,' Ellen broke in, excusing James, even though she doubted that their York relatives knew the real reason for his leaving. 'And why not?' she insisted. 'If young men want to go and seek their fortunes elsewhere, then we shouldn't stop them. But I fear our menfolk are depleted. James and Mark, they've both gone off to seek experience or adventure, and if they find their fortunes too, they will do well.' She looked across at Tom and Billy who were standing side by side. Both were tall: Tom, broad-shouldered and strong, Billy, slim and willowy, one dark, one fair, yet both from the same stock. 'But we are lucky, are we not,' she smiled, 'to have two such deep-rooted and dependable young men as Tom and Billy?' She gazed from one to the other. 'These two, I feel, have more Foster character than any other of our kinsfolk. They will stay and make their mark here as their forebears did. They won't be found wanting in any respect.'

Billy grinned at his mother and then, catching sight of someone over her shoulder, he raised an arm and waved.

Local townspeople, who knew the names of Billington and Rayner, had gathered to see the bride and the fashionable guests, and were now moving away. Only a straggle of poorly dressed women and barefoot children were still standing watching. One of the children was waving her hand.

'Surely you are not familiar with those people,

Billy?' Henrietta asked humourously. 'Friends of yours!'

'Not friends, Aunt. But I know them, some of them, yes.'

Sammi chuckled. 'Have you got an admirer, Billy?'

Billy laughed and shook his head, then waved again as their carriage arrived. 'Remind me to talk to you about her later, Sammi. There's something I want to ask you.'

After the formal reception was over, a party was to be held in the evening for those who wished to stay. The ladies retired to a sitting-room to rest before the festivities began, while some of the men went off with Arthur Rayner to look at the trains and the engines in the station, and William went to Anlaby to sit with his brother Isaac and tell him all that had happened at the wedding.

'Try not to mention the child or James, dear,' Ellen said as she saw him off from the front of the hotel. 'It won't do him any good to become distressed. I wouldn't be surprised if the upset of it all was the cause of his illness.'

He promised that he wouldn't. 'I feel so sad for him,' he said. 'It doesn't seem fair that he should miss his son's wedding.'

'Shall I come with you? Two of us could cheer him, perhaps, and it is such a strain talking to Mildred.'

'No, my dear. It would seem odd if you didn't stay. Bear up if you can and come later after the dancing.'

She leaned towards him. 'And who shall I dance with, my love, when you are not there? There will be no young swain wanting to dance with an old woman like me, when there are so many bright-eyed young lovelies around.'

He bent to kiss her. 'They don't know what they are missing then, these young men. Poor things, they have to wait until they reach maturity to appreciate real beauty.'

But have you seen your eldest daughter, William? she

mused as she waved him good-bye. *Sammi's last veil of childishness is about to float away. I could see it as she dressed for the wedding today. She looks so lovely, she's hovering on the brink of womanhood, yet she is ruining her chances of a good marriage in her concern for the child. I only hope* . . . She sighed and turned to go back into the hotel. She could only hope that her impulsive daughter didn't become involved with anyone unsuitable. *I must watch out for her. And Betsy, ah, Betsy, there is some dangerous excitement simmering there. She, too, must be watched. Growing up is not easy – so many temptations.*

Ellen rejoined Mildred and Harriet's mother and some other ladies to drink tea; Gilbert and Harriet were having their wedding photographs taken with their attendants, and Betsy and Sammi, bored of sitting, took a stroll around the foyer of the hotel until the festivities began. They had taken a second perambulation around the floor when a man and woman came through the doors. Sammi and Betsy merely glanced at the couple and went on with their discussion of who was wearing what, and what a very fashionable crowd had been invited, when the man came up to them.

The woman, colourfully dressed in a red-and-black gown and yellow silk shawl, stood back and gazed fixedly at the flowers which were arranged in urns around the foyer.

'Miss Rayner, I think?' He bowed, holding out his hand flamboyantly.

'Yes!' Sammi disregarded his hand. As far as she was aware, she didn't know him. She couldn't remember seeing him in church, but perhaps he had been sitting at the back.

'I thought so. You can tell a Rayner anywhere with that lovely red hair.'

Sammi raised her eyebrows at the compliment, but it wasn't well received. *Pure flattery*, she thought. *Who is he to make such familiar compliments?*

'May I introduce myself, Miss Rayner? Charles Craddock. I'm a good friend of your brother Gilbert.'

Betsy giggled and put her hand to her mouth, and Sammi, trying not to laugh, raised her chin as she spoke. 'Then your friendship is lacking in intimacy, sir, if you think that Gilbert is my brother, for he is not.'

Craddock's mouth opened then closed, and he appeared so lost for words that Sammi, against her better judgement, took pity on him. 'He is my cousin, therefore we share the same name – and the red hair.'

Craddock bowed again, recovering his composure instantly. 'A thousand pardons, Miss Rayner. Gilbert has spoken of his sister, and I assumed – wrong to do so, of course, one should never—' He turned to Betsy, who was watching with obvious amusement. 'And another cousin, perhaps?' His eyes paid court to her low-cut bodice. 'Or – a friend? Gilbert is a lucky man indeed to know such lovely ladies.'

'Second cousin,' Betsy replied brightly. 'Elizabeth Foster. We don't bear the same name or the red hair as our kinsfolk.' She glanced across at Craddock's companion who was tapping her fan against her hand. 'Your wife is getting impatient, Mr Craddock, she is feeling neglected. I think you are about to receive a rap on the knuckles.'

'Not my wife,' he replied with a cavalier attitude. 'My, er, my companion for the occasion; may I introduce—'

'We must look for Mama, Betsy,' Sammi intercepted. 'Perhaps some other time, Mr Craddock. Please excuse us.'

'Sammi!' Betsy murmured as they moved away. 'I didn't know you could be so disparaging. You are usually so polite.'

'I was not impolite, Betsy,' Sammi protested. 'My manners were commendable, I'm sure, unlike his. What a fawning, grovelling toad.' She shuddered. 'He made me quite angry, pretending that he knew

Gilbert so well. I'm sure that Gilbert wouldn't entertain such company as his.'

Betsy turned her head towards Sammi. 'We are merely country girls, Sammi,' she laughed. 'We know nothing of business life, when people of differing personalities are thrown together. Mr Craddock may well be a colleague of Gilbert's. And he *has* been invited to the wedding!' She inclined her head gracefully as Mr Craddock looked in their direction. 'I wonder if he's rich? His clothes are well cut and his watch chain is gold.' She pulled an impish face and said shockingly, 'And I rather think the lady with him is a—' she whispered from behind her hand into Sammi's ear.

'Betsy!' Sammi stared shocked and wide-eyed at her cousin. 'How can you say such a thing? You don't know. How do you know?'

Betsy laughed and adjusted her dress about her shoulders. 'I just do, that's all.'

They heard the sound of music and wandered back into the reception room. A pianist and a violinist were playing a medley of waltzes by Johann Strauss, and groups of people were sitting or standing and tapping their feet or fans in time to the music.

'I don't see Tom or Billy anywhere.' Sammi glanced around the room. 'Mama is here, and Aunt Mildred, and Mrs Billington, and here are Gilbert and Harriet just come back.'

'Here they are.' Betsy looked towards the door. 'And just look at them. They've had a drop or two to drink!'

Not inebriated by any means, but certainly quite merry, Tom and Billy stood in the doorway with their arms around each other's shoulders. 'Hello, Sammi – Betsy. We've been looking at the choo-choo trains.' Billy beamed at them as he and Tom weaved their way towards them, 'But we got bored, so we sneaked off for a glass of ale.'

'Or two,' Betsy commented. 'Now who is going to

dance with us, for neither of you will be able to waltz without falling over.'

'Not true, Betsy,' Tom admonished her. 'We are perfectly sober, we simply shared a jug of ale and our sorrows.'

'Sorrows?' Sammi and Betsy cried simultaneously. 'What sorrows?'

Billy hung on to Tom's arm. 'Tom has told me – in confidence – of his feelings for a young lady and I—'

'Ssh. That's enough.' Tom put up a finger to silence him. 'No more.'

'Tom! Don't tell me you have a secret passion?' Betsy teased her brother. 'Not you – old sober-sides!' When Tom didn't respond, she said cynically, 'It doesn't seem fair, does it, Sammi, that men can have grand passions but ladies cannot?'

Billy came to her and put his arm around her waist. 'I am of the opinion, and I will discuss it with you, my dear cousin, when I am not under the influence of alcohol, but I am of the opinion that there are many discrepancies and injustices in our society which need to be swept away.'

'A reformer, are you, Billy?' she said a shade bitterly. 'Then start with the women in society, for they are the ones who lose every time.'

'No!' Sammi protested. 'Start with the children. They are the ones that we should look to first.'

'I quite agree, Sammi,' Billy said. 'You took the very words out of my mouth. Excuse me.' He staggered away. 'I must go and sit down.'

'You shouldn't have let him drink so much, Tom,' Betsy admonished. 'Now he'll go to sleep and miss the dancing.'

'I didn't!' Tom complained. 'We didn't have much, but the Hull ale is strong.'

The dancing had started, and Betsy looked around the room wondering if anyone might ask her. She saw Charles Craddock looking her way and, catching his eye, she feathered her fan about her face.

'Miss Foster. If you are not engaged, may I have this dance?' He bowed towards her and Tom, who was standing next to her.

Tom started to say something, but Betsy took Craddock's arm and allowed him to escort her to the floor.

'Who's he, Sammi?' Tom frowned. 'Have we met him?'

'Yes,' she answered flatly. 'He introduced himself earlier.' She felt strangely deflated, yet couldn't reason why. 'He thought I was Gilbert's sister.'

Tom looked down at her. A wisp of hair had fallen about her face and he abstractedly smoothed it back from her cheek. 'Why?' he asked softly.

'What?' He was looking at her so strangely, as if he was preoccupied. She was bewildered by his mood, and caught up in a web of irrational confusion.

'Why did he think you were Gilbert's sister?' He still gazed at her with his dark, dreamy eyes as if he was half-asleep.

'Er – I don't know.' She looked away from him; she felt mesmerized, uncertainty flooding over her when her eyes met his. 'The red hair, I think.'

He touched a ringlet that was coiled on her neck and she felt the brush of his fingers. 'Oh, yes. Of course.' He blinked and seemed to give himself a mental shake and wake up. 'But still – I hope the fellow is all right.'

She had her doubts about Craddock, but her lips trembled unaccountably as she replied, 'There you are again, Tom, constantly watching over her.' *Who is Tom harbouring a passion for? And why haven't Betsy and I known of it? It must be someone in Holderness, but who?*

'Come on, you two. Tom! Invite Sammi to dance.' Gilbert swung by with Harriet on his arm. 'Come on, everyone must dance.'

'I can't, Sammi. I'm sorry. I don't know how.' Tom made his excuses.

'I'll show you, if you would like to,' she said slowly. 'It's quite easy to waltz.'

Reluctantly he took her hand and led her to the floor and, with his hand on her waist and hers on his shoulder, she guided him around the floor; they swung in triple time, and as there were so many other couples dancing, it didn't seem to matter if they missed a step or two.

'That was lovely, Tom,' she said as the music stopped. 'You did very well.'

He raised her hand to his lips and thanked her, and was about to say something more, when there was the sound of a shrill voice which carried above all the others.

'Hello, Billy, my old darling. Aren't you going to talk to me?'

'Billy?' Sammi said in concern. 'Who is talking to Billy like that?'

'Not your Billy.' Tom still held her hand and drew her towards him. He could see over the tops of heads, heads which were looking over to one side of the room. 'Your Billy is still asleep in the chair.'

They walked to the side of the floor. Betsy was standing there with a look of merriment on her face. 'It's Mr Craddock's friend,' she whispered. 'She's three sheets to the wind; he's gone to rescue her before she upsets the party. She's found someone she knows.' She nodded knowingly at Sammi. 'Told you, didn't I?'

The crowd parted and then reassembled as the music began again, and they saw Charles Craddock and his lady friend talking to Harriet's father. Austin Billington, with a brief nod, moved away from them and came towards Sammi, Tom and Betsy, who were the nearest group of people who were not dancing.

'Now, my friends,' he said vigorously, 'I haven't yet had the chance to talk with you.' His face was rather red and he glanced over his shoulder at Craddock and the woman, who appeared to be arguing.

'Gilbert's cousins if I remember correctly,' he said, as he put out his hand to Tom. 'How do you do, sir – Miss Rayner, Miss Foster.' He bent forward conspiratorially and indicated over his shoulder. 'I don't know how those two came to be here.' He pursed his mouth. 'Not my sort at all.'

Gilbert joined them. 'I've lost my wife already,' he nodded towards the floor where Harriet was dancing with an elderly man. 'Betsy, will you take pity on a fellow whose wife has gone off?'

'Well, married men are not my style,' she replied flippantly, 'but as it's you, Gilbert, I'll make an exception.'

She took his arm and as they turned to the floor, Craddock's lady friend appeared once more at Austin Billington's side. Her face was blotched and her dress was awry.

'Come on, Billy-boy, aren't you going to have a dance with your little Letty?' She crooked a finger under his chin. 'I don't usually have to do the asking, do I?' She giggled. 'You're the one who generally asks me to dance.' She lifted her skirts, showing her ankles and waved a foot provocatively.

'Look here.' Billington wiped his forehead with a handkerchief. 'I don't know who you are, madam. You've obviously confused me with someone else. Where's the fellow who brought you?' He looked wildly around for Craddock who was sitting in a chair with his pin-striped legs crossed, his jacket open showing his red braces, obviously enjoying his host's discomfiture.

'She's only having a bit of fun, Billington, old chap!' he called out. 'She don't mean any harm.'

'Excuse me, Sammi.' Tom stepped forward and bowed towards the woman. 'Perhaps, ma-am, you would give me the honour of a dance?' He took hold of her arm and led her away from Sammi and Billington. 'Now be a good girl,' he whispered in her ear, 'and come with me, and if you don't, then I shall have the manager of the hotel show you to the door.'

She gazed up at him with pencil-smudged blue eyes. 'Ooh! You're just 'sort of man I've been looking for,' she hiccupped. 'Somebody masterful and 'andsome. And rich.'

'Then you don't want me, Letty. You'd better stick to your Mr Craddock.' He pushed her into a chair in the foyer. 'Now stay there and don't move.'

'He's not my Mr Craddock,' she pouted. 'He only brought me to make a stir. He's like that. Nowt but a trouble-maker.'

Tom went back to the dance and sought out Billy, who was just stirring from sleep. 'Hello, Tom. What are you doing here?' He looked around. 'Oh,' he groaned. 'Have I been asleep? Have I missed anything?'

'Not a thing.' Tom hauled him to his feet. 'But I need you to help me out. Come on.' They walked across the room to where Craddock was still sitting, swinging his legs and cradling a glass of wine. 'Craddock!' Tom greeted him like an old friend. He was much taller than Craddock and towered over him. He put out his right hand.

Craddock looked up. 'Yes.' He put down his glass and raised his hand. 'Have we met? Forgive me if I don't get up, old fellow.'

Tom's hand closed around his and gripped it hard. 'I'd rather you did, *old fellow*, there's someone waiting for you.' He pulled and, like a cork from a bottle, Craddock was sucked from the chair.

'I say,' he protested, but said no more as he was marched, with Tom holding one arm behind his back, and Billy close by his side holding his other elbow, towards the hotel exit.

'Miss Letty wants to go home,' Tom said. 'See that she gets there and don't come back. The party is over.'

21

The chimes of two longcase clocks in the hotel foyer, one in deep profundo, the other a pause behind in bell-like melody, were striking eleven. The guests ceased their chatter and gathered together their wraps and cloaks, their top hats and greatcoats, and prepared to leave. Gilbert and Harriet had already been waved off in their carriage, to spend the night in their house in Charlotte Street, before leaving the next day to spend a few days in Scarborough.

Ellen and Victoria and the York Rayners had left with Mildred for Anlaby, where they had been invited to stay the night, and although conversation between Ellen and Mildred was a little strained, it was decided that to refuse would appear churlish. Because there was insufficient room for them all, Sammi, Betsy and Tom were to spend the night at a small respectable hotel which had been booked for them, and Billy was returning to his lodgings.

Billy walked with them to their hotel, which was across the town near the Market Place, and they all smiled as Tom put his hand in the air to feel the quality of the breeze. 'I hope Da and George have got finished milling,' he said seriously. 'There's not been much of a breeze here today.'

'Yes, it's very sultry,' Sammi agreed. 'I think we're in for a storm.'

'I want to show you something before you go to the hotel.' Billy led them towards Holy Trinity Church and the street down the side of it. 'You especially, Sammi.'

He pointed down towards some cellar steps and a

low doorway which had cardboard and sacking draped across it. 'Look. Look down there.'

'What am I looking at?' Sammi peered down but could see nothing.

'It's someone's home,'·he said. 'Dozens of children live there.'

'They live there? Under the ground?'

He nodded. 'I've been in. That young girl who was waving to me earlier, she took me in to show me. It's horrible, Sammi; yet they'd rather live there than in a children's refuge. They say they have their free-dom.'

Sammi bit her lip to stop it trembling. 'I've seen the children in the hospitals. They're so cowed. They're kept clean and fed, but there's no love, no-one to tuck them up at night. Does no-one care?' she cried. 'And this is how Adam might have lived.'

Tom gripped her arm. 'Those who should care are not doing so.' His voice was tight and restrained. 'If James is accountable for the child, he shouldn't be leaving the responsibility to you. What kind of a man is he? He didn't even turn up for his brother's wedding!'

'I know,' Sammi whispered. 'Something's wrong. It's not like him.' This was the first time Tom had made any comment about the situation. 'But I can't send him away, Tom. Not while there's the smallest chance that he has Rayner blood.' She looked down the cellar steps. 'I couldn't see him here – no, not any child, not if I could help it.'

'Sammi's right. You wouldn't believe the conditions that these children live in,' Billy said passionately, 'and yet down there, in that depressing damp hole in the ground, they consider it a palace compared to the hovels they have lived in before.' He was silent for a moment and they all stood watching him as a great flood of emotion spilled out. 'Some of them have lived in filthy lodging houses that you wouldn't keep your pigs in, Tom! They've shared the same bed

as their parents and eked out a bowl of broth between them when there has been nothing else. Their
mothers and sisters become prostitutes to earn money
to eat, and then become pregnant again, and so the
vicious circle begins again.'

'We're lucky, aren't we, Billy?' Betsy said softly. 'To
live as we do. I wonder how we would survive in those
conditions.'

'We wouldn't. We would go under. We haven't the
stamina – and yet, do you remember, Sammi, when
Grandmama told us that her parents had once been
very poor? Her father had an accident which meant
he couldn't go to sea any more.' He shook his head.
'But they were not like these people: these people
are in the lowest level of society. They have no hope
of pulling themselves out of the gutter unless someone puts out a hand to help them.'

'And that hand is yours, Billy.' Sammi stared at her
brother. 'That's what you are saying, isn't it? You're
going to help them?'

'I think so.' He looked at them in turn, his eyes
vague, not seeing them but something else. 'I don't
know how, as yet, but I'll do something, somehow.'

They were silent as they made their way back
towards the hotel, each wrapped in thought: Billy with
a vision in mind of an ideal world and Sammi
wondering why James hadn't come to the wedding,
hurt that he hadn't written to enquire of Adam, and
puzzled as to why Tom seemed angry with her.

Betsy let her mind drift over the day and considered
her future, not knowing what she wanted. *Billy has his
ideals, Tom's rooted at the mill, and Sammi, well, one day
she'll marry a rich landowner if she doesn't spoil her chances.
I wonder if Harriet is finding it wonderful in Gilbert's arms?
I wish! I wish! What do I wish? That Luke was sharing my
bed tonight? How shocked everyone would be if they could
read my thoughts.* She had thought of Luke often
during the day and evening, even when she was
dancing with Charles Craddock, who had intimated

to her that he was interested in her. He wore expensive clothes, his hair was sleek, he had the air of a
rich man. *But he is not a gentleman*, she mused, *though
he may think he is.* Not like Billy or her brothers Tom
and George or even Mark in his way, were gentlemanly in their manners.

But then, she wondered, *do I deserve a gentleman, for
I am not a lady in the proper sense of the word! And I could
use you, Charles Craddock, if I'd a mind, just as you would
use me, given half the chance.*

Betsy squeezed Billy's arm as they mounted the
steps of the hotel. 'I wish you luck with your life,
Billy.'

He blinked and came back to the present. 'And I
wish you the same, dear cousin.'

The landlady brought in tea and chocolate and
small sweet cakes. 'Nothing for me.' Billy seemed
absent-minded and preoccupied. 'I'll say goodnight
to you all.'

'I'm going to bed too,' Betsy said. 'I'm tired and I
feel rather sick.'

'Too much champagne. We're not used to such
lavish living.' Sammi sat down and poured tea for
herself and Tom, and said she would come up shortly.

Tom stretched his arms and then loosened the
stock about his neck. 'I shall be glad to get out of
these fancy clothes,' he grinned, 'and back into my
boots and breeches.'

'But these clothes suit you very well, Tom,' Sammi
said shyly. 'Yet you seem different – not the same
person that I know so well.' She hesitated, should she
ask the question that had been bothering her? 'I – I
wanted to ask you something,' she began diffidently.

'What is it, Sammi?' He came and sat beside her
on the small sofa, and she moved up to accommodate
him. Crinolines took up a ridiculous amount of room,
she thought.

'I shall be going back home in a day or two,' she
began. 'You know that I said I thought that Mark had

gone away because of me?' He started to protest, but she interrupted him. 'I know. You did explain that it wasn't anything to do with me, and I accept that, but – but I think that it is better that I go, though I will come back to visit if Luke Reedbarrow should call on Betsy.'

He frowned but she continued, 'Mrs Bishop has agreed to nurse Adam for six months, so there is no need for me to stay in Tillington any longer. But I also realize that it was unfair of me to come and stay as I did. It was unfair because I realize now that I was imposing on *you*. I shouldn't have done that, and though you haven't complained, I can tell that it has been a strain on you, having me there all the time.'

He gazed at her for a moment, a bemused expression on his face. 'Whatever do you mean, Sammi? A strain on me?'

'Oh, I can tell, Tom.' She hunched her shoulders and then gave a sigh. 'I have known you all of my life. I know when something is troubling you. You've been uncomfortable with me living at the mill. You haven't been your natural self at all.'

A smile broke on his lips and he reached for her hand. 'Have I not behaved in my usual cousinly manner, Sammi? Have I been impolite?'

'Oh, no, Tom. I didn't mean that!' Her eyes searched his face, begging for understanding. 'You have always behaved well towards me. I have always been assured of your regard and affection.' She looked away again. This was the whole point, if she could only explain it properly. She could not now hold a proper conversation with him. She was almost tongue-tied and embarrassed, as if she didn't know what to say. 'It's just that things seem to be different between us now, Tom,' she said softly. 'It's as if we don't have the friendship we once had; we seem to have lost something – as if we have grown away from each other.'

He still held her hand and gently ran his long

fingers across it, tracing up and down her fingers. His hands were surprisingly smooth, in spite of his rough work, and there was something soporific about the movement. 'I'm sorry that you feel like that, Sammi.' His voice was almost inaudible. 'I don't quite know what I can do about it.'

He lifted her hand to his lips and closed his eyes. She watched him in amazement; that was the second time he had done that. She gazed at his wide forehead, his thick eyebrows, his straight nose and the way his dark hair curled behind his ears. He must be very unhappy, she puzzled, and was taking some comfort from her presence.

He opened his eyes and saw her watching him. He gave a slight smile but kept his lips on her hand.

'What is it, Tom?' she whispered. 'Have we lost something, you and I? Do say that we haven't?'

He kissed her hand and gently lowered it. His smile disappeared and he touched her cheek. 'Yes, Sammi. I'm afraid to say that I think we have.'

In the house in Charlotte Street, the maid had left a small brass kettle filled with water in case they wanted a drink. A fire was burning in the sitting-room, and when Gilbert ran upstairs to check the fire in the bedroom, he saw that the covers had been turned back on the bed and there was a vase of roses on the bedside table, just as he had ordered.

He divested Harriet of her cloak and she took off the flowered coronet from her hair. She moistened her lips with her tongue and whispered, 'Has the girl gone to bed?'

'Yes. I told her not to wait up. She can clear the things away in the morning.' He glanced at the tray with the china cups and saucers, milk jug and sugar bowl. 'Would you like anything before, er, retiring, Harriet?'

She shook her head and looked at him with her large eyes. It had been her eyes which had first attracted him to her, those and her gentle manner. 'No thank you, Gilbert. I'm very tired. It has been a long day.'

'But an enjoyable one, my darling.' He came towards her and gently stroked her face. He felt her cringe. Only slightly, but it was there, nevertheless. He put his arms around her and pulled her towards him. 'You don't need to be nervous,' he whispered, his lips touching her hair.

'But I am, Gilbert. Even though I love you, I am afraid.'

'But why?' He held her away from him and looked at her. She was shaking, her lips trembling and her lowered eyes brimming with tears. 'I'm not going to hurt you. Not if I can help it.'

She lifted her eyes to his. 'I know that you will be considerate, Gilbert. And I know that this, this has to be done. I will be a good wife to you. I will try to keep you contented and bear your children, and look after your home so that you will always be glad to come back to it. And I shall put up with, with – what a woman has to put up with, without complaint.'

'Put up with?' He stared at his new wife in disbelief. 'Put up with? Who has told you this?'

'My mother. She says that there are some things that women must endure, as she has had to do all these years.'

He turned away. He was so angry. Devastated by what she had said. How could anyone believe that this act of love should be simply for a man's satisfaction and a woman's discomfort?

An image came into his mind, an image that he had fought hard to diminish. A mental picture of a young girl, dark like Harriet, who had lain with him and loved him and had not complained. Had she simply put up with it? He thought not. She didn't have to stay, but she did, all night, and nor did she expect any payment, for the next day she had gone, disappearing from his life until her mother had brought her child and said that she was dead.

He took Harriet by the hand and led her up the narrow stairs. He had remained celibate since that night, not wanting any other woman. Tonight was his wedding night, but he would not force his wife. He would wait. Wait until she was ready. He opened the bedroom door. The lamp by the bed was lit, giving a glow to the yellow roses. The firelight flickered and the room looked cosy and inviting.

'Turn around,' he said, and started to undo the buttons and ribbons on her gown. It slipped to the floor and he helped her out of the wide cage. Beneath the cage she wore a silk shift and white stockings, and she put her arms across her breasts and bare arms and looked at him, her eyes wide with apprehension.

Without speaking, he took the pins and combs from her chignon and her hair fell onto her shoulders in a mass of dark curls; he twisted a curl around his finger and then bent to kiss her bare shoulder. He felt so sad. Thoughts of birth and death mingled with his marriage vows, and he couldn't have made love to her tonight, not now, not even if she had been willing.

He cradled her face in his hands and kissed her tenderly on the mouth. 'Go to bed, my love. Sleep well. I'll see you in the morning.' He turned on his heel and went out of the door, closing it behind him.

'Well, Da, 'wedding will be over. They'll be starting 'music and dancing about now. Our Tom will be trying out his few steps.' George sipped a mug of tea and bit into a slice of bread. 'I hope they think to bring us a few treats back, a bit of cake or pie or summat.'

His father stretched himself out in his chair and grunted. 'They'll not be thinking of thee, they'll be too busy enjoying themselves. I'm sorry tha couldn't go, lad. Would tha have liked to?'

George shook his head. 'No, not me, Da. I'd rather

be here. I don't care for 'town life. I'd rather be here in Tillington where I belong. Besides, somebody has to be here for 'mill and 'builders and all.'

Thomas smiled and lit his pipe. There wasn't often time for conversation with his sons, they were always so busy. *Perhaps that's been my mistake,* he thought. *Maybe that's why Mark has gone off. If I'd had the chance to talk to him he might not have felt he wanted to leave.* He looked at his youngest son sitting opposite him in the kitchen. All the furniture except for two wooden chairs and a table had been moved into the parlour. The kitchen extension at the other side of the wall was slowly being built up, and in another few days the dividing wall would be knocked down.

'Hast tha got a young lady, George? Or anybody that's caught thine eye?'

George blushed at his father's directness. 'No, not me, Da. I haven't met anybody I'm partial to. Though there's plenty of lasses in 'village who give me 'eye.' He grinned. 'They all think that 'miller's sons are a good catch.'

'But not 'miller's daughter?' Thomas queried. 'Don't young fellows think that our Betsy is a good catch?'

'Nay,' George said disparagingly. 'Betsy let them know a long time ago that she wasn't in 'marriage market for 'lads round here. Farmers' sons maybe, or somebody wi' a bit of land, but she'll not let herself go cheap, won't our Betsy.'

So you haven't heard about Luke Reedbarrow, his father mused. *It's not general knowledge then. Or maybe Betsy hasn't made up her mind.* He fretted. *Yet she's been seeing him on the sly. Now that worries me. He's a fine-looking fellow, but some of 'family are not stable. It's not fair to judge 'lad on his forebears I know, but . . . !* He sighed. *Aye, that worries me a lot.*

'Da? What will happen if our Tom should get wed? Would I have to move out? It's not likely that a young woman'd want three men to look after.'

'Can't see Tom getting wed. He's like our Betsy, a cut above 'village lasses. So, tha'll probably be wed afore him, George, and want to find a nice little house in 'village for thyself and thy wife. Aye, that's how it'll be.' He bit on the stem of his pipe and gazed into the fire and painted an idyllic picture. 'And afore I know where I am I'll have grandchildre' riding on my back and playing around my knees.'

They both sat up as they heard a sudden gush of wind down the chimney and a scattering of soot fell into the fire; both men reached for their boots, which they had taken off while they had their supper.

'We'd better get aloft.' Thomas fastened his laces. 'I'd hoped we might have had a night off tonight.'

'There's a storm brewing up. I can smell it,' George said. 'It's been that clammy all day.'

They went out into the mill yard. The air was heavy, and a huge black cloud over the sea was moving swiftly towards Tillington.

'I don't like 'look of that,' George muttered, 'and I don't like 'sound of that wind getting up. We'll have all on, Da, without Tom here to give us a hand.'

'We'll manage.' His father knocked the dead ash from his pipe and put it in his pocket. 'As long as we don't get tail winded.'

George nodded. The greatest fear of all millers was when the wind changed its course and gusted onto the backs of the sails, wrecking the shades and the main shaft. His father had had a fantail fitted many years ago at the rear of the domed cap, which alleviated most of the problems of tail winding, but it was a danger of which they were always aware, and after stormy weather they often heard reports of caps being blown off and mills being so badly damaged that they had to be dismantled and rebuilt.

George went into the bagging room and started to shift the sacks of grain to be ready to hoist onto the chain, which, propelled by wind power, travelled up to the bin floor, passing through a series of trap doors set into each intervening floor and which opened on leather hinges for its entry and closed with a thump behind it.

He called to his father who was mounting the access ladder to open up the trap doors. 'There's a drop of oil needed on 'drive wheel, Da. 'Sack hoist's not been running smoothly.'

His father shouted back, 'I'll do it! I'm going up into 'cap. I don't like 'sound of that wind. We might have to abandon if there's a storm. Check 'balance of 'weights on 'vanes, wilt tha?'

As George went out into the yard, the wind caught the door, pulling it out of his hand and crashing it back against the hinges. He closed it firmly and looked up at the sails. They were set at rest in the St Andrew's Cross position, with the shades open to reduce the wind pressure and to ensure no damage was done during a high wind. The sky was dark above him, the storm seemed to be gathering over his head. He dashed round to the rear of the mill and, putting his hand to his forehead, he peered up at the fantail. He narrowed his eyes: there seemed to be a wobble on one of the fly posts beneath the fantail sheers, and he hoped that it wasn't loose. A flash of lightning momentarily lit up the sky and he saw it more clearly. Yes. He was sure that it had come adrift.

He ran back inside to warn his father; there would be no milling tonight, it would be far too dangerous if the fantail came loose or the wind reversed its direction, for it could then quite easily turn the shades inside out.

'Da!' He shouted up to the top of the mill. 'Da! 'Fantail's adrift. I'd better come up and try to fix it.'

His father's muffled shout echoed down to him. 'I'm up here already. I'll take a look.'

George chewed on his lip. He wished that Tom was here, he didn't like the idea of his father leaning out of the access door to check the fantail, even though he had been doing it for years. They had all noticed .

that he was not as agile as he once had been, and often the pain he felt in his aching legs was etched upon his face; in the last few months he had given way to Tom and let him do the jobs which previously he had insisted on doing himself.

'Let me go out, Da!' he called again. 'I'm a bit thinner than thee!'

Before his father could reply there was another sudden gust of wind, and at the base of the mill George felt the building shake and the sails rock. 'Fantail's gone, Da!' he yelled. 'Now we're for it!'

The air was heavy with ominous thunder growls, and the sky was filled with a mass of sombrous clouds whose edges were lit with an opaline hem at each lightning flash. Thomas felt like a god in this lofty elevation. *A god or a mariner, like the grandda I don't remember*, he meditated, as the dome above him creaked and shifted its timbers. He opened the access door leading out to the fantail and looked out across the fading vista. Across the fields and beyond the village of Monkston, he saw in the dim light the foaming white sea crests and the great waves breaking and dashing against each other in their run to the shore.

'There'll be more land lost tonight,' he muttered, narrowing his eyes to define his vision. 'William won't be ower happy. It won't be much longer afore they'll all have to move back.'

The wind dropped, and in the temporary stillness he heard the rhythmic banging of wood against wood, and saw the loose flypost swinging against the fantail blades. He cursed beneath his breath: he'd have to go out and try to secure it. He looked up and the heavens seemed not so far away. The eye of the storm was above him and the dark sky hovered above the mill in a simmering, pulsating agitation, threatening that at any moment in a boiling convulsion it would rip apart and destroy.

He put his foot out and searched in the darkness

for the narrow ledge, then felt the sudden thrust of wind catch him. He held onto the wall of the cap and, carefully easing himself out, he reached for a handhold. The crash of thunder startled him and, as the lightning flashed, illuminated below he saw the empty hay cart, the mill yard and the fields and copses beyond it lit in a flood of daytime brightness. For a moment he was mesmerized, and forgetting caution he straightened up and stared at the scene which he knew so well but which now was so different, as if he was looking from another world.

The thunder cracked again and hid the sound of the fantail breaking, but he felt the shake of the cap as the blades flew off above his head, whisked away into the darkness with a whistling hiss. He bent quickly to crank the gears and avert more damage but as he did, the remaining flypost broke and crashed down upon his head. He raised his hand to his head, dazed by the blow and, straightening up, put out his other arm to steady himself.

The rain started to fall, sheets of torrential rain wetting him through in seconds. He put his foot back, searching for the narrow ledge to balance on. His head throbbed, his vision blurred by the blow, and he felt the trickle of blood on his forehead. He shifted his feet again and turned to reach the door. He searched for a handhold. He was dizzy and nauseous. George would have to come up. He put out his foot; the ledge was wet and slippery and he misjudged the distance; there was nothing below him, only a void, a deep black hollow which gathered him up as he plunged in a swift and sudden descent.

George heard his cry and the heart-stopping thud out in the yard. He ran out of the door and into the yard and stopped, horror-struck at the sight of his father's twisted body lying motionless, half in, half out of the hay cart.

'Da! Da!' His shocked and whispered voice cracked as he bent over him. He touched his father's face, patting it, trying to wake him, for his eyes were closed and he lay so still. 'Don't die, Da. Please, don't be dead. What shall I do? I don't know what to do! Da! Who's going to help me?' He stood up and ran to the gate to look down the lane. There was no-one about, the rain had been threatening all evening; people had finished their work and scurried home before the storm broke. He ran back to his father, the rain lashing against him.

'I'll have to get thee indoors, Da, but I don't know if I can lift thee.' He knew that he couldn't. His father was a big man and heavy. The only thing he could do was try to drag him out of the cart and into the mill, yet he was so afraid of hurting him further. He could not accept that his father was dead, but he knew that he must move him inside out of the rain. 'Then I'll run for 'vicar. He'll know what to do, Da. He'll send for 'doctor, then tha'll be as right as can be.'

George put his hands beneath his father's shoulders and was sickened at the sight of his bleeding head and contorted legs. His head sank down and he started to sob, weeping great tears that ran unchecked. A clatter of hooves made him look up and through his blurred vision and the torrential rain, he saw a figure leaning from a horse, trying to open the gate.

'Richard! Richard! Thank God tha's come. Help me. Please.' He sprinted to open the gate and let him in. 'Da's fallen from 'top of 'mill. I can't lift him.'

Richard slipped from his mount's back and ran across the yard. 'Oh, God! Is he dead?'

George, his face sheet-white, shook his head. 'I don't know. He doesn't seem to be breathing.'

Richard put his head to his uncle's chest. 'I think I can hear a beat.' He stood up. 'I'll go for the doctor, but let's cover him over first. Fetch that tarpaulin that's covering the sand; that'll do – anything that will keep him dry.'

The rain was falling in torrents, they were soaked

through, their hair plastered to their heads, but together they dragged the heavy canvas over George's father, draping it over the top of the cart to keep the weight off his body.

'I'll ride as fast as I can.' Richard re-mounted. 'Let's just hope that the doctor is in and not out on some other errand of mercy.'

As he rode off, George crept under the tarpaulin with his father and held his limp hand. 'Please don't die, Da,' he kept repeating. 'What'll I tell our Tom? He'll wish he'd never gone to 'wedding. How shall we tell Mark when we don't know where he is? It's my fault. I should have gone up to 'top instead of thee.' He shivered and started to weep again. If he had insisted on taking his father's place, he might have been the one lying broken in the cart instead of his father, his life shattered and at an end before it had even started.

Richard returned with the doctor within fifteen minutes, having caught him returning from another call and just descending from his carriage; he immediately climbed in again, turned around and arrived at the mill just as Thomas made a small sound.

'He's alive, Doctor!' George cried. 'There's some hope, isn't there?'

Doctor Wilkins bent towards Thomas's crooked legs. 'Hope, George?' He knew all the miller's sons and daughter, having delivered each one of them into the world. 'What hope is there for a miller with a broken body?'

He straightened up. 'Cease your weeping, lad, and let's bring your father inside. There'll be more tears shed before long. I can do nothing for him.'

22

Betsy had said she wanted to spend an hour shopping before they returned home and Sammi had agreed, although Tom insisted that they should spend no more time than that, as he was anxious to get back to the mill; but when they awoke the morning after the wedding, Betsy had changed her mind, she complained that she still felt nauseous.

She put her hand to her midriff and winced. 'I'm not used to such rich pastries and tarts, and I'm sure the butter must have been rancid.'

'Didn't stop you eating any of it though, did it,' Tom remarked. 'I saw you stuffing yourself with *bon bons* and *petit fours* or whatever they were called.'

Betsy groaned. 'Oh, what a feast, and how I'm paying for it. Is no-one else suffering?'

Sammi and Tom both shook their heads and tucked into a breakfast of omelette and ham, whilst Betsy sipped a cup of lemon tea.

Austin Billington had spared no expense at the wedding breakfast, and had employed French pastry chefs to make exotic breads and sweet cakes, and pies filled with partridge, chicken and veal, while the English chefs had cooked roast beef and dumplings, cold ham and tongue for those with a plainer taste in food. Lobster, poached turbot, quails' eggs and salmon tempted those with a delicate constitution, and an array of rich desserts and a succulent pyramid of peaches, apricots and grapes scattered with glistening spun sugar completed the meal, and they had all eaten to capacity.

After breakfast, they set off on the journey home,

but the coachie was ordered to stop several times as Betsy felt sick and had to get out to take deep breaths of air. Sammi stepped out, too, and looked across the meadows and corn fields, and cherished the sight of the poppies which swayed in a scarlet profusion in the breeze. In the deep ditches of Holderness the tall feathery flowers of meadowsweet raised their creamy heads, and beneath their feet, the fragrance of pineapple rose up from the greeny yellow flowers of crushed mayweed.

'The corn is looking good, Tom. You'll be kept busy.'

'If we ever get home, I expect we shall be.' Tom was impatient. 'Whatever is Betsy doing?'

'She's coming.' Sammi took her seat beside him. 'I think her sickness is going.'

'I trust we shall be busy,' he responded to her previous comment. 'The crops will soon be ready, but the farmers are complaining that they're not getting the price they need to make a living. Wheat is coming in from America and Canada which is cheaper than ours, and they say it makes better bread.' He glanced across at her. 'The small farmers will lose their land if they can't sell their crops and pay their rent; it'll be left to go fallow, for not all landowners are like your father and farm it themselves, and whatever happens,' he added with a sudden grin to this gloomy tale, 'the miller will get the blame for the high price of bread. He always does!'

Betsy, her face pale, climbed back into the carriage, and Sammi pondered morosely on what Tom had said. Her father had spoken of the hard times that some of the farmers who rented land from him were having, and though he understood their needs, being a working landowner himself, there wasn't much more he could do to help them.

Sammi had seen for herself some of the farms where the farmer struggled to make a living and keep his family well fed. And she had seen, too, the cottages of labourers who worked on neighbouring farms, where the wind whistled through the door and the rain poured through the roof, and the pinched faces of the children looked out through the cracked windows and ate only bread and potatoes.

Her father was also having difficulties because of the land loss every year, and although he had perceptively bought farms inland when they came on the market, he became more worried every winter as another piece of Monkston land slid into the sea.

'They've had some rain out here.' Tom looked out of the window as they continued their journey. 'The road's flooded, and just look at the corn! It's been flattened. There's been a storm all right.' He opened the window and leaned out as they approached Tillington. Another minute and they would turn the bend in the road and see the church steeple on the rise, and to the left of that the mill.

''Fantail's gone!' He gave a sharp exclamation. 'The sheers are swinging. Why haven't they been up to secure them? Something's wrong!' He turned towards his sister and Sammi. 'Something's wrong!'

'Don't be such a pessimist, Tom.' Betsy was indifferent and languid, and kept her hand on her midriff. 'Da's probably waiting for you to go up and fix it.'

Tom shook his head. 'You know Da's not like that. It would be his first job as soon as the rain stopped, or even before it did!' He jumped out at the gate and opened it for the driver to pull in.

'Off you go, Tom.' Sammi realized that he was waiting to hand them down. 'Betsy and I can manage without—' She stopped as the house door opened, and it was only then that they all realized how quiet it was. There were no builders working on the house, the sand in the yard was still piled as high as it had been when they left, and George's face as he stood in the doorway was pale and working with anguish.

248

'It's Da,' he whispered, his eyes shadowed and enormous. 'He tummelled off 'cap. 'Doctor says there's nowt – nothing can be done. He's concussed. His right leg is shattered and so is his left ankle.' He moved away from the entrance as Tom strode past him into the house, and his eyes filled with tears of remorse as his sister and Sammi hesitatingly approached.

Thomas lay on a makeshift bed in the parlour where they had taken him, his face almost as white as his beard. His eyes were closed, but his features contorted and his body flinched as if in pain.

Tom knelt beside him and with his elbows resting on the bed put his head into his hands. 'I should have been here,' he said, his voice muffled. 'I shouldn't have been gallivanting off enjoying myself.'

Betsy made no sound; she stared at her father and sank into a chair and began to weep. Sammi moved towards Tom and put her hand on his shoulder. There was nothing she could say or do to comfort him, she knew, but still she whispered, 'Don't blame yourself, Tom. Uncle Thomas wanted you to go to the wedding. And had you been here, it might still have happened.' A small tremor ran through her at the thought that it might have been Tom lying there instead of his father. Milling was by its very nature a dangerous business, full of potential hazards and imminent perils, from toppling down the narrow ladders to losing fingers in the sail blades, or falling from the cap as her uncle had done. She squeezed Tom's shoulder and he put his hand over hers and patted it.

'I know. Thank you, Sammi. I'm glad that you're here.'

But I'm supposed to be going home, she thought, as she went up the dusty stairs to take off her outdoor clothes. *Perhaps I had better stay a few days longer.*

The doctor came again and gave Thomas a dose of opium and told them, 'He appears to be coming out of concussion. I'll splint his leg and we'll keep him as free of pain as we can. Just make him as comfortable as possible. That's all we can do.'

Ellen and William came as soon as they heard the news from Richard, and sat by Thomas's bedside. William was shocked and anxious. 'Two of our men to be struck down so suddenly.' He shook his head despondently. He was as close to and as fond of his cousin Thomas as he was of his brother Isaac. 'I feel so helpless – it's as if the family is being wiped out.'

'Nonsense, William,' Ellen remonstrated with him. 'How can that be when we have all these fine young people about us?'

Sammi came and put her arms around him to comfort him. 'We'll never be wiped out, Pa. The Fosters and the Rayners will go on for ever. Tell him, Tom – we will, won't we?'

Her father sighed but smiled at her earnestness. 'Yes, of course we will, Sammi. How could I think otherwise with all of these kindred?'

Tom looked up at the question and gazed at her. He didn't answer, but a deep hurt filled his eyes. He excused himself and abruptly left the room.

'Please stay, Sammi,' Betsy had pleaded with her. 'I can't manage on my own. I don't know how to cope with sickness – and if Da should die I wouldn't know what to do. Please, please stay.'

Sammi agreed that she would stay a little longer. Betsy was in a deep shock, her face was pallid, she couldn't stop trembling, and she could hardly bear to go near her father's bedside. The doctor came in every day to administer the medication, and arranged for a woman to come in and change Thomas's bedding and take it away for washing, whilst Sammi, at frequent intervals, bathed her uncle's face with cool water when he sweated with pain. Sometimes he became lucid and tried to speak to them. He asked for Tom and gave him instructions on who he should send for to help them with the milling while he was incapacitated; he had forgotten the details of his accident and thought that he was laid up with some sickness.

At other times he was delirious and called out for his father and mother as if he were a child again; or he would shout for his wife to bring him a jar of ale into the mill.

Betsy became increasingly more depressed and each day pressed Sammi for assurance that she wouldn't go home.

'But *you* must tend your father, Betsy,' Sammi admonished her. 'He needs you more than me.' She felt so tired, her uncle's demands were beginning to exhaust her, yet she felt compelled to sit by his bedside and watch over him when Tom and George were working so hard and so long, and Betsy spent more and more time lying on her bed weeping and saying that she felt ill.

The fantail had been replaced on the cap, and the farmers were starting to harvest the barley which spread across the land like a layer of golden sand; the wheat was on the turn from its verdant hue to pale gold, and Tom said if they didn't do the milling, then the farmers would take it elsewhere.

'There are plenty of other millers willing to do it,' he said, wiping his forehead with a cloth and accepting a jug of lemonade which Sammi had brought in for them, and replying to her scolding that they were working too hard. 'But we could do with some help.'

'Could you not get a young lad to help with the sacks?' she asked.

'He'd have to be strong.' George took a gulping draught from the jug. 'Those sacks are not exactly full o' feathers. We couldn't tek on any recklin'.'

'Would you take on Luke Reedbarrow, Tom? I saw him in the lane the other day and he asked how your father was. He said if there was anything he could do—'

Tom's face became tense. 'We'll manage,' he muttered.

'Aye, he's a big strong fellow,' George interrupted, wiping his mouth with his sleeve. 'He wouldn't have any bother lifting 'sacks.'

'I'll think about it.' Tom turned away. 'Come on, let's get a move on or we shall be here all night.'

That evening Uncle Thomas seemed quite rational and asked Tom quite clearly where Mark was. 'I need to speak to all of my lads, Tom, to make things clear. This illness is taking its toll on me. My head hurts and my legs ache summat terrible. I can't seem to move 'em, and it seems to me that a miller is no good wi'out his legs, no good at all.'

'Your legs are broken, Da.' Tom, conscience-stricken, endeavoured to be honest with his father. 'You won't be milling again. You can take it easy now; George and I will take over.'

His father pondered this for a long while; Tom wondered if he had done the right thing in speaking out, when his father spoke again in a whisper, 'Tha'd better try and find Mark then, for tha'll not manage wi' just two of thee. See if he wants to come back, equal partners with thee, though it's not as I planned; and George, well, George isn't cut out to manage, though he's as good a worker as any, but I know tha'll see that he's treated fair.'

'Aye, Da. I'll look after George. He's just a babby in arms where money and business is concerned. But I don't know where Mark is. He's not written home yet.'

His father gazed up at the ceiling. 'Then tha'll have to get some help. We can afford it. And Tom—' he reached out a limp hand towards his eldest son, '—everything's taken care of if owt should happen to me, if sands o' time should run out and I snuff it, sudden like.'

Tom felt a lump come into his throat and he tried

hard to swallow. 'You'll be all right, Da. You'll soon be up and able to take care of 'accounts and farmers' bills and such like.'

His father ignored his stammering and turned to gaze out of the square window to the sky beyond. On the window-sill were pots of bright red geraniums and sweet-smelling musk and a bowl of roses which Sammi had brought in, in an attempt to brighten up the sick-room.

'All accounts are up to date,' he went on. 'We don't owe anybody; tha'll find everything tha needs in my strong box when time is right. And Tom,' he turned his gaze back to him, the effort to speak was becoming harder, 'tha'll need to get wed. It's doubly hard running a mill wi'out a good woman by tha side.' He gave a weary sigh. 'I know. I know how hard it is, and 'bed is cold and lonely at night.'

'I'll leave it to George to get wed, Da,' Tom said in a bid to amuse. 'He's the one that 'lasses chase, not me.'

'Nay, it has to be thee, Tom. Firstborn needs a wife at 'mill, aye and some sons to carry on after. Find thyself a helpmate, somebody who'll share thy troubles and joys. And find George a good strong lass to look after him. Ask Sammi, she'll help thee find somebody to suit thee both.'

'And what about Betsy, Da?' Tom joked, though he had no laughter in him. 'Do you want me to find a husband for her, too?'

His father wearily shook his head and closed his eyes. 'Betsy is a law unto herself. She'll go her own way. She's not like 'Fosters at all. I don't know who she's like. Somebody from a long way back, I reckon. No, Betsy'll make her own bed and happen she'll lie on it too.'

Tom waited until his father dropped off into an exhausted sleep, and strode off down the lane and into the village. He crossed over a dirt road and turned down a narrow lane which led to a cluster of cottages and the thatched house and smallholding where the Reedbarrows lived.

Mrs Reedbarrow answered his knock. She was a tired-looking woman who had borne six children after Luke; one child had died, two of the girls had gone to work in Hull, and the three younger ones were still at home. She wore a handmade tucked and pleated bonnet on her fading fair hair and a sacking apron wrapped around a loose black skirt, which did nothing to hide her pregnancy. She pointed with a wooden spoon towards the long garden where she said Luke was working.

He had his booted foot on a fork, digging up a bucketful of early potatoes and throwing the haulms onto a heap where there was other rotting vegetation. The garden was neat and orderly. Rows of onions, their straight stalks green and lush, stood next to a row of young cabbages, and beyond them were the feathery tops of carrots.

'Everything growing well, Luke?' Tom bent to pick up a potato and rubbed off the skin with his thumb. 'You've got a good crop of spuds.'

'Aye.' Luke straightened up. He towered over Tom by about three inches. 'I've got green fingers like thou hast miller's thumb. But growing 'taties and carrots doesn't bring in as much brass as milling corn.'

'No,' Tom agreed. 'I don't suppose it does.' He threw the potato back into the bucket. 'I wondered if you could spare some time to help out at 'mill? You'll have heard about my father's accident? We'd be pleased to have some extra help. Usual labouring rate.'

Luke scraped the heavy soil off his boot with the fork. He nodded his big head and pushed back his fair hair out of his eyes and looked Tom straight in the face. 'I wondered when tha'd get round to asking. Are there any conditions?'

Tom hesitated, then before turning on his heel

replied, 'No. None but the usual when working in a dangerous place.'

'Right then.' Luke stabbed the prongs of the fork into the earth. 'I'll be round first thing in 'morning.'

23

James read Gilbert's letter and noted that although Gilbert had said how ill his father had been, the emergency was now passed. *If anything should happen to my father then I won't go home again*, he pondered. *Mother doesn't care about what I do, nor does Anne, and Gilbert will soon be married to Harriet and will be busy in his new life. I should always keep in touch of course, with Gilbert − and with Sammi*, and guiltily he bethought himself, *I must write to Sammi. I cannot explain of course, that I'm now sure I haven't experienced sexual union, but I'll tell her that I am almost certain that the child isn't mine and therefore do not feel compelled to support him. She will be upset, I expect, as she will have grown fond of him. But it cannot be helped*, he debated, *it will be hard enough making a living for myself without providing for someone else's offspring.*

However, as the days passed, he began to grow anxious about his father and decided that he would, after all, pay a short visit. He put on a velvet jacket which Madame Sinclair had bought him as a gift, and, looking in a mirror, he adjusted his cravat. She often gave him presents: a pair of silver cufflinks, a Venetian glass bottle for holding hair-dressing, a pair of kid-skin gloves which she insisted he wore to protect his artistic hands and blithely describing them as mere trinkets when he demurred over accepting them.

He would call upon her this morning and tell her that he must travel to Yorkshire to visit his sick father.

'Oh, my poor James. How very sad for you, of course you must go.' She greeted him once more in the conservatory when the maid took him through. 'But it is a great pity that you must go at this time, for I was about to send a message asking you to call on me tomorrow.'

How lovely she is. He gazed longingly at her in her simple gown of white muslin which draped and folded its softness around her.

She invited him to sit beside her on the chaise longue and gave him her hand to kiss.

'Tomorrow, Madame? Is there something special about tomorrow?'

'Ah. Every day is special since meeting you, James,' she said softly. 'But I wanted you to meet someone, a friend from Italy.'

'A friend?' He was struck by a pang of jealousy. He knew nothing of her life before she came to London, and she had always deflected his questioning when he had asked her of it.

'Is he a lover?' he blurted out. He couldn't bear it if the answer was yes. He felt so gauche, so young and inexperienced in comparison with her, for she teased him and flattered him, and he felt that she was inviting him to proposition her, yet he didn't dare.

'A lover, James? Would you care so much if he was?' She playfully teased him.

'Yes,' he replied vehemently. 'I would mind very much. I would probably kill myself.'

'How?' She gazed at him and stroked his thigh with her fingers. 'How would you kill yourself?'

He drew in a sharp breath. She knew so well how to disturb him. 'I would drown myself in the Thames or throw myself beneath a train,' he said huskily. 'I have told you that I love you. I cannot bear it if you love someone else.'

'But if I have loved someone else in the past, that is all right, *si*?'

'I cannot help what has gone before.' He touched her cheek with his fingers, her skin was soft and fragrant. 'But I want you to love only me now.'

'I haven't said that I love you, James.' Her eyes were

dark and deep, and the scent of orange blossom in the conservatory was overpowering; he was suffocating with the perfume and the desire to hold her in his arms. 'But I think that perhaps I could,' she whispered.

He couldn't believe what he heard. Did she mean what she said? Or was she teasing him yet again? But her face was gentle, not playful or tantalizing but tender, with a seductive softness in her eyes.

'Madame – Mariabella,' he breathed, 'I ache for you. Please, don't torment me! Either send me away or let me stay and show you that I love you.' He clasped both her hands and pressed them to his lips, then raised his eyes to hers. 'I adore you. I have never loved anyone else.' His ardour threatened to engulf him as she drew him towards her and he bent his head to kiss her on the mouth.

He trembled and closed his eyes. Her lips were warm and soft. He kissed her again, taking courage when she hadn't spurned him, and held her in his arms, feeling the shape of her body between his arms.

She pulled away. 'I'm sorry,' he began. 'Forgive me.'

'No. No. There is nothing to forgive, *amore mío*,' she whispered, touching her fingertips to his lips. 'But not here. *Viene.* Come with me.'

He followed her in a vacant, dreaming reverie, barely noticing where they were going as she led him out of the conservatory, through the cool hall, so cool after the heat of the conservatory that he shivered, up the curving staircase to a landing lit by a tall window, and with two closed doors.

She put her hand on the door-knob of one of the doors and ushered him inside. '*Un momento*, James, and I will come to you.'

James sank down and put his head in his hands. At last, she would be his to love, but— He was filled with self-doubt. What if he made a fool of himself? She would surely know that he was unskilled in the art of love; perhaps she would expect more from him than he could give? She was foreign after all, and a married woman! Beads of perspiration gathered on his forehead. Suppose her husband came to visit unexpectedly? Suppose the maid came in whilst they were *in flagrante delicto*? It didn't bear thinking about. Perhaps, after all, he should make his excuses and leave and come back another day?

He began to pace the oriental carpet. This was her sitting-room. He hadn't been in here before. It was so obviously her own private sanctum. A satinwood veneered and inlaid writing desk stood by an open window, which was draped with billowing curtains and revealed the river frontage below. Murano glass in vibrant colours stood on the veined marble fireplace and reflected in the mirrored overmantel above it. A day bed with a dark velvet shawl thrown over it stood invitingly in a draped alcove at the side of the room, and a circular, lace-covered table beside it held a vase filled with the slender green stalks and white wax-like flowers of heavy-scented lilies. He began to shake. Would this be where . . . ?

An inner door opened into the room and Maria-bella stood in the doorway. She had changed from her muslin gown and was wearing a black satin robe. Her hair was loosened and hung down her back to her waist. Around her bare throat she wore a thin thread of gold with a small gold cross attached to it. She held out her hand to him, '*Viene!* Come, *amore mio.*'

In the room behind her he saw a four-poster bed, its drapes partially drawn around the downy pillows and the covers pulled back to expose white linen. The light in the room was veiled, for the blinds were drawn at the window and the sunlight filtered through in slanted strips of pale gold.

'*Viene,*' she repeated. 'I am ready for you, James.'

*   *   *

He awoke from a doze with her dark hair streaming across his face. He gazed down at her. '*Bella. Bella,*' he whispered and leant to kiss her bare shoulder.

She stirred and opened her eyes. 'You speak Italian, James?'

He shook his head. 'No. Only *grazie, molte grazie, amore mío.*'

Her eyes softened and she smiled teasingly. '*Di niente. Prego!* It was nothing. You are welcome.'

'I was not a very good lover, was I?' he asked diffidently. 'Too impatient, too hasty. I did not satisfy you.'

'Too eager, James. You had waited too long. This time was good. Next time will be more good, *si?*'

'*Si.*' He sighed and turned her towards him. 'It was beautiful. *You* are so beautiful.'

'Phww,' she pouted, and drew a line with her finger down from his chin and throat, through the dark hairs on his chest, down to his navel which she circled with her finger-nail, making him gasp. 'I am not so beautiful – and the first time with a woman, it is always wonderful for a man, I think?'

'The first time?' he protested. 'Why do you think it was my first time?' Her fingers sank lower and he groaned softly and closed his eyes. 'I have to confess to you, Mariabella, that I have possibly fathered a child.'

She gave a little chuckle and took his hand and placed it between her thighs. 'Possibly? You mean that you cannot remember? James, *amore mío.* You are telling me that you can forget something like this?'

'No. I won't ever forget,' he whispered as, aroused again, he sought her tenderness between his fingers. 'Never.'

'I am your first, yes?' she murmured in his ear.

He didn't answer, unable to utter one single word as tenderly and this time, so slowly, they came together again.

* * *

'So who is this man that you are so anxious for me to meet?' James refastened his cravat and put on his jacket.

'He was a great friend of my father, and was – what do you say – my protector, until I married.' Mariabella lay on the bed and idly toyed with her hair.

'Your guardian? Ah, I see.' James felt relieved. There was no rival then. He looked into the mirror and straightened his hair. He felt ten feet tall. *I look older*, he mused and started to hum beneath his breath.

Mariabella smiled. 'You are happy, yes? You are a man now? No longer a boy!'

He leant over her and kissed her. 'So happy, Mariabella. I can't believe how wonderful it was.'

'And you will come tomorrow, or will you go home?'

He nodded. 'I think another day won't harm, and anyway my father would understand if I was detained on business.'

But it isn't just business that delays me, he thought as he gazed down at her. *I must see her again tomorrow, make love to her again. She has awakened such an appetite in me, that I don't know how I shall appease my hunger until then.*

She held out her hand for him to kiss. 'Go now, James, and close the door quietly behind you. And James, when you meet my friend Romanelli, you will remember to address me as Madame Sinclair?' She rose from the bed and stretched, and her robe parted, showing a glimpse of pale flesh. 'You will be discreet, yes?' She ran her fingers around his face and pressed her mouth against his. 'It is our secret,' she whispered against his lips. 'We must not share it with anyone else, *amore mio*, or it is finished for ever.'

When he returned to the studio, Batsford had gone out and Miss Gregory was drinking a glass of ale and eating a meat pie. 'It's too hot to go out,' she said, 'and Batsford wants me again later when he gets back, so I thought I would have a bit of a nap after I've eaten.'

'Can I sketch you while you're sleeping?' James asked eagerly. He felt so buoyant, so full of energy and verve, that he was convinced he could create a perfect drawing of Miss Gregory's form, even though he would have in mind the image of someone else.

'I thought you were going away?' She wiped her mouth of frothy ale with the back of her hand.

'I was, but I've been detained. Will you? Please?'

'All right, but it'll cost you extra – and I won't sit nude,' she added. 'You've got a look in your eye that I'm not sure about.'

'Oh, I'm in love, Miss Gregory,' he said impulsively. 'You have nothing to fear. There is only one woman in the world for me; I can look at no other, except in the aesthetic or symbolic sense.'

Miss Gregory rolled her large eyes to the ceiling and uttered a sigh. 'Come on then.' She got to her feet. 'If the muse is upon you, then we'd better get on with it.'

He worked feverishly and heard Batsford come in and then go out again, but was so consumed by inventive imagination that he didn't stop or call out to him. As he sketched the sleeping form of Miss Gregory, draped by her lace shawl, which he surreptitiously moved without waking her so that her shoulder and one breast were bare, he remembered all that had happened that morning with his beautiful Mariabella, and wanted to tell the world.

He arrived early the next morning, hoping to see Mariabella before the Italian, Romanelli, arrived. He had consulted a Bradshaw and saw that the following day he could catch the six-fifteen fast train, on the Great Northern Railway line from St Pancras, to arrive in Leeds Wellington at half-past one. If he hurried then across the northern city he would be just in time to catch another train to Hull, and from there hire a hansom cab to take him to Anlaby.

'Madame is not yet ready to receive you, sir,' her maid announced. 'But if you would be good enough to wait, she will be with you shortly.'

He was a little embarrassed to be so early, but he wished to be the first there. He wanted to assess Mariabella's and Romanelli's greeting of each other, to ascertain if, in fact, they had ever been more than friends, more than just guardian and dependant. He waited in her drawing-room, a cool, elegant room decorated, not in the overdressed style so in vogue at present, but of an earlier period, with pale pastel colours and elaborate friezes, and pedestal cupboards topped by Grecian urns.

He heard Mariabella's foot on the stairs at the same time as the carriage drew up outside the door, and he stood by the window to glimpse the man descending from it. He saw his face as he turned to pay the driver; not a tall man, but stockily built, a long nose and a short, pointed beard. He wore a dark frock-coat and a top hat on his dark hair, and was carrying a bouquet of flowers in his hand. James cursed beneath his breath for not having thought of bringing flowers for Mariabella also. He waited and listened as Mariabella went to the door herself to greet her friend and heard her happy exclamation as she bid him enter.

'*Buon giorno, carissima.*' He heard the deeper tones of Romanelli. 'It is so good to see you after so long.'

'*Buon giorno, buon giorno,* Massimo. You look so well!'

He heard their laughter and a language that he couldn't understand, and felt young and vulnerable again and wished that they would come in and introduce him so that he might get the moment over.

They came into the room, Mariabella holding on to her visitor's arm, and James saw, now that Romanelli had removed his hat, that he was quite a handsome fellow, his hair dark and curly with white streaks about his temples and in his beard, blue eyes which creased at the edges when he smiled. But he was much older than Mariabella, and then James remembered that she had said that he had been a friend of her father's.

'James! How good to see you.' She extended her hand as if she hadn't seen him in a long time, and James bent formally and kissed her wrist.

'You look well, Madame. So good of you to invite me,' he murmured and was gratified to see a look of approval in her eyes.

She turned to Romanelli, '*Posso presentarie*—? Massimo, may I introduce James Foster Rayner. James, this is my very good friend, Massimiliano Romanelli, who is on a visit from Florence. I wished for you to meet. I think you will have much to discuss.'

James put out his hand. 'Signor Romanelli. How are you, sir?'

Romanelli took his hand and shook it and gave a small formal bow. '*Molto bene, grazie.* Any friend of Signora Sinclair, I am very happy to meet.' He gazed thoughtfully at James. 'You are a painter, yes?'

'Yes, sir. At least that is what I hope to be. I am taking instruction from Batsford.'

'Aah. How is Batsford? I must call on him. He is a good teacher, you are lucky to have him. He is a better teacher than painter. He knows better how to tell it than how to do it himself.'

'Are you a painter, sir?' James asked diffidently, not wanting to show his ignorance if the man should be famous. 'Your name seems familiar.'

Romanelli shrugged. 'It is a common enough name, but I am known as an art critic, not as an artist.'

'He could have been the very best artist,' Mariabella interrupted, tapping Romanelli on the arm with her fan, 'if he had wanted to be.'

'If I had not been lazy,' he laughingly agreed. 'If I had not had a rich wife and had to earn my own living.

264

I had no fire in my belly for painting – my passions were directed elsewhere.' He looked tenderly at Mariabella and smiled. He took her hand and raised it to his lips, and once more James was filled with doubts. 'But,' Romanelli turned to James, 'your name, too, is familiar. Many years ago I knew a family with the name Foster-Rayner.' He rolled his r's as Mariabella did. 'They lived in Yorkshire. They were very fond of the arts and music, and invited artists and writers and musicians into their home.'

'Oh!' James was astonished. 'It must have been my aunt and uncle, Arthur and Henrietta Rayner. They live in York. Foster is our middle name, from my grandmother. All our family have it.'

'Yes, yes, that was the family.' Romanelli rubbed his hands together. 'And you, you have taken the full name, yes? It will look well on your paintings, that is why, I think.'

James blushed. 'That is what I thought. Yes.' *Did it seem terribly snobbish?* he wondered. Romanelli seemed to be scrutinizing him rather intensely. *Perhaps he thinks that I am pretentious – but then it is my name! Why shouldn't I use it?*

'And you, too, are from that ancient city of York? A place where Italians can feel almost at home.' Romanelli spoke to Mariabella in their native tongue and James guessed that he was describing the Roman remains of York, for he caught the words of *Eboracum* and *colonia, principia*, and *via praetoria.*

He turned again to James. 'Yes. It was a wonderful time for me. It was a long time ago – nearly twenty years, but I have never forgotten that period of my life.'

James nodded. 'It is a wonderful place, that is where I found my love of art. I was at school there, though my home was not there. I live – lived, east of York, in the village of Anlaby near the port of Hull. My father is in shipping.' His voice trailed away as Romanelli's eyes flickered intently over him.

Romanelli stroked his beard. 'Indeed? May I sit down, my dear?' he asked of Mariabella who was still standing.

'*Si, si.* Excuse me. Of course. How remiss of me. And you will take a little wine or coffee?' She rang the bell for the maid and Romanelli sat down on one of the sofas and continued to peruse James.

'Then I have met your parents.' Romanelli gave a dry cough. 'The – erm – Rayners in York had a brother and his wife staying with them at the time. They were from Anlaby. I visited them at their home.'

James was even more astonished. 'Really, sir? How extraordinary.'

'Yes,' Romanelli murmured, cupping his hands together and tapping his fingertips. 'Isn't it!'

They had coffee and cakes with Mariabella and then Romanelli asked James to accompany him to see Batsford, where he would look at his work and hear what was happening in the art circles of London.

James reluctantly said goodbye to Mariabella; she did not invite him to return with Romanelli, and he kissed her hand and wished that he could have spoken to her privately before leaving. She expressed the wish that he would find his father improved, and requested that he call on her on his return.

'William Morris is the man to look out for,' Romanelli said as they walked along the riverside. 'He has much talent. One day he will be famous the world over. You will do well to study him.'

'Yes, indeed,' James agreed. 'I have met him and had conversation with him, and with Burne-Jones; but the painter I most want to meet is Rossetti.'

'He will be returning to London in a few days, I met him in Paris only last week. I will introduce you.'

James felt a quiver of excitement. 'I would be so grateful. Do you know him well?'

Romanelli nodded. 'Well enough. We have known each other for a long time. His father came to England as a political exile, and his home in London was always open to other Italians. But to talk again of your family,' he added. 'Your father is sick, I heard you say?'

'I received a letter from my brother saying that he was, and so I decided that I would return home for a few days.'

'I'm sorry,' Romanelli murmured. 'I trust that he will make a good recovery. And your mother? She is well?'

'I believe so,' James said dismissively. 'Gilbert said that she was worried.'

'Gilbert? Your brother? I remember him also, I think. He was only a small child but I remember his orange hair.'

'His red hair!' James laughed. How Gilbert would hate to have his despised hair described as orange. 'Most of my family, my cousins and uncles, have various shades of red or fair hair. Except me,' he added. 'I take after my mother.'

'Of course.' Romanelli glanced at him as they neared Batsford's studio. 'She was very dark – and quite beautiful. Is she still?'

'My mother?' He had never thought of his mother as ever having being beautiful. No. His mother, he was convinced, had never been remotely beautiful, she was too sullen and morose, there was no inner light within her to give any kind of loveliness.

Romanelli slowed down and then stopped to look over the river. He stood with his arms folded in front of him and gazed out towards Battersea Bridge. '*Si*,' he said softly. 'You perhaps would not think it of your mama, children rarely do. But – *si*, she was very beautiful. She was enchanting and joyous. *Milly*.' He dropped his voice to a mere whisper. '*Milly bella*.'

24

Gilbert was convinced that Harriet was softening towards him. He had been attentive and devoted towards her during their stay in Scarborough, making sure that she enjoyed her visit to the fashionable spa resort without any nervous apprehension. He even tenderly bathed a blister on her foot, which came from walking in unsuitable shoes down the cliff path from the Esplanade to the Spa, where she desired to try the efficacious mineral waters so recommended by doctors and health seekers. Gilbert declined to do the same, being quite put off by its russet colour and odd smell, and declared that he would rather bathe in the sea, for it would surely do as much good. Harriet was reluctant to bathe publicly, although the bathing machines appeared to be discreetly situated, and so they both decided that as the wind was cool, perhaps they would leave the experience for another time.

From the Spa Terrace they looked down at the wide sweep of sands and viewed the lighthouse at the end of the Vincent Pier: the cluster of red-roofed houses nestling in the shelter of the tree-covered headland, and to the right of the picturesque ancient church of St Mary, which clung to the side of the hill, the remains of the castle stood dominant, defiant and protective above the town.

They crossed the ornate iron Cliff Bridge to visit the town and could still hear the faint strains of music coming from the Spa's Gothic Saloon, but which was almost lost by the screech of seagulls, such an integral sound of Scarborough.

Harriet appeared puzzled by his attitude towards her, expecting, it seemed, that he should be demanding of her and not so attentive and thoughtful as he obviously was; and he thought that she was trying in little ways to please him, as if she felt guilt over the conflict between her desire to be an obedient and good wife and the abhorrent fear within her of what lay ahead in the marriage bed. He did not demand anything of her, and left her each night to sleep alone while he slept on the daybed in the sitting-room of their suite.

On their last evening before returning home, she had been particularly tender towards him, giving him her whole attention during their conversation, and holding his hand in a caressing, loving way as they listened to the concert in the New Hall. Yet still he did not suggest that he came to her bed, and she retired with a sad and confused look on her face.

He awoke at about two o'clock in the morning; the moon was shedding its light into the room and he was startled to see Harriet standing there, clad only in her bedgown. 'What is it, Harriet? Are you unwell?' He threw the blanket from him and went towards her.

'No, I'm not ill, Gilbert. I couldn't sleep, that's all. I'm sorry to disturb you – I thought perhaps a little wine or cordial, if there was any, might help me relax.'

He smiled. Harriet drank very little wine, it was unlikely that she would crave it to help her into oblivion. 'Come here,' he said softly. 'Sit by me.' She did as he suggested and lay her head on his shoulder. He kissed the top of her head and put his arms around her. 'There,' he whispered, 'is that better?'

'Yes, thank you, Gilbert. You are so good to me. I don't deserve you.'

He turned her head towards him and kissed her tenderly on the mouth. 'What nonsense is this?' he whispered. 'It is I who does not deserve you.'

'No,' she protested. 'I have failed you. I have not fulfilled my duty towards you.'

He tensed. So she still had this idiotic idea that it was a woman's duty to please her husband. He said nothing, but stroked her arm and shoulder, running his hand up and down her soft skin. His hand brushed against her breast and he felt her tremble. He touched her gently, his fingers feather-light against the curves beneath her cotton bedgown, and she gave small gasping breaths. He kissed her again, small loving kisses against her cheeks, her ears, her throat, while his hands explored her breasts and tiny waist. She looked at him, her face white in the moonlight, her lips parted and her eyes enormous.

'Come,' he whispered and pulled her to her feet. 'Look.' He led her to the window. Below them, across the Esplanade, the sea was bathed by the bright light of the moon, the white wave crests sparkling with silver as they rushed to the shore and the sands bleached white. 'See how beautiful it is.'

'Gilbert,' she breathed. 'I think that perhaps I am ready for you.'

He kissed her once more on her mouth, holding her face between his hands. 'Not yet,' he said softly. 'Not yet. Goodnight my darling, go back to bed,' and he turned her around and propelled her towards the bedroom door.

She barely spoke on the journey home; they travelled by train, and in the company of other passengers there wasn't the opportunity to talk privately, but Gilbert was bright and breezy, pointing out various items of interest in the fields and villages as they passed through, which Harriet looked at with large soulful eyes, but made no comment.

When they arrived back at Hull's Paragon Station, he took her home in a hired carriage, and said that he was just slipping out to the office to see if all was well and that he would be home for supper. As it was late, most of the clerks had gone, but Billy was still there, as was Hardwick, who greeted Gilbert with some relief.

'I don't want to bother you now, sir, when you have just got back,' Hardwick looked worried, 'but we have no news of 'Star Two; she hasn't been seen since leaving 'Shetlands.'

'Good heavens, man. It's far too early to start worrying, she won't have reached the ice fields yet.'

'No, we know that, Gilbert,' Billy interrupted. 'It's just that the Frances May returned early with a damaged hull and reported that they hadn't seen sight of her, even though they left at the same time.'

Gilbert dismissed their worries. 'I'll make enquiries tomorrow, but I still think it is too early to have any fears about her. Have you heard news of my father?' he enquired of Billy.

'My father said he looked quite well when he left him the day after the wedding, but there is bad news of Uncle Thomas.' Billy told him of their uncle's fall from the top of the mill. 'Sammi is still there with them; Betsy has taken it very badly, and Tom and George are working like ten men, now that Mark has left.'

Gilbert commiserated and said that he would try to get out and see them, though he knew deep down that he wouldn't, especially if Sammi was there and there was a chance that he might see the child again. His conscience was very troubled when he thought of them, and he was still in a quandary as to what to do. *How I would hate Harriet to find out.*

He bathed when he got home and changed for supper, and saw that Harriet had arranged flowers on the dining table which was set with the silver and crystal they had been given as wedding presents.

'I think the maid will do very well, Gilbert,' Harriet said. 'So I hope that we can keep her. As for Cook, well, we shall see tonight whether she is worth the money we are paying her.'

Gilbert grimaced, the payment for servants had

never before occurred to him; his mother had always taken care of that matter and, as far as he knew, she never had recourse to his father over any difficulty with them.

Cook excelled herself at this, their first meal in their new home. Turtle soup was presented first, followed by plaice fried in butter and lemon juice, a sorbet to cleanse their palates came next, and a third course of mutton pie in small pastry cases was served with mushrooms and parsley.

'I asked Cook to keep the supper light,' Harriet said as Tilly brought in the dessert of gooseberry pie and cream. 'I thought after our journey it was best not to eat too heartily, as we shall probably want to retire early.'

'Quite right, my dear.' Gilbert poured another glass of wine. 'I am a little weary. Will you take more wine?'

'Yes please.' She finished off the wine in her glass. 'It is quite pleasant.'

He glanced at her in surprise, he thought she had pulled a wry face on taking her first sip. 'Here,' he smiled. 'Put a little sugar in it. You may prefer it.' He passed her the silver sugar bowl which had been brought in with the dessert. 'Not that you need sugar, my darling. You look sweet and lovely enough.'

She blushed, a soft pink on her cheeks, her hair fell in dark ringlets around her face, and the white bodice of her gown was cut low, emphasizing the rounded swelling of her breasts.

'I don't recall seeing you in that gown before, Harriet. Is it new?'

She shook her head. 'The skirt I have had since last year, and the bodice even longer.' She lowered her eyes. 'It was a high neck, you may remember, and — and I decided to adapt it.'

'I see.'

She had been busily sewing in her room when he had returned home and had glanced up in some confusion when he looked in at her. The bodice was very revealing and he hoped that she wouldn't wear it when they were out in other company. He didn't want his wife's charms on display for other men to see.

At half-past ten he made a great show of yawning and stretching, and announced that he would go up to bed. 'I'll see you in the morning, Harriet.' He bent over and kissed her on her cheek. 'I'll look in on you before I leave.'

She looked up at him in bewilderment. 'But Gilbert,' her voice wavered, 'you don't have to use the spare room.'

'It's all right,' he said lightly, 'there's no need to worry; I shall sleep perfectly soundly. It's a very good bed. Don't stay up too late and overtire yourself. Goodnight.'

He saw tears glisten in her eyes and her lips trembled, but he turned away and closed the door behind him.

The clock was striking eleven when he heard her come up the stairs and enter the bedroom next door. He was beginning to feel some remorse at leaving her alone downstairs and at not persuading her to share his bed, but he was passionately hoping that she would, by now, be feeling some yearning and want him as much as he wanted her. This celibate state did not suit him and he was filled with desire for her – desire which he did not want to persuade upon her. Yet if she kept him waiting much longer, he may well have to.

He was just drifting off to sleep when the door opened. Harriet was standing there, looking as she had done when they were in the hotel in Scarborough. Her hair was floating about her shoulders and she wore a loose bedgown. She held aloft a lighted candle whose flame illuminated her face. 'Gilbert?' she whispered. 'Are you awake?'

He gave a sleepy grunt and smiled in the darkness and muttered inaudibly, 'What? Who's there?'

'It's only me, Gilbert.'

He didn't answer but turned over with a deep sigh and flung an arm outside the bedclothes. He felt her touch his arm, gingerly at first and then growing bolder, she stroked it gently. He watched her through half-closed eyelids as she put the candleholder on the bedside table then, bending, she blew out the flame and turning back the covers crept into the bed beside him.

He had never worn nightclothes before he had married, and though he now had several sets of new nightshirts, tonight after undressing, he had as usual, slipped naked into bed. Harriet lay perfectly still beside him and as he turned towards her he put his arm over her and moved closer, still feigning sleep. He heard a small gasp as she felt his nakedness next to her, and then her hand moved against his chest; her fingers explored across his shoulders and down to his waist and hips, stopping short at his buttocks.

He could stand it no longer. He drew her towards him. His hands searched her body, his mouth her lips. 'Harriet,' he murmured, 'I love you. I want to show you how much.'

'I love you too, Gilbert,' she whispered back, 'and I want you too. I'm not afraid now. I'm sorry that I was so foolish. Love me now, Gilbert. Please.'

Gilbert breakfasted alone in the dining-room and helped himself from the dresser. He dined heartily on porridge and herrings rolled in oatmeal, bacon and eggs, toast and marmalade and a big pot of coffee, and then went up to say good-bye to Harriet, who was sitting up in bed with a breakfast tray on her lap. She looked flushed and pretty in her lacy bedshawl.

'I'll try to get home at midday,' he said as he kissed her. 'But if not, I shall see you this evening. I hope you have a pleasant day.'

She put her arms out to pull him back towards her.

'I shall call on Mama,' she smiled. 'I want her to see how happy I am.'

He was late. He hurried across the town. His gig and pair were stabled at the company as there were no stables attached to this house. It wasn't far to walk to the office, but he never could get up in the morning, and always seemed to be rushing at the last minute. He smiled to himself, and if Harriet was going to be as delightful and willing, as warm and indulgent as she had been last night, then he could quite see that he might be late most mornings.

He was in such a state of pleasurable gratification, so transported by their rapturous night, that he almost bumped into Harriet's father, who was coming towards him as he took the usual short cut between the buildings to Lowgate.

Billington looked slightly embarrassed, then gave a bluff cry. 'Well! Well! Look who's here,' and shook Gilbert by the hand. 'And how is my daughter?' he boomed. 'Did she miss her papa?'

'I don't think so, sir,' Gilbert answered boldly. 'She's very well indeed. I believe she is calling to see her mother later today to tell her of our excellent holiday in Scarborough.'

'Oh! Well. Good, good.' He bumbled on for a moment and then with a glance at the house behind them, he bent his head towards Gilbert and lowered his voice. 'I've only got a moment, I er, I have an appointment, and then I must get back to the bank, but, now that you are family, I wanted to tell you that I can put one or two things your way, in the financial sense, I mean.'

'Really, sir? In a private capacity, do you mean?'

Billington pursed his lips. 'Well, if you had a thousand guineas to spare, you could double it within a month, but,' he waved his hands negatively, 'I know how it is when you're just married, and I wouldn't like to think you were using Harriet's dowry for a gamble, even though, come rain or shine, it is an absolute certainty. But if your company could bring themselves to dabble, it would go a long way towards buying a new ship.'

'What kind of business are we talking, sir?' Gilbert asked curiously, thinking vaguely that if Billington would hurry up and hand over Harriet's dowry, there would be all kinds of things they could do with it. 'Shares or . . . ?'

Billington tapped the side of his nose. 'Can't say. Not now. Everybody would want to be in if word got out, and that would spoil the profit for the rest of us, those who have already taken a stake.'

Gilbert questioned to know more, but Billington stood firm, and when Gilbert suggested a smaller stake, say a hundred, Billington chortled. 'Not a chance, dear boy. This is going to be a good one.' He pulled out his fob watch and then looked up the stairs at the house nearby. The door was ajar and he waved his hand to someone inside. 'Must go. You know how it is.' He looked Gilbert in the eye. 'Well, perhaps you don't. Not yet. But you will, take my word for it.' He turned to go. 'Think about the other business. I'm telling you as family, so don't let it go any further. But you can't afford to miss this, Gilbert. It's a certainty.'

Gilbert watched him skip jauntily up the steps of the house and heard the sound of female laughter. He, too, glanced at his watch. Nine-fifteen and Billington was visiting a brothel. He felt vaguely sorry for the man in view of what Harriet had said about her mother's view of the marriage bed.

How sad to think he had no comfort in his own bed but had to resort to a place like this. Gilbert took a deep breath. How lucky he was to have such a sweet and loving bride. He felt warm and contented when he thought of Harriet. He would do his best for her: work hard, give her every comfort. He would think seriously about what Billington had said. If only he had the money.

He had almost reached the corner when he heard his name called. 'Rayner!'

He turned and saw Billington beckoning to him from half-way down the steps. He walked back, and Billington came down to speak to him.

'All right.' He inclined his head towards Gilbert's ear. 'Under the circumstances – only don't tell a soul, make it five hundred and I'll put the other half in. I don't want you to miss out. But I must have it today, no later than three o'clock or it will be too late.'

'Oh, that's very good of you, sir. Thank you very much indeed.'

Gilbert was so swept away by his father-in-law's generosity that he gave no thought of where he would find five hundred guineas before the middle of the afternoon, until he had walked away again. Then he deliberated, and already being in a bold, dauntless mood, he became assertive. *Well*, he insisted, *where is the sense of being the acting managing director of a company, with power of attorney, if I can't draw a measly five hundred from the account, which will in the long run benefit the company. It isn't as if I am doing it for myself.*

He turned his steps away from the High Street and his office, and headed for Salter's bank to see Mr Collins.

The meeting did not go well. Collins wanted to know what the money was required for, and when Gilbert refused to say, and although the banker couldn't refuse the transaction, he became very tight-lipped about it.

Gilbert became angry, though he tried not to show it. 'Mr Collins! While my father is incapacitated I make the decisions, and I have to say that in view of your attitude towards me, I shall now seriously recommend to my fellow directors that we move our business elsewhere.'

Collins blustered and mumbled that there had never been any dissatisfaction before, and that he, Mr Rayner, in view of his inexperience, would be well advised to take the bank's advice in view of the difficulties that the shipping industry was experiencing. Gilbert made no reply, but picked up his top hat and wished him good day.

I shall call a meeting, he thought victoriously, as he swept through the door held open for him by the commissionaire. *I shall show that old fool that he can't impose on me the way he has done with my father. It's our money that he's handling after all, not his. I shall write immediately to Uncle William and Uncle Arthur, and speak to my father tomorrow. He will be persuaded that it is for the best. We need a fresh start. A new push forward. Billington is the man to watch out for us. He will have our best interests at heart. He's family, after all.*

25

'Gilbert and Harriet will be home today, I think.' Mildred sat by the window in Isaac's room with her sewing in her lap. 'I'm so pleased that the weather kept fair for them; Scarborough is lovely at this time of the year.'

'Any time of the year,' Isaac wheezed. 'I always enjoyed Scarborough. We used to go when I was a boy, you know. We had relatives living there, an aunt and cousins; we've lost touch now. The uncle was a fisherman, he used to bring such delicious fish for our supper, and lobsters. Oh yes, we had such happy times. There was horse-racing on the sands, and pierrots and morris men and such, but now I understand the sands are full of bathing machines, and even ladies are bathing in the sea. I'm not sure what to make of that.'

'Perhaps we should go when you are feeling better? The air is so beneficial at Scarborough.'

'It's a nice thought, my dear.' He lay back on the pillow. 'But I'm afraid I'd never get up the hills, you need a good deal of breath for Scarborough.'

He watched Mildred as she sat, framed by the afternoon light from the window. She had been so much warmer, more loving, since his illness. More like the sweet wife she had once been, before her encounter with the man who became her lover and who had left her feeling lonely and bereft, despite giving her a child.

Thinking of James as a child, he thought about the infant for whom Sammi was still caring. Mildred, he was convinced, had dismissed the infant from her mind, refusing to even think about him. The wheel had come full circle, he reflected; a child has been abandoned once again, just as James's own father abandoned him.

But James has had me. I am his father. He is my son. The son whom he had always thought of only as his, the boy who had been more of a son to him than Gilbert, who had always been Mildred's favourite; more favoured even than Anne, who, he sighed, was spoiled and indulged and not the considerate daughter he would have liked her to be.

'Have you missed him?' he asked. 'Gilbert, I mean?'

'Yes.' Mildred turned her gaze to the view of the garden. 'I have. It will be strange to think he won't be living here any more. The house will be very quiet, especially when Anne gets married.'

'If!' Isaac commented breathily. 'Young Tebbitt hasn't popped the question yet. Not to me, at any rate.'

'He will.' Mildred drew out a fresh thread from her wicker sewing basket. 'He's only waiting for you to recover, I'm sure of it.'

He might have a long wait then, Isaac pondered. *I feel very weak. I can't stand for long and the thought of going downstairs fills me with dread.* 'I hope James comes soon. I keep expecting him every day. I wonder if Gilbert expressed the urgency to him?'

'Don't fret yourself, Isaac.' Mildred put down her sewing and came and sat on the edge of his bed, being careful not to jolt him. 'You know how vague James is, he probably hasn't opened his post.'

'Yes,' Isaac answered absent-mindedly. 'I don't know who he takes after.'

Mildred gave a start and Isaac immediately realized his error. 'I'm sorry, my dear,' he began. 'I didn't mean—'

Her face was pale and drawn. 'I know you didn't, Isaac, and there is no reason for you to apologize to me.' She bowed her head and he thought how vulnerable her slender neck looked. 'When I think of how you have carried this secret for so long and never once reproached me. Any other man would have turned me out long ago.'

'That is because I always lived in hope that you would come back to me in spirit; that one day you would love me again,' he said softly.

'I never stopped loving you, Isaac, never once. It was just – just that I can never rid myself of his memory. There is always an empty space within me. I thought – I thought that when James was born he would fill it; but he didn't, he only served to remind me more.' A tear trickled down her face. She had done so much crying lately and yet still could not expurgate her guilt, not of her passion for the man, nor of her indifference towards the child he had given her.

'You won't ever tell James, will you, Mildred?' Isaac's voice was weak and quavery.

She looked up, startled, and shook her head.

'You won't ever tell him that I am not his father? It would break my heart if he knew. He was always my son, you see.' There were tears in his eyes and a catch in his voice. 'More than Gilbert ever was, and especially when I saw that you didn't care for him as much as you might have done.'

'No, Isaac.' She wiped away her own tears and put her hand over his. 'I won't ever tell him. On my life, if you can ever trust me again, I won't.'

At supper time she carried up a tray to Isaac's room; he was eating little, but he had said he would try a drop of soup. She had placed a pretty cloth on the tray and set a fresh rosebud from the garden next to the soup bowl.

He held the flower to his nose. 'Beautiful,' he said softly. 'The perfume is delightful. Sit with me, will you, Milly, after you have had your supper?'

She said she would, and after she had eaten and Mary had cleared away, she washed and changed into her bedgown. It was nine o'clock and Isaac would soon be wanting the light turning down and preparing himself for his medication and sleep.

'You always did look lovely with your hair loose,' he said when she drew wide the curtains as he requested, and the light from the summer moon poured into the room.

She turned and smiled, and in the half-light he saw again, or imagined he did, the young bride of twenty-five years ago.

He held out his hand. 'Come here, Milly. Hold my hand.'

Mildred moved towards him and took his hand, then bent to kiss his cheek. 'May I come into your bed, Isaac?' she said softly. 'It has been a long time. Can you bear it? Can you forgive me?'

He put his arms out towards her. 'I never thought . . .' he began brokenly. 'I never thought to hear those words from your lips ever again, my darling.'

She lifted aside the covers and eased herself in beside him and turned towards him, gently holding him in her arms. 'Help me to forget, Isaac,' she whispered. 'Help me to forget. For as God is my witness, I want to.'

As morning broke, Mildred awoke and felt a chill. She got up to close the open window and looked out at the garden. A river mist was breathing over the shrubs and lawns and flower borders, lacing them with a diaphanous veil. The moon had disappeared and the sky was flooding with flashes of yellow light and slender streaks of purple. She paused for a moment, exulting in the beauty. She heard the first call of a blackbird and then another, and then the sound of a wren, the throaty coo of a wood pigeon, and it seemed as if the air was filled with their music.

'Are you awake, Isaac?' she said softly, anxious not to disturb him, but wanting him to share her joy in

282

the morning. 'It's the start of a new day. A new beginning.'

She stood at the side of the bed looking down at him. How peaceful he looked. How happy he had been that she had at last come to him. Content just to be cradled in her arms. She, too, felt a peace of mind which had deserted her for so long. The long shadow of the past which had lain so heavily for so many years, had shifted, easing some of its heavy weight from her.

A warmth enveloped her, the act of loving made her feel again more like the woman she had once been, and not the sour, disillusioned and incomplete person she had become. She had robed herself in a hypocritical, sanctimonious cloak of pretence, even to her style of dress, with her high-necked plain gowns and severe hair styles. It was as if she had been hiding her real identity, not wanting anyone else but the man she had lost to see her as her own self.

'I will try to make amends, Isaac,' she whispered. 'Before it is finally too late for us.'

He didn't stir, his eyes were firmly closed in a deep sleep. She gave a gentle smile at him in his serene contentment and put out her hand to hold his which lay folded on the bedspread. His hands were cold. So cold. As she gazed down at him, despair washed over her, displacing her brief happiness. Isaac would never feel warm again. Would never feel the warmth of the sun on his face. Would never see another dawn, not on this earth. And neither would she hold him in her arms again. It was too late for both of them.

She sank to her knees, and pressing her lips to his cold hands, she started to weep.

26

Sammi was packing her bag to go home, when Billy arrived once more, this time with the news of Uncle Isaac's death.

She sat by Uncle Thomas's side as Tom broke the news to him.

'He should have waited on a bit,' his father said morosely and shifted himself awkwardly. His right leg was splintered and stretched out on his bed, but his left ankle hung limp and useless. 'We could have travelled together. We'd have been company for each other.'

Tom protested and Sammi declared that he shouldn't think that way, that he was much improved.

'Aye, in my mind, lassie, not my body, and I've no fancy for hanging around with broken shanks. I'm no use to anybody in this state.' A gleam came to his eyes as he tried to lighten their mood. 'Why, I'd such notions of finding myself a rich young widow woman and leaving our Tom to carry on at 'mill. Now I'd know they'd onny be after me for my money.'

Tom and Sammi smiled bleakly at his joke, but Billy, standing by the door, didn't.

'Come, lad,' said his uncle. 'Don't be so despondent. Death comes to us all sooner or later, and both your Uncle Isaac and I have had long lives, long enough to do what we wanted.'

'Then you've been fortunate in that, Uncle,' Billy said grimly. 'There are some who don't get that chance, no matter how long they live.'

They all looked at him. He seemed so bleak. *It cannot surely be unhappiness only for Uncle Isaac's sake,* thought Sammi. 'You're thinking of those children, aren't you, Billy?'

He nodded. 'Yes. I need to talk to you about them, Sammi, about one of them, anyway.'

After he had gone, Sammi unpacked her bag again, for Betsy once more took to her bed when she heard of her uncle's death.

'I don't understand you, Betsy,' Sammi taxed her. 'We were fond of Uncle Isaac, but you were never so close to him to take on so.'

'I'm just so afraid,' she sobbed, 'I can't cope with unhappiness, Sammi. I only want to be happy, to have pleasure in life. I hate misery.'

'We have to have one to know the other.' Sammi grew impatient. 'I don't understand what is happening to you, Betsy. You must have some indisposition. I think we'd better ask the doctor to take a look at you next time he comes to visit your father.'

Betsy was so opposed to that suggestion that Sammi went downstairs in a huff and vowed that she didn't know Betsy as well as she thought she did.

Uncle Thomas asked Tom to attend the funeral on his behalf. They would shut down the mill for the day, George and Luke could clear up after the builders, who had finished the kitchen extension and almost finished the engine house, and Betsy would stay and look after her father's needs.

'It's not for me to say what tha should do, Sammi,' her uncle said thoughtfully. 'I expect tha'll want to pay 'last respects to Isaac; and go home if tha must, but I'll not fare so well with my own daughter's ministrations as I've done with thine.'

She bent down and kissed him. 'You've been a good patient, Uncle Thomas, but be tolerant with Betsy, I don't think she is well.'

'What ails her then?' he asked sharply. 'Has she some sickness that I haven't been told about?'

'I don't know. I'd like her to see the doctor, but

she won't hear of it. She's unhappy, she needs something to cheer her up.'

She suggested that Betsy read to her father after supper, and asked Tom if he would take a walk with her. He nodded and put on his boots. They took the path towards the copse. The harvest had been gathered in before the rains of the last few days and the golden stubble glistened in the evening light.

''Farmers should be happy,' Tom commented as they linked arms. 'It's been a good harvest.'

'And the mill cap is restored and working again, but your father isn't,' she added softly. 'Poor Uncle Thomas. I feel so sad for him.'

Tom squeezed her arm. 'Aye, it's a bad business, but at least he's still with us. I was so afraid he would die.'

They walked on, both looking out at the cropped fields and over the undulating meadowland which stretched like a great prairie as far as they could see, broken only by clusters of hawthorn bushes and hedges or thickly planted copses.

'I shall return home after the funeral, Tom.' Her words hung in the stillness.

Tom said nothing for a moment, then murmured, 'We shall miss you, Sammi, Da particularly; but if you feel that you must . . .'

She glanced up at him, but he kept his eyes straight ahead. She hoped that he would understand: it wasn't that she didn't want to stay. 'Betsy is relying too much on me. She'll perhaps manage better if I am not there. She is mistress after all, and Nancy is working well since you spoke to her, and does as she's told.' She shook his arm. 'You do understand, don't you, Tom? I realize now that I was most inconsiderate to impose on you because of Adam, but he is doing so well now under Mrs Bishop's care.' *But I shall miss him,* she thought sadly. *He knows me now, and his little face smiles when he sees me. Oh, dear. I don't know what to do.*

'Ah, yes,' he said, grim-faced. 'I quite forgot that Adam was the original reason for your coming to stay.'

'But also, Tom,' Sammi felt that she had to find some other justification for leaving, 'I have to make amends with Mama and Pa. They are unhappy about the situation. It has to be resolved.'

'So we all need you, Sammi!' They reached the copse and turned again for home, and as they reversed their direction he moved to the other side of her so that she might be away from the over-hanging hedge. He put his hand on her shoulder. 'We shall have to chop you into little bits,' he said lightly, 'so that we can all have a piece of you.'

'Silly,' she chided. 'You will manage perfectly well without me.' She remembered what Billy had said at Gilbert's wedding about their shared confidences, and asked hesitantly, 'Have you ever thought of marrying, Tom?'

The question was so sudden that he stopped in his tracks and she nearly fell over him. 'Sorry,' they both said, 'my fault.'

She looked up at him and couldn't make out the emotion which was so evident in his face; his eyes narrowed and he clenched his lips firmly together: she couldn't tell whether it was anger or dismay that he was feeling.

'I'm sorry,' she said in confusion. 'That was an intrusion. I shouldn't have asked such a personal question. Please forgive me, Tom. I'm sorry.'

'It's all right, Sammi!' he said brusquely. 'Are we not friends that you can ask me anything?'

'We always were,' she murmured and wondered why she felt so miserable.

'As a matter of fact, my father said only a little while ago that I should marry and bring a wife to the mill house.' He turned towards her, his eyes searching hers. 'He even suggested that I should ask *you* – to find me someone suitable.'

She stared at him, her eyes wide. 'Oh! I couldn't possibly do that, Tom. I should never be able to find anyone that I would approve of sufficiently.' *And if I did*, she thought, *it would mean that I wouldn't be able to visit so often, for any wife of Tom's would surely disapprove of my friendship towards her husband.*

She saw his face lighten at her words as he assured her, 'Then I will have to remain a bachelor all my life, Sammi, for I have no inclination to look for myself.'

So he didn't have a secret passion after all, as Betsy had suggested, she reflected, and felt quite light-hearted at the thought. They turned off the path into the lane; dusk was falling rapidly, and long shadows from the horse chestnut trees were spreading in dark pools.

''Evening, Master Tom, Miss Rayner.' Luke Reed-barrow with Annie Greaves, a girl from the village, by his side, were about to take the path which they had just left.

The girl looked at them curiously. Sammi knew her by sight, her family used to live in Monkston on her father's land until their cottage was devoured by the sea, and they had been rehoused in Tillington. Tom nodded to them, but barely spoke; he and Sammi looked at each other incredulously after the pair had disappeared from view, and Sammi knew that they had both had the same thought. Why was Luke Reedbarrow walking out with another young woman when he had been given permission by her father to court Betsy?

Betsy waved them off on the day of Isaac's funeral as the Rayners' carriage turned around in the yard. Sammi and her mother were dressed in black. Aunt Ellen in matt black crêpe, and Sammi in one of her mother's old velvet gowns which had been hastily altered and trimmed with white lace at the neckline to relieve the blackness. Uncle William was clothed in full mourning suit for his brother, Richard and Tom both wore black armbands on their jackets.

She closed the door and prepared a drink for her father and George, and sent Nancy upstairs to clean the bedrooms of the dust which was still settling from the new building work. They now had a new bathroom with a proper cast-iron bath, and Tom had bought a new marble wash-stand and a flowered jug and washbowl to stand on it. An additional bedroom had been built above the kitchen which, though small, would be suitable for a live-in maid.

Betsy doubted if they would find a village girl. They were all moving to Hull to go into service, and she felt something of a pang of envy at what she thought of as their good fortune.

I almost wish I could do the same, she thought dejectedly. *I can see myself being stuck here for ever, with no prospects at all of moving out. Not now, not with Da as he is.* And she thought of Mark who had escaped to fresh pastures. *Though he might well be dead for all we know, for the devil still hasn't written to us.*

Her father, having asked constantly if they had heard from Mark, no longer asked if they had received a letter, and seemed to have resigned himself to the fact that his second son had gone for good.

There was a knock on the door and Luke put his head around, and seeing that she was alone, stepped into the kitchen. 'Is your da sleeping?' he whispered.

'No,' she answered in a low voice. 'Why would he be sleeping at this time of the morning?'

'I was just hoping that he was so that I could come and have a chat with thee.' He put his arms around her. 'It's been ages, Betsy, since – you know. I've missed thee.'

She pushed him away. 'Don't. Not here. The girl's upstairs.'

'She won't hear owt. Come on, just give us a little kiss, nowt else.'

She put her face up to his and felt the tingling sense of want that came every time she was near him.

'Meet me later, Betsy. I need thee.' He ran his hands around her waist and hips. 'We haven't been together for weeks.'

'I've not been well.' She moved away as she heard Nancy clattering upstairs and her father cough. 'And I don't know how I can get away now, not with Da confined to the house.'

'Come tonight,' he persuaded. 'After they're all in bed. Tha'll not be missed.'

She considered. Perhaps she could. Sammi would have gone, she said she was returning home with her parents after the funeral. 'All right,' she smiled, and felt a sudden lightening of her spirits. 'I'll try to come at about ten o'clock. Wait for me by the footpath.'

He took the jug of tea from her and with one more brief kiss he left her and went back to the mill. Nancy came downstairs, wiping her brow and complaining about the dust.

'If you don't like the work, I can soon find someone else who does,' Betsy said irritably. 'You'd better watch your step, my girl, or you'll find yourself given notice and no reference.'

Nancy sulked and muttered, 'Sorry, Miss Betsy. I weren't complaining. Shall I take 'maister's drink in to him?'

'No, I'll do it.' Betsy relented a little. 'Make yourself a drink to slake your throat and then clean the bath tub. Only don't scratch it.'

'No, miss.' Nancy took the kettle from the side shelf of the new range and placed it on the fire, where it was soon steaming. 'It's grand, Miss Betsy, having all these conveniences – makes life a lot easier. I suppose if Master Tom and Miss Rayner should ever wed, she'd expect summat a bit grand, seeing as she's used to it.'

Betsy turned back from the doorway, a tray in her hands with her father's teapot and large cup and saucer on it. 'What did you say? Whatever do you mean?'

Nancy looked embarrassed. 'Sorry, miss. It's onny what I heard.'

'What?' Betsy put the tray back on the table. 'What did you hear?'

Nancy hung her head. 'I suppose folks are jumping to conclusions, Miss Betsy. But Annie Greaves asked me if it were true what she'd heard, that 'young babby at Mrs Bishop's was Miss Rayner's and was Master Tom his fayther? It's 'cos she's living here. She'd seen them together, walking together all comfortable like.'

Betsy stared at her. Mark had warned them that people would talk, that they would assume the child belonged to one of them. 'How ridiculous!' she snapped. 'You of all people, Nancy, should know that Miss Sammi has stayed on to help look after my father. She has long been a good friend of all of us, not just Master Tom.'

'I said that there was nowt in it, miss. But babby's there for all to see, and there's no mistaking it's got red hair just like Miss Rayner. And somebody else said,' she added defensively, 'that they thought it was Master Mark's bairn and that was why he'd left in such a hurry. They said as how Mr Rayner was coming after him with a shotgun.'

Betsy sank down on a chair. The very idea was ludicrous. Such rumours. Sammi marry Tom! How ridiculous. Why, her parents would have very different plans for her. She was bound to marry someone with land and estate, someone with more wealth than Tom. Then a doubt slowly crept in. Had Sammi spoilt things for herself by taking on this child? This child who was supposed to belong to cousin James? It wasn't Sammi's child, Betsy knew that, but no-one else knew. Anyone who didn't know would think that he was hers. And if there was a doubt, no-one of quality would take the risk of marrying her.

Her father shouted, 'Betsy! Where's my tea?' and

291

she got up from the chair and picked up the tray again.

'The child is not Miss Rayner's as you very well know, Nancy, nor is it Master Tom's or Mark's. The rumour is malicious, obviously started by a trouble-maker, and I will hear no more of it.'

And what if, just if, Tom should marry her? Then what would happen to me? I wouldn't be mistress in my own home. I would take second place to Sammi!

We were travelling this road joyfully so little time ago, Ellen mused. *First a wedding and now a funeral. Poor Isaac.* She felt sad at her brother-in-law's death, but little sympathy for his widow, having considered for a long time that Mildred had not given much consideration to Isaac. *I wonder if she knows that Adam is Gilbert's child? Hmm. I think not. She would view the situation quite differently if she did. Gilbert was always her favourite. It would still have been wounding to her sensibilities of course; she would have been angry, but I'm sure some provision would have been made for him.*

And James, how is he going to feel when he hears the news of his father? He will be devastated. Quite bereft. I hope that he will be there and not miss his father's funeral as he did his brother's wedding. My poor William. She glanced at her husband sitting with his chin in his hand, looking quite miserable. *He has taken this very hard, he was very fond of his brother.* Sammi was gazing out of the window, her face expressionless. *And what shall I do about you, Sammi?* Her mother watched her. *She worries over Adam. As I do too.*

Gilbert must be confronted, she thought positively. She was reluctant to risk Gilbert's marriage by challenging him, yet annoyed and distressed that he should so blithely let someone else take responsibility. Her gaze fell on Richard. He was looking out of the window at the stubble and the set ricks standing high, at the teams of men and horses who were harrowing the fields. There would be no problem there. Richard would find himself a sturdy farmer's daughter to wed and lead an uncomplicated life.

Tom is a good sensible lad, she thought, giving him a sideways glance as he sat, his eyes on his clasped hands. *He'll do well at the mill; he's steady and reliable.* She watched him as his gaze lifted to Sammi, still staring out of the window as they bumped along the potholed road; and there was something in his expression which made her look at him again a few minutes later. *There is something troubling him,* she puzzled. *He is unhappy over something.* He was gazing at Sammi with such a brooding, longing expression, that Ellen was quite startled.

What could it mean? She shifted in her seat; Tom looked up and caught her watching him. He gave her a slight smile but with such a look of intense sorrow, which for a brief moment he wasn't able to hide, that her heart went out to him. He looked away and she turned her thoughts to other things, but when she surreptitiously glanced at him again as they rattled into the streets of Hull, she saw that once more he had turned wistful eyes to Sammi.

Tom? Not Tom? Not Tom and Sammi? For a moment she was disturbed and confused; then as she discerned that what she saw written on Tom's face was unrequited longing, and on Sammi's was unsuspecting innocence, she became calm and practical. Gone were her thoughts of Tom's steadfastness and reliability, and in their place was a picture of frustrated manhood. Sammi must come home immediately! *She is still unworldly, no matter that she thinks she knows about life. I must protect my daughter! Not from Tom, he wouldn't harm her, of that I am sure, but from herself! She is so compassionate and warm-hearted that if she should discover how Tom feels about her, she might be swayed by his emotions before she is aware of her own.*

27

There was something wrong! Dusk was falling as James arrived at his home, but there was no sign of lamplight from behind the tightly drawn curtains at the windows. There were two carriages outside the door. One he recognized as belonging to the doctor, but the other he didn't know. It was completely black and shiny and drawn by two black mares. He walked slowly up the steps. He could think only the worst. He turned the door-knob. The door was locked and he hadn't a key. He rang the bell and waited, like a stranger to his own home.

Mary opened the door. Her eyes were red as if she had been weeping. 'Oh, Master James. You've come at last. We were all hoping that you would.'

'What's happened, Mary? Is my father worse?'

His mother stepped out of the sitting-room. Her face was deathly pale and her words were tremulous. 'Your father died early this morning, James. He knew no pain. He passed peacefully away in his sleep.'

She moved towards him and he kissed her cheek. 'I didn't realize, I didn't know,' he stammered. 'I would have come before.' *If I had come immediately*, he thought, *I would still have had only a short time with him. Guilt hit him like a blow. But I could at least have told him what I was doing, and about the people I had met. He would have liked that. He was interested in me, unlike Mother. I would have told him about Batsford, and about Mariabella, and about Romanelli who has promised to introduce me to Rossetti. Now it is too late. He will never know.*

He put his hand to his eyes to quell his tears, and

his mother took him by the arm and led him into the study which had been his father's. 'Stay here a moment, James, until you have recovered,' she said quietly. 'Then, when you feel able, come into the sitting-room. The doctor is here, and the undertaker. The funeral service has been arranged for tomorrow.'

'And Gilbert? Where is he?' *Surely*, he thought, *Gilbert should be here making arrangements, not Mother!*

'Gilbert has been here most of the day, he came as soon as he received my message. He sent off a telegram to your lodgings this morning, and has been busy notifying everyone who needed to know. He has only just gone home, you have missed him by only half an hour.'

'Gone home?' He looked at her with dull eyes. 'But this is his home.'

She put a nervous hand to her throat. 'Not any more. He and Harriet are married.'

He stared at her. 'Married?' Anger took place of sorrow and he raised his voice. 'Without telling me? Am I so unimportant that I wasn't told?'

'It was a lapse on Gilbert's part that you were not told,' his mother admitted. 'Your father was very angry with him, but it was because of your father's illness and all the extra work that Gilbert had to do, that he forgot to mention his marriage in his letter to you.'

'Some marriage!' James said bitterly. 'If Gilbert forgot about it. It doesn't bode well for it.'

'I'm sorry, James.' His mother was contrite and it occurred to him that she didn't normally apologize. 'You are right to be upset. Gilbert can't forgive himself for the lapse.'

And nor can I, James resolved. *But at least I know now exactly where I stand. When my father is safely put to rest I shall leave this house and never return.*

It was stiflingly hot in the town, even though it was only just ten o'clock in the morning. At Gilbert's decree, Masterson and Rayner had closed their office for the day out of respect for his father. A large gathering of shipping magnates and business people, as well as employees, were expected at the service at St Andrew's Church in the parish of Kirk Ella, where the parishioners of Anlaby worshipped.

Billy dressed and ate breakfast and walked into the town to meet his parents' carriage at the appointed time. He was early, so he cut across The Land of Green Ginger where the banks were just opening their doors, and crossed the junction of Silver Street and Whitefriargate.

A group of women and children from the workhouse were standing around in random fashion outside the Custom House, and two uniformed policemen were bearing down on them in a highhanded manner, which could only mean, Billy thought, that they would be moved on. He gave a quick glance at their situation and continued on down Trinity House Lane towards the church of The Holy Trinity and the cellars.

He put his fingers inside his high collar and eased it a little. It was so hot; he wrinkled his nostrils, the air was close and muggy, permeated with the smell of blubber and fish oil.

Jenny was sitting at the top of the cellar steps, she had an old frayed blanket around her shoulders and her feet were bare. "Morning, Master Billy.' Her face was pale and she seemed to have lost her normal cheerful manner. 'You're about early,' she commented. 'I'd have thought tha'd be in thy nice office at this time of day.'

'I would be normally, Jenny, but I'm going to a funeral and the office is closed today.'

She pursed her lips in sympathy and nodded.

'Are you not well, Jenny? You look pale. Paler than usual, I mean.' *Though what a fatuous remark*, he thought. *How can anyone look well, living down in that rat hole?*

'I'm all right. It's just that I'm so tired I could sleep for a fortnight. I've been up all night, you see. One of 'bairns down there was sick. He was vomiting all night and I couldn't stand 'stink any longer, so I came up to 'street and thought I'd kip out here.' She shook her head in disapproval. 'But I was bothered all night long. Allus some fellow nudging me with his boot. I got quite ratty in the end. I told 'em straight – get off to Leadenhall Square, I told 'em, plenty of willing girls there, and don't be bothering decent women. By,' she said, an impish grin lighting up her face, 'I could have made a packet o' money, Master Billy, if I'd been willing.'

He froze in disbelief. Jenny didn't seem to realize that she had been lucky. Sooner or later some man would come along who wouldn't take no for an answer and would force himself upon her, regardless of her wishes.

'Jenny?' How could he couch the question?

She looked up at him and smiled. Her eyes were shadowed beneath the lids, but so bright and trusting.

He swallowed. 'Jenny? Erm – have you . . . have you ever been with a man? Has a man ever—'

'Taken me, does tha mean, Master Billy?' she asked candidly. 'No. I've managed to dodge them up to now, though I've had a few narrow squeaks. Mark you,' she folded her arms about her thin chest, 'it can't be all that bad. I heard tell of a friend, she's a bit older than me, about fourteen, and she's got herself fixed up regular. And she's got a room to share with only a couple of others; 'windows are broken and roof leaks, but she's got money for food, and a nice frock to wear for her customers.'

'Jenny!' He spoke on impulse. 'Would you like to move away from here if I could manage it?'

She gazed at him suspiciously. 'Where to?'

'Perhaps as a kitchen maid in my mother's house?'

'She'd never take me!' she said, a touch of derision in her voice. 'Why should she?'

He didn't know why she should, *But I'll ask*, he thought. *Or at least I'll ask Sammi first and see what she thinks.*

'Anyway,' Jenny eyed him questioningly, 'what about 'other bairns who are here? They rely on me. How can I go and leave 'em?'

'You'd have to, Jenny.' What a caring girl she was, in spite of the life she was leading. 'You'd have to think about yourself for once. Surely the others would understand?'

'Would I ride in that little carriage?' Her face was brightening with expectancy.

'Possibly.' He grinned as the idea took hold. 'But think about it and I'll speak to my family about it.'

'All right,' she beamed. 'I'll think about it and ask other 'bairns what they think I should do. They probably wouldn't mind, they'd be glad for me. Some of 'em, anyway.' Her face clouded again. 'Some of 'em are too sick to care one way or other.'

'What's the matter with them?' he asked. 'What sort of sickness have they got?'

She shrugged. 'Vomiting and sweaty – some is worse than others. Must have ate something disagreeable,' she said dryly. 'Too much rich food, Master Billy!'

He set off back, walking along the Old Harbour side where there was a slight breeze blowing, and towards the North Bridge where he had arranged to meet the carriage. It was waiting for him already and he started to run. 'Sorry, Ma, Father. I've just had a meeting with someone. I've been arranging a new maid for Sammi.' He studied the astonishment on their faces. 'I hope you'll approve.'

After the funeral, the family and a few close friends returned to Humber Villa while the company of black carriages, carrying employees and former shipping colleagues of Isaac Rayner, snaked its way back through the villages into Hull.

Some of the men withdrew into the smoking-room,

but the close family gathered in the drawing-room and talked quietly while they ate and drank the refreshments which had been provided for them.

James stood slightly apart and observed them. His mother appeared to be remarkably calm, yet when in church, as he sat at one side of her and Gilbert at the other, he had noticed that, although her face was unseen below the thick black veil, her shoulders shook and her hands holding the prayer book trembled.

Sammi had caught his eye once or twice during the service as she'd sat in the pew across the aisle and had given him a sympathetic nod. He knew that he would have to speak to her before she left and tell her of his decision about the child. Her father, Uncle William, was very sombre, he seemed to feel the loss of James's father very keenly; James had observed him several times during the service, surreptitiously blowing his nose with a large white handkerchief, and Aunt Ellen taking his arm and patting it.

Uncle Arthur, on the other hand, who had made the journey from York, was quite composed; he had a glass of wine in his hand and was chatting to someone about financial shares, and which were the best to buy, while his wife sat nearby, sipping tea. Gilbert was busying himself playing host, and James thought that the role suited him well. They had barely had the chance to do more than greet each other, and he guessed that Gilbert was embarrassed over the wedding lapse. Harriet was sitting in a corner talking to someone and James decided that the nicest thing about Gilbert was Harriet. But he needed to talk to Gilbert about financial arrangements their father might have made; he had very little money, the fifty pounds sent to him was almost gone. His father's lawyer had been at the service and he assumed that his father's will would be read shortly.

Uncle Arthur turned his attention to Tom. 'Any

news of your brother, young Tom? Has he written yet?'

'No, sir. Not yet. But he will, in time,' Tom answered firmly. 'When he has something to tell us.'

Arthur grunted at the response and then confronted James. 'So, James. How is life in London? Starving yet, are you? Isn't that what you artist fellows do?' He clapped a hand on his shoulder. 'Wearing hair long in London, are they? I thought it was the fashion to have it short these days, like Gilbert's?'

Gilbert looked up as he passed, his curly hair was cut short and parted in the centre.

James threw back a lock of dark hair. 'I don't go in for following fashion, Uncle, I have my mind set on other things.'

His uncle pulled a face. 'Oh, of course. An *aesthete*! But you'll be giving up all this arty nonsense now, won't you? You'll be joining the family firm and giving your brother a hand?'

'Why should James give up his career?' William chipped in. 'Give him a chance, Arthur, he's only just got started.'

James cast a grateful glance at Uncle William. 'I'm not cut out for business. I'll leave that to Gilbert. Anyway, Billy has joined the firm, I don't see that I am needed.'

'Not for long,' Billy muttered out of the corner of his mouth and added as James turned towards him, 'I'm not cut out for it either.'

'Well, I suppose if you are really dead set on it,' Arthur pursed his mouth, 'perhaps we shall have to see what we can do to promote you.'

James bristled. He didn't need to be promoted. He would get where he wanted with his talent, if he had any, or not at all.

'Now let me think. Who do we know, my dear?' Arthur turned to his wife. 'Ideally, he needs a patron.'

'Thank you, it's kind of you,' James interrupted. 'But I already have a patron who has seen my work, and I have the promise of support from a well-respected art critic.'

'Indeed!' Arthur's attitude was one of disbelief. 'So soon?'

'She is Madame Sinclair, and he is Massimiliano Romanelli.' James rolled the name majestically and eloquently around his tongue. 'He's from Florence.'

'Romanelli?' Aunt Henrietta said curiously. 'Did we not once meet someone by that name, Arthur?'

'Oh, indeed you did, Aunt.' James turned to her. 'I almost forgot, but he did mention that he'd met you in York, many years ago.'

'Well, bless my soul,' Arthur broke in. 'So we did. The very same fellow. How extraordinary! You remember, Mildred, don't you? You remember the Italian fellow, Romanelli? Didn't he come here a time or two?'

James's mother, who had not been taking part in this conversation, had nevertheless overheard and turned her head towards their group. 'What?' Her hand fluttered to her neck, a nervous gesture which James noticed she had been using frequently. 'Who did you say?' Her fingers strayed to her mouth.

'Romanelli!' Arthur boomed. 'Didn't he come over here to see you and Isaac? Wanted to paint the river or ships or somesuch?'

'Yes,' she whispered. 'What about him?'

'It's just that I've met him,' James explained. 'Through my patron. He's quite taken with my work. He's promised to introduce me to Rossetti.'

Mildred bit anxiously on her lips, she was very pale and her hands were shaking.

'You don't look well, Mildred.' Ellen took pity on her sister-in-law. 'I think the day has been too much for you. Would you like us to leave so that you can go and rest?'

'No. No, please don't go. I shall be spending enough time alone in the future. I'm grateful that you are all here now.' Her gaze was drawn back to

301

James. He had his back partly turned to the window; the curtains, tightly drawn before the funeral as was the custom, had now been opened, and his profile was etched in silhouette. She drew in a succession of short sharp breaths. '*Massimo*,' she whispered, and only James heard and understood the name and wondered why his mother would use the familiar shortened first name when he had only used it in full.

'He said he remembered you very well, Mother,' he said softly, realizing that she was unwell. 'He asked if you were still as beautiful as you once were.'

'Did he?' Her eyes were vague, her voice a mere breath. 'And he? How does he look?'

'Well, his hair is dark, but he has a lot of silver streaks in it, particularly in his beard and sideburns. He's quite distinguished-looking, I suppose – very Italian, with his long nose and dark eyes.'

'Ah. Yes.' A smile hovered briefly on her lips. 'He used to joke about his Roman nose.'

'My patron, Madame Mariabella Sinclair, jokes about her nose too.' He smiled tenderly as he thought of her. 'But she is nevertheless very beautiful.'

'Mariabella?' His mother's hand again fluttered to her throat and played with the string of jet around it.

James nodded, aware that all of his relations were now listening with interest. 'She is Italian, married to an Englishman. Romanelli was her guardian until her marriage to Sinclair, it was she who introduced me to him.'

'And so she is promoting you?' Arthur commented. 'Is she very rich?'

James bridled and felt his face flush. 'She is not promoting me, Uncle,' he said thinly. 'She is helping me to get started by introducing me to the right people, people who know about Art, like Romanelli.'

Arthur shrugged. 'Sounds like the same thing to me.'

Mildred rose shakily to her feet. 'If you will excuse

me, I will, after all, go and lie down. Please feel free to stay as long as you wish,' she assured the relatives and guests. 'Gilbert and Anne will attend to you. James!' She put out her hand. 'Would you help me upstairs?'

28

Tom sat by his father's bedside in the parlour and told him of the events of the funeral, then, saying that he was tired, he said goodnight to him and to George and Betsy who were in the kitchen, and went up to his room. He sat on the edge of the bed. The house felt empty without Sammi, even though she had only been gone a few short hours, and both his father and George had said that they were missing her already. Betsy hadn't commented, but then Betsy didn't seem to be saying much at all lately, having become tearful and morose since their father's accident. Tonight though, she seemed to have recovered a nervous energy, busying herself constantly since supper, and telling him and George that they could get off to bed and that she would lock up when she had finished doing what she had to do.

Sammi had collected her belongings after they had returned from the funeral, and Aunt Ellen had come inside and waited for her; Tom thought that they both seemed preoccupied.

'Will you be able to manage, Betsy?' Aunt Ellen had asked. 'I'll find you some more help as soon as I can.'

'Don't worry, Aunt Ellen.' Betsy was much more cheerful than usual. 'I'm feeling much better. I can manage well enough, with Nancy's help.'

But I can't manage, Tom thought, as he leant with his chin in his hands. *At least I can, but I don't want to. I miss Sammi so much already. How can I cope for the rest of my life without her?* For he was in no doubt whatsoever that Sammi was destined for someone other than him; someone with more money, prestige, and position. He looked at his hands and turned them over. They were strong hands, used to rough work, brown and hard and with his right thumb flattened, just as his father's was.

He sighed and got up and opened the window wider to look out across the night sky. There were few clouds, which promised a fine day tomorrow, and he breathed in the heady summer night air. There was a scent of honeysuckle, lavender and roses, a sweetness which reminded him so much of her; and an earthy smell of harrowed earth, the rich balmy smell of grain and, blowing on the slight breeze, the salty aroma of the sea. He leaned on the window-sill and looked across to where Monkston lay. *She doesn't notice me, of course,* he reflected. *I've always been here. I've always been part of her life, one of her kinsfolk, and although we were always close, I have been just as one of her brothers. And today, at Uncle Isaac's funeral, someone upset her and I suspect that it was James. He said something to her out in the garden – but what? I felt jealous, angry even, when I saw her with James, and I don't know why. But they had had their heads together as they walked around the garden, and I felt excluded. Yet,* he mused, *when she came inside again, she came across to me and sat beside me as if she wanted to confide, but didn't know what to say. Everyone was on edge, understandable under the circumstances – James, Gilbert, Aunt Ellen, Aunt Mildred more than anyone. There was a strange atmosphere.*

As he started to undress he thought of Mark, which he did most nights, and wondered where he was, thinking that, if it hadn't been for Mark's chance flippant remark, he might never have opened his own eyes to Sammi. *She's so young,* he mused, as he slipped between the sheets and lay wide-eyed in the darkness, with his arms behind his head. *She must never suspect how I feel; yet I sometimes think that everyone in the whole world must know, that even Sammi wonders, and that is why she questions me. Have we lost something, Tom? she asked after Gilbert's wedding, and I kissed her hand in reply, when really I wanted to hold her in my arms. Yet I would never want her to suspect that what she had lost was a friend, and found a lover.*

Betsy smiled up at Luke in the darkness of the copse. 'I've missed you, Luke. I have to admit it.'

He grinned down at her. 'Tha misses what I do to thee. Go on, say it. Tha likes what I do.'

She sighed and drew him closer. 'Yes. I shouldn't, but I do.' She nibbled his ear. 'My da told me again, we can court if we want. Do you want?'

He pulled away. 'I don't know,' he muttered. 'I've told thee afore, I'm not ready to settle down. I've no money for one thing.'

'But we could have an understanding, like people do, until you were ready.'

Luke gazed at her anxiously. 'Is that what tha wants, Betsy? I never thought that tha did.'

She sat up and brushed the grass from her skirt and contemplated. 'No. It isn't. I'm fond of you, Luke, but I don't think that I'm ready for settling down either.'

He put his arms around her and squeezed her. 'Tha's best thing that's ever happened to me, Betsy. I'm greedy for thee. I can never wait to see thee and hold thee.' He ran his big hands so gently and sensuously over her. 'You're beautiful; so round and soft. I could eat thee.' He kissed her passionately on the mouth and she pulled him down towards her. 'Maybe one day, eh? Maybe one day we'll get wed, and then we can do this all 'time.'

'But then we won't want to, Luke,' she mumbled beneath his lips, and eased herself slightly to move his crushing weight from her. 'I don't think married folk do.'

Sammi sat by her window, red-eyed and drained of weeping tears which she had held back until she reached the sanctity of her own room. It was all so familiar and well loved, and it was only now that she realized how much she had been missing her home. She had missed, without realizing it, the spaciousness of the rooms, the sweep of the wide staircase, the smell of polish on the floors and furniture and the soughing of the sea which was so constant. And yet there was a turmoil inside her, an emptiness and unhappiness which wasn't wholly the fault of James, who had so cruelly and decisively told her that Adam was most definitely not his and he could not therefore accept any responsibility towards him.

'But how do you know now, James, when you didn't know before?' she had asked, as with a terrible understanding, she realized that if James had been duped and Adam wasn't his, then no-one else would claim responsibility for him.

'I can't possibly tell you that, Sammi.' A blush had come up on his face. 'But I know.'

As they came back into Aunt Mildred's house from the garden, she had seen Tom standing on the steps by the door and he had looked angry about something. And if it hadn't been for that intense expression on his face and realizing that he had some troubles of his own, she would have confided in him; it had been on the tip of her tongue to do so as she sat beside him.

She had wanted to cry when she left the mill house. Uncle Thomas had patted her hand and although Tom hadn't said much, she wondered if he would miss her not being there. *I do hope so*, she'd thought as they'd driven away, and she'd turned to see him standing at the gate, with Betsy and George waving at the door, *for I shall surely miss him.*

How foolish I am, she pondered as she leaned on the window-sill and breathed in the sharp salty air and felt the breeze ruffle her hair. *I shall see them all again in only a few days, but it won't somehow be the same.*

*   *   *

Sammi tiptoed into Victoria's bedroom early the next morning. A kettle of water on a burner at the side of the bed was steaming gently to help her breathe. Victoria was hot and restless, her chest heaved and sighed in an effort to draw a deep, satisfying breath.

'I need some sea air,' she heaved. 'It's the only thing to cure me.'

Sammi got up and opened the window wider; Victoria always said that when she was ill, but, she thought, *we can't get any nearer to the sea than we are. We're practically sitting in the water now.*

'I wish Grandmama Sarah was here. She would know what to do.'

Sammi turned at her sister's breathless words. Victoria had always had a special empathy with their grandmother, who made up her own potions and medications for anyone – villager or landowner – who was sick, and her reputation was widespread. When she had died, Victoria, more than any of them, was devastated and took to long solitary walks where, she said, she felt she could be close to her once more.

'I'll take you for a walk along the sands,' Sammi promised now. 'Just as soon as you are feeling better and able to get up.'

'Sammi?' Victoria whispered. 'Will you bring Adam that I might see him?' Their mother entered the room as she spoke and Victoria gave her a weak smile. 'I would like to see him.'

Sammi and her mother exchanged glances and Sammi felt her heart sink. She would have to tell her what James had said. It wouldn't be fair otherwise. 'Yes,' she answered dully. 'I will bring him.'

'Mama!' Victoria held out her hand to her mother, who sat beside her and bathed her forehead with a cool cloth. 'Mama! If I should die, will you let Sammi bring Adam here to take my place?'

Their mother gave a start and put her hand to her mouth; Sammi felt tears welling up beneath her eyelids and spill over and down her cheeks.

'I'm quite serious, Mama, and you must try not to be sad. I shall be with Grandmama and she will take care of me. And it will be good to know that Adam is with a family who will love him rather than with strangers.'

Sammi watched with streaming eyes as their mother, too choked to speak, patted Victoria's hand and murmured something.

'But you're not going to die, Victoria.' Sammi, her lips trembling so much that she could hardly speak, knelt by the bed. 'We won't let you. Will we, Mama?'

Her mother got up and walked across to the window and looked out as she sought to overcome her emotion. Then she turned back to the bed and with bright eyes and a cheerful manner, said, 'Of course not, Victoria. You mustn't think such morbid thoughts.'

'They're not morbid, Mama, but I must plan, just in case.' Her face was pale and her hair hung in strands around her thin cheekbones, but her eyes were wide and determined.

Her mother didn't answer for a moment, then she said, 'This has gone on long enough. You mustn't worry about Adam, either of you. It will be resolved.'

29

During the course of that morning, Ellen's house-keeper, her lips in a tight thin line, asked to speak privately to her. Martha drew herself up straight and folded her hands in front of her. 'It's like this, ma-am. And it's better it comes from me as knows it isn't true, as for you hear it from some busybody.'

'Very well, Martha,' Ellen sighed. 'If it's something I should know, you'd better tell me.'

'Folks are talking in Tillington, ma-am. Tongues have been wagging ever since Mrs Bishop took 'child on, but since Miss Sammi went to stay at 'mill house with 'Fosters it's got worse, and it's just come to my notice, for nobody would have dared say such a thing to my face, that now they're saying that 'bairn is Miss Sammi's and his fayther is Master Tom Foster.'

'Surely no-one would think such a thing!' She was shocked and angry, her worst fears realized.

'Folks can be very petty when they want to be, ma-am, particularly if they see somebody set above them succumb to 'perils of 'flesh.'

Martha, who had never been married or strayed from the path of virtue, set her lips even more firmly together; Ellen thanked her for her confidence and loyalty, and hardened her resolve to visit Gilbert the very next day.

As Martha turned to leave, Sammi appeared in the doorway. She moved aside for Martha and then said, 'Mama. I need to speak to you.'

Her mother stretched out her hand to invite her in to her sitting-room, which everyone referred to as 'Grandmama's room', even though Sammi's mother had now claimed it as her own. It was the room in which Grandmother Sarah had been born and which she used to say was a special place that held many memories. It caught the morning sunlight and, although they had moved out the old tester bed and replaced it with an upholstered sofa, some of the old chests of drawers and wooden chests were still there, gleaming with beeswax polish which the maids so assiduously applied, and smelling of lavender and rosemary which still lingered within the drawers.

'Yes, we need to talk, Sammi.'

Sammi leaned on the window-sill and looked out over the garden towards the sea. The day was bright and the sea, with its glistening wave crests, appeared to be just below the paddock where Boreas was grazing. 'It's getting nearer, isn't it?' she said. 'Sometimes I don't notice it, and then suddenly I realize that the band of water below my window is wider than it was and that means that more of the cliff has gone over.'

Her mother came and stood beside her. 'Field House is right on the edge. Your father told me and I went to look at it the other day. It will go over this winter.'

Sammi felt so sad. Field House had been the home of Grandmother Sarah's parents, the Fosters, when they had first come out to Monkston from Hull. It had been empty for years, but she and Billy and Victoria used to play in it when they were children. They would pretend that it was their own house and furnished it with discarded furniture and wooden boxes, and once Billy made a fire in the grate and burnt his hand. Then they were banned from using it, their father saying that it was no longer safe and that he would lock the door on the memories and keep them fast.

'Mama. I have something to tell you.' Sammi clasped and unclasped her hands. 'It's about Adam – and James.' She took a deep breath and said huskily,

'Adam isn't James's child! He told me most emphatically that he wasn't. Therefore he said that he couldn't be expected to contribute towards him. Not that he has anyway,' she added. 'Not a penny piece!'

'I know,' her mother said quietly.

'You know? How can you know? I have only just found out – James told me at Uncle Isaac's funeral. He hasn't told anyone else!' Sammi stared at her mother incredulously.

'I, er, I said I knew, yet I haven't any proof. I mean, I guessed as much. Almost from the beginning.' Her mother fingered the collar of her gown.

'But why didn't you say? You let me become fond of him when all along you thought that he didn't belong to James!' Sammi's voice rose and she couldn't hide the anguish at her mother's seeming insensitivity.

'What was I to do, Sammi? Throw the little mite onto the care of the parish? Send him to the workhouse? You had already left home because of him.'

'I'm sorry.' Sammi bent her head. 'I'm so miserable, Mama. I just don't know what to do.'

'People are talking,' said her mother. 'They are saying that the child is yours. The matter has to be resolved!'

A flush came to Sammi's cheeks. 'Gossip isn't worth listening to!'

'It is if it affects your life! Your chances of a good marriage are already diminished, you must realize that?'

'I would not consider marrying a man who did not trust or believe in me,' Sammi said hotly. 'I will stay single for ever if a man cannot take me as I am. And what choice have I?' she demanded. 'James has disowned him. I can't abandon him now. You said yourself—' Something occurred to her. 'But, but – if you guessed that he didn't belong to James, then does that mean you know who the father is?' She gazed blankly at her mother.

A hesitation showed briefly on her mother's face. 'I have no proof as yet. It is merely a suspicion, therefore,' she added swiftly, as Sammi opened her mouth to respond, 'therefore it would be unfair to voice my supposition. I will tell you when I am certain.'

Sammi sat silently as she absorbed this revelation. 'It still doesn't help the situation, does it? Whoever it is, if he hasn't been brave enough to admit responsibility before, he's not going to want to take Adam now. He'll probably just pay for him to be put somewhere.' She shook her head and whispered, 'He will be out of our hands. He maybe won't live in the cellars like Billy's children, but he'll still go to strangers.'

'I don't know, Sammi,' said her mother. 'I just don't know.'

Ellen told Sammi that she was going to Hull the next day. 'We need new linen and a few other things,' she explained and was taken aback when Sammi said she would like to come, too, as she wanted to see Billy. She couldn't think of any reason for refusing her. Victoria was up and dressed and said she would be perfectly all right without either of them, and she reasoned that, if Sammi was meeting Billy, there would be a legitimate reason for calling on Gilbert. She had told Gilbert at his father's funeral that she would be calling on him, and he had stammered that he would be glad to see her as soon as he had sorted out his father's affairs.

Well, he has had time now. I'm quite sure that Isaac would have left everything in order, she thought, as she waited to be shown into his office.

Billy had taken Sammi off to a coffee house, so Ellen arranged to see her later in the day. 'When I've finished all my calls, Sammi,' she said. 'There's no rush.'

'Aunt Ellen. Please come up,' Gilbert greeted her

from the top of the stairs. 'How good of you to drop in.' He kissed her on the cheek and complimented her on how nice she looked.

What a charmer you are, Gilbert, she mused. *We can't help but like you. You mean so well and can't help but get into scrapes and muddles.* 'How is Harriet? And your mother?' she said pleasantly. 'And have you heard from James?'

'We haven't heard from James, but Harriet is very well indeed, and Mother seems to be improving daily, she is much more positive than she was. She has asked if we would like to live out at Anlaby with her and Anne. The house will be too big for her if Anne should get married, but although Mother promised to keep herself quite separate, Harriet is not so very keen on the idea.'

'I should think not, indeed,' Ellen murmured. 'You have a dear little house of your own, and so handy for the company.'

'It's just the expense, Aunt Ellen,' he said with an imploring look. 'You have no idea how expensive it is setting up a home these days.'

She smiled. 'It always was, Gilbert. But you are surely in a better position now than you were previously?'

'I shall be,' he said. 'Just as soon as the bank situation has been attended to. We are changing our banker. I have discussed it with Uncle William and Arthur. I have been dissatisfied with the previous bankers for some time; we are going to use Billington's bank. We shall get a good deal from them!'

So, new brooms sweep clean, she thought. *I hope it bodes well for us; our fortune is in your hands too, Gilbert.* 'You know, of course, why I have come, Gilbert?' she said directly. 'It was not to discuss business.'

For a moment she thought he was going to deny her, then he shifted his gaze away from her and looked down at his desk. 'I can imagine why you have come.'

'I have waited, Gilbert, for an approach from you,' she said, a hint of reproach in her voice.

'I know. I have put it off. There has been so much to do; Father's illness, our marriage, then the funeral—'

'I do understand.' She was calm and patient, but determined. 'That is why I haven't pressed you. It hasn't been easy for you, I know. We all make mistakes in our lives, everyone of us, but we sometimes have to acknowledge them. You do not deny, then, that Adam is your son?'

Gilbert took a deep breath and then looked up at her. *There is no denying it*, she thought. *It is so obvious that I don't understand why I am the only one who sees it.*

'No, Aunt. I do not deny it. He is mine.'

There was a silence between them; it was as if a heavy weight had been lifted and the problem beneath it could now be examined and resolved.

'But I don't want Harriet to know,' he pleaded. 'I can't bear to think that she might turn against me. I will support him as soon as I am able – if we could find someone who wants a child, I would do all I could to help them.'

'Would you want to see him?'

'I do want to see him.' He stared into space. 'Please don't imagine that I never think about him, for I do; ever since the day he was brought to our home, on that very first night when I heard him cry. I went to Sammi's room,' he said quietly and candidly, and she wasn't shocked. 'And I saw him there, and I knew that he was mine, and I remembered his mother and how beautiful she was.

'It wasn't shameful or sordid, Aunt Ellen. I loved her that night, and I think that she loved me.' He lowered his head and whispered, 'I looked for her, but I couldn't find her. I don't know what I would have done if I had, for I was promised to Harriet; yet I felt bound to her.'

'I'm so sorry, Gilbert. So very sorry.' Her heart went out to him. *He is not bad,* she thought, *merely weak.*

'But I know that although I might want to see him, I cannot; if he is to have a life without me then I must deny myself that pleasure.'

'So you will look for a foster home for him?'

He looked at her in alarm. 'But then it will get out! If I start making enquiries here in Hull everyone will know.'

She watched him steadily. 'So what do you propose?'

'Well, I thought that perhaps you might . . . ? What about the woman who is nursing him now?'

'No,' she said firmly. 'He has to leave Holderness. Rumours are flying that he is Sammi's child.'

He looked shocked. 'Oh. I'm sorry. I never thought—'

'No, you wouldn't, and neither did Sammi; but her whole future could be affected by this.'

He nodded. 'Yes,' he muttered, 'I do see. Does she know?' he asked. 'About me?'

'Not yet. But she must be told, as must James. *He* has told her that he no longer thinks that he is the father, so it won't be long before she puts two and two together. She won't be pleased, Gilbert, to think that she and James have been duped, especially by a member of family.' She rose to leave. 'If I make enquiries about a foster home, it will fuel the rumour about Sammi, so the decision about his future must be yours; but there are two stipulations that I will make. One, that I or someone I nominate will monitor the home, and the other is that James must be told.'

He clenched his hands together and pressed them to his mouth as he deliberated. 'Yes. James has suffered enough on my account. There is nothing else for it,' he muttered.

She nodded and rose to leave. '*We* won't betray you

to Harriet, Gilbert. Not if we can help it. That decision is between you and your conscience.'

'I don't know what to do, Sammi.' Billy watched as Sammi poured the coffee into small white cups. 'I can't stop thinking about those children. They refuse to go into the children's homes, and some of them are quite good places, you know, they're not all harsh, though they are strict and regimented.'

'I suppose they want to stay together too, do they?' Sammi looked at her brother over the rim of her cup.

'Yes, brothers and sisters do, but mostly, you know, they need to be directed. They're quite sharp some of them, they would make good traders or artisans if only someone would teach them.'

'Can I meet them?' she asked. 'Only don't tell Mama; I'm in enough trouble as it is over Adam. He doesn't belong to James after all,' she confided. 'Mama thinks she knows who the father is, but she won't say, not until she's sure.'

'Good heavens! I wonder who?' Billy looked astonished. 'Does he look like anyone we know?'

'Yes.' Sammi said grimly. 'He looks like me.'

'So . . . ?'

She raised her eyebrows. 'There appears to have been a terrible mistake, Billy. I can't say any more than that.'

He took her down to North Church Side, but the children were not out in the street. 'They might be sleeping,' he said. 'They stay up late begging at the theatres and concerts and sleep during the day. Pity,' he glanced down the cellar steps, 'I especially wanted you to meet Jenny. She's the young girl I told you about. I didn't choose the right moment though, did I?' He grinned.

'Hardly,' Sammi agreed. 'Mama wasn't in the mood for discussing any more waifs and strays, let alone bringing one home.'

They turned away and walked back towards the

317

Market Place, when suddenly they heard screaming. 'Get tha dirty hands off me!' a voice was crying. 'Don't touch me. I'll have 'law on thee.'

'It's Jenny,' Billy said. 'Come on!'

Sammi hurried after him as he ran towards the King William statue, where Jenny was struggling with a man, and a crowd of onlookers were enjoying the scene.

Billy pushed his way through the crowd and laid his hand on the man's arm. 'What are you doing? Leave her alone.'

The man looked Billy up and down, then released his grip on Jenny. 'It's just a bit o' fun, mister. Nowt else. She's allus hanging round here, she's waiting for summat or somebody.'

'I'm not waiting for thee,' Jenny glared. 'Nobody puts their hands up my skirt!'

The man raised his hand threateningly, but before he could do or say anything, Sammi's parasol was laid across his arm.

'I think you had better go,' she said coldly. 'Before I call the constable. I saw you molesting this child and will gladly be a witness in court if necessary.'

The crowd started to disperse; the fun was over and no-one wanted to be part of any court procedure. The man shrugged and started to walk off. 'Little bitch!' he spat at Jenny. 'Just let me catch thee out here again.'

They walked back with her to the cellars and Sammi was conscious of Jenny casting surreptitious glances up at her, at her gown and bonnet, then smoothing down her own torn and dirty dress as if to tidy it, and running her fingers through her tangled hair.

'Goodbye, Jenny,' she said. 'I hope you're not bothered again.'

'Thank you, miss.' Jenny bobbed her knee. She looked at Billy and then again at Sammi. 'Did – did Master Billy say, did he say about—' She hesitated.

'Yes?' Sammi smiled encouragingly.

She shrugged and looked disappointed. 'It doesn't matter.'

'I'll see you again, Jenny,' Sammi reassured her. 'I'll come and talk to you, if I may?'

Jenny looked at her with parted mouth and adoring eyes. 'Oh, yes please, miss. Any time.'

Sammi and Billy looked at each other as they walked away. 'Oh dear,' Sammi said. 'Whatever are we to do?'

30

What Sammi and Billy did was to ask their mother if Sammi could stay over in Hull. She would stay at Billy's lodgings; Mrs Parker wouldn't mind in the least, Billy said, and she would call on Harriet, *For*, Sammi appealed, *I would like to become better acquainted with her*. Their mother agreed, not least because she was anxious to avoid any questioning by Sammi for the time being, and so she returned home alone and the carriage would return to collect Sammi in two days' time.

Sammi called on Harriet that very day, hoping that she was at home, which she was, and therefore justifying her reason for staying, should her mother enquire. Gilbert arrived while she was there and appeared ill at ease, though he put on a show of welcome, and, she thought, seemed relieved when she refused Harriet's offer that she should stay with them.

Sammi thanked her and started to explain that Billy had arranged for her to stay in his lodgings, when the doorbell rang and there was Billy himself.

'Mrs Parker is preparing supper now,' he said. 'I called to tell her you wished to stay and she's delighted.'

'Oh, such a pity, Sammi. You could have stayed with us, couldn't she, Gilbert?' Harriet was crestfallen. 'It would have been so nice.'

'Indeed, indeed,' Gilbert bumbled and Sammi looked at him curiously and promised that next time she was coming to Hull she would write and tell Harriet and would come to stay.

'What they need – the children, I mean – is a sponsor.' Billy took Sammi's arm as they walked to his lodgings. 'They need a place where they can feel at home and learn a trade. We need the help of someone philanthropic, someone with money and influence. Public-spirited enough to see that the way these children live is a disgrace on our society.'

'It's a pity you are not ten years older, Billy.' Sammi's manner was abstracted. 'If you had made your mark you would be the perfect person for it.'

'Yes.' He stared straight ahead. 'It's what I would like to do.' He stopped walking and turned to her. 'It's what I *will* do,' he said emphatically. 'I will do it, Sammi. But I can't do it alone. I'll have to find somebody to help me. But who?'

'You're serious, Billy?' She saw the earnest expression on his face. 'What's Pa going to say? He's expecting you to take up his shares in Masterson and Rayner!'

Billy smiled. 'Oh, I'll have to stay for a while to earn my living while I'm planning. But the first thing is to find someone of influence who can help me get started.'

'Gilbert!' Sammi breathed. 'He's the one!'

'What a joke, Sammi,' Billy laughed. 'He hasn't a sou! He's spending all of his money on his house. Besides, he's not in the least philanthropic.'

She shook her head. 'No. I didn't mean that.' She drew her brows together in a frown, then blinked rapidly as if to clear a mist. 'Gilbert,' she said, 'can help us! He'll know men of influence; there are surely many in the shipping industry?'

'Mm – yes,' Billy agreed. 'But will he? Will he be willing to introduce them?'

She gave a thin smile. 'Oh, yes, I'm sure he will. In fact I'm absolutely positive!'

'Gilbert!' Billy popped his head around Gilbert's door. 'Sorry to bother you, but Sammi and I wanted a word with you, but Sammi insists that I say if you are too busy we will call on you at home. We have something to ask you.'

Gilbert bit on his lip. 'Erm – what – erm? Well, no, we'd better have a meeting here. I'd rather not bother Harriet.'

Billy was puzzled. 'No? She might be interested in what we have to say, Gilbert. She's a very caring person.'

'No.' Gilbert was brusque, yet awkward. 'Ask Sammi to come up.' He muttered under his breath, 'We'd better get it over with.'

Sammi sat in the chair which was offered to her and smiled in a very friendly manner, but Gilbert chose to stand and tapped his fingers on the desk top. 'We're sorry to interrupt your busy day, Gilbert,' she said. 'But you are the only one we can think of with the answer to our problem.'

Gilbert sank down onto his chair. 'All right, Sammi,' he said wearily, 'what is it that you want to know?'

'I can't believe how helpful Gilbert was,' Billy said for about the third time since the meeting with Gilbert.

Sammi looked out from the carriage window and nodded thoughtfully. 'Yes, he was indeed. He couldn't have been more willing. You'll let me know what happens if you manage to get an interview with Mr Pearson?'

He agreed that he would, the minute he heard; he waved her off and went back into the office. *Amazing*, he thought. *I've never known Gilbert to be so accommodating and agreeable. And if he can arrange for me to meet the Mayor, Mr Pearson, I'm sure he's just the person to help.*

Billy had explained to Gilbert that he needed to meet men of business who would give not only of their wealth, but also of their time and experience. 'For what is wanted,' he'd said, 'is a proper charitable trust, and I have neither the experience nor the knowledge to set this up.'

Gilbert had seemed quite eager to help, and his face broke into wreaths of smiles when he suddenly exclaimed that he knew just the man: Zachariah Pearson, the Mayor of Hull and a great philanthropist. 'He might not be able to assist personally,' Gilbert had said, 'but he will know who to ask. My father knew him well, of course, and I also know him. I'm sure he will agree to meet you, Billy.' He'd drawn himself up and exhaled a deep breath. 'I'll do what I can.'

Sammi had stood up from her chair and looked him in the eyes. 'I'm sure that you will, Gilbert. We're counting on you.'

He'd lowered his eyes for a second, then raising them, he said softly, 'You have my word on it, Sammi.'

'Johnson!' Sammi called up to the coachman as they pulled out of the yard. 'I have a call to make before we go home.'

'Yes, Miss Sammi. Where to?'

'Will you go down by the Holy Trinity Church? I need to see someone.'

'Aye, miss, all right, though it'll be busy. I'll have difficulty getting through 'market.'

Johnson manoeuvered the carriage through the Market Place, calling to the traders to move their sacks of produce and shouting to the crowd, who were milling around the stalls, to get out of the way. He turned down by the side of the church and went on a few paces before stopping.

Sammi put her head out of the window. 'A bit further, Johnson. Near that old warehouse.'

Johnson drew to a halt and jumped down to open the door. 'There's nothing here, Miss Sammi. Who is it you want to see?'

'Someone who lives in these cellars, Johnson. A young girl. I want to see if she's in.'

Johnson stared at her. 'Oh, no miss. I can't let you

323

do that. What would Mr Rayner say? He'd have my hide.'

Sammi contemplated. That was perfectly true. Her father trusted Johnson implicitly with his wife and daughters. He would consider that he'd let him down if she should do anything untoward. She couldn't really compromise him. 'I suppose you wouldn't knock on the door either, would you, Johnson?'

Johnson glanced down the cellar steps to the battered door. 'No, Miss Sammi. I wouldn't.'

'Then we'll just have to sit and wait,' she said and settled herself back against the cushions. 'I just hope she isn't too long.'

Johnson cast a look of resignation at his young mistress. 'Ten minutes only, Miss Sammi, and then we'll have to be off. 'Master's expecting us back before 'day's out,' and climbed back up onto the box.

Five minutes only had gone by when Sammi became aware of movement behind the door. Gaps between the strips of cardboard became wider, and she could see eyes peering out, then almost before she could blink, the door shifted, opened, then closed just as swiftly, and Jenny appeared at the carriage door.

'Here! What do you want?' she heard Johnson shout. 'Get off! We want no beggars.'

Sammi opened the carriage door and stepped out. 'It's all right, Johnson. This is who I was waiting for.'

Jenny smiled up at her. 'Hello, miss.'

'Hello, Jenny. I said I would come and see you, didn't I? I'm on my way home now, but I wanted to say good-bye.'

'Do you live by 'sea, miss, like Master Billy?'

'Yes, I do.' Sammi scrutinized the girl; her features, though thin, were animated and lively beneath the grime.

'Wish I could see it. 'Sea I mean. Master Billy asked me—' She stopped and looked away.

'What did he ask you, Jenny?'

324

She scoured the dust with her bare toes. 'He said, would I like to go and live somewhere else – as a maid, I think he said, and I asked 'others if they would mind and they said no they wouldn't.' She lifted her gaze to Sammi and blinked. 'He said he would ask his ma, but maybe he forgot.'

'No, he didn't forget. But we were on our way to a funeral and our mother said to ask her later.' Sammi gave a small smile as she thought of her mother's actual reply. 'For heaven's sake, Billy, don't you think I've enough to think of at the moment?'

'Would you like me to ask her?' she said.

'Oh, yes, miss.' Jenny's mouth opened wide. 'I'll just get me things,' and she turned on her heel and shot down the steps.

'But, I didn't mean – Oh dear!' Sammi gazed after her. 'I think she misunderstood me.'

Johnson got down from the box as Jenny lugged a dirty brown paper bag towards them and a crowd of ragged children crowded behind her.

'You were not thinking of letting the young person ride inside the carriage, were you, Miss Sammi?' he said firmly. 'Your mother would not be pleased.'

'Perhaps not, Johnson.' Sammi hid a smile. Jenny was probably crawling with fleas. Perhaps some of them would blow off, she thought, if she sat on the outside, though Johnson would probably object if he could.

He helped Sammi back into the carriage. 'Where do you wish me to take the young person, Miss Sammi?'

She stared unblinkingly at him. 'Home, please, Johnson,' and as he gazed stoically back at her, she added, 'You'd better not sit too close.'

31

When James arrived back in London, his first call was to Mariabella. *Mariabella!* he breathed. *I just can't wait to see you.*

But she wasn't there. She'd gone away, her maid told him, she thought to Brighton, she said, when he questioned her; and no, she didn't know for how long.

'Damn,' he muttered. 'What shall I do?' His mind raced on various possibilities. *Should I go to Brighton and look for her? But what if Sinclair is there? Or Romanelli?* And the latter possibility bothered him more than the former, for he was still a little unsure of the relationship between her and Romanelli.

He moped around the studio for a few days and then, because the weather was fine, he took his canvas and went off to the London Docks, where he settled down to paint the busy scene of shipping – of canvas sails flapping, of steamers and their passengers, of porters and their sleds – and soon became engrossed in his subject.

It was here, three days later, that a shadow fell across his canvas. He didn't turn around, for passers-by occasionally stopped to look and he knew that eventually they would walk on again; but this time, though the shadow moved so as not to interrupt his light, he was aware that someone was still standing there by his shoulder.

He turned and squinted up. Romanelli! 'How good to see you.' He started to rise, his paint-stained hand held out.

Romanelli patted his shoulder. 'Don't get up,

please. I do not wish to disturb you. I was told by Batsford that I might find you here.'

'I've finished for now. I was about to stop for a bite to eat. Will you join me? I've arranged with one of these fellows to put my canvas in one of the sheds out of harm's way.'

Romanelli shook his head in mock despair. 'One day, James, people will be fighting for your paintings, and you leave them lying around in a shed on the docks!'

James laughed. 'It's a good joke, sir. But I don't think anyone is likely to steal it; besides the paint is still wet, I can't carry it with me.'

Romanelli shook a finger at him. 'I tell you, James, if I should see such a painting abandoned so, then I should certainly steal it. But still, it is yours to do with as you wish. Come, let us eat.'

They found a small bar where the porters ate. The ale was strong, the food nourishing and plentiful, and James sat back, replete. 'I don't think that I can paint any more today,' he said. 'I shall need to walk that off.'

'Then you can walk and observe and absorb all that is happening around you and put it onto canvas another day, yes?' Romanelli lit a cigar, and through the aromatic smoke regarded James.

'Have you seen anything of Madame Sinclair?' James ventured. 'I called on her, but her maid said that she had gone away.'

Romanelli drew a breath and the tip of the cigar glowed a fiery red. 'Yes,' he said. 'She is in Brighton. I have been there also, I left her only yesterday.'

James felt such a sinking feeling that his body felt like lead. 'Oh,' he managed to say. 'I trust she is well.'

Romanelli nodded his head and then tapped the cigar ash onto the wooden floor. 'Quite well. The sea air is doing her good. Come, James, we will collect your painting and get a cab, and I will go with you to Chelsea. I wish to talk with you.'

The cabbie dropped them at James's lodging and, after depositing his paints and canvas in his room, they returned to the river side and sat together on a wooden seat, gazing out at the river.

'How is your father?' Romanelli asked after a while.

James was startled; he had not thought of his father all day and yet he had been constantly on his mind until today. 'He is dead. I was too late, he had died the morning I arrived.'

'I am so sorry to hear that. You will miss him, James.'

'Not so much here,' James admitted, 'for he was never part of the life I lead here. But I missed him terribly at home. The house seemed so empty without him.' He remembered how he had climbed the stairs to his father's room. The first thing he had seen were his slippers lying abandoned by the bed, and then his father's body lying so cold and still and vacant.

'He was a good man – a good father to me.'

'Yes, indeed. It is hard to be a good father, but I am sure that he was one,' Romanelli replied softly.

They watched the sun throw golden shafts of light on the water as it lapped below their feet, and listened to the shrieks of the gulls as they followed the ships up river.

'And your mama, how is she? Is she very unhappy?'

'She is coping very well.' *She has changed*, James thought. *It is as if my father's death has made her softer, kinder, more understanding.*

'You must not blame your mama too much,' Romanelli said suddenly. 'Mothers have much to worry them.'

James looked curiously at Romanelli. Whatever did he mean? 'Did you know them well?' he asked. 'My parents? I don't remember them ever mentioning you.'

'It was a long time ago.' Romanelli shifted his position and recrossed his legs. 'But yes, I did know them well, for a short time, anyway. I stayed at your home. I – I wanted to paint the river.'

'And did you?' James kept his eyes on Romanelli's face.

'No. I was not in the mood; too restless to concentrate. But later, when I returned to Italy, then I painted. I painted what I remembered. And that is what you must do, James.' He turned to him and gazed candidly into his eyes. 'Do not waste any of life's experience, be it happy or sad. Store it away, and one day you will use it.'

'And what did you paint, Signor, when you returned home? What was it that you remembered most of all of our northern country?'

'I painted your mama, James. I painted her so that I would never forget.'

The sun started to sink as they sat there, changing the golden river into a rippling ribbon of scarlet. Presently James broke the silence.

'Did you love my mother?'

'Yes. I loved only two women in my life, and she was one.'

It's strange, James thought. *I never thought of my mother in that sense. She seemed incapable of showing any emotion, except – except—* From the recesses of his mind came an image of himself as a child sitting on his mother's lap, and of her arms around him as she wept. *How odd that I should remember that now.* 'And she loved you?'

'Yes.'

'Did my father know?'

'No. At least, I don't think so.' Romanelli got up from the seat and walked to the river's edge. He stood for a few moments contemplating its flow. Then he turned around to face James. 'I let her down very badly; but what was I to do? We were both married to other people, and she would not have run away with me to a foreign country. And I, well, I was worse, I could not have given up my wife; she was rich, her family was influential, I would have been ostracized in my own country.'

'Love can be a terrible thing,' James said passionately. 'Sometimes I think that it is unbearable. But still,' he added quietly, 'there is no harm done. It is over with.'

'No, James.' Romanelli sat beside him again. 'It is never done with. Love and its consequences can stay for ever.'

James stared bewildered. 'What are you saying, sir?'

'I am saying, James, that you are my son. That your father, Isaac, who was surely a better father than I could ever be, was not your own, but that I am.'

James felt tears fill his eyes. *My father! But my father – he loved me as only a father can, whereas this man—!* He felt that his head would burst. He could not take it in, and yet so many things fell into place. He had always been different from Gilbert and Anne. Different even from the rest of the Rayner family.

'You left my mother to suffer this alone?' he stammered.

Pain showed in Romanelli's eyes. 'I suffered too,' he defended himself. 'And your mother had the love of a good man to sustain her.'

'But you had the love of your wife,' James declared defiantly. 'You said that you loved her.'

'No!' Romanelli looked away. 'I did not say that! I said that I had loved only two women in my life, but perhaps I should have said three. One was your mother. The other was Mariabella's mother. Mariabella is my daughter.'

James mentally reeled as the significance of Romanelli's words struck him. *Mariabella! Not Mariabella! But I love her – have loved her. What shall I do? Does she know?*

'When I met your mother, Mariabella was eight years old. Her mother and I had been lovers when we were very young, and she was the consequence. Our families disapproved of our relationship and she

330

was forced to marry an older man. She was very unhappy, and she died of a fever within a year.' Romanelli gazed into the distance, lost in the past. 'Mariabella was looked after by a relation until I was able to support her. She was the reason that I married my wife; with her money I was able to bring up Mariabella in a proper way.'

'But Mariabella said that you were a friend of her father's!' James struggled to comprehend.

Romanelli nodded. 'Her uncle; she always referred to him as her *padre* – her papa. We did become friends over the years. Mariabella did not know then that I was her father.'

'And now?' said James, his voice breaking. 'Does she know now?'

'*Si*, James. Now she does. That is why she has gone away.'

After Romanelli had left, and James returned to his lodgings, he let his emotions rise to the surface and wept. 'I must never see her again. Never hold her in my arms. How shall I ever bear it?' He blew his nose and rinsed his swollen eyes and paced the floor. *I will kill myself. There is nothing left for me. I have no life without her. My sister! Mariabella is my* sister*!* He broke into a fresh spasm of weeping. *I have no-one. No-one that I can turn to. I cannot speak to my mother of this, and my father, the only one who would understand, is dead.*

His thoughts stopped him short in his pacing. *But thank God that he didn't know. How I would have hated him to know that my mother had been unfaithful and that I wasn't his son. My poor father; it would have killed him! But my mother, how she, too, must have suffered.* For the first time in his life, he felt empathy with his mother. *I know now how she must have felt – to have loved in vain.*

He contemplated how he would die: should it be by poison, or should he throw himself under a train as he had once told Mariabella that he would? But he didn't know about poisons and he might buy the wrong one and suffer a lingering death. *No. It must be quick. The train is the thing. But how? Should I throw myself from the platform under the wheels, or buy a ticket and leap from a moving train?*

His stomach rumbled while he was considering, and he cut himself a slice of bread and poured a glass of wine. He had a headache with all the weeping, and, after he had eaten and drunk his wine, he lay down on the horsehair sofa and closed his eyes.

When he opened them again, his neck was stiff and his legs cramped, the morning sunlight was creeping in through his basement window and someone was hammering on the door.

It was Romanelli, bearing a warm crusty loaf, a hunk of cheese and some ham. 'I remember that I never had any food in the house when I was a young artist,' he said as he bundled in at the door, 'so I bought all of this. I will make you a proper breakfast and then we can talk. Today you can think better, yes?'

James gazed at him through bleary eyes. He had nothing to say to the man – the man who had ruined his life and Mariabella's.

'You will feel better after eating, you cannot think on an empty stomach.'

James watched him sullenly as he busied himself. He put the bread in the middle of the table and sliced the cheese and ham and laid it out in a concentric circle on a plate. 'We have good food in Italy, you know. We have delicious fish, delectable fruit – oranges, the sweetest melons which drip juice down your chin, tomatoes, olives.' He kissed the tips of his fingers in an extravagant gesture. 'And of course the juice of the grape. You will love it, James.'

'I have no plans to go there,' he answered bitterly. 'I have no plans at all.'

'No? That is because you have suffered a shock. But you must consider, you have had only a short life so far; you have been comfortable and had a stable existence.' Romanelli pointed with a knife. 'Your parents have supported you. Now is the time for you to think for yourself what you will do with the rest of your life.' He pulled out a chair and invited James to sit down and eat. James smelled the warm bread and realized that he was hungry.

'And I can help you. If you will allow me. I would like to.' Romanelli tore off a crust of bread with his hands and began to eat. Then he looked at James with an appeal in his dark eyes. 'You must remember, James, that I, too, have been deprived all these years. Your father, Isaac, has had the love of my son, and I have had nothing.' He slowly wiped the crumbs from about his beard and mouth. 'I beg of you, James, to let me make up for the loss of those years. Come back with me to Italy.'

32

'Sammi! You're not content with bringing one child here, but must bring another! What on earth am I supposed to do with her?'

'We thought, Billy and I—' Sammi knew very well that her mother had an extra soft spot for her brother, 'that she could be trained as a kitchen maid. She hasn't a chance of employment in Hull, Mama. No-one would take her, and she is so vulnerable.'

'Yes, yes. So you told me. But we don't need another kitchen maid. Cook will not be pleased.' She tapped her fingers together. 'How old is she?'

'About thirteen, I think.' Sammi felt hope rising. 'She's so very bright, and quick-witted.'

'The right age,' her mother agreed, then frowned. 'But is she honest? If she's been begging for food, then the chances are that she has also stolen in order to exist. It's a risk for us to take.'

'Possibly so, Mama. But if you saw those children for yourself perhaps you would understand, if indeed they do steal. When I saw them for the first time,' she implored, 'I thought of Adam. If we hadn't rescued him he might have shared the same fate.'

'Yes, yes,' her mother repeated testily. 'But we cannot be expected to rescue the entire destitute population of Hull. Someone in authority should be attending to the situation!'

'Yes, Mama.' Sammi smiled. 'We knew you would agree. At least, Billy said that you would.'

'What?'

'He's waiting for an interview with a benefactor.

334

Gilbert is arranging it,' she added. 'Billy wants to get something organized to help these children.'

Her mother groaned. 'Oh, goodness. Whatever am I to do with the pair of you? I don't know what your father is going to say!'

'If you approve, Mama,' Sammi said slyly, 'he won't say a word. You know he won't.'

Martha knocked on the door. 'Beg pardon, ma-am. May I speak to you for a moment?'

'Yes, what is it?'

'Beg pardon, Mrs Rayner, it's just—' She glanced at Sammi out of her eye corner. 'Well, what am I to do about 'young maid?' She indicated somewhat disparagingly over her shoulder toward the kitchens. 'She's filthy! Full o' fleas!'

'Oh heavens! Could she have a bath?'

'That's what I wanted to ask, ma-am. If she's staying she's not going between my clean sheets in 'state she's in now.' The housekeeper gave a snort. 'And 'other maids won't want her in 'same bedroom as them.'

'Then give her a bath and some clean clothes, and she looks half-starved from what I saw of her, so give her something to eat.'

'Oh, she's had that already, ma-am. Cook gave her some chicken broth and she sat and ate it on 'kitchen doorstep. She said she didn't want to come in 'house and was there a shed or somewhere she could sleep.'

'Oh we can't have that.' Her mistress was definite. 'Is there somewhere we can put her until we decide what's to be done?'

'There's 'small box-room on 'top landing, ma-am. I could put a truckle in there.'

'Very well, and when she's cleaned up, send her in to see me.'

Sammi said not a word as her mother rose from her chair and paced the floor. Then she stood by the window and gazed out. 'I won't promise anything, Sammi, but we'll see how she turns out. If she thieves but once, she goes straight back where she came

335

from.' She turned towards her daughter. 'But if she's suitable, honest and hard-working, and if Martha is willing to train her, then perhaps she can go to the mill house. She might be the answer to Betsy's problem.'

Sammi gave her a quick hug. 'Thank you so much. She'll be good, I know she will. She was so eager to come. I hadn't the heart to turn her away.'

'I've heard that before, Sammi,' her mother rebuked her. 'But please don't let me hear it again.' She gave an impatient gesture. 'What a pretty kettle of fish you have brought about, Sammi. First Adam—'

'Not me, Mama,' Sammi said bluntly, 'or James. It's Gilbert, isn't it? He is Adam's father!'

'You know?' A frown crossed her mother's forehead. 'Did Gilbert . . . ?'

'Oh, no!' Sammi's lips tightened as her mother's words confirmed her suspicions. 'Gilbert did not say! He was hardly likely to, was he?' she mocked. 'He let James take the blame and let me take charge of Adam without saying a word. He certainly didn't tell! I don't know why I didn't realize before,' she raged. 'It is so obvious now that we do know.'

'He told me,' her mother said softly. 'He knows he has made a terrible mistake.'

'But will he admit it to anyone else?'

Her mother sighed and shook her head. 'Only James. I insisted on that. He's afraid of Harriet finding out. He's a foolish young man,' she said, 'but he has agreed to give an allowance for Adam, and he says he will find someone to take him.' She gazed candidly at Sammi. 'It's up to us whether or not we tell, Sammi. Do we ruin his marriage before it has begun? Or do we wait for Gilbert's own conscience to dictate?' As Sammi remained silent, she added, 'He will be a better man for his own admission of guilt.'

'So everyone else must suffer? We keep his secret, James is banished to London, and my marriage chances are *apparently* lessened.' Sammi gave a small sob. 'Perhaps I, too, made a mistake, Mama. Perhaps I should have left Adam to the tender mercies of the workhouse guardians. It would have been so much better for everyone, wouldn't it?'

'Sammi!' her mother reproached her.

Sammi went towards the door. 'Excuse me, Mama. I am going to my room.' She put her hand on the door-knob. 'But Gilbert will answer for this. Sooner or later he will repay his debt.'

'*Nothing much is happening, I'm afraid,*' Billy wrote to Sammi three weeks later. '*Gilbert hasn't been able to see Mr Pearson yet, which is very disappointing, so in the meantime I have been calling on traders to ask for their support.*'

Not that that had been very successful either, he thought as he walked down Whitefriargate to post the letter. He had approached various tradesmen to enquire if they would be willing to contribute to a scheme to help the destitute children of the town. Some of them gave their names willingly, prompted, he felt sure, by their desire to appear philanthropic; others stated flatly that they wouldn't give so much as a button, because in their opinion the children were nothing more than ruffians and thieves in the making. He courteously thanked even the most impolite and made a note of their names in a separate list from those who were willing, and vowed to himself that he would return and ask again, once a scheme was under way.

Three days later, in immediate response to his letter, Sammi arrived in Hull with a clean, well-scrubbed Jenny, who dipped her knee when she saw him.

'Martha said Jenny needed some shoes and other things. She's been wearing old clothes belonging to one of the other maids, but they're all too big for her, so I volunteered to bring her in,' she explained.

'But really I thought that I would speak to Gilbert and ask how he's getting on with Mr Pearson.'

Billy shook his head. 'But I told you in my letter, he hasn't seen him yet. Gilbert just hasn't had the time.'

'Really?' she said. 'Poor Gilbert. So busy! Is he in now?'

'Yes. Shall I tell him you're here?'

'No.' She smiled sweetly at her brother. 'I'll surprise him.'

Gilbert had his back to her when she opened the door after perfunctorily knocking. He turned from the filing cabinet and started on seeing her. 'Sammi! Why – what brings you here? Nothing wrong at home, I trust?'

'Nothing more than usual, Gilbert. Just the daily traumas of life. The usual ups and downs of family life: quarrels, misunderstandings, retribution and so on, you know how it is.'

She stared him in the face, then burst out, 'How could you? How could you let James take the blame? How could you let your father go to his grave thinking that it was James who had fathered Adam?' She hadn't intended to confront him, merely insinuate that she knew, in order to persuade him to help Billy. But her resentment, which had been simmering for the last weeks over the injustice of the situation, suddenly boiled over.

He stared back; his eyes had a helpless look, then his face crumpled. 'Because of Harriet,' he said. 'I wanted the marriage to go ahead and I knew her father wouldn't allow it if word got out.' He sat down heavily behind his desk. 'We were a good match,' he went on, 'both families wanted it.'

Sammi's mouth turned down. An arranged marriage, she judged; but she softened as he continued, 'But now I'm terrified of her finding out. I care for her so much, Sammi,' he said. 'I never thought I could care for anyone the way I care for

338

Harriet. I don't know what I should do if I lost her.'

She remained silent; this, then, was why her mother felt sorry for him.

He blinked and looked up at her. 'I have promised your mother I will find a place for him. What else can I do or say, apart from I'm sorry?' He rose to his feet, mindful of his manners. 'I beg your pardon, Sammi. Won't you sit down?'

She shook her head and remained standing. 'What I want you to do, Gilbert,' her voice was husky, 'what I want you to do is write to James, if you haven't already done so, and tell him; whether you tell your mother is up to you. And the other thing I want you to do,' she took a deep breath, 'is to try to make amends in another way.'

'Yes, yes. I'll do what I can. I really am sorry, Sammi,' he pleaded. 'I wanted to tell you that first night, but I didn't dare, and then it was too late. James decided to go and you took Adam, and so I left things as they were,' he added miserably.

She hardened herself towards him, though she felt uneasily that perhaps she, too, had acted hastily. 'What I want you to do, Gilbert, is to make amends by helping other children, children who might well have been born under similar circumstances.'

She couldn't help but add this rider and, embarrassed at her candour, he looked away.

'I know, I did say that I would speak to Pearson,' he agreed; then as she made no reply but waited for him to continue, he said, 'There's a Chamber of Commerce meeting tomorrow, he's sure to be there. If I promise to speak to him then will that be . . . ?'

'Perfect. You'll tell Billy the outcome?'

'I will,' he assured, relief showing as he smiled at her. 'Thank you, Sammi. I won't let you down this time. I will speak to Mr Pearson.'

She nodded. 'I shall be relying on you, Gilbert, and so will others. Children like Adam, who through no fault of their own are in intolerable situations.'

His smile disappeared and she saw him swallow and take a breath. He bowed his head. 'Trust me, Sammi. I beg you.'

On their way home, Sammi decided to call at the mill house and introduce Jenny. The girl was learning fast, and Martha had said that she wouldn't have minded keeping her at Garston Hall as she was such a willing soul; but Sammi's mother had said no, she would go to the Fosters', where she was needed.

But first she called on Mrs Bishop to see Adam. She leant over his crib and fondled his toes. 'He will be leaving us soon, Mrs Bishop. A foster home is being sought. He has done well under your care.'

Mrs Bishop gazed at her frankly. 'Breeding and feeding is what I'm good at, miss. And, I have to say, that I hope that this bairn will one day be grateful to thee for what tha's done for him. But, Miss Sammi, I warned thee already and I say again that there's some who will – are – judging thee; true they're nobody much in 'scheme of things, common folk whose opinions maybe don't count, but gossip spreads, and it'll spread upwards.'

'You're saying there are those who consider that I am a fallen woman? That he is my child?' she said bluntly. 'Because I have cared for his well-being they paint my character worse than it is?'

'Aye, miss.' Mrs Bishop nodded. 'That's about 'strength of it.'

Betsy wasn't in, and Uncle Thomas was sleeping, so she searched out Tom in the mill. 'Betsy's gone off somewhere, Sammi, but I don't know where.' Tom rubbed his hands together to shake off the grain. 'She doesn't always tell us.' He followed her outside, where Jenny was waiting by the carriage door. She looked a trifle apprehensive as he approached, but he tried to put her at ease as he said, 'So, you're coming to look after us, are you, Jenny?'

She dipped her knee and looked at Sammi for

confirmation, then shyly said, 'When I'm ready, sir. Mrs Martha said I wouldn't be long. I'll do my best for thee, sir.'

He nodded. 'Thank you. I'm sure that you will.'

Aside to Sammi as Jenny moved away, he murmured, 'She's very young. Will she do, do you think?'

'I'm sure, Tom. Betsy will be able to train her into her own ways. She's a good worker, Martha says so.'

'Well, if Martha says so, who am I to question? I hope Betsy takes to her; it's a pity she's out.'

'Never mind.' She felt his gaze upon her. 'They'll meet another time.'

'What's that nice smell, miss?' Jenny asked as she climbed into the carriage beside Sammi.

'Smell?' Sammi was watching Tom's retreating back as he walked back towards the mill, his head slightly bent. Was his demeanour different? Had he heard the gossip, and if he had did it worry him?

'Like at 'baker's shop!'

'It's the grain,' she murmured, 'balmy and warm. I used to think it was a comforting, soothing kind of aroma when I was a child. It's the scent of a good harvest gathered in.'

33

Betsy put on her best yellow gown and her prettiest bonnet, and looked in the bedroom mirror. The gown had been decidedly tight around the waist, but she had eased the seams and adjusted the lacing on the bodice and now it felt much more comfortable.

'Is tha putting on weight, Betsy?' George had asked as she sat unpicking the seams, and she replied no, not at all, it was more fashionable to wear a looser style. When he laughed and asked who would see her wearing it, she replied mysteriously to wait and see.

Tom had looked at her questioningly, but hadn't asked, so she casually dropped the remark that she and Sammi were thinking of having a day out.

'I don't remember Sammi mentioning it,' Tom said, and she retorted that Sammi didn't tell him everything, even if he thought she did, she'd added meaningfully.

And that shut him up straight away, she mused as, with a final glance in the mirror, she picked up her shawl and went downstairs. *I wouldn't be too surprised if he's sweet on her after all.*

'Are you sure you'll be all right, Da?' She hesitated by the parlour door.

'Aye, don't worry about me, lass. Go off and enjoy thaself and give Sammi my love. Or is she calling in?'

'No. I said I would meet her in the village. Save turning the trap around.' She spoke nervously. She didn't like to lie to her father; it was the first time she had ever done so, but she knew very well that she wouldn't be allowed to go if she told the truth.

'Ask Tom to give thee a shilling or two,' her father

said. 'Go on, tell him to get it out of 'box. Treat thaself.'

When she asked for the money, he asked, 'How much did he say?'

'A guinea or two.' She kept a straight face. 'But I shan't want so much,' she added, when she saw his look of astonishment and worried that he might check with their father. 'Just a guinea will do.'

'I'll see you later,' she called gaily and hurried down the lane to catch a lift on the carrier's cart into Hull.

The idea had come to her when, on returning from an errand in the village, she had seen the carrier on his way back from Hull to Hornsea. A woman she knew had climbed down and called up to the driver that she would see him the following week.

They stopped for a few words and as the cart drew out of the village, she had exclaimed, 'Drat. I'd forgotten that our Nellie's coming next week. I shan't need 'lift after all.'

'I have to go into Hull next week,' Betsy had said impulsively. 'I could take your place.'

Mrs Glover had nodded. 'It'll be busy. They're opening 'park on Monday.'

Later in the week Sammi, too, had mentioned the opening of the park. 'Billy is going as an official guest,' she said. 'He's going to meet Mr Pearson. I wish we could have gone, Betsy, but I have to stay home with Victoria as Mama and Pa are going up to the Wolds.'

But I could go, Betsy thought. *Only I won't tell anyone, or else I shan't be allowed. How annoying it is to be a woman; a man can go wherever he wants, but a woman is always so restricted.*

She knew that, up to a point, that was untrue, for married women like Mrs Glover regularly travelled alone, as did young girls like Nancy, who were not afraid for their reputation. But Betsy had been kept on a tight rein by her father and brothers, ever mindful for her safety and well-being.

Well, I'm breaking free, she exulted as she signalled for the carrier to stop. 'I'm taking Mrs Glover's place,' she said climbing up. 'Her daughter is visiting her today, so she can't come.'

'Righto, miss. It makes no difference to me. I haven't given thee a lift before, have I?'

'No.' She gave him a winsome smile. 'My brother generally brings me in, but today he can't, and I wanted to go to the opening of the park.'

'Why, miss, 'park is nowt special for country folk like thee! It'll be full o' trees and flowers same as out here. It's for townies and them as don't have a bit o' grass on 'doorstep. Mind,' he flicked his reins and the pair of greys picked up their heels, 'there'll be brass bands playing and sodgers marching, so it'll be a good day out.'

Betsy was filled with excitement; she was going to have such fun, a whole day to herself. The sun was shining and she had money in her purse to spend on whatever she wanted.

When they arrived at the outskirts of the town, however, the roads were jammed with jostling coaches, carriages and carts all trying to join the procession on its way up the Beverley Road towards the new park, given by and named after the benefactor and Mayor of the town, Zachariah Pearson. They crossed the North Bridge and turned into the High Street, then came to a full stop at the junction of Salthouse Lane.

'Tha might as well walk in, miss,' the carrier said after they had sat immobile for twenty minutes. 'By the time I get into 'Market Place, 'show is going to be over.'

Betsy agreed and stepped down, calling up to him to ask what time he would be going back.

'Two o'clock as a rule, but I doubt I'll make it that time today.' He touched his forehead. 'Be at 'Reindeer between two and three if tha wants a lift back.'

Betsy followed the crowd into the Market Place.

344

Already the streets were crowded and the townsfolk very lively. Flags were hanging from shop and office doorways and people were claiming their places in windows ready to watch the procession, and stray streamers were floating down onto the heads of the crowd below.

I had no idea that it would be like this, she thought as she was jostled by the crowd. *I thought there would be a fête at the park, but I never dreamt that the whole town would be celebrating.*

The town was filled with soldiers, bandsmen and police, all getting in place to form the military and civic pageant; crowds were spilling out in their thousands from the railway station where special trains were bringing them in from all over Yorkshire, and the steamers at the pier were discharging hundreds of passengers. The whole of the town, the thoroughfares and side streets, were thronging with residents and visitors all come to enjoy the day.

'What time does the parade start?' She stopped a young woman with two young children.

'One o'clock,' the woman said, 'but we're making a start for 'park now, otherwise we'll never get there to see owt. Bairns don't want to miss seeing sodgers marching, or 'side shows.'

Betsy decided that she would make a start also, for if she was to see the planting of the first tree by the Mayor when he arrived at the park, and get back into Hull in time for the carrier's cart, then she would have to hurry along.

She was half-way along the Beverley Road when a cheer went up and someone shouted that the parade had started. As Betsy strained her ears, she could hear the striking up of the kettledrums and the blast of trumpets as the bandsmen began their performance, and the procession started on its route through the town.

Over the Whitefriargate Bridge they marched, Junction Street, Prospect Street, where the nurses and not so sick patients waved from the windows and grounds of the Infirmary, and on up the Beverley Road towards its destination at the park. Carriages and horse-back riders were preceding the procession, and as Betsy approached the park gates, which were decked with flags and evergreens, she moved aside to let a gig through. She looked up at the driver as he manoeuvred past and stared. Charles Craddock!

He saw her and called out, 'Miss Foster! How delightful to see you.' An official was moving him on, and his black gelding was prancing and throwing its head as he held it in check. 'Are you alone?' he called. 'Come on, jump in if you are.'

She hesitated only for a second and with a quick hitch up of her skirts she scrambled up. 'No,' she said breathlessly and rearranged herself, 'I'm not alone, but I've lost sight of my companion.'

He flicked his reins and they moved on again. 'You'll never find her in this crowd, unless you've made an arrangement to meet somewhere.' He turned to smile at her. 'Now why do I assume it is a female companion? I am wrong. It is bound to be a sweetheart when you are looking as lovely as you do.'

She assumed a coy look. 'It is, of course, a female companion, Mr Craddock. We came for a day's shopping and got caught up in the festivities.'

He handed her down as they entered the park, and a boy took his horse and gig to a compound. 'Then if you have lost your companion and as I am alone with a spare ticket' – he fished two tickets out of his jacket pocket – 'perhaps you would join me up on the platform?' He pointed into the centre of the grassy area where a huge platform had been erected with seats covered in red cloth and a canvas top covering the whole.

She hesitated. 'Come on,' he persuaded. 'They're the best seats, right in the middle; it's a shame to let one go to waste.'

'All right,' she decided. 'Why not?'

346

They took their seats and Betsy surmised that these seats had been reserved for the élite of the neighbourhood, for the occupants were expensively dressed, the ladies in pretty veiled hats and crinolines of silks and velvets, and some of the gentlemen in formal attire, whilst the people in the side seats, though well dressed, did not have the air of gentility the others had, and she was glad that she was dressed in her best yellow gown.

'Fifteen hundred seats on this platform,' Craddock whispered into her ear. 'And I'm lucky enough to be sitting next to you!' He put his hand along the back of Betsy's seat and fingered her shoulder beneath her shawl.

She looked at him and then lowered her lashes. 'I trust you are not going to take advantage of me, Mr Craddock, just because I have accepted your offer to sit beside you.'

He immediately removed his arm. Then he took her hand and raised it to his lips. 'I beg your pardon, Miss Foster,' he said softly. 'It's just that I have thought of you so often since we met at your cousin's wedding, that I cannot believe my luck in finding you here. Please forgive my impertinence.'

She arched her eyebrows. Had he really been thinking of her? But whether he had or not, it was quite nice to flirt a little. *I can't really flirt or dally with Luke*, she thought, *he is so basic.*

She allowed him to keep hold of her hand, and he ran his fingers up and down hers and stroked her wrist. Everyone stood up as the procession entered the park, and Craddock put his arm around her waist to support her.

First came the Police followed by the Park Committee, then the brass bands of the East and West Riding, and the East Yorkshire Militia; the Artillery Volunteers and East Yorkshire Rifles, and members of various lodges. There was a great variety of uniform, the Lincolnshire volunteers in grey tunics and trousers trimmed with red, the corps from Lincoln wore dark green with black facings, and on their heads the peaked and plumed shakos.

'Here come the dignitaries,' Craddock said, as the civic procession rolled towards the dais below them. First came the beadles carrying the sword and mace, followed by the Mayor in his robe of office and gold chain, and riding with him in his private carriage was Lord Wenlock, the Deputy Lord Lieutenant of the Riding. Lord Hotham, Member of Parliament, was in private dress, and the Town Clerk wore ceremonial wig and robe of office.

Everyone cheered and then sat down again once the Mayor had passed and watched the remaining procession from their seats. The Sheriff and Deputy Sheriff of Hull, both in Court dress, were followed through the grounds by Members of Parliament, Wardens and Brethren of Trinity House, Foreign Consuls and the members of the Dock Company.

'There's my cousin!' Betsy exclaimed.

'Ah, you found her?' Craddock smiled. 'It was Miss Rayner who came with you?'

Betsy was about to deny it, then said, 'I meant Gilbert. Look there he is, walking with the men from the Dock Company.'

Gilbert's tall figure stood out from the others in the procession.

'Ah, yes. Gilbert,' Craddock mused. 'I had forgotten that he might be part of the official party.'

As Betsy watched the next part of the proceedings, she suddenly thought of her lift home. 'Mr Craddock! What is the time?'

He consulted his pocket watch. 'Two-thirty exactly.' He looked at her quizzically. 'Not tired of me already, are you?'

'Not at all.' Worriedly, she contemplated her situation. 'But I – we – had arranged to meet between two-thirty and three o'clock in the Market Place if we got separated.'

'Too late, I fear. You would never get there in time, the crowds are still swarming in.'

'What shall I do?' she said anxiously. 'I've arranged for a ride home.'

He stared out at the tableau that was just arriving through the gates, an allegorical scene put on by the theatre managers of the Royal Queen's Theatre, Wolfenden and Melbourne. 'Would you allow me to drive you home?' he asked. 'Would your family object?'

She thought of the response she would get from her father and Tom if she should arrive home with a stranger, having ridden alone with him along the lonely country roads of Holderness. 'I think they would be very grateful that I had been delivered safely,' she said, and knew as she uttered the words that he believed not a word, any more than she did.

'Then that's settled,' he said with a smile and a penetrating gaze from his small eyes.

It's a pity that he isn't more handsome, she thought wistfully. *He has rather a mean look about him. But still, it's better than being here alone, and I wouldn't be here in the best seats enjoying myself if it were not for his generosity.* She settled down again, secure in the knowledge that she would get home eventually. *I'll think up an excuse later*, she decided. *I shall be in trouble anyway when I get home and they find out that I'm not with Sammi.*

The tableau which drew the loudest cheer of all was designed as a temple, with children dressed as the muses of poetry, comedy, tragedy and dancing and singers of songs for lovers, who stood poised in decorated niches. Shakespeare appeared on the platform, being crowned by the Three Graces, and following the tableau came six horses ridden by young boys dressed in Old English costumes and led by six Beefeaters.

'We shall have a glass of wine to refresh us when this is over,' Craddock remarked as the last of the procession completed its circle around the arena and

349

the Mayor descended from his carriage to walk to the dais, where he was to make his speech before officially planting the first tree.

'Are you hungry?' he asked. 'Did you eat lunch?'

She shook her head. 'I'm starving,' she claimed. 'I have had nothing since six o'clock this morning.'

'My dear young lady,' he said in concern, 'just as soon as the ceremony is over we shall go to the tent and have a feast. Do you like champagne?'

'Yes.' Her eyes sparkled. 'I had it at Gilbert's wedding for the first time.'

'Then that is what we shall have: champagne to whet your appetite, oysters to stimulate you.'

'I'm more in need of a meat pie and onion gravy,' she laughed. 'I might faint at your feet otherwise.'

'Then I should have the pleasure of reviving you.' His voice was soft. 'But you may have anything your heart – or body – desires.' He looked into her eyes and she saw an intense flame lingering there. He took her face in his hands and kissed her on the lips. From behind she heard someone gasp and a voice complaining.

She smiled at him and then pulled away. She was playing with fire, she well knew. He had the same look of desire that she saw in Luke's face when they were alone, and it was the power of knowing that they wanted her which excited her.

I could perhaps put up with his plainness, she mused. *He is not handsome like Luke, but he has finesse; though I feel sure that he is not a gentleman. He knows how to treat a woman, he's generous and attentive, and I do believe he is very taken with me.*

They joined the crowd in the refreshment tent after the ceremony and Craddock bought a bottle of champagne and two dozen oysters. He insisted she drank a glass of champagne first and then, holding her chin up with his forefinger, he slipped an oyster into her open mouth.

'Now swallow,' he said, wiping her lips with his fingertips.

She gazed at him, her mouth apart. The wine was going to her head, she felt quite swimmy. She took hold of his arm. 'Oh,' she gasped. 'I feel very strange.'

'You'll feel better after another glass,' he urged. 'Come on, drink up.'

She took another sip and held her mouth open again whilst he slipped in another oyster. She felt the touch of his fingers as he slid it into her mouth. She swallowed and momentarily closed her eyes.

He smiled down at her. 'Feeling better now, my beautiful Betsy?'

She drew herself up and looked around. The afternoon seemed to have taken on a brilliant clarity. The sun was shining, and the array of greenery and banks of flowers were bright and resplendent in their colours. Charles Craddock seemed suddenly to have grown taller and more handsome, and he was holding her arm so protectively and caringly.

'Yes,' she said brightly, 'I feel wonderful.'

34

Billy took his seat on the front row of the platform immediately behind the dais where the Mayor would make his speech and plant the *Wellingtonia Gigantia*, the emperor of all pines. He wished that Sammi could have come. It was through her intervention that Gilbert had arranged the meeting with Pearson. But the Mayor was so very busy that he hadn't a free occasion for weeks, and had suggested to Gilbert that Billy came to the opening of the park when he might have a moment to speak to him as he chatted to various members of the public.

He listened to the presentation speech and transfer of conveyance, clapping when the spade struck the sod and the tree was planted. As the ceremony finished and the crowd headed for the refreshment tent, he turned and glanced up at the platform behind him. There was a sea of faces: a colourful pattern of bobbing hats and rustling, swaying gowns, a sprinkling of greys and blacks from the men's formal suits and top hats. Some colours predominated: red, green, purple, white. There was a young woman in a yellow gown who had a look of Betsy. How she, too, would have loved the day if she could have come.

There had never been such an event in Hull before. Not even the Hull Fair could compare with an event such as this, when all members of society were here to join in the celebrations. Rich and poor, all were here to enjoy the opening of the first public park. He caught sight of the Mayor as he was escorted to the refreshment tent, and saw him stop to have a word with the people who were standing around watching. Ragged people, some of them, with dirty-faced children, tradespeople, ladies in elegant dress, all mingling harmoniously and sharing the pleasure of the day.

Then he saw Gilbert walking across towards the Mayor. Zachariah Pearson spoke briefly to him and Gilbert put his hand to his chin, nodding earnestly, then made his way across to Billy.

'Billy! Sorry to disappoint you, but Mr Pearson said he would prefer to see you at tomorrow's event. He's very busy you know, old fellow. You're lucky I've been able to arrange something so quickly.' Gilbert seemed to be puffed up with his own importance after being chosen to take part in the parade with other members of the Chamber of Commerce and Shipping.

'Oh!' Billy was cast down. He had been so buoyed up with anticipation, so keen to get on with organizing something for the children.

'Tomorrow will be more suitable,' Gilbert pressed on. 'The Mayor's children are planting another tree, and all the children from the town are being invited. You could even invite your young ruffians if you wanted,' he condescended. 'There'll be games and Aunt Sallies, juggling and so on.'

'Yes, I know.' Billy wasn't able to hide his despondence. 'I have already told them.'

'What a wonderful gift Mr Pearson has given the town.' Gilbert looked around at the throng, his expression conveying that he, too, had been involved with the great act of beneficence. 'A day when people can forget their grievances and miseries!'

Billy shook his head. 'They're not forgotten, Gilbert,' he said quietly. 'They're simply put on one side.'

Betsy climbed into the gig with some difficulty, even though Charles Craddock had hold of her by the waist. She giggled as he tickled her and pushed his

353

hand away. 'Behave yourself.' She gave him a playful slap and he pinched her cheek.

They waited in a queue of traffic to move out of the park gates and he bent towards her. 'Do you have to go home yet? Can you not stay a little longer?'

She felt so light-headed and her legs were wobbly. She hadn't had enough to eat. They couldn't get near the food table for the crush of people, and so they had had only more oysters and another bottle or two of champagne, or was it three, she wondered.

'You could come back home with me for supper,' he said persuasively. 'And then watch the fireworks and the procession.'

'I'm so hungry,' she wailed.

'Then that's settled.' He bent to give her a kiss and she put her mouth towards him. 'We'll eat first and then decide what to do afterwards.'

A shout from the carriage behind telling them to get a move-on disturbed them, so Craddock flicked his whip and turned out of the park to head for town.

A maid opened his house door as he rattled on the knocker. He nodded to her. 'Tell Smith to put the gig away and then get off home. I shan't need him again. Is supper ready?'

'Yes, sir.' She bobbed her knee. 'I've left a tray. Will that be all, sir?'

'Yes.' He motioned Betsy through into a small drawing-room and dismissed the maid, who slipped away down a staircase.

Betsy shook her head to clear it. Wouldn't they need the gig again? Or perhaps he had another carriage in which to take her home?

He took off her shawl and then unfastened the ribbons on her bonnet. They had knotted and he fumbled impatiently.

'Let me,' Betsy giggled. 'I can see you are not used to ladies' fripperies.'

He smiled and put his hands around her waist. 'I'm not.' He drew her close. 'You'll have to teach me.'

'Naughty.' She tapped his hand. 'Now, what about my supper?'

He pointed to a table. A lamp was burning on it and a tray of food was set: bread, slices of beef and ham, boiled eggs, sweet apple tart, a bottle of red wine and two glasses.

'You were expecting company?' she asked. 'Two glasses?'

'The girl knows that I often bring a fellow or two back with me after I have been out.' He scrutinized her as she gazed around the room. 'Do you like it?'

'It's very lavish.' She observed the luxurious red velvet curtains, the opulent silk cushions scattered on the deep buttoned sofas and chairs, and the soft glow of the lamps in the corners of the room. 'But it doesn't seem like a man's room.'

The corner of his lips twitched slightly. 'I will show you the rest later, after we have eaten.'

They ate their supper and as Betsy relaxed onto a deep sofa she began to feel very tired.

'You're not looking forward to that long drive home, are you?' he asked, bringing her another glass of wine and coming to sit beside her.

'I confess I'm not, and I feel so guilty that you will have to drive back again. We have no spare guest room, I'm afraid.' *And I can't imagine Tom or George wanting to share their beds with you*, she thought soberly.

'Ah,' he said softly and then put his glass down on a side table and stroked her hand. 'And I would find it very difficult to sleep on a sofa, knowing that you were only a flight of stairs away.'

She smiled, seeing the desire in his eyes, and the way in which they followed the curve of her neck down to her breasts. *I don't want to go home yet*, she thought. *I'd rather stay and watch the fireworks and the procession. Perhaps I could persuade him to let me stay the night; he has a maid here, it would be quite a proper thing to do.*

He picked up his glass of wine again and held it to

355

her lips. 'Do you have to go home, my sweet little Betsy? Would your family be very anxious?'

'Yes, probably. Though they think I am with my cousin.' She gave a small gasp as the truth slipped out.

'Ah! So they don't know where you are?' His eyes gleamed with interest. 'What a naughty girl you are to deceive your mama.'

'Not my mother,' she said petulantly. 'I haven't a mother. I have a father and three brothers.'

'A father and three brothers!' Alarm showed on his face and she laughed, the wine was making her feel quite merry again, her tiredness disappearing.

'My father is a cripple and one of my brothers has gone away.' She leaned towards him and put her face close to his. 'So there would only be two who would come chasing you.'

'I remember one of your brothers,' he said grimly. 'He was at your cousin's wedding.' He pondered for a moment. 'But they don't know where you are?' He fingered the buttons on her bodice. 'Does anyone else? Do you not have a sweetheart whom you confide in?'

She thought dreamily of Luke, his big strong body, his head of golden hair. If only he had more delicacy, more refinement, instead of his vital needs, how perfect he would be. 'No,' she whispered, and felt a twinge of guilt. 'There is no-one special.'

He started to unfasten the buttons. 'You're lying, my beautiful Betsy,' he whispered and put his hand inside her bodice and eased out her breasts. 'But I don't mind if you are, my plump little pigeon.' He licked his lips and lowered them to her nipples. 'I'm fond of a little intrigue. It's what makes life so enjoyable.'

She lay back on the sofa and watched his soft white hands as he took off her boots and lifted her skirts to unroll her stockings. *It's too late now, Betsy*, she thought hazily and closed her eyes. *Too late to change your mind.*

*　　*　　*

He caught her wrist as she was about to slip out of bed. 'Where are you going?' he asked and roughly pulled her back.

'Ooh!' She rubbed her wrist and tried to prise off his fingers. 'I was only going to look at the fireworks.'

He rolled on top of her. 'You little firecracker, you don't have to look outside, there are enough explosions going on in here.'

'You said we could watch the procession.' She breathed heavily beneath his weight.

'So we can, what's left of it.' He swung off her. 'Get up,' he demanded. 'Go and stand over there, by the lamp.' She picked up her cotton shift. 'No,' he said. 'Leave that. Just as you are.'

She felt embarrassed in her nakedness. It had been all right beneath the sheets, but now she felt exposed. But she did as he asked and stood with the light shining on her and her hands clasped in front of her.

'Turn around.'

She turned her back to him, facing the window. The night sky was lit by Shooting Stars, by Catherine Wheels and great flashes of colour to the accompaniment of crashes and bangs as the fireworks were set off.

He came and stood behind her, pressing himself close and nuzzling his head into her hair and neck. He ran his hands around her belly and breasts. 'Perfect,' he murmured into her ear. 'Magnificent. As round as a dumpling. Just as a woman should be.' He dug his fingers into her flesh, kneading and squeezing and pinching and then turned her round. His lips were wet and the dark pupils of his eyes dilated. She swallowed. Not again. How many more times? Did the man not tire?

It seemed that he did not, for once more he took her and then fell asleep, his arms flung across her so that she couldn't get up without disturbing him. She looked around the room. This, too, was lavishly furnished with heavy curtains and drapes, and mirrors on the wardrobe doors so that she could see herself as she lay in bed beside him. She felt mildly shocked, with a sense of dismay that he would have been watching all that they were doing.

She slid under his arm and, checking that he was still asleep, crept out of bed and stood in front of one of the mirrors. She had never seen herself completely naked before. They didn't have full-length mirrors at home, and if they had, she wouldn't have thought of looking at herself like this. *It's like looking at a picture,* she mused, *only the women in the picture are always draped in something flimsy, but I've always thought that that made them seem more erotic.*

As she gazed past herself in the mirror, she saw the lamp glowing by the bed and the swathed hangings from the tester, and then blinked as she realized that Charles Craddock was leaning on his elbow watching her, an amused smile on his face.

'Do you like what you see?' he asked.

'I – I don't know,' she said. *I only know that I am getting plumper,* she thought, as she turned to face him. *But still, he likes the way I am.* 'Do you like what you see?'

'Oh, yes. I do.' He held out his hand for her to come and she climbed back into bed. 'I've been thinking as I was watching you, my romping country wench. Why don't you stay a few days? You'll probably be in trouble if you go home now, so why not stay? Write a letter to your father and tell him that you are staying with friends. What about it?'

She looked dubious. 'Well, I don't know. And I haven't a change of gown.'

'Phww. That's nothing. Tomorrow we will buy you a dozen gowns, and a new bonnet.' He put his hand under her chin. 'And tonight, if I don't take you home, I shall take you to a party.'

'A party!' she exclaimed, her eyes lighting up. 'What kind of a party?'

'A gambling party. And if I win, then you shall have a present.'

A party! And a present! She had made up her mind already. What had she to go home for? There was no fun, only dreariness, with three men to look after. She felt a brief pang of grief as she thought of her father. She would write immediately and go out and post the letter.

'All right,' she said, with seeming reluctance. 'I'll stay.'

'I thought you would.' He smiled and drew her towards him. 'Now, come here.'

35

Tom went again to the gate and looked down the lane. He called to George. 'Go down to the village, will you, and see if there's any sign of them.' He was beginning to worry. It was seven o'clock and still no sign of Betsy and Sammi.

'I can't think what's keeping them, Da,' he said as he went back into the house. 'They must have cleaned the shops out lock, stock and barrel by this time.'

'They'll be back.' His father pressed his hands against the arms of his chair, taking his weight on his arms and stood on one foot for a moment, before dropping back into the chair again. 'Two lasses together, they'll be having a fine old time. It's good for Betsy to get out, she's been looking peaky lately.'

Tom nodded. It was just that he had a sneaking suspicion that Betsy was up to something; she'd been so vague about her trip out with Sammi. 'Where did she say she was going, Da? Was it into Hull or Hornsea?'

'Well, I don't rightly know. I don't recall her saying exactly.'

That's right, she didn't, Tom pondered. Nor did she say how they were going. 'Were they going in Sammi's trap, or was Johnson driving them in the carriage?'

'They must have been going to Hornsea. She said summat about Sammi's trap.' His father shifted uncomfortably and winced. 'I can't remember what. Summat about meeting her in 'village to save turning round. So she'd never drive all 'way to Hull in 'trap, would she?'

'No. No, of course she wouldn't.'

'There's no sign of 'em.' George came back inside. 'So we'd best get our own supper.'

At half-past eight, Tom strode into the village himself and walked down the main street and stood looking down the long road which led into Hull. The road curved sinuously over the hummocky plain, dipping and gently rising, disappearing below the hollows and then reappearing again a few miles on. It was empty. Not a horse or cart or carriage, not a man or woman to disturb its tranquillity. It was as empty as it had been when he had last waved good-bye to Mark.

Then he turned and walked to the other end of the village and stood on the rise, looking down the road leading towards the coastal town of Hornsea. There was a lone rider coming towards him, a farmhand by the look of him, riding on a shaggy hooved plough horse. He was about to call and ask if he had seen anything of Miss Rayner's trap, when he thought better of it. No point in spreading the word around the whole village unnecessarily; instead he called as the man drew close, 'I'm waiting of a delivery. Have you seen anyone else on the road?'

The farmhand tipped his cap and shook his head. 'I've not come far, only from Redshaw's, but there's nobody else on 'road.'

Tom walked back to the mill. The sun had gone down and though it wasn't yet dusk, the evening was grey with low-hung clouds, threatening rain.

'I'll wait a bit longer and then ride over to Garston Hall,' he announced. 'Betsy's perhaps gone back with Sammi to spend the night there, though I think she might have called home first.'

His father looked worried, though now an angry frown creased his forehead. 'She'll feel 'sharp end of my tongue when she does get in,' he said. 'Nine o'clock and not yet home! Unless summat's happened,' he added anxiously.

'Nowt'll have happened, Da.' George bit into a slice

of raised pork pie. 'She just gets mad at us allus watching out for her. She'll be staying out late on purpose.'

Tom put on his jacket over his flannel shirt and brushed his dark hair in front of the mirror.

'Tha doesn't have to get toffed up to see thy kin.' George eased a piece of meat from a hollow tooth with his tongue. 'Unless tha's expecting to be invited to supper.'

'And you don't have to talk with your mouth full, but you do,' Tom answered back sharply. 'Watch out for Da. I'll be back as quick as I can.'

The road to Monkston was pot-holed, some of the hollows had been filled with sand and pebbles, but his Cleveland bay picked his way steadily on powerful limbs. There was a rush of white wings as a barn owl flew past, and in the hedgerow he could hear the rustling and twittering of disturbed finches, buntings and wrens.

A light was showing in one of the bedroom windows, and Tom assumed that it was Victoria's room. She hadn't been well again and everyone was worried about her. Another lamp was burning in a downstairs sitting-room, though the drawing-room window was in darkness. He rang the bell and waited. He had a strange feeling in the pit of his stomach. The maid who opened the door gave him a bright smile. 'Good evening, Mr Foster,' she said and bobbed her knee.

'Er, good evening.'

'You don't recognize me, do you, sir?' She opened the door wider to let him in.

He shook his head. 'Oh,' he said. 'Yes, of course. It's Jenny. How are you? Are you enjoying your work here?'

'Yes, sir, thank you. Though I'm coming to your house soon.' She gave him a beaming smile. 'As soon as Mrs Rayner thinks I'm ready, I'll be coming.'

'We'll look forward to that.' *She's a merry little soul,* he thought, *she'll cheer Father up no end.*

'Are Mr and Mrs Rayner at home, Jenny? I need to speak to them. Or Miss Sammi?'

'I regret Mr and Mrs Rayner are not at home.' She answered parrot-fashion as if she had been rehearsing. 'But Miss Sammi is,' she added eagerly. 'Shall I take you through?'

'Please,' he said, and followed her across the hall. 'Is my sister with her?'

'No, sir!' She looked blank at his question, then, knocking on the sitting-room door, she opened it and announced, 'Mr Tom Foster, Miss Sammi.'

Sammi was sitting on a sofa by a low fire, an opened book lying at her side. 'Hello, Tom! What brings you here?'

'I'm looking for Betsy. Isn't she here?'

A frown creased her brow. 'No. I haven't seen her for a few days. Why did you think she was here?' She motioned him to sit beside her.

Tom bit his lip. Something was wrong. Betsy had lied. 'She said something about a shopping trip. We're sure she said you were going too.'

'No. Betsy knew that I had to stay here with Victoria,' she disclosed. 'I told her that Mama and Pa were going up to the Wolds for a few days. Victoria is feeling a little better,' she added, 'so they made the most of the opportunity.'

'Who else might she have gone with?' Tom asked, perturbed that he couldn't think of the name of a single female whom Betsy had befriended.

'No-one,' Sammi said slowly. 'She has never had much time for anyone in the village.' She tapped her finger on her lips and he followed the curve of her mouth with his eyes. 'What time did she go?'

'Early. She was rather vague, yet she mentioned something to Da about you.'

'I think she's gone into Hull!' Sammi thought it through. 'I told her about the opening of the new park, and what fun it was going to be. Billy and Gilbert were both going. If she has gone, she will have gone in with the Hornsea carrier!'

'Which park?' Tom frowned. 'And why would she go without telling us?'

'The People's Park,' she said. 'Billy told me all about it. There's to be a fête, and entertainment with fireworks this evening. That's where she'll be, Tom. And you wouldn't have let her go alone.' She looked at him frankly. 'That's why she didn't tell you.'

There was a knock on the door and it was immediately opened. Martha stood there with a rigid expression on her face.

'Yes, Martha?' Sammi looked up in surprise. 'What is it?'

'Beg pardon, Miss Sammi. But I wondered if there was something wrong – Master Tom being here so late, I mean.' She looked from one to another as they sat side by side, and Tom gave a slight smile at her hostile expression. She wavered. 'With Mr and Mrs Rayner being away and it being so late for calling,' she repeated, looking again at Tom. 'I wondered if there was anything I could assist with?'

Tom rose to his feet. Anyone could, of course, misinterpret his visit. 'I'm anxious about my sister, Martha. She hasn't arrived home from a shopping trip and I thought she was with Miss Sammi.'

'Not arrived home! My word!' Martha was aghast. 'Where in the world can she be at this time of night?'

'Thank you, Martha, that will be all. Master Tom is leaving shortly.' Sammi grimaced as Martha closed the door behind her, and she and Tom exchanged a smile. 'She's like a mother hen when Mama is away,' she whispered. 'I've been thinking.' She rose to her feet. 'If Hull was very busy because of the fête and Betsy missed the carrier to come home, the most sensible thing she could do would be to go and stay with Gilbert and Harriet, and catch the carrier again tomorrow.' She nodded reassuringly. 'That's what she will have done.'

'Do you think so?' His mind was drifting away from Betsy. *This setting is so right for her,* he reflected. Sammi seemed to be framed in the backcloth of the room; her back was to the overmantel mirror and he saw the red curls hanging down her back. Flowers were on a side table, blending with the pale green walls and the gold damask covers on the furniture.

'Tom? Don't worry.' She shook his arm gently, breaking his reverie. 'She will be all right, I'm sure. But come tomorrow and tell me, won't you?'

Without thinking, he leaned forward and kissed her on her cheek. 'Good-bye, Sammi.' He swallowed. 'Thank you. Yes. That's where she'll be. There's nothing I can do tonight anyway.'

She opened the sitting-room door for him and he begged her not to come out; there was no need, anyway, for there was Martha hovering in the hall, waiting to usher him out.

'I'm sorry, Martha,' he apologized. 'I had no idea that Mr and Mrs Rayner were away, but even if I had, I would still have come. I'm very anxious about my sister.'

'I do understand, sir. But I hope you understand my position too.' She pursed her lips. 'When young Jenny said as it was you calling on Miss Sammi, well, I thought there was something up.'

He laughed softly. 'You did perfectly right, of course, but I've been coming here all of my life, you surely know that I wouldn't compromise Miss Sammi?'

She didn't smile back but regarded him in a deliberate manner. 'It's not me as is the problem, Master Tom. It's tittle-tattling of others that we have to watch. Miss Sammi is of an age, and we have to mind her character.' She opened the door and ushered him out. 'Good night to you, sir.'

As he slung himself into the saddle, he felt more despondent than ever. He wished he could believe that Betsy would have gone to Gilbert's. It would be just like her to spend her money on a hotel, and a woman alone would not be viewed with respect. He sighed and dug his heels into the horse's flanks. And as for Martha, as she was so mindful of Sammi's reputation, even with him whom she knew so well, did it mean she was aware that there was a suitor somewhere on the horizon? And why had Sammi's parents chosen to go to the Wolds at this particular time? Were they anxious to arrange a marriage before rumour of Adam reached other ears? Was there a rich farmer up there considered suitable enough to ask for Sammi?

The next morning Tom walked down into the village to wait for the carrier on his journey into Hull. He hailed him as he waited outside the Raven Inn.

'Did you pick up a young lady yesterday morning?' he asked. 'Dark hair, yellow dress?'

'Aye, I did. Right bonny she was too. Going to 'opening of 'new park, she said. By, what a crush. Tha should have seen 'crowds. Did she get home all right?' he asked. 'I waited 'till gone three, like I said, but she didn't come.'

Tom rubbed his chin absently. 'No, she didn't. She must have stayed with a relative.'

'Aye, well that doesn't surprise me. Forty thousand visitors they reckoned they had in town. And it'll be 'same again today, 'cos Mayor's bairns are planting another tree and there'll be more festivities.' He clicked his tongue and the horses pulled away. 'So don't be too surprised if she doesn't get back tonight either. But I'll keep an eye open for her if tha's worried,' he shouted back. 'She said as how her brother generally took her in.'

Did she now? Tom's anxiety was replaced by anger. *It seems to me that Betsy has planned this escapade and given no thought to anyone else. Not Da, who needs her, and not George or me who might be worried about her.*

She didn't arrive back by the afternoon carrier, and George, who had been down to meet it, reported that the carrier had said that the town was still brimming with visitors.

'Dammit!' Tom struck the kitchen table with his fist. 'I don't know what to do.'

His father called through from the parlour, he'd obviously heard his exclamation. 'Tha'll have to go into Hull and look for her. Go to Monkston and see Sammi, ask her where she thinks she might be. She might have an idea. Then tha can go first thing in 'morning.'

Tom didn't think for one moment that Sammi would know where Betsy was staying apart from with Gilbert and Harriet, but he felt the need to be doing something, and he had also promised to tell Sammi as soon as he had news. *Which I haven't, I'm as much in the dark as I was yesterday. Where on earth has she got to?*

Martha opened the door to him this time. 'Still no news, Master Tom?' She pursed her lips. 'That's bad. I don't like 'sound of it at all. Who's looking after Mr Foster?' she asked keenly.

'My brother and I.' He was off-hand. *I could do without this badgering*, he griped. *I've enough to think about without your curious questioning.*

'Have you food in 'house, Master Tom?'

'Yes, thank you, Martha. Is Miss Sammi about, or are her parents back yet?'

'No, they're not,' she said anxiously. 'I wish they were. Miss Victoria's been poorly again today.'

'Oh, I'm sorry. Perhaps I should go?'

'No, come along in, sir. Miss Sammi could do with company maybe. She's had a tiring day.'

She's had a change of heart towards me, he thought grimly as he waited in the sitting-room. *I'm not such a threat after all.* He glanced around the room, everything was the same, firelight flickering, the flowers shedding petals and a slight fragrance, yet it seemed somehow empty without Sammi's presence. *Just as home does*, he mused. *It hasn't been the same since she left.*

'Miss Sammi said will you go up, Master Tom.' Martha stood in the doorway, a look of disapproval on her face.

'Up?' He looked questioningly at the servant.

'To Miss Victoria's room,' she said primly. 'Nurse has gone for a rest and Miss Sammi doesn't want to leave her sister. She said as you were to go on up,' she added, as if to say that the decision wasn't hers. She showed him upstairs and held open the door, then left, leaving it slightly ajar.

He tiptoed across the room to where Sammi was standing close to the bed. She wore a simple gown of grey, the folds falling softly about her. The room was lit by one low lamp and a small flickering fire; Victoria was asleep in the large bed, her face was pale but her breathing was regular.

Tom stood looking down at her. How long would they keep her? he wondered. She had suffered since childhood with her respiratory problems. Every harvest brought her difficulty as grain dust filled the air, and every winter the cold brought her low with bronchitis.

Sammi gave a deep shuddering breath beside him and he turned to her and took her hand. 'I thought she was so much better yesterday?' he whispered.

'She was,' she said quietly. 'And then she had another attack. I'm so glad that you are here, Tom,' she said tremulously. 'I felt so lonely. So worried.'

He pulled a long stool up to the bed and bade her sit down, then sat beside her so that they could both keep watch. He put his arm around her and she leant against him. 'You should have sent for me, Sammi. I would have come.'

'I almost did,' she said and put her head against his shoulder. 'Then I thought of how worried you had been about Betsy and Uncle Thomas, and I didn't want to bother you.' She turned her face towards him. 'Has Betsy come home?'

He shook his head. She was so close, so trusting. He would have to leave, he couldn't bear the nearness of her, it was cutting him in two.

'Tom! Where can she be?'

'Still enjoying herself I shouldn't wonder,' he said acidly. 'While we are all worrying about her.'

She didn't answer, but anxiety showed on her face and he noticed dark shadows beneath her eyes as if she hadn't slept.

'Rest for a moment,' he said, pulling her close once more. 'You look tired.' *It is enough,* he thought, *that I can be of comfort to her. If it is the least I can be, then so be it.*

Her hair brushed his cheek as she sat with her head against him and presently she mumbled softly, 'I'm so glad that you are here, Tom.' He didn't answer, but just listened to her steady breathing and watched Victoria as she turned her head on the pillow and slipped into a deep slumber.

His arm began to get cramped and he shifted slightly. 'Sammi,' he whispered, 'I have to go.'

She didn't answer and he leaned his head forward to look at her: her eyes were closed and she was lost in sleep. He manoeuvred himself to his feet, and lifted her into his arms. Her head was in the crook of his arm and he stood for a moment just looking at her. Then he bent his head and kissed her lightly, his lips on hers. She moved slightly and sighed; he moved towards the door. Martha was coming up the stairs and she stopped as she saw them.

'Ssh,' he said softly. 'Show me to Miss Sammi's bedroom. She's fast asleep.'

Martha, with tight lips, turned at the top of the stairs and took him along the landing to Sammi's room. He remembered where it was, for he had been in it when they were children, but he didn't recognize it now without the childish toys and hangings. This was a woman's room, with swathed drapes and soft fragrance.

He carefully placed her on the bed and turned to go. 'Miss Victoria's asleep too, Martha,' he said quietly, 'but you'd better rouse the nurse to sit by her.'

'Aye. I will. You can leave everything to me, Master Tom. You'll want to be getting back home,' she said firmly.

He nodded. He wanted to smile. If she had appeared a moment sooner, she would have thrown him out on his ears; as it was, he could sense her bristling disapproval at finding Sammi in his arms. But she wouldn't say a word, of that he was sure.

Jenny was standing in the hall. She was wearing an outdoor cloak and a small bag was on the floor by her feet.

'I hope I'm doing right, Master Tom.' Martha followed him down the stairs. 'I don't want to step out of turn, and I would have asked Miss Sammi if she hadn't been asleep, but I've told young Jenny she's to go back with you.'

He stared at her.

'She can ride up behind you,' she said. 'And she can stop until 'mistress gets back, then she'll decide what's to be done. But I can't think of thy poor fayther with no woman to tend him.'

'Thank you, Martha.' He was moved by her concern. 'It's kind of you.'

Martha surveyed Jenny and then brushed a speck of dust from her cloak. 'She's a good girl, you'll have no bother with her. And she was coming to 'mill house eventually, anyway.'

Tom gave a small smile. *She doesn't trust me with Sammi, yet I'm allowed to ride through the darkness with this young maid!*

They went outside, the moon was just breaking through the clouds, edging them with translucent light. Across the sea, it drew a path of silver and sparkled on the breaking wave crests, which sighed and lamented as they broke against the cliffs.

'All right, Jenny?' he asked as he put her bag at the front of the saddle and prepared to mount.

She was staring, transfixed, at the sight of the ocean. 'Yes,' she breathed. 'It's so big, isn't it? It makes me feel so small, as if, as if I'm of no account, of no importance.' She looked up at him waiting for her on his mount. 'It frightens me, Master Tom.'

'Then you won't mind coming to Tillington with me?' he said, holding out his hand to hoist her up. 'There's no sea at Tillington.'

She put her foot on the mounting block and took hold of his hand to heave herself up. 'No,' she said. 'I'm glad to come, though this is a nice house and they've been good to me. But I just wish—'

They trotted on down the long winding drive which led down to the old lane of Monkston; a stoat bounded in front of the horse's hooves, its moulting red coat showing streaks of white in the moonlight; they heard the scuttle of a rabbit and then its scream as the spitting predator struck.

'What, Jenny? What do you wish?'

'I just wish that Miss Sammi was coming too.'

'Ah,' he breathed, so that she couldn't hear him. 'So do I, Jenny. So do I.'

36

Billy stood by the refreshment tent the next day and waited for the proceedings to finish. The Mayor's children planted the second tree to the sound of great cheers, and the festivities began once more. A horde of children stampeded towards the tent where they had been promised, by a clown in curly wig and false red nose, that they could have a free coffee and piece of cake at his expense.

He moved out of the way and found a convenient place to stand where he could watch out for Mr Pearson to become free. He looked again at the crowd and judged that there were as many people as the day before, but the crowd were not quite so elegant; there were also many more children, as the children of the workhouses and Trinity House had been admitted free of charge. *There's the girl in yellow again; she does have an appearance of Betsy,* he thought, *though her face is shadowed by her bonnet.* He narrowed his eyes to observe her and her companion. *He looks familiar.* Billy stared harder. *Craddock! That's who it is. So it can't possibly be Betsy. He's quite a libertine according to what I hear. Perhaps it's the woman he brought to Gilbert's wedding who caused such a scene with Harriet's father, and whom Tom escorted to the door! Craddock won't forget that evening in a hurry,* he mused wryly. *I can't understand why Gilbert invited him in the first place, he's surely not a friend?*

A young barefoot boy walked past him, his cheeks bulging with cake and Billy scanned the crowd to see if he could find any of the children from the cellars, for if he could, he thought, he would take some of them with him to meet the Mayor. But strangely, he couldn't see one familiar face.

Nor had he seen them last evening as he had walked back into the town to see the firework display and the German Working Men's torchlit procession as it wound its way around the town. The crowds had followed them and, with their torches held high, they sang their vigorous songs outside the Royal Station Hotel where the Mayor and his party were celebrating the end of the festive day with a splendid banquet.

The Mayor had come out to thank them and pledged his continued support to the working classes of the town. A great cheer went up and Billy joined in. *He's the man*, he'd thought exultantly. *He's the one who can help.*

The Mayor was free! The crowd surrounding him had moved away and there was only a handful of people by his side. Billy hurried across and approached one of his aides. Mr Pearson glanced up as his aide spoke to him and then, excusing himself to his other guests, came across to Billy. He shook him by the hand. 'Your cousin has explained a little of what you have in mind, Mr Rayner. Do you not think that the orphans of this town are catered for sufficiently? We have our workhouses, our hospitals and Children's Unions, a school even, for children of seamen.'

'And excellent establishments they are, I'm sure sir, with some exceptions,' Billy said bluntly. 'But I have in mind an establishment especially created for the children who live on the streets: a home which they can call their own and where they can attend workshops and gain education and training. They are independent, most of them, used to fending for themselves,' he implored earnestly. 'Their energy needs to be channelled in a direction other than foraging, so that they can eventually go out and earn their own living.'

Mr Pearson drummed his fingers together. 'You say they live on the streets?'

'Yes, sir. They live in cellars below ground, with rats and mice for company. I've seen them trying to keep dry when the rain pours in and the *mud*, for want of a more descriptive word, seeps into the cellars. The situation, sir,' he said boldly, 'is a stain on our society.'

The Mayor viewed him candidly. 'Do you have an occupation, Mr Rayner?'

'I am at present working with my cousin at Masterson and Rayner, sir.'

'And would you be willing to give up your position if such an organization was set up?'

Billy felt a surge of hope. 'Yes, sir. I would.'

'Why?' The Mayor was blunt. 'What motivates a young man like you to give up the promise of a good career, position and standing in society for the sake of down-and-outs who probably won't appreciate what you do for them?'

'I have so much, sir. Family, friends, security,' Billy said quietly. 'And they have nothing, no hope or expectations, through no fault of their own. Circumstances dictated that they should live in the gutter. They are young, they deserve more than they have at present.'

Mr Pearson nodded in agreement. Then he put out his hand. 'Let me think it over,' he said. 'I think I might know one or two people who would be interested. Yes. Benevolent men who have money and time to spare.'

'Thank you, sir.' Billy beamed. 'I would be so grateful.'

The Mayor started to move away and then turned back. 'Have you thought of a name for this venture?'

Billy swallowed. 'I have, sir.' He felt so full of emotion. 'Three words only. Three words without whose aspirations we are all lost.'

Pearson gave a compassionate smile at his youthful earnestness. 'And they are?'

'Faith, Hope and Charity.'

He walked back into town, elation giving a spring to his step. *I must write to Sammi and tell her, she will be so delighted. And Jenny too, she must be told that her friends are to be given a chance such as she has had. She was the first to escape from that Devil's Hole. I'll go to the cellars before I go to my lodgings,* he decided. *Though I'd better not say anything yet, just in case the plans don't materialize. But I'll find out why they didn't come to the park. It's not like them to miss out on a treat.*

There were several boys sitting on the cellar steps as he approached. They all had their heads scrunched down into their jackets and their hands in their pockets. Tim, one of the smaller boys, looked up. His skin looked yellow and flaky, and his eyes were small and sunken in his cheeks.

'What's up, Tim? Somebody pinched your space?'

He shook his head and then looked down at the floor. 'No.'

'Have you had anything to eat today?'

Again he shook his head. 'Not hungry.'

Billy sat on the wall and looked down at them. 'You didn't come to the fête at the park today! There was food and drink and games. I was expecting you.'

'Some of us was sick,' Tim muttered. 'That's why we didn't come.'

Billy glanced from one to another. Something was wrong.

'Some of us is very sick,' said another. 'That's why we're out here. 'Stink's making us sicker.'

'That's not why I'm out here.' Tim put his head onto his knees. 'I'm out here 'cos our Mary's asleep in 'bed. I can't get warm 'cos of her.'

'What do you mean, Tim?'

The boy sniffed. 'She's that cold I can't get near her.'

Billy got to his feet. 'When you say they're sick – how sick do you mean?'

One of the older boys said, 'Some of them's been

sick since 'weekend, only it's gotten worse.' He wrinkled his nose. ''Other end as well, Master Billy. We tried to clean 'em up but we've no water. Them that's sick has drunk it all, they were that thirsty, and when we went to get another bucketful from 'tap down yonder,' he indicated with his thumb across to a nearby court, ''folks there chased us off – said as we were up to summat.'

Billy descended the steps. 'I shouldn't go in if I was thee,' one of the boys called after him. 'Tha can't tek a deep breath down there. Not unless tha puts 'scarf round tha nose.'

Billy pulled out the silk scarf which he had had inside his jacket collar and put it around his mouth and nose, then pushed aside the planks of wood and sheets of cardboard at the entrance. He couldn't at first discern anything in the gloom, but his nostrils were assailed by a fetid stench. He retched but resisted the urge to turn around and rush back outside. Instead, he put his hand over his nose and ventured further into the dank and gloomy interior, and as his eyes became accustomed to the dimness he saw several children lying together in a corner. Some were on makeshift beds, others were lying on sheets of cardboard, covered by pieces of old carpet and rags. Pools of vomit lay festering beside them.

'God in Heaven,' he muttered. 'What has happened?' He moved cautiously over to them, speaking in a low voice so as not to frighten them, for above all they were mistrustful of adults, seeing them all as dictatorial authority.

'It's Billy,' he whispered. 'Billy Rayner. I've come to help you.'

There was a low moan from a bundle of rags and someone half sat up. It was Dinah, she was a friend of Jenny's and about her age. 'Master Billy.' She licked her dry lips. 'I'm that thirsty and I've got terrible cramps in me belly. I think I'm dying!' She started to cry. 'I want me ma.'

He put his hand on her forehead. It was cold and her skin was wrinkled and dry like an old woman's. 'How long have you been like this?' he asked urgently. 'Are you all the same?'

She nodded, she had hardly the strength to speak. 'Since Sat'day,' she said weakly. 'Some of little children are worse. They haven't been able to keep owt down.' She pointed to an empty bucket and then flopped down again onto the floor. 'We've drunk 'bucket dry.'

He stumbled across to another of the beds. It was made of wooden boxes and was off the ground. He carefully pulled away the coat which was covering the child beneath. It was Mary, Tim's sister. She was lying still and silent; Billy put out a tentative finger and touched her cheek. It was icy cold.

He faltered for a moment and then staggered away. 'I'll fetch help,' he croaked, though he doubted that anyone was listening and headed for the entrance and fresh air. He retched and retched. He couldn't stop himself, he was so horrified and nauseated at the sights he had seen below ground. The boys watched him with unblinking expressions. It was as if they were inured of all feelings and emotions.

He wiped his mouth and straightened up. 'I'm going to fetch a doctor. I'll be back as soon as I can.'

'They won't take them into 'Infirmary, will they?' asked Tim. 'Our Mary won't want to go. Not without I go with her.'

Billy's eyes smarted. How could he explain to this small boy that his sister wouldn't be going anywhere ever again? He turned away. Where to go? Not all doctors would be willing to come to patients who couldn't pay.

Then he remembered Doctor Fleming, who had often been called upon to attend casualties at Masterson and Rayner; mainly to porters or seamen who had injured themselves during the course of their work. *I can but ask*, he thought as he set off at a run towards Lowgate where the doctor lived.

A carriage was waiting outside the doctor's house and the doctor just emerging into the street to enter it.

'Doctor Fleming,' Billy said breathlessly. 'You're needed urgently. There are some very sick children—'

'There are sick people all over this town, young man.' The doctor looked at him from over his round spectacles. 'But I cannot attend them all. You must find someone else, I fear.'

He put one foot on the step of his carriage. 'Where are they, these children? Are they within walking distance? And how many of them?'

'They're in the cellars in North Church Side. It's only five minutes, sir. If you could just come. There are about seven or eight of them, all very sick.'

The doctor stepped down and confronted Billy. 'In the cellars? Which cellars?'

'Where the warehouse burnt down, sir.' Billy spoke quickly, trying to impress the urgency upon him. 'That's where they live.'

'Beggar children, are they? Vagrants?'

'Yes, sir,' Billy said despondently. So now he wouldn't come. He'd have to find someone else.

The doctor put his foot back onto the carriage step and entered. After closing the door, he pushed down the window. 'I can't come. I'm on my way to a woman about to give birth. Ring the bell on my door. My nephew is there. Tell him I told him to go with you. It'll do him good to see life in the raw rather than reading about it in his text books.'

He tapped on the roof of the carriage with his cane and it pulled away, leaving Billy feeling guilty for his erroneous attitude towards the diligent doctor.

Doctor Sheppard was a brisk, eager young man who grabbed his bag and hurried after Billy as soon as he was told of his uncle's directive. 'Thank heavens,' he said. 'I thought I was going to be twiddling my thumbs all night.'

'Why didn't you go to the birthing?' Billy asked curiously.

'The woman wouldn't have me,' he said cheerfully. 'She said having one male there was more than was seemly. It's a breech and likely to be a forceps job, otherwise she wouldn't have had my uncle either. You know what women are like,' he added. 'They think that men are in the way at such a time.'

Billy reflected that they were probably right. How could men be expected to understand the rigours of birth? The only births that he had seen were those of lambs and calves and small animals like kittens and pups in the stables at Garston Hall, when he had watched in awesome fascination.

'Where are we going?' Doctor Sheppard looked around the street as Billy slowed from his fast trot as they neared the cellar steps.

'I'm afraid it's pretty rough down here,' Billy said, and the boys who were still sitting near the steps moved back to let the doctor through. They ducked their heads as they went through the low opening and entered the dark and musty interior.

'What in God's name is this place? It's as black as *Hades*.' The doctor slipped and almost stumbled. 'Surely no-one lives in this wretched place? Is there no light?'

'There is no light,' Billy said grimly. 'Not down here, or in their lives. Wait a moment and your eyes will become accustomed. These are all children living alone,' he explained, 'though there are other people living further back; families and some single people – some drunks, some escaping from the law. But no-one interferes with the other, everybody keeps to themselves.'

'I'm going to be sick,' the doctor muttered. 'The air is foul.'

'Try not to breathe too deeply,' Billy advised him.

'Thanks for the advice, *doctor*,' Doctor Sheppard said sardonically. 'I'll try to remember.'

Billy gave a spontaneous grin in the darkness, though he felt far from humorous. Here was a man he could relate to. 'Here they are,' he whispered as they reached the children. 'One child is dead. They've been drinking from a bucket of water which smells putrid.'

'That doesn't surprise me. The water is still being drawn from the River Hull, and we know well what gets thrown in there.' Sheppard pulled back the coat covering Tim's sister and hastily threw it back again. 'She's dead all right, has been for some time. We'll have to get the body out before it starts decomposing.'

Billy put his hand to his mouth as nausea overtook him.

'Breathe through your mouth if you feel faint,' Doctor Sheppard said. 'Never mind the stench, and if you're going to be sick, go and get it over with.'

'No, I'm all right,' Billy gasped. It was not the nauseating stench but the thought of the poor child, Tim's sister, spoken of in such basic terms that had sickened him.

'This is Dinah,' he said, going to where the young girl lay. 'She said they'd been sick since Saturday.'

Doctor Sheppard put his hand on Dinah's forehead as Billy had done less than half an hour ago. 'I don't know if we can save her,' he said. 'We have to get them out of here. They need fresh water; saline.' He put his hands to his head. 'I've not seen it before. But I'm almost sure.'

'What?' Billy asked, staring open-mouthed at his stricken face.

'It's cholera.'

37

Gilbert leaned back and put his feet up on the desk. He felt rather pleased with himself. He had been included in the assembly of notable shipping personages of the town in the procession to the new public park, and had had discussions with eminent members of the shipping and commerce professions on the state of the whaling industry. At least, he had listened and sagely nodded his head when points had been brought up, and he had agreed that the industry wasn't what it had once been, now that there were fewer whaling ships sailing from Hull.

The Greenland Yards, which prepared and boiled the blubber for processing into oil, were in the process of being closed down, while other industries were springing up as new machinery was developed; seed oil was displacing whale oil, and coal gas for street lighting had long ago supplanted the product of the whale. But, Gilbert had considered complacently, theirs was a well-established firm, which ran smoothly on standards of good sense and practicability set long ago.

He was gratified, too, by his own personal finances. The money borrowed and speculated at Billington's suggestion had proved a sound investment. He had paid back the original loan and with the interest accrued he had reinvested again, once more on Austin Billington's advice. He had transferred the company's business to Billington's bank and severed all connections with the previous bank.

Yes, things are going pretty well, he thought smugly. *Billington's the man for us; he's sharp and forward-looking,*

*not afraid to take a bit of a chance, unlike that old stick
in the mud, Collins. I might even have a wager,* he mused.
*It's quite some time since I had a game of crib. Although
Harriet wouldn't approve. I shouldn't have to tell her.*

He had been prompted towards this fancy when
he'd caught sight of Craddock in the town. Craddock
had a large parcel beneath his arm and he'd crossed
over the road deliberately in order to speak to Gilbert.

'Don't see you these days, Rayner,' he said fa-
cetiously. 'Little wifey keep you under lock and key,
does she?'

'Not at all,' Gilbert replied stiffly. 'I've been very
busy.'

'Of course.' Craddock smiled. 'I do understand.
But there's a game on this evening if you're interested. Bring Mrs Rayner if you think she'd like a
gamble.'

'She wouldn't.' Gilbert wouldn't dream of taking
Harriet to such places. Gambling dens were not
suitable for ladies of Harriet's sensitivities.

'Can't blame you, old fellow.' Craddock gave him
an insidious grin. 'It's cost me a fortune.' He indicated the parcel. 'My little lady saw me win last
night and wheedled a new gown out of me.' He
winked. 'I told her if she was specially nice to me, I
would come out and buy her one from Madame
Schubert.'

'Indeed?' Gilbert had moved away. 'Must be off.'

'Don't forget then!' Craddock called out. 'Tonight
at the Squirrel Club, ten o'clock. If you're allowed
out!'

Ten o'clock, he pondered, taking his feet off the
desk and reaching for the hand bell. *It's tempting,
though I don't know what excuse I would give if I went out
at that hour.*

'Yes, sir?' His clerk answered the bell.

'Ask my cousin to come up will you, Jennings.'
Gilbert busily shuffled some papers around his desk.

'Mr Billy hasn't come in today, sir.'

Gilbert looked up. 'Not come in? Have you had word from him? Is he sick?'

'We haven't heard, sir. We knew that he wasn't going to be in Monday or Tuesday, but expected him as usual today. Should I send round to his lodgings?'

'Yes, you'd better – mm, no, on second thoughts, don't bother, leave it until later in the day. Perhaps he's been held up with something.'

The clerk turned back to the door.

'Send Hardwick up then. Ask him to bring the accounts that he was working on yesterday.'

'I'm sorry, Mr Rayner. Mr Hardwick isn't in either. He had a message to go down to 'docks while you were out earlier and he hasn't got back yet.'

Gilbert sighed. 'All right. Send either of them up if and when they get back.'

Jennings closed the door behind him. Gilbert rose and stood by the window. Below him, in the Old Harbour, barges and tug boats were packed into the narrow waterway, and on the quayside the porters and tally men were counting coils of ropes and checking crates of equipment before despatching them down the river to the docks, where some of the old wooden whaling ships were laid up for further strengthening.

The *Polar Star Two* and *Arctic Star* were iron ships, powered by steam, and although they had both had successful voyages, the seamen who sailed on them were less than satisfied, being of the opinion that the wooden ships rode the waters of the Arctic and withstood the pressures of the ice much better than the iron vessels. But there was still a disparity of opinion as other men told of the long journeys tracking through the ice before the advent of steam arrived to quicken their voyage through that harsh landscape.

Perhaps we should diversify, he thought. *We have had good catches of seals over the last couple of years, better than the whales. Maybe it's true that there are fewer whales than there once were. Perhaps on the next voyage we'll try for seals in Newfoundland rather than the Davis Straits for whales.* He sighed. *Decisions, decisions. I wish Father was here.*

There was a pad of running feet on the stairs and an urgent knock on the door. He turned from the window and returned reluctantly to his desk.

'Sorry, Mr Gilbert. But can you come down to 'docks?' Hardwick, whose forefathers had been with the firm for almost a century, stood flushed and breathless in the doorway.

'What's happened? Is something wrong?' It wasn't like Hardwick to be so agitated. He was not given to panic.

'Some of 'other whalers are in.' He stood in front of Gilbert's desk. 'Two of Brown's; *Lara*, belonging to Wymark's, and two more of Samuelson's are off 'Shetlands.'

'Yes – and?' There was more to come, judging by Hardwick's anxious face.

'They've none of them seen '*Polar Star Two*, not since they set off from Shetlands on 'outward voyage.' He took a deep breath. 'And they've not seen '*Arctic Star* since she was in Melville Bay.'

'Plenty of time. Plenty of time. Another month yet before we need to start worrying.' Gilbert sounded more confident than he felt.

'For '*Arctic Star*, yes, perhaps, sir. But not for '*Star Two*. *Lara* was 'last to see her. Nobody has seen her since. She's disappeared. She's gone from 'face of 'earth.'

'Rubbish! There are other ships due in. Somebody will have seen her.' He frowned. 'There's something else bothering you, Hardwick?'

'Yes, sir. That's why I wanted you to come down to 'docks. There was a message for you to go earlier, but you weren't here, so I went instead.' He tapped the desk top with his fingertips. 'There are some women waiting by 'dock side. Wives of men from both ships. They're a bit agitated as well they might be. But –

but, they're blaming 'company, sir. They're saying that '*Star Two* voyage was doomed from 'start.'

'Doomed from the start! What is that supposed to mean?' Gilbert exploded. 'She's a good ship. Seaworthy!'

'It's because no-one from 'company saw her off, Mr Gilbert. I know that you sent her a message, but they're saying that that wasn't good enough, that there should have been somebody there.'

Gilbert stared at the man in front of him. Hardwick would understand these women more than anyone. His was an old seafaring family, and he would know of all the old superstitions and customs, and although seeing off the departure of company ships had been instigated by the senior members of Masterson and Rayner themselves, the tradition was now firmly entrenched and had become part of a ritual, so important to the superstitious sea-going folk.

'I'll come down.' He strode from behind his desk and reached for his hat from the stand. 'You'd better come with me, Hardwick, and we'll sort it out together.'

Some of the women gathered on the dock side had taken time from work; many were from the fish yards and were wearing their wooden clogs, and with swollen reddened hands were clutching the woollen shawls which were draped around their heads. Others had small children clinging to their skirts or babies at their breasts.

Gilbert was uneasy. He didn't know how to speak to these women; he felt, too, that they didn't really trust him, not in the way they had trusted his father, who, he suspected, they regarded as their guardian while their husbands, brothers or sons were sailing in his ships.

'What seems to be the problem?' he asked heartily, rubbing his hands together as he spoke. 'You know as well as I, that a whaler can be overdue for all kinds of reasons.' As he spoke the words he realized that he had spoken unwisely. At the word *overdue*, the women looked at each other anxiously and muttered uneasily.

'Mr Rayner is not saying that the ships *are* overdue,' Hardwick broke in. 'They are not expected back just yet, as you well know. There is no need to start worrying unnecessarily. I have a cousin on *Polar Star Two*, it's a fine ship – as is the *Arctic Star*. Our company has a good record.'

A woman stepped forward. She was almost as tall as Gilbert, and twice as broad, and he stepped back as she waved a finger towards him and Hardwick.

'We know that tha's a company man, Hardwick, and well paid for thine efforts I don't doubt. But we're not complaining about 'ships being overdue, we're here because 'ships haven't been seen in weeks and 'reason is because there wasn't a Rayner there to see *Polar Star Two* off on her voyage.'

'That's ridiculous,' Gilbert began, but was silenced by the woman who raised her voice at him.

'Can I remind you, Mr Rayner, *sir*, that 'custom was started by thine own grandfayther who sailed in 'company ships.' She had a sneer in her voice as she implied that Gilbert did not. '*He* knew how it felt to sail from these shores, and he was allus there.'

'My father was ill and I was at his bedside! Don't you understand? I couldn't be there. A message was sent.'

Was it sent? he asked himself. *I asked Billy, I think, but I can't remember signing anything. And if anything should have happened to the ship I shall be blamed. Oh, what superstitious nonsense!* But he knew deep down that it wasn't nonsense. If the men on board had been uneasy about the omission, it could quite easily affect their attitude during the whole voyage; they could become depressed and pessimistic and filled with foreboding.

'I was there for the *Arctic Star*,' he declared. 'How do you account for that not being seen?' Again he made a mistake. He was being negative. He should be bolstering up the confidence of these women instead of arguing with them.

''*Arctic Star* was last seen in Melville Bay. She could be trapped in 'ice and we all know what that means, and we must bide our time and wait, but '*Star Two*—'

The woman's mouth trembled and her eyes filled with angry tears. '*Polar Star Two* was ill-fated, 'cos of thee. Thy fayther would have forgiven thee for not being with him. She'll not come back. Our men'll not come back. Tha'll have to live wi' that on thy conscience. I hope tha sleeps easy in thy bed at night.' She turned away from him and marched off, her clogs clattering on the cobbles and dragging two small boys by the hand. Then she stopped and turned back. 'Tha'll have no more of my lads, Mr Rayner, sir. I'll not let them work for thy company again. We're finished with thee.'

Gilbert stared after her. This mustn't get out. A company could be finished if the men refused to work the ships. He turned back to the other women who were standing silently. 'Please don't worry,' he said in his most appealing manner. 'Our ships are the very best; efficient, well run, built to the highest standards which we consider our men deserve.'

One or two of the younger women caught his eye as he appealed to them, smiled at him and nodded, but some of the older ones turned away, muttering, and as he finished speaking, the crowd dissolved and broke up, leaving Gilbert and Hardwick standing alone.

'It's a bad business, sir.' Hardwick rubbed his chin thoughtfully. 'Very bad.'

'You surely don't believe all of that nonsense, Hardwick? Not a man like you!'

Hardwick avoided his employer's eye. 'You mustn't forget, sir, that I'm from a long line of seamen: whaling men, harpooners, ship's carpenters, and even though I've never been to sea as they did, 'sea is in my blood and I understand their ways.' He turned then to Gilbert and looked at him in the face. 'One of my cousins was on 'Polar Star Two. I was at 'dock side that morning when she sailed. He wasn't happy and neither were 'other men. Our family have lost two of their men in 'Arctic, sailing in Masterson-Rayner ships. I wouldn't like to think that he'll be 'third.'

Hardwick hurried back to the office alone, leaving Gilbert to walk back slowly, pondering over the morning's events and not really wanting to return to the uneasy atmosphere which he knew would be simmering, both in the office and the yard, when there was a possibility that a ship might be lost.

He glanced up as a running figure approached him. 'Billy! Where have you been?' Gilbert stared at Billy's dishevelled appearance. He was unshaven, his hair was uncombed and his clothes looked as if they had been slept in. 'Why are you not at the firm?' he demanded. 'You're needed. We have a crisis on our hands.'

'A crisis?' It was Billy's turn to stare. 'Has something happened?'

Gilbert told of the women at the dock side. 'Did you send that message, Billy? I particularly asked you to.'

'Yes.' Billy's reply was equally terse. 'I did. And I signed your name as you were not there.'

Gilbert's relief was short-lived as Billy continued, 'But it wasn't your message, was it? It was mine, even though I signed your name. Therefore it doesn't count.'

'Doesn't count! What do you mean? *You* surely don't believe . . . ?'

Billy shook his head and wearily put his hand up to his eyes. 'I don't know what I believe – but – you can't trick Fate!'

'But you're a Rayner,' Gilbert stuttered, beginning

to half believe the irrational notion. 'Doesn't that count for something?'

'I don't know, Gilbert, and I'm far too tired to work it out. I must go. I, too, have a crisis on my hands.'

'But – where are you going? Why are you not at the firm? And why do you look such a mess, as if you have been up all night?'

'I look a mess because I *have* been up all night. I've been at the cellars with the children, they're very sick and—'

'For God's sake, Billy!' Gilbert broke in angrily. 'I've just told you there's an emergency. You're needed back at the company. Now get yourself cleaned up and back at your desk!'

Billy exhaled a deep breath. 'I'm wasting time here, Gilbert. I'm about to call on the doctor and bring him out again. There are a dozen children in those cellars with cholera. Doctor Sheppard and I have been with them all night, fetching clean water, giving them saline fluid and opium. He came back for an hour's rest, but now two more are ill.'

Gilbert stared in horror. 'Cholera! But you might catch it! Don't go back. You're not a medical man. What can you do?'

'The children know me, they trust me,' Billy said patiently. 'I have to go back. It's true I can't do much, but just being there seems to be enough for some of them. And – and I'm not coming back.'

'Not coming back? What do you mean?' He was starting to panic. He was relying on Billy to placate the men if there was a dispute, especially now that Hardwick seemed to be opposing him. 'You have work to do. Important work,' he insisted. 'One day you will be a director of our company. Now, I gave you yesterday off to see Pearson, and I suppose you'd better take the rest of today as well. There's no point in coming in looking as you do, but tomorrow—'

Billy sighed. 'You're not listening to me, Gilbert. I'm not coming back. If we don't get this epidemic under control, then it could spread throughout the town. Oh, you do right to look alarmed,' he added as dismay showed on Gilbert's face. 'Cholera is no respecter of status, but I doubt if you, or I for that matter, will get it. But the people who live in damp alleys or holes in the ground like the children do, are very vulnerable.' He turned away and stepped towards a nearby door which had a brass plate outside. He rang the bell. 'And when I said I wasn't coming back, I meant just that. As from today I resign. You can keep my month's salary in lieu of notice if you wish.'

Gilbert continued to stare as Billy waited for someone to answer the door. 'You'll regret it!' he snapped as the door opened. 'You can't live on fresh air and charity!'

'A lot of people do.' Billy turned away and stepped inside the open door.

'When did you decide?' Gilbert called him back. 'Don't be hasty! You might change your mind!'

Billy popped his head around the door; he suddenly looked animated and refreshed. 'I won't.' He grinned, his teeth looking white in his grimy face. 'And I decided about two minutes ago.'

38

When Tom came down the stairs the morning after he had brought Jenny back to the mill house, the fire was blazing in the hearth, the kettle was boiling and there was a smell of porridge cooking in the pan. George was already seated at the table, an empty bowl by his elbow, enthusiastically dipping a thick slice of bread into a plate of eggs.

''Morning, sir.' Jenny looked up from the range as he entered the kitchen. 'I'm sorry I can't cook any bacon, 'cos there doesn't seem to be any. But I collected some eggs from that big garden at 'back where 'hens are. Was it all right to do that?'

'That's 'paddock.' George interrupted with a mouthful of bread. 'Where 'hens are, I mean.'

'Beg pardon, Master George, I didn't quite catch what tha said.' A slight grin played around her mouth.

'You'll have to excuse my brother, Jenny,' Tom apologized wryly. Martha had taught her well in such a short time. 'He has the manners of a goat.'

She smiled back at him. 'It'll not take me long to find where everything is. But it seems funny out here in 'country without shops to buy bread and stuff. Cook at Garston Hall showed me how to knead dough, but I'm not very good at it yet. I couldn't get my teeth into 'last lot that I made.'

'Tha can't be any worse than our Betsy,' George remarked, 'she's worst cook I've ever known. Doesn't tha want thy porridge, Tom?'

Tom moved his dish out of George's reach and started to eat. 'I'll take you through to my father when

I've finished this, Jenny, and we'll see what he wants. He doesn't eat much, but we try to persuade him if we can. Then I'll help him up.'

'Oh, I've been in already, sir,' she said quickly. 'Mr Foster heard me moving about and called to me. He's had porridge and a boiled egg and a slice of bread, so he's set up 'till dinner time.'

Tom and George glanced at each other. Their father wasn't usually in the best of moods in a morning, especially if he had had a painful night, and it was all they could do, as a rule, to persuade him to eat a morsel of bread.

'I have to ride into Hull.' Tom finished his porridge. 'I, er, have some business to attend to. Is there anything I can get for you?'

'Is tha going to look for our Betsy, Tom?' George interrupted. 'She should have been back by now.'

Tom sighed and pushed back his chair. 'Thank you, Jenny. That was good.' Outwardly he was polite but inwardly seething at his brother's lack of reticence in front of the girl. He leaned towards him and whispered, 'I'll put a bit and bridle on your tongue before you're much older, just see if I don't.'

'Oh, Master Tom! I nearly forgot.' Jenny turned from the sink. 'First post has come. I left 'letter on your fayther's bed. He said he'd wait for you to go in and read it.'

'How are you this morning, Da?' Tom picked up the envelope and turned it over. It was good quality paper, with a C embossed in the corner.

'Not so bad,' his voice was low and he spoke with effort, 'though I haven't slept much 'cos of worrying over our Betsy. Then I got to thinking about Mark and wondering where he is! They've got wanderlust, those two, and no mistake.'

He threw back the bed coverings. 'Yon young woman is a cheerful little soul, isn't she? She'll have us all eating out of her hand if we don't watch her.' He frowned his beetling eyebrows as he watched

Tom's eyes scanning the letter. 'What's up? Is it trouble?'

'I'm not sure.' Tom held the letter loosely in his hand. 'It's from Betsy. She says she's staying with friends in Hull for a few days, maybe a week.' He glanced at the letter again. 'She says she's sorry she wasn't able to get back home. She missed her lift because of the crush of people in Hull and bumped into some friends who invited her to stay with them.'

'Friends! What friends does she have in Hull? Who does she mean?' His father barked out the questions and then grimaced as Tom helped him out of the bed and into his chair.

'I don't know.' Tom shook his head. He was ready and dressed to ride into Hull. Should he still go, and where would he start looking?

'Who does she know that we don't? Could she mean Gilbert's wife?'

'She would surely have mentioned them by name, if that's who she is with.' Tom deliberated. There seemed no sense in going on a wild-goose chase if Betsy was enjoying herself with friends. She wouldn't be pleased to see him and be returned home; even if he knew where to find her.

'I'll ride over to see Sammi again and ask her what she thinks, and then leave it at that. No sense in worrying. Her letter is very cheerful. She must be all right, Da. She just doesn't consider anybody else, that's the trouble with Betsy.'

Once more he arrived at the door of Garston Hall, but this time he was shown in to see Aunt Ellen, who was in her sitting-room with an opened letter on the table in front of her.

He greeted her with the query that he hoped her visit to the Wolds was a pleasant one, and she nodded, regarding him intently, and said that it was. 'I hope your correspondence was good news, Aunt, for ours was rather perplexing.'

As he was telling her about Betsy's letter, Sammi

came into the room and listened as he finished his explanation.

'I'm worried, Tom,' Sammi said softly. 'I can't think who Betsy will be with; and I really don't understand her behaviour.' A small frown appeared between her brows. 'I acknowledge that she has not been well lately, and felt the need to get away, but even so!'

'What kind of illness does she have?' her mother asked. 'Perhaps she should see the doctor?'

'She says she's all right now,' Tom said. 'She was nauseous and tired; Da's accident upset her, but now she seems much better. She wouldn't have gone jaunting into Hull, would she, if she was not well.'

'I'll speak to her when she returns and try to find out what is troubling her.' Ellen glanced up at him. 'Did she walk out with Luke Reedbarrow, Tom? Your father said that she might.'

He shook his head. 'No. I don't think anything will come of that. And he obviously doesn't know where she is, either, for he has asked several times where she is.'

'If you wait for me, Tom,' Sammi said, 'I'll come back with you.'

Tom and her mother both looked at her. 'Why? Where are you going?' her mother asked.

Sammi glanced from one to the other. 'I shall go and stay at Tillington until Betsy comes home. Jenny won't be able to manage alone.'

'No!'

The exclamation burst from both Tom's lips and his aunt's, and a significant observation from one and an eloquent appealing glance from the other, left both in no doubt that they were of one and the same mind.

'You are no longer a child!' Ellen faced her fractious daughter after Tom had left. 'You are a young woman and cannot stay alone in a household of men. It just won't do!'

'But they are my cousins!' Sammi's response was irritable. 'At least Uncle Thomas is Pa's cousin, so it's almost the same thing.'

'It's not the same at all, and even if it were, you still couldn't go. You have your reputation to think of. Besides,' her mother turned to her desk and picked up the opened letter, 'I wanted to talk to you about something. Two things!'

Sammi waited impatiently whilst her mother dithered. It was so ridiculous that she wasn't allowed to go to Tillington. But even Tom didn't want her to go. Surely he didn't have such old-fashioned ideas? An image came drifting into her mind, but as it was about to take shape, her mother spoke briskly and, Sammi thought, rather too heartily.

'Do you remember my friend Rebecca Hartscombe, Sammi? They live up near Pickering. We stayed with her five or six years ago.'

'Yes.' Sammi only half listened, busy with thoughts of when Tom had kept her company on the night Victoria was ill. *He was so kind and caring, the least I can do is go and help him.* She touched her cheek and remembered the sensation of his flannel shirt against her face as she leaned against him. *I was so tired and worried, and he was such a comfort.* The hazy vision flickered back again. *I must have fallen asleep for I don't even remember going to bed; only waking up as Martha pulled off my skirt and stockings – and she was such a cross-patch.*

Her mother's voice drifted back. 'And so she said she would be delighted if you and Victoria would go and stay again. I told her that Victoria was not well enough to travel at the moment, but I was sure that you would like to go. Cecily and Edgar would be so pleased if you would.'

'Edgar?' She blinked and cringed. 'You don't mean her horrible son?'

'Sammi! How rude!'

'I'm sorry, Mama. But he was such a cringing,

sneaking toad. I couldn't endure him. I remember him coming back from school and completely ruining our holiday. We were having such a nice time until then.'

'Why, how strange,' her mother said lightly. 'And he has such good memories of you. He said he couldn't wait to meet you again.'

'Mama!' Sammi stared at her mother. 'Mama! You weren't – you haven't been . . .' Her face paled. 'You're not trying to marry me to him? You wouldn't?'

'Of course we wouldn't, Sammi. Don't be so silly.' Her mother rose and crossed to where Sammi was sitting bolt upright in the chair. 'But it's time you went out and about and met some more young people. You won't ever meet a marriage partner until you do.' A doubt crept into her mother's eyes. 'We only want you to meet other young men so that you have a choice.'

'A choice?' Sammi whispered. 'But I didn't ever want to choose! I just wanted something magical to happen and then I would know that it was right.'

Her mother patted her hand. 'Perhaps it will, my darling. But sometimes Fate needs a helping hand to push us in the right direction.' She sighed and then looked down at the letter in her hand. 'But that wasn't all I wanted to talk to you about. This is from Aunt Mildred. She has had a change of heart over Adam: she says that she will accept responsibility for his well-being and will write to James and tell him.'

Sammi stared. 'So Gilbert hasn't told her?' she whispered.

'Seemingly not.' Her mother looked at the letter again and began to read. ' "*If I am doing this for anyone,*" she says, "*then I am doing it for Isaac. He was a good, kind, caring man and this is what he would have wanted.*" She says, strangely, that she has many things on her conscience and this is a way of repaying.'

She handed the letter to Sammi. 'You may read it; she asks if we will call for a discussion, though she stresses that she will take personal financial responsibility. And she has heard of someone in Beverley who wants a child.'

She saw the disbelief on Sammi's face. 'I don't understand it any more than you, but she says she realizes that she was too hasty. It was the shock, I suppose,' she added. 'But she says she will accept that he is James's child.'

39

James put on his coat and looked around the small room for the last time. 'Farewell,' he murmured. 'I haven't been here long enough to say that I'll miss you. There are other things, other people, that I will miss more. The river glinting every morning, the companionship of my fellow artists. I cannot call them my peers, for I am not yet their equal; not William Morris or Burne-Jones, or Batsford, but one day, one day I will be.' He locked the door behind him and put the key through the letter box, and strolled across to the river bank. *And Mariabella; how I will miss you most of all. My darling, my loved one. My sister!* He stifled a sob. *How can I bear it? If we should ever meet again we must pretend that there was never ever anything between us. I am finished for ever with love*, he declared. *I shall throw all my passion into my painting. Never again will I love another woman.*

He searched in his pocket for a handkerchief and felt alongside it the envelope with the letter inside that had come this morning. He noisily blew his nose and proceeded towards Batsford's studio where he would wish him good-bye.

His mother's letter had come in the same post as the letter from the lawyer with a copy of his father's will. Both had surprised him. His father had been more than generous towards him, leaving an inheritance, payable when he was twenty-one, and an annuity, which would enable him to live comfortably, though not luxuriously, until then.

There were no shares in the company left to him, and he was relieved about that, for he had no business inclination. Gilbert, on the other hand, had been left all of his father's shares but only a small legacy. But the surprise was that, as well as providing for his wife and daughter, Isaac Rayner had also left money to be invested in a trust fund *'for the child known as Adam Foster Rayner, at present in the care of Sarah Maria Foster Rayner'*. The instructions were that the child would inherit at twenty-one, but if it was found that he was not a son of the Rayner family, then the fund should be halved.

And he is not mine, James denied as he walked briskly along. *And I thought that Father believed me! Yet he still left the child an inheritance! What a kind, generous man he was. Like Sammi, she is the same, and how cruel I was that day. She was so hurt when I told her that she must do what she would with the child, for he was no concern of mine. And now my mother is changing! I don't understand! She says in her letter that she will now accept him. I must write again,* he thought vaguely, *and try to explain.*

He stopped and put down his bag and, taking the letter from his pocket, read it once more.

'Try to forgive me, James. Passion is a fearful emotion and one which, one day perhaps, you will experience; but by accepting this child and caring for him, perhaps in some way I can make amends. If you see Massimo again, tell him that I have no regrets; not for loving him, or for choosing to stay with Isaac.'

He folded up the letter and returned it to his pocket. It had been written in reply to one he had sent her when he had learned the truth about his parentage; and in the days of indecision following Romanelli's plea for him to return with him to Italy, he had in his misery and anger poured out a torrent of abuse, berating her for betraying his father and destroying his own life, and had posted the letter before sanity finally prevailed and he saw opportunity in front of him.

He regretted it now; he felt shame and remorse, and vowed that he would write again and tell her. *I will write and tell her that I love her, that I have always loved her, in spite of pretending to myself that I didn't. It is what we all want. The reassurance that we are loved.*

He wiped his eyes and walked across to Batsford's studio. He opened the door cautiously, expecting him to be working, but only Miss Gregory was there, idly flicking through a magazine. She was wearing a loose, Grecian-style muslin dress with a blue sash, her hair was loose around her shoulders, and once more he was struck by her resemblance to Sammi.

'I'm leaving,' he announced. 'I was hoping to see Batsford before I go. I'm going to Italy to study.'

'I know.' She rose to her feet which he saw were bare. Bare and small, with pale pink toe-nails. 'Batsford told me. He said he will meet you later at Romanelli's rooms.'

'Good-bye then,' he said nervously, as his departure and new life loomed nearer. 'We don't seem to have got to know each other very well, but wish me luck!'

'Oh, I do.' She came towards him and brushed away a breadcrumb from her mouth. He smiled. He had never known a woman eat as much as she did. Yet she had such a lovely body, curvaceous hips, a small waist and full, round breasts.

'I'm sorry that you are going,' she said softly and took hold of his hand. 'Is your lover going too?'

'My lover?' He felt a flush creep up his neck.

'You said that you were in love.' She gave a slight smile. 'You said that you could only look at other women in the aesthetic sense.'

He shook his head. 'It's finished. All over. That's one of the reasons why I am going away – to forget her.'

She raised her eyebrows and looked at him with her head on one side. 'That's a pity. Could you not forget about her here?'

He swallowed. Why was it that he felt more embarrassed with her fully dressed and so close to him,
than he ever did when she was posing naked? Perhaps
it was because he knew that she always expected him
to take advantage of her, in spite of his protestations
that he never would.

'Romanelli has offered me the opportunity to study
in Florence,' he said. 'Batsford says that it would be
foolish to refuse his offer.'

'Well, don't forget us, will you? And come and see
us if you come back to London.'

'I will,' he promised. 'And thank you for sitting for
me. You are – really beautiful, you know.' He gazed
at her. 'One day I will paint you. I have the sketch
already, and then perhaps we both will become
famous.'

She still had hold of his hand and she squeezed it
gently. 'You're not a bad sort of fellow. Come here.
Give us a kiss, just this once, just to set you on your
way.'

She put her face up to him and he kissed her gently
on her mouth. Her lips were full and soft and he
closed his eyes. He had vowed never to kiss another
woman after Mariabella, but when he opened his eyes
he saw her fresh young skin, a bloom on her cheeks
and a brightness in her eyes, and realized with a
quickening of his pulses that he might well change
his mind.

'Off you go then, Mr Rayner,' she said softly, 'and
don't tell anyone, for I don't give away my kisses
lightly.'

He put his arms around her and gave her a hug. 'I
won't, Miss Gregory. And thank you, thank you so
much.'

He walked away, down the riverside towards the
city, and then turned back for one more glimpse of
the tall terraced houses of Cheyne Walk and the vista
of Battersea Bridge, whose ancient leaning structure
was etched against the skyline. The tide was running

strong and the surging river rushed and broke against its wooden piers.

Coal-carrying tugs and barges, iron frigates, ocean-going cutters, ferry boats and the new English clippers, built in the London Docks, filled the waterway. What was once the main highway of London and was still the shimmering commercial lifeline, was throbbing and heaving with craft, their sails creaking and sighing atop the tall masts, the paddle wheels gyrating in the churning water and the steam-propelled engines clanking and hissing; and as James watched the scene, he thought tenderly of his father, who used to take him down to the Humber bank at Hessle near his home, or take him to watch the great whaling ships leaving the harbour on their long voyage to the Arctic.

An idea started to form in his mind. *I will paint the river*, he determined. *I will capture it in all its dark brooding glory. It will be filled with triumphant billowing sails as the whaling ships return to port.*

He became filled with enthusiasm. He felt joy flooding through him once more as he anticipated the prospect in front of him. 'I will paint the river,' he declared out loud. 'But not the Thames. I will paint the Humber, and I will dedicate it in memory of my father.'

40

Billy and Doctors Fleming and Sheppard stood outside the cellars. Billy and Doctor Sheppard both gulped in air, while Doctor Fleming lit a cigar. Doctor Sheppard had asked his uncle to come back with them the following day to confirm that the disease was cholera, which he did unhesitatingly.

'Have you notified the sanitary committee?' the older man asked his nephew and drew heavily on the cigar. 'They'll need to be told so that they can set up cholera stations.'

'I haven't, sir,' Doctor Sheppard confessed. 'My main concern was treating the sick – and dying.' His face was drawn, his eyes shadowed. 'I haven't come across anything like this before.'

'No, they teach you how to look for symptoms at medical school,' Doctor Fleming said bluntly. 'But they don't teach you, can't teach you, how to cope with the mortally sick.'

Billy passed his hands over his eyes. He had been shocked when Jenny's friend Dinah had succumbed so quickly, her frail, thin body stretched lifeless on the dirty floor.

Doctor Fleming nipped his cigar out to extinguish it and threw it into the gutter. 'Very well,' he said briskly. 'Let's get on. You do what you can here, Stephen, and I'll notify the authorities. They'll clear the bodies, and then set out tar barrels, I expect. Those who want to can be taken to the hospitals, they won't get much treatment but they'll be isolated. Try to persuade them to go if you can.'

'And if they don't want to, sir?' Billy asked. 'I know that some of the children will be afraid to.'

'If they don't want to, they won't be forced, but somebody will have to look after them here, and you won't find many willing helpers, too many people remember the last epidemic.'

Doctor Fleming hunched into his coat. 'That was a bad business. Nearly two thousand people died, *two thousand people*,' he repeated. 'Five hundred died during one week in September.'

'There's no wonder there's disease,' Billy cried vehemently, 'when people have to live under these conditions! Something must be done!'

'I quite agree, Rayner,' Stephen Sheppard broke in. 'These places want boarding up; they're nothing more than death traps.'

'Yes, yes, all these arguments have been heard before,' Doctor Fleming broke in crisply. 'Yet still no-one can agree. Why, in one cholera epidemic – in 'thirty-three it was, I was a young student then – I can remember the story going around of doctors arguing and even fighting over the cause and the cure. Alderson and Ayre, both respected men, yet neither would compromise.'

Doctor Fleming departed, leaving them with the question of where they would put the people from the cellars, for the courts and alleyways were already overflowing with humanity.

'They are just stinking middens, most of them.' Billy bent his head to re-enter the gloomy interior of the cellars. 'And the people down here think they are living in luxury!'

At times he felt as if he was living in a nightmare. He was so tired that he almost fell asleep on his feet. Men came and went, bringing lamps to light up the cellars, thus revealing the true state of the dank interior; the green vegetation on the oozing walls and the rat holes in the muddy floor; they carried, too, white winding sheets over their arms.

He had heard the sound of retching, the shout of drunkards and the cries of babies, and he'd stooped almost double beneath the archways with a flickering candle in his hand, to reach the far corners of the subterranean shelter to find others sheltering there. Grey faces stared out at him from the darkness, others covered themselves so that they would not be discovered, and he called to them not to be afraid but to come out if they needed help. Women pushed children towards him, and as he stumbled back towards the entrance, with the children holding onto his coat and a baby in his arms, he heard their mothers weeping.

He sat outside on the cellar steps and closed his eyes. He was so tired and dirty, but now he felt that he knew how the people of the courts must feel all of the time. The sense of lethargy, hunger – for he had not eaten for hours – and hopelessness, which he would dispel in some measure, by a bath and a good meal, was forever with them; for them there was no release.

Some of the children had agreed to go to the paupers' hospital or the workhouse where there was a bed for them, and the regulations were to be relaxed to allow one other person to go with them to attend them or give them water. The air was filled with the smoke and smell of burning tar which had been set alight in barrels in streets around the town, as a preventative measure against further infection, and to warn people of the high-risk areas which they were entering, and Billy felt as if he couldn't get a deep breath without filling his lungs with the acrid smoke.

He heard someone calling to him. 'Master Billy! Master Billy!'

He peered through the dusk at the group of young people who were hovering nearby. 'Who wants me?'

One of the youths who had been at the cellars on

the first night stepped forward. 'We thought you ought to know about young Tim.'

'What about him?' He hadn't seen the boy since his sister's body had been taken away. 'Don't tell me that he's sick too?' he asked wearily.

The boy shook his head. 'No. Though he'll be sicker afore long,' he said cynically. 'He's clapped up in gaol. 'Constable caught him smashing windows in 'Market Place. He was in a right state, they had to put him in a strait coat.'

Billy stared aghast. 'But why? He's a good lad! Why would he do that?'

'He said somebody had to pay for his sister. He's got nobody now. We said we'd look after him, but he wouldn't listen.' These youths were set apart from the other children; they were older, twelve or thirteen years of age, and had said that they didn't need any adult to mind them, that they could fend for themselves. But already they were becoming hardened, and what they couldn't obtain by working for or begging, they would steal.

'There's glass all over 'Market Place,' the boy continued, 'he used a brick to smash 'windows.' He sneered derisively. ''Butcher's got a queue outside his shop, he's selling meat off cheap 'cos of glass in it.' He opened up his tattered coat and showed a loaf inside the deep pocket. 'And 'baker's giving bread away for 'same reason.'

Billy stumbled back into the cellars and called to Doctor Sheppard. 'I'll have to go across to the gaol. Young Tim has been taken in. He's been smashing windows in the Market Place. Someone will have to speak for him.'

Stephen Sheppard looked up from where he was bent over a young girl. 'You can't.' His words were dragged out as if he hadn't the energy to speak. 'You'll have to fetch more help, Rayner. I can't cope on my own any more. Go to my uncle. Tell him he'll have to badger the Board of Health and the

Guardians. They must find more places for these people, it's getting out of hand. Take a look at this child.'

Billy bent over and peered at the young girl on the floor. She was tossing feverishly and her face, which had a purple rash across it, was wreathed in sweat.

'What is it?' Billy asked in a low voice. 'It's not the same as before?'

Stephen Sheppard pressed his fingers to his brow and heaved a deep breath. 'No,' he said. 'It isn't. This is typhus.'

Betsy wavered over a box of chocolates. Should she have the coffee flavour or the marshmallow? She decided on the marshmallow and popped it into her mouth, chewing appreciatively on the sweet and sticky concoction. Then she idly rose from the sofa and wandered to the window. She was alone and bored. She had had fun here in Craddock's house. New gowns were hers for the asking, a new bonnet and shoes. She had been horse racing and to the theatre, and she had been gambling. Craddock had given her a wad of money and she had gambled it all away.

She thought that he might be angry with her, but he had merely laughed and said that he would make her pay for the loss one way or another. She smiled, she knew well now how to please him and what made him happy, and she had, she thought, got him eating out of her hand.

But then he surprised her by saying that he must go away for a few days and that she must stay in the house and not go out. She protested, but he was adamant. 'I don't want Gilbert Rayner seeing you, not unless I'm with you.' He clasped her face in his hands and kissed her roughly. 'He might send you home, and that would spoil our fun, wouldn't it?'

Then he pushed her onto the bed and was neither caring or tender, but wanton, without regard for her desires, and she was left with the thought that perhaps she didn't know him quite as well as she had imagined. She watched him as she lay exhausted on the bed while he carefully tied his cravat and slipped on a dark jacket. He was dressed more soberly than usual, and she asked in a small voice where he was going and when would he be back.

He turned towards her and looked her over. 'To see my mother,' he replied lazily, fastening a gold pin to his cravat. Then he bent over and sought her mouth. 'I shall be back,' he breathed. 'Don't worry, little dumpling, I'm not abandoning you. Now be a good girl and don't go out. There's cholera in the town, anyway, and I don't want you catching that and bringing it back here.'

So she had stayed in, but now the day was irksome. There was nothing to do but gaze out of the window onto the street below, or read, and his choice of books and magazines were few.

The maid who lived below stairs had an insolent manner, bringing her meals at the appropriate time and leaving without a word, and when Betsy had attempted to make conversation with her, she answered only indifferently.

It must be me, she thought. *I don't have a way with servants. Now if it had been Sammi, she wouldn't have answered her like that. But then*, she reflected, *Sammi wouldn't be here in this situation, would she?* She reached for writing paper and pen and ink, and resolved to write to Sammi, but she had no sooner started the letter, than she realized that if she wasn't very careful how she phrased her words, Sammi would guess who she was with and would probably tell Tom, who would fetch her back home and give Charles Craddock a bloody nose into the bargain.

I'm not ready to go back yet, she decided. *If at all. If Charles becomes really besotted by me, he may want me to stay for good; though*, she mused, *I don't think that he is the marrying kind.*

She reached for the paper again and wrote a brief

note to her father, telling him that her friends insisted on her staying a little longer.

> '*Please don't worry about me, Da. I am having a splendid time. My friends are most hospitable and can't do enough for me. I have told them that I must return soon in order to look after you, but they seem to think that my prospects will be very good if I stay a little longer. I'm sure that you know what I mean.*'

She sealed the envelope and, searching in Craddock's desk, which he had carelessly left unlocked, she took out a postage stamp and stuck it to the envelope, put on her new cloak which he had so generously bought her, went down the stairs and out into the street. The house was in Percy Street, a quiet, discreet area and not one that she knew, but she determined her direction and set off towards where she thought the shops might be, for she still had coins in her purse which she had brought from home and a little money which Craddock had given her.

She slightly misjudged her direction, for she found herself in a narrow street. Children were playing on the ground near pools of stagnant water, and several men were lounging in grimy doorways and listlessly watching two dogs worrying a dead rat. Women were bent over water tubs, presumably doing their household washing, though the wet articles that they were hoisting out of the tubs looked as grey as the ones lying on the floor beside them.

One of them looked up at her and stared. She was smoking a pipe and had a man's hat on her head. She called to a man nearby who got up from his seat on a window ledge and walked towards Betsy. He looked so dirty and evil that she turned around and fled back from where she had come, to the sound of raucous laughter behind her and then the rattle of a stone which hit the ground near her feet.

She hurried on, taking note of where she was so

that she could avoid the street on the way back, and eventually came to an area that she knew slightly better. These were the streets of Whitefriargate and Lowgate, the shopping and business areas, where she had been with Sammi, and near where they had stayed when they came to Gilbert's wedding.

I must watch out, she thought, *in case Gilbert is about, though he would probably only think I was here for shopping if he should see me. I doubt that he would know I haven't been at home.* But as she turned a corner she walked slap into Billy, who was hurrying in the opposite direction.

'Oh, so sorry, ma-am,' Billy gasped. 'My fault entirely – Betsy! I didn't realize it was you. You will excuse me if I don't stop?' He looked gaunt and pale and was obviously in a great hurry. 'It's good to see you, you look *very* well. Betsy, do me a favour, will you?'

She nodded. *Anything*, she thought, smiling at him. *He obviously hasn't heard about me either.*

'When you next see Mama or Sammi – she's not come into Hull with you, has she? No? Well, would you tell them that I will come home to see them when I can. It's just that, well, I'll explain when I see them. There's such a lot happening just now. And Betsy – ' he called back as he set off at a run, 'take care, disease is rife in the town. You'd be advised to stay at home.'

She watched him as he hurried away, his long legs loping along the pavement and his fair hair flopping on his coat collar.

Idly she window-shopped, made a purchase of stockings and gloves, posted the letter and then decided that as the day was turning a little chilly she would return to Percy Street and ask the reluctant maid to make her tea. She heard raised voices and loud banging as she retraced her steps, and she looked towards a building on the corner of the street, where a large group of men and a few women were standing. Some of the men were standing on the steps of the building and with their walking sticks and fists were banging on the doors which were firmly locked.

'They won't open the door!' she heard someone shout. 'Put your boot on it.'

She looked with interest as more people arrived and spilled over onto the road. It was then that she saw Gilbert. He was standing at the door of the building, but looking down at the crowd and not at the door. His lips were moving silently and his eyes moved amongst the crowd as if he was searching for someone. He looked in her direction and she moved back into the crowd, but though he gazed straight at her it was as if he didn't see her. He looked as if he was wracked with despair, as if he had suffered a great shock.

'The bank's failed,' a voice called from the crowd. 'They can't pay out! We're finished!'

It was Hardwick who had come in with news of the rumour. He had entered Gilbert's office and closed the door firmly behind him. 'I don't know how true it is, sir, but there's a nasty whisper going around that Willard's bank is in trouble.' He looked anxious. 'I thought you ought to know.'

'No!' he said in disbelief. 'Surely not? Do you – do you think I should go down there?' he asked, unsure of what to do in such a situation.

Hardwick's eyes flickered over his employer's face, then he said decisively, 'I think you should.' He'd paused. 'Would you like me to come with you?'

Gilbert felt a great cloud descending on him and he stared at Hardwick as he considered. Then he rubbed his brow and said, 'No, you'd better stay here. Keep the clerks busy, don't let them chatter. I don't want them to hear of this. It's probably nothing,' he added half-heartedly. 'Somebody panicking; that's how these stories start.'

He knew that Hardwick wasn't convinced. He

wouldn't have come to him in the first place if he hadn't thought that there was some truth in the report. He wasn't a man for gossip or hearsay, but he always had his ear to the ground; he had a shrewd knack of knowing all that was happening in the business and shipping world; which ships were in, which were sailing, which whalers were coming in full and which had had a bad voyage. He discerned the details almost as soon as the shipping masters themselves.

Gilbert stood now on the top of the steps outside the closed and bolted bank doors. He felt no anger, as did some of the men beside him, who were banging on the doors; but only bewilderment and despair, and struggling below these emotions, a surge of shame. Shame that he alone might have brought his company to the brink of failure. For it was at his insistence that the company capital and shares were moved to Willard's bank and into Billington's safe keeping.

He looked down into the crowd, all below him looked anxious, some showed wide-eyed fear. Some of the men were tradesmen, bakers in their white coats, cobblers in leather aprons, as well as businessmen in top hats and morning coats. There were seamen who had maybe saved their money rather than swilling it away in ale houses, and it was as he looked at the latter that he remembered that he had transferred the insurance of the *Polar Star Two* and the *Arctic Star* to Billington, who was acting as agent to an underwriter.

'We'll be all right,' he murmured. 'Billington will have made sure that everything is watertight. He's family – he wouldn't risk his daughter's future.' He cast his eyes around the crowd looking for someone that he could count on for support, someone who would reassure him that it was all a ghastly mistake. But there was no-one.

'If only Father was here,' he muttered. 'He would

know what to do. But he's not. There's no-one who can help me.'

Someone pulled on his sleeve. It was Hardwick, and he whispered into his ear, 'A message has just come from Mrs Rayner, sir – your wife that is, not your mother – she requests that you go to her mother's house immediately.'

Gilbert nodded absently; if Harriet and her mother had heard the rumour they would be bound to be worried; Austin Billington might have been absent from home for a day or two if the bank had been experiencing difficulties. Yes, he would go there straight away and find out what Mrs Billington knew. No point in hanging around here.

'I'll be as quick as I can, Hardwick. I, er, I don't suppose you have heard anything more?'

Hardwick unrolled an umbrella and handed it to Gilbert. It was just starting to rain. 'No, sir. But I'm afraid 'rumour is spreading around 'town. I've just had 'accounts clerks from 'ropery and 'chandler's office asking if any outstanding monies can be paid immediately.'

'Great heavens!' Gilbert raged. 'They don't waste any time, do they? Do they think that we're not going to pay their paltry little bills?'

Hardwick stood silently for a moment, the rain became heavier and started to run down his face. 'I don't think that is the situation, Mr Gilbert,' he said quietly, with just a hint of reproach in his voice. 'But both companies bank with Willard's. They may find it difficult to pay their men.'

'Oh. Of course. Yes. I wasn't thinking,' Gilbert said, crestfallen. He turned to move away and then on impulse handed back the umbrella. Hardwick was wearing only his office suit, which already was soaked about the shoulders.

'Take this,' he said. 'I've got my coat and hat on, and I'll call a cab.'

But he didn't; several hansoms slowed down as they

approached him during his walk across the town towards the Billingtons' home, but he waved them on. He put his head down and hunched into his collar, letting the rain engulf him.

'Oh, Gilbert! What a terrible thing to have happened. Mama is distraught, I can do nothing with her. She only talks of the shame.' Harriet grasped his hands as he entered the drawing-room.

'But what have you heard? What has happened? No-one seems to know. The bank doors are locked, and rumours are flying that the bank has failed.'

She sank into an armchair and put her hands over her face. He knelt beside her. 'Harriet. Tell me what you know,' he said quietly. 'I have to know so that I can act. Our livelihood depends on it.'

Suddenly he felt stronger; he would be more capable of making decisions once he knew the facts.

She raised her head. 'We shall have no livelihood. Not if you have banked with my father.' She searched for a handkerchief in her skirts and Gilbert took one of his from his pocket and handed it to her.

'Don't you see, Gilbert?' she said tearfully. 'We're ruined, and it is *his* fault.'

'You're being melodramatic, Harriet,' he said firmly. 'Now take a deep breath and tell me what in heaven's name has happened.'

'*I'll* tell you what has happened, Gilbert.' Mrs Billington's voice boomed from the doorway and Gilbert rose to his feet as she entered. Her hair was dishevelled and her eyes were dull with fatigue, but behind the tiredness was a glimmer of anger.

'For years I have put up with his whores and his mistresses. No, I make no excuse for my language, Harriet,' she said, as her daughter drew in a sharp breath. 'You have to know all of the truth — you too, Gilbert — and we'll soon know if you are man enough to stand by us.' Her mouth twisted in a sneer. 'Your father, Harriet, has been spending *my* money for years

414

on his excesses. *My* money! *Old* money, not tainted money of doubtful origin, as I discovered his was.' She lowered herself into a chair. 'But now,' she said bitterly, 'an official has been from the bank. He says that he's been using the bank's money for his own schemes. He's been speculating with clients' accounts.'

Gilbert felt himself grow cold. He had given everything over to Billington, trusting him to open the accounts and accepting only his signature. He had disregarded Hardwick's misgivings on the procedures. 'But what – what did he say? It can't be the sole reason for the closure.'

She nodded. 'He said he is solely responsible for the mismanagement of funds. The liabilities are eighty thousand pounds, and the bank's assets only twenty thousand.' She clasped her hands to her chest. 'They will notify the authorities that he has committed fraud.' Her voice was a muffled whisper. 'He will go to prison.'

'Where is Mr Billington now?' Gilbert asked in a low voice. 'Is he at the bank?'

Mrs Billington lifted her head. 'He's upstairs. Locked in his room. He refuses to come out.'

'May I go up?'

'He won't speak to you, Gilbert,' Harriet grieved. 'I've tried, but he refuses to answer.'

Gilbert walked to the door, and Mrs Billington called after him, 'There's nothing he can say. Nothing that can change anything. He has ruined my life.'

And not only yours, dear lady, Gilbert deliberated as he walked up the stairs. *There are many who will be cursing his name this day.* He tapped on Billington's door and called out to him. 'Mr Billington! It's Gilbert Rayner. Can I come in?'

'No. You can't. Leave me alone.' Billington's voice was clear and decisive.

'I must speak to you, sir. Your wife and Harriet, they are most distressed.'

'Ah! My wife! Yes, she will be. But tell Harriet not to worry, she's got you to look after her, after all. Are the constables here yet?' he asked suddenly.

'No.' Gilbert had his face pressed against the door. 'Won't you let me in, sir? You need to be represented. I could arrange for a lawyer to act for you.'

'Hah! Too late for that, old fellow. One gamble too many, I'm afraid.'

There was silence and Gilbert waited for Billington to speak again. He could hear the sound of drawers being opened and closed. 'Sir!' He knocked softly on the door. 'Arrangements have to be made. I need to know what must be done. What about Mrs Billington? How does she stand financially?'

There was no answer for a few moments, then Billington answered in a low voice, 'I expect her relatives will rally round,' he said, 'and the house is hers anyway.' He sounded very weary. 'And I expect that you will help out. You're a decent sort of fellow.'

Gilbert was suddenly angry. 'How can I help if I'm bankrupt?' he said sharply. 'I trusted you. I moved all our assets over to you when I could have left them where they were safe.'

'You wanted a gamble, Rayner. A bit of excitement, a chance of making more money.'

'I didn't want to risk the company, lose our ships, throw the men out of work.' He was full of emotion. 'I didn't know that that was the risk. My family has worked hard for their good name. I trusted you.'

Again there was silence, then, 'Yes, I know. I'm sorry.'

Gilbert turned away. Harriet was right, it was no use. There was nothing he could do. Only wait and let events unfold. He had reached the bottom of the stairs when a shot rang out. He stopped and turned, his heart racing. Harriet and her mother appeared at the drawing-room door.

'What was that?' Harriet's shocked face stared at him and her mother clutched her arm.

'Send for a doctor!' Gilbert raced back up the stairs to Billington's room. 'Tell him there has been an accident.' He put his foot up and crashed it against the door. It was solid and held, jarring his foot. He moved back and kicked again and he felt the lock shudder. Once more he put his strength behind it and the lock broke, bursting the door open.

Sickened, he stood in the doorway and surveyed the scene in front of him. Austin Billington lay, unrecognizable, his face down on his desk, a pistol in his hand and his brains splattered over the carpet.

41

Luke Reedbarrow stood at the door of the mill, blocking Tom's way out. Though Tom was tall and broad, Luke towered over him, his wide shoulders filling the doorway.

'Where's Betsy?' he demanded. 'I'm sick of being fobbed of wi' excuses. Tha's sent her away, hasn't tha, so that she can't see me?'

'Don't be ridiculous, man.' Tom flushed with anger. 'Why would I do that?'

'Because tha doesn't think I'm good enough for her! Tha'd somebody better in mind. Somebody with a bit o' brass, not a common labouring lout.' Luke's blue eyes glared at his employer. He was taking a risk in talking in such a manner.

Tom stared back at him. He didn't dislike the man, but he disapproved of his careless lackadaisical attitude. Though he was generally polite to those of higher rank, he also appeared indifferent regarding their opinion of him.

'You do yourself a disservice, Reedbarrow. If Betsy wants to go out with you, she can. My father said as much.' Tom made to go through the door but his way was barred as Luke put his brawny arm across the doorway.

'Thy fayther said – but what about thee? Tha doesn't approve?'

'Look!' Tom grew exasperated. 'It has nothing to do with me. Not any more. Betsy can do as she likes – she does do as she likes. She doesn't ask my opinion.'

'So where is she then, if tha hasn't sent her away?

418

She's been gone over three weeks and never a word.'

Tom took a deep breath. 'I don't know. She's staying with friends in Hull. She hasn't given us an address.'

Each time she has written, he thought, *she has left off the address. Neither has she mentioned her friends by name. Why hasn't she?* A niggling doubt rose to the surface as it had so many times recently. *Why doesn't she want us to know?*

'Tha doesn't know?' Luke Reedbarrow's face creased in disbelief. 'That's a bit odd, isn't it? Somebody must know. Miss Rayner – doesn't she know?'

Tom shook his head. 'No, she's as flummoxed as we are. But Betsy's letters are cheerful,' he added. 'She's enjoying herself while we're here worrying.'

Luke folded his arms across his chest as he pondered. 'She's not been 'same since she went to that wedding.'

'What? What do you mean?'

'Well, I know it was a shock when tha got back and found thy da injured, and then Betsy was ill, but after that she was restless somehow, as if she couldn't settle.'

He's right, Tom thought. *She was jumpy and nervous; she didn't want Sammi to leave at first, and she spent time in bed and wouldn't get up, saying that she was ill, but wouldn't have the doctor.*

'Right then,' Luke said determinedly. 'I'll go and look for her.'

'No.' Tom was adamant. He had made the same decision. 'No. You stay here, there's plenty you can be doing and I'll have to dock your wages if you go.'

'I'm not bothered about that,' Luke began. 'I'll manage.'

'I'll go,' Tom insisted. 'If there are official enquiries to make, then I can make them as her brother. Besides, I shall ask our relatives first; if she's in Hull they might have seen her.'

Luke clenched and unclenched his big fists. 'If

she's in trouble tha'll tell me?' he said. 'I'll stand by her.'

For two pins I'd fight you, Tom considered as he discerned Luke's meaning. *But I might get the worst of it and I can't go into Hull with a black eye or a cut lip.* He had seen the results of Reedbarrow's temper in the shape of a blooded farmhand who had the misfortune to say something disparaging about a member of the Reedbarrow family.

'I'll tell you,' he said tersely. 'Now, can we get back to work?'

He didn't have to visit Garston Hall to ask Sammi one more time if she had any idea where Betsy might be, but he did. He left George and Luke to bring the sails to rest and lower the stones after they had finished milling, saddled up and rode over to Monkston.

It was a beautiful evening, it had rained during the morning, but the sun had come out in the late afternoon and the sky was shot with wide streaks of red and orange, even the darkening clouds had shades of soft pink within them. He could hear the murmuring of the sea as he trotted down the lane which led through Monkston and towards the long drive of Garston Hall. It was a calming, somnolent sound. A soothing lullaby which could rock a child to sleep.

He stopped before turning up the tree-lined entrance, and listened. He wasn't misled by its gentleness. He had lived all of his life at Tillington; he was a landsman, born to work the earth and its fruits, but his ancestors had been seamen and the sea was in his blood. His great-grandfather, Will Foster, the common root which he shared with his Rayner relatives, had been a whaling man, and Tom knew of the sea's capriciousness, when, as if on a fickle whim, its mood could change from caressing waters to a vicious pounding sea, bent on destruction.

*   *   *

420

'Sammi has gone for a walk before supper, Tom.' Aunt Ellen invited him in to the drawing-room where she and Uncle William were sitting. 'I don't suppose she will be long. Will you stay and eat with us?'

'I suppose I ought to get back,' he hedged. 'I intend to go into Hull tomorrow to see if I can find Betsy. I thought I would ask Sammi where she thought I should begin.'

'Do you – do you really think something has happened? That she is not with friends after all?' Ellen sat forward in her chair.

'I don't know what to think,' he said worriedly. 'I just don't understand.'

'I'm driving into Hull tomorrow, Tom,' William offered. 'You could come with me, though I'm staying over a few days and you'd have to make your own way back.'

'I'd appreciate that, sir. It will save me taking the trap, and I can get a ride back with the carrier if I finish in time; otherwise I'll stay the night.'

William nodded and rose to stand by the fire. 'I'll pick you up at about six. I have to go in and talk to Gilbert. You'll have heard about this business with Billington and the bank?'

'Yes, it was in the newspaper. A terrible affair. I hope it doesn't affect you too much?'

William pursed his lips. 'We shall have lost out, certainly. How much, we don't know as yet. The worrying thing is the two missing ships. If they're lost and we're not covered, then the company is finished.'

He stared down into the flames of the fire. 'I blame myself as much as anyone,' he said in a low voice. 'We should have assessed Billington more thoroughly. Gilbert was obviously swayed by him. Not his fault,' he muttered. 'Not his fault.'

'Tom. Why don't you go out and look for Sammi?' Ellen sought for a change of subject. 'She won't be far away. Probably down on the sands – she's taken the dog. Bring her back and we'll have an early supper.'

When Tom had gone, she stood up and put her arms around her husband and laid her head on his chest. 'You mustn't blame yourself, William,' she said softly. 'You are merely a silent partner. You have never had much to do with the running of the company.'

'There was never any need when Isaac was alive; but I should have known that that boy, for that is all he is, couldn't run it alone; he hasn't had the experience, nor has he the acumen. No, I should have watched over him better.'

'What will you do?' she asked quietly. 'Is it very bad for us?'

'Bad enough,' he said grimly. 'But we shall survive. Thank God for land, even if some of it is being washed away. What I shall do—' he put his arms around her so that they were locked in a close embrace, '—is spend a few days with Gilbert; Arthur is coming over from York and we'll go over the details of the accounts to see where we stand, what money we have to come in and so on; and I shall suggest that we trim our sails, so to speak, and form a smaller company. One that is easier to handle, and then,' he looked down at her, 'I shall resign my directorship. My heart isn't in it, Ellen. Isaac had all the sea water in his blood. It's enough for me to watch it from the land. Billy can have my shares if he wants them, he'll be able to take a more active part with Gilbert.'

'And if he doesn't want them?' she murmured. 'What then?'

'Then Gilbert can have them. I'll sell them to him for one penny and then I won't feel so bad about resigning, and at least he will survive. It's the least I can do to help him. He is my brother's son.'

'William!' She drew away from him. 'I need to talk to you about Adam. Mildred says she will accept responsibility, I know, but—'

'Hmph. She didn't want anything to do with

him before, why the change of heart now? Has she accepted that he belongs to James?' Ellen didn't answer, but he didn't appear to notice as he went on, 'I don't understand her; she was never very fond of children, not even her own.'

'No.' Ellen was thoughtful. 'She wasn't.'

'Not like you, Mother Hen, with ours.' He dropped a kiss on the top of her head.

'Another thing,' she murmured, deciding to leave the issue for the moment. 'Have you noticed anything about Tom lately?'

He frowned. 'Tom? No. He's always in the mill when I call on Thomas. He works hard, that boy. Is he having some difficulties? Apart from worrying about Betsy?'

'He might consider them difficulties,' she said warily. 'Though they might not be.'

'Oh, come, Ellen, don't be so mysterious. If he has a problem, you'd better tell me and have done with it. If Thomas is not well enough to guide his sons, then I must.'

She smiled. 'There can be no guidance in the matter of the heart, William. You of all people should know that.'

'*Oh.*' He grabbed her by the waist and held her fast. 'What are you talking about, woman? Matters of the heart? What would I know about that? You know I only married *you* for your money! So tell me. Has Tom fallen in love with someone unsuitable?'

'He loves Sammi,' she said simply. 'It's as plain to see as the nose on your face!'

He rubbed his fingers through his beard. 'Sammi! Our Sammi do you mean?'

'How many are there?' she queried, as she ascertained his reaction.

'You've sent him out looking for her,' he said distantly. 'Was that wise?'

'They've been walking on the sands since they were children,' she said softly. 'I know that she is safe.'

'But, how do you know of this? Has he spoken to you of it?'

She shook her head. 'No. But I know.'

He sat down heavily in his chair. 'Sammi! Well, it was bound to happen sooner or later. But Tom! I never expected . . . ! Not from that quarter.' He looked up at his wife. 'He's a good man. Reliable, hard-working. And his prospects are good. Thomas was always a shrewd old devil.' His face lit with humour as he mentioned his cousin's name. 'He'll have a fair nest egg put by for his sons and daughter.' He stretched out his long legs as he contemplated the news; Ellen sat down opposite him. 'He told me once that he'd bought some railway shares. He'd been talking to Arthur, and he bought them at a good price, then sold them at a profit. And I know that he bought one or two parcels of land over near Beverley, not vast acreage, but near enough to other larger estates who might be interested in buying one day.

'Yes, he's an opportunist, is Cousin Thomas. He also bought a few acres over at Hornsea, and if the railway line comes as they say it will, it will double in value.' He nodded. 'If anyone was looking for a suitable husband for one of their daughters, Tom would be a good candidate.'

'But?' Ellen queried. 'He's a miller's son. Do you want more for *your* daughter?'

He looked bewildered for a moment at her question and then hurt. 'I have never been pretentious, Ellen, you surely know that. I only want my children's well-being. Besides,' he gazed thoughtfully into space, 'I was taught never to forget my beginnings. My mother was the daughter of a common seaman. She never forgot it, she was proud of it almost, even though she became mistress of this great house.'

'I know,' she said gently. 'I was only asking. But the difficulties I was speaking of are Tom's. You see, he has more pride than you.'

'I don't understand what you mean, Ellen,' he

424

replied a trifle irritably. 'Why do you have to speak in riddles? Pride! What has pride got to do with anything?'

'It has to do with Tom! He won't ask for her, I'm convinced of that. No matter that he loves her.'

'Why not?' he demanded. 'Doesn't she care for him?'

'I don't think she knows yet.' She smiled wistfully. 'But he won't ask for her. He's such a gentleman, is Tom – only he doesn't know it.'

'For heaven's sake, Ellen! What are you talking about?'

'I'm talking about you being a landowner, William.' She shook her head at her husband's obtuseness. 'Whilst Tom knows he is only a miller's son.'

Sammi looked up from the sands and saw Tom on the cliff top silhouetted against the red and gold of the sunset. She knew instantly that it was him, even though she couldn't see his face. She knew his tall figure, his head of thick dark hair, his unmistakable long-legged stride.

How well I know him, she thought as she waved to him. *He has always been there whenever I needed to talk to someone. He must have known that I need someone now.*

He slithered down the cliff face, his boots making score marks in the oozing boulder clay as he jumped over the broken hummocks and ridges where there had been another fall.

'Tom,' she chastised him. 'I remember you telling me never to do that! You once told me that I must always use the steps.'

'Do as I say,' he laughed, rubbing the mud from his hands, 'not as I do! And that must have been a long time ago, for I can't remember.'

'I was about ten, I think, and I fell half-way down. You scrambled down and rescued me.' She laughed at the recollection. 'I was covered in mud and I lost my shoes.'

'Yes! That's right, I do remember. You were such a harum-scarum child. Always into mischief. Trouble always seemed to find you.' He smiled down at her, his eyes gentle.

'It still does. But sometimes it's my own fault.' She looked up and was about to say more, but couldn't understand his expression and changed her mind. 'Is something wrong, Tom? Why are you not at the mill?'

'The first thing is that I have come to fetch you home for an early supper – orders from your mama.'

Oh, she thought, *so you didn't come especially to see me, just when I wanted to talk to you.*

'And secondly, I wanted to tell you that I am going into Hull to try and find Betsy, and to ask where you think I should start looking?'

'You could start with Billy and Gilbert.' They linked arms as they retraced their steps, and she thought of the extra problems that Gilbert now had over the bank's closure, and of her own angry pronouncement that one day he would pay for his misdemeanour. *Should I tell Tom about Gilbert and Adam? Perhaps not; he would be so angry; he would think him dishonourable.*

The waves lapped close to their feet, leaving a frothy lacy edge on the sand and a damp edge to Sammi's skirt. 'Would you like me to come with you?' she asked. 'Would I be able to help?'

'No. I don't think so.'

She bent and picked up a pebble and hurled it into the sea; the dog leapt in after it, barking joyfully.

'Ooh! Why the temper?' he asked quietly.

'It wasn't temper!'

He stopped. 'I think it was. What's wrong, Sammi?'

'I only wanted to help; to come with you and look for Betsy. But I am only a woman and of course I'm not allowed!' She hung her head and scuffed the sand with her shoe. 'And I'm very mixed up about Adam. Aunt Mildred says she will take responsibility for him after all.'

I don't understand her motives, she thought. *James has*

denied to me that Adam is his, and Gilbert hasn't yet plucked up the courage to tell her that he *is the father. There is something very strange happening.*

Tom frowned. 'Why has she changed her mind?'

'I don't know!' Sammi cried fractiously. 'No-one wanted him when I brought him here, everyone was prepared to let him go to a charity home, or anywhere out of sight – except Mama,' she added softly. 'She wasn't so cruel.'

'It doesn't seem to make sense,' Tom admitted. 'But you should be pleased that she has had a change of heart and is prepared to accept him.'

He looked away down the long sands which stretched towards the high cliffs of Dimlington and the slender fingertip of Spurn peninsula. 'You are naturally curious about her reasons, but you have to think of your own future, Sammi. One day you will marry,' he said, tight-lipped. 'Your parents want what is best for you, and the longer the child stays here, the more gossip there will be.' He turned to look at her and found that she was gazing stonily out to sea. He put his hand under her chin. 'Look at me.' She lifted her head and gazed at him; her brown eyes were moist and he wanted to kiss away her tears. 'The child has red hair! He *could* be yours.'

She couldn't tell him the truth about Gilbert, but said passionately, 'I only want what is best for Adam. How I hate gossipmongers – mischief makers. And – and why should my virtue be so important in the general scheme of things?' A flush touched her cheeks as she spoke, but she continued to gaze defiantly at him. 'When I was a child I was brought up to be independent, to think for myself.' Her voice dropped and there was a note of resentfulness. 'But now that I am a woman, I must change my disposition and only do what is expected of me, because of what others might think!'

'There have to be rules, Sammi,' he said gently. 'Society falls apart without them.'

'Don't tell me that you believe in this – this social disease of narrow-mindedness, Tom? I can't believe that of you!'

'No. I don't. I believe that we must do what we think is right at the time, as you did over Adam.' He hesitated as he looked down at her fervent expression. 'We must adhere to what we believe in, and we shouldn't ignore our convictions of principles and scruples, even though—' he touched her cheek with his fingers, '—even though it might bring us unhappiness in the long run.'

'So, so we are agreed then, Tom?' she whispered, suddenly confused. 'There is no – no – dispute between us? We are of the same mind?'

He smiled and stooped to kiss her cheek. 'There never was any dispute between us, Sammi. Whether we are of the same mind is another matter altogether.'

She put her hand up to her cheek and her shawl slipped from her shoulders. Tom rearranged it, lifting her hair from beneath it and quite illogically caressed the back of her neck with his fingers. He felt the smooth vulnerability of her neck, the downy softness of her hair, and instinctively kissed her gently on her lips.

He saw her air of bewilderment and quickly gathered himself together. 'We only want what's best for you, Sammi.' He patted her face in a friendly, fraternal gesture. 'That's what we all want.'

42

'Perhaps I won't stay for supper, Aunt Ellen,' Tom said lamely, when they returned. 'I ought to get back.'

'Oh, but a place is laid,' she insisted. 'George is with your father, isn't he? And young Jenny? Do stay.'

Sammi sat opposite him at the table and listened vacantly as he exchanged conversation with her parents and Richard and Victoria. *Why do I feel so strange?* she thought. *I want to weep, yet I am not so unhappy, only confused over so many things.* She drew her hair away from the back of her neck and remembered the caress of Tom's fingers, firm and strong, yet delicate in their touch. She watched him as he ate. She saw his expressive dark eyebrows as they rose and fell during conversation, the curve of his mouth as he spoke or laughed, and wondered why she hadn't noticed these features before.

She touched her mouth with her serviette and thought of his tender kiss, and again a half-remembered image floated into her mind.

'Sammi! You're miles away,' Richard teased. 'What or *who* are you thinking of?'

A blush came to her cheeks, but she stressed that she had been thinking that perhaps she and her mother should travel into Hull the next day with her father and Tom, and call on Aunt Mildred. 'And I also want to see Billy,' she maintained. 'I want to find out if he met Mr Pearson, and if he was willing to help with the project for the children in the cellars.'

Her father raised his eyebrows to the ceiling and emitted a deep sigh. 'Yes. Very well, Sammi. If your mother wishes to, we will all go and resolve all the issues.'

The meeting with Mildred was cordial enough, though Sammi still found it hard to understand her treatment of James or Adam; but she seemed willing enough to finance the child, and had already made enquiries about the foster home in the town of Beverley.

'They are honest people,' Mildred said, 'and kind, and lost their only son when he was young, and although they are perhaps older than we would have wished, they seem very suitable.'

I wonder what Gilbert thinks of the arrangement? Sammi felt aggrieved. *He has got away scott free!* 'He cannot leave his nurse yet, you do realize that, Aunt Mildred?' she said doggedly. 'He is too young to be weaned.'

Mildred gave her a slight smile and nodded. 'Yes, Sammi. I am aware of that. We are now in September; if we said just before Christmas? He could then be put onto a bottle and pobs.'

And we can give him away like a Christmas present, Sammi grieved. *But I am his Godmother; his only one. I can visit him surely?*

Mildred drew Ellen to one side as they were leaving. 'I'm sorry, Ellen, about our harsh words over the child. I cannot ever explain why I behaved the way I did, but I had my reasons, and only Isaac understood. And now he has gone,' she added in a whisper.

'Everyone was hasty.' Ellen leaned forward and kissed her cheek. 'Including Sammi, but she is young and impetuous.'

'As once we all were,' Mildred said softly.

'Does Gilbert know of your decision?' Ellen ventured. 'What are his feelings?'

Mildred shook her head. 'He has so much to worry him just now, that I hardly ever see him, and I would not add to his burden; but I have written to James and told him of my decision.'

Sammi and her mother journeyed back to Hull in silence, Ellen debating whether she should tell Gilbert of his mother's decision. *He is in deep water I know*, she pondered, *but he must strike for the shore himself if he is to survive.*

And Sammi thought broodingly of the Christmas to come and the departure of Adam whom she had come to love, and who was going to strangers.

'There's Billy!'

Ellen leaned towards the window and pulled it down. 'Stop, Johnson!'

Johnson had already seen Billy striding along the road and was drawing to a halt.

'Ma! Sammi! What are you doing here?' He got into the carriage beside them and they moved off again towards the High Street. He gave his mother a hug and grinned at Sammi. 'You shouldn't be here yet, you know, the epidemic is still lingering.'

'Epidemic? What epidemic?' His mother's face showed alarm.

'Didn't you hear? There's been cholera and typhus. It was reported in some of the newspapers.'

They shook their heads. 'Is that why you haven't been home, Billy?' Sammi asked. 'I've wanted to know about the children.'

'Why yes! I explained to Betsy that I was busy, and I told her that there was disease in the town. Didn't she tell you? I asked her to.'

They both gazed at him, eyes opened wide. 'When?' Sammi asked. 'When did you see her?'

'Phew, so much has happened – I don't know, about three weeks, maybe, nearly four. It was after the opening of the park anyway, and at the start of the epidemic.'

He was on his way to the company, he said. He had promised Gilbert that he would help in any way he could while there were so many difficulties. The closure of Willard's bank had rocked the town, causing ripples of alarm throughout the business community. Gilbert had also told him that his father was coming into town and he needed to speak to him regarding the plan he had for his own future, and to ask if he would fund him until his inheritance was due.

Tom was standing in the door of the stables, chatting to Johnson. 'I was hoping to see you, Billy.' He came over to greet him. 'Gilbert said you were coming in. Your father and Arthur are about to begin a meeting with Gilbert, so I decided to wait out here.'

Billy nodded. 'I've just heard about Betsy. I saw her one day; it was during the epidemic and I advised her that she'd be better staying at home. She looked very well, Tom; I wouldn't have thought that anything was amiss.' He pulled a wry expression. 'I wondered afterwards what she must have thought of me, for I'd been up all night and looked like a scarecrow, whereas she looked so lovely in her blue bonnet and cloak.'

'Blue bonnet and cloak?' Tom queried. 'Surely you were mistaken? She was wearing a yellow dress and shawl when she left home that morning!'

'She's probably borrowed some finery. You know how ladies are; she would want a change of clothing if she's staying with friends. Or else she's bought something new. Don't worry about her,' Billy assured him, though he felt uneasy. 'If she's said she's all right, then she will be.'

'I hope so,' Tom agreed, and went off again to look around the town.

'Sammi, can you stay over? May she, Ma?'

His mother agreed and they decided to ask Harriet if she could stay the night with her and Gilbert, as she had promised previously.

Billy ran upstairs and knocked on the door of Gilbert's office. 'Just wanted to tell you that I'm here, and could I have a talk with you before you leave, Father?'

His father beckoned him in. 'Gilbert says that you have resigned, Billy!'

'Yes, that's why I wanted to speak to you. I need your advice.'

'Are you sure that you are doing the right thing?' Arthur spoke up. 'This company isn't finished yet. We shall diversify, which is what I've been saying we should do all along! We should go into other forms of shipping, fleeting perhaps, or even some other commercial business, not just whaling.'

'That isn't why I resigned, Uncle. I had decided before all this business at the bank flared up,' Billy said hastily. 'Gilbert will confirm that, won't you?'

Gilbert nodded. He had his chin hunched over his hand as he sat behind the desk. He looked tired and had lost weight. He had taken the blow very hard.

'I want to go into local politics. I want to do something for the people of this town,' Billy began.

'Hmph. There's no money in that,' his uncle scowled. 'None whatsoever. You'll need something else to keep hearth and home secure.'

'Can we leave Billy's problems for the moment,' his father broke in. 'They have no place in this discussion. What is important is who is going to partner Gilbert if Billy leaves the company? Even with a smaller, more compact enterprise, Gilbert still needs a working partner. I don't wish to do it and neither do you, Arthur, so if the company is to survive then we have to think of someone else. Someone who has initiative and knows the industry.'

There was silence as they thought over the implications. Then Gilbert shook his head. 'There is no-one else if Billy leaves, there's only James and he isn't interested.'

'Does it have to be family?' Billy asked. 'For if it doesn't, then I can think of the ideal person!'

'Well, we're looking for loyalty. That is the most important thing,' said his father. 'Would we get it from a stranger?'

'Well, that's just it; he isn't a stranger,' Billy said enthusiastically, 'and his loyalty is unquestionable. Make him a director, give him some shares and the company is on the way up again.'

'Why – do you mean who I think you mean?' Gilbert rose to his feet, a gleam of hope in his face.

'Yes.' Billy beamed. 'Hardwick!'

'I want you to meet Stephen Sheppard, Sammi. We've become great friends.' Billy took Sammi's arm and they hurried across the busy Market Place towards a coffee house where he had arranged to meet Stephen. 'And I also wanted to tell you the good news about the children's project, though I must say it has paled significantly since hearing about Betsy not coming home. I don't like the sound of that at all.'

'She has written and apparently she is well and happy,' Sammi took off her gloves as they sat down at a table in the window, 'but it is very strange that she doesn't say where she is staying. We're all very worried.'

He ordered coffee and chocolate, and gave her the details of the cholera epidemic in the cellars. He told her that Zachariah Pearson was arranging for him to meet two businessmen in the town who might be willing to fund the project for a children's home.

'Billy,' she began, 'have you thought about where this could lead you? I have thought so often about what might have happened to Adam. Will there be room for abandoned babies in your children's home? Will there be a place for young women like his mother, who might have been turned out of their homes in disgrace? Will one home be enough?'

'No, it won't,' he said. 'So much to do. Where shall I begin?'

'Begin at the beginning,' a voice interrupted. 'Wherever that might be,' and they looked up to see Stephen Sheppard standing there.

Billy made the introductions and ordered more coffee. 'We're talking about injustices, Stephen, and how to eradicate them.'

'Then you can start with me.' Stephen gazed gloomily at them. 'My uncle and I have been rebuked for spreading alarm around the town! There has been a meeting at the hospital and none of the other doctors would confirm that they had attended any cholera cases.' He stirred his coffee vigorously as he explained the situation. 'I tell you, Billy, I'm sickened by the whole thing. Why should politics interfere with the treatment of the sick or dying? It was definitely cholera. I'm convinced of it! Why damn it, I beg your pardon, Miss Rayner, there was even a *blue* stage, and you only see that with cholera!'

'Why won't the authorities admit it?' Billy asked. 'Why are they now saying it was acute diarrhoea and typhus, when you and Doctor Fleming were so sure that it was cholera?'

'It was that last case of typhus. They said that the symptoms were so similar that we were mistaken. Of course, what it really is,' he said bitterly, 'is that the doctors can't agree on a cure, and as the authorities won't clean up the sources of infection, it's stalemate.' He leaned forward and whispered, 'They are still arguing about the water at Springhead. They say that there isn't enough to supply the town, and the councillors won't allow Warden, the engineer, to continue boring. That water is as pure as it is on the Wolds, which is where it comes from,' he asserted. 'Yet they still insist on using the water drawn from the Stoneferry works.' He screwed up his face in disgust. 'And no matter how much it's filtered, we're still drinking river water which has had dead dogs and sewage in it!'

He sat back glumly. 'We badly need a fever hospital, and neither the Board of Health nor the town Guardians will sanction one. They've been using the Citadel and the old hulk in the river for the foreign seamen, but they've nothing remotely suitable for the townspeople.'

He finished his coffee and asked Sammi if she would like more chocolate, but she declined, adding, 'But what, then, is the answer, Doctor Sheppard?'

'I honestly don't know where the answer lies. They say they can't take precautions or enforce the Prevention of Diseases Act unless the town is under threat, and in my humble opinion it is under threat with those *pestilential privies* that people have to live in!'

'So are you in trouble, Stephen?' Billy asked anxiously. 'Will this affect your career?'

'No!' The young doctor was determined. 'It won't. But I think my uncle will retire; he says he is sick of petty-fogging politics. I shall go on fighting, but I'm a medical man, I haven't the time to go in for local politics as well as attend the sick. What I sorely need is a friend on the Board of Health or the Sanitary Committee; someone in authority who isn't afraid to say what he thinks.'

Sammi pondered before asking, 'How long could you wait for someone like that?'

'As long as it takes, Miss Rayner.' The doctor smiled at her. 'This problem won't go away in a hurry.' He looked at them both as they stared thoughtfully at each other. 'Why? Have you someone in mind?'

'Yes.' Billy leant back in his chair and folded his arms. 'We have. Me!'

43

Charles Craddock pulled off his shoes and threw them into a corner and flopped down into a chair. 'Get me a brandy, I'm spent.'

Betsy was about to tell him to get his own, but there was some ill humour in his eyes that made her change her mind, so she crossed the room to a side table and poured him a large measure from the decanter. 'You've been away ages, Charles. I've been so bored,' she said petulantly. 'Where have you been?'

'Don't start that again,' he growled, taking the glass from her. 'I've told you before to mind your own business.' He pulled her down onto his knee. 'Just keep that pretty nose out of it. God, Betsy, but you're getting heavy.' He pushed her out of the chair. 'You're eating too many chocolates.'

'Well, there's nothing else to do when you're not here. I might just as well be back at home as sit here alone.'

'Well go, then,' he said carelessly and drained his glass in one swallow. 'See if your father and brothers will welcome you back after being some man's whore.'

She drew in a sharp breath. He couldn't mean what he said? Surely he didn't want her to go? A doubt crept in; he had been spending more time away from home of late, and when she had questioned him he always said he was going to see his mother. But he often arrived back during the early hours of a morning smelling of spirits, and she was sure that he had been gambling, for there was often a wad of money in his pocket; but he hadn't asked her to accompany him recently.

'Charles? You don't mean that? You are teasing me?' She tickled his ear with her fingertips.

'Mean what?' he said, catching hold of her hand.

'Being a – *whore*, that's not a nice thing to say about me!' She stroked his face. 'I mean more to you than that, don't I?'

He caught her other hand and held her fast, and then yawned. 'God, I'm tired.' He let go of her hands. 'Get me another brandy and then I'm going to bed for an hour.'

'You haven't answered my question, Charles,' she persisted.

He sighed. 'Which question? For God's sake, woman!'

'You said I was a whore!' She whispered the words. She was beginning to be afraid.

'Yes! And? That's what you are, isn't it?' He folded his arms and scrutinized her. 'How else would you describe yourself? You live here with a man who feeds you, gives you money, tumbles you in bed. Is there another word?'

'I, I thought that I meant more to you than that,' she stammered. 'You seemed to care for me.'

'So I do, little dumpling.' He put out his hand to draw her near. 'I think you are delightful, but don't start questioning me about where I have been or what I have been doing; just keep on pleasing me the way that you do, and everything will be fine.'

'But won't there be more than just that?' Still she questioned. 'Don't you want more from me than just to tumble me in bed?'

He laughed. 'You'll be saying next that you expect me to marry you!'

'No,' she said slowly. 'I don't think I expected that, not yet anyway. But I didn't expect to have to stay in the house while you went out. We had such fun to begin with, horse racing and the clubs and parties. Now you don't take me any more.'

'Oh, I got bored with all that,' he said lazily. 'And

438

anyway, there's hardly anyone around at the moment with this business at Willard's bank. No-one dares gamble for fear of losing their precious businesses.' He put his hand beneath his chin and speculated thoughtfully. 'I wouldn't mind taking a wager with your cousin Gilbert at the moment,' he sneered. 'I'd like to bet his failing company against a deck of cards.'

'Gilbert's company?' She was shocked. 'Masterson and Rayner, you mean?'

'Yes.' He guffawed. 'Didn't I tell you? Your precious Gilbert married a swindler's daughter, who, when he was found out in his thieving enterprises, shot himself through the head. They say his brains were splattered all over the walls!'

Betsy was sickened, she felt tears come to her eyes. Poor Harriet. She was such a gentle creature; to have her father do such a thing must have devastated her! She started to weep as she thought of her own crippled father; and here she was, living a life of debauchery. Yes. That's what it was. And it was true what Craddock said about her. She was a whore!

'Come here,' Craddock said invitingly, stretching out his arms and reaching for her. 'I like it when you cry; you seem so defenceless and vulnerable – so innocent, and yet I know very well that you are not.'

She rose early the next morning and stood by the window looking out. *What a fool I am*, she thought. *What can I do?* She pushed to the back of her mind the reasons for not going home and concentrated on the present, rather than the future. *I'll have to be nice to Charles, so that he will want me to stay.*

'Betsy!' Craddock's voice came from the depths of the bed. 'What are you doing?'

'Just looking out at the day,' she said brightly. 'It's a beautiful morning, sharp but sunny. What shall we do? Would you like to go out or,' smiling she came towards the bed, 'would you prefer to stay in bed?'

He raised himself onto one elbow. He wasn't

smiling, he had a most disagreeable scowl on his face.

'Who's a cross-patch in a morning?' she teased as she turned back the covers.

'Go back to the window!' he demanded. 'Go on, stand where you were before.'

Inwardly she cursed him as she returned to her place by the window. She ached from the night's activities and his insatiable appetite. The light was strong and her bedgown transparent, they wouldn't be going out again this morning.

'You bitch! You whore!'

She put her hands to her face. 'What? What is it? What have I done?' The venomous expression etched on his face frightened her. He looked at her as if he could kill her.

'You tricked me!' He shot out of bed and grabbed her. 'Or tried to,' he hissed. 'But it won't work, my beauty, not on me!'

'I don't know what you mean! Charles, you're hurting me!' Tears came to her eyes.

'Oh, don't start that. It won't work this time. You bitch!'

She tried to step back, away from his gripping hands and violent expression.

'You thought to trick me! Thought to claim the bastard was mine! Well, I know that it isn't. So you can clear out. Get your things and go. Why I didn't notice before, I don't know!'

She shook him off and involuntarily clutched her midriff. 'I don't know what you mean,' she whispered. 'Why should I trick you?'

'That's it,' he spat. 'Mother's instinct – protect the child.' He gave an assumed punch towards her and she flinched.

'You're mistaken,' she panicked. 'I've put on weight. You said you liked me this way.'

'You're pregnant!' He pushed his face into hers. 'You're pregnant, and it's not mine! I can't sire children, thank God, for if I could I'd have half the women in the town claiming I'd filled their bellies.'

'No. No. I'm not. I'm not!' Her voice didn't seem to belong to her as she disclaimed the issue that had confronted her so often, and which she had rejected. 'I can't be! It's not true.'

He put his head back and laughed. 'Not true! Just look at you.' He forced her over to the mirror and gathered her bedgown close to her body. 'Turn sideways. That's not chocolate! What a joke!' He let go of her and rolled onto the bed and laughed to split his sides. 'Chocolate!' he gasped. 'Chocolate!' He suddenly stopped laughing and sat up. 'Now get dressed and clear off!' he snapped. 'I want no pregnant women or bastards here. Whatever would my wife say?'

'Your wife?' she stammered. 'You have a wife?'

'Of course I have a wife!' he barked. 'How else could I afford to live the way I do?'

She stared at him for a moment, then without a word she turned and opened the wardrobe door and took down a gown.

'Not that one,' he said brusquely, putting on a dressing robe and going towards the bedroom door. 'The one you came in. You take nothing that I bought you.'

She didn't answer, but put back the gown and took down her yellow one, which in comparison to the others hanging beside it, now looked very shabby. It was also too tight. *I've put on weight, that's all,* she deliberated as she strove to fasten it over the whalebone cage. *He doesn't know what he's talking about.* She stifled a sob. *It's not true. It isn't.*

She couldn't fasten the bodice and she took a silk scarf and pushed it into the neckline, hoping he wouldn't notice that it was one of his gifts, then she looked around the room to see if there was anything else of hers. Only her shawl and empty purse, nothing more; but on the chair were his jacket and trousers where he had carelessly thrown them.

441

She tiptoed across and slipped her hand inside the jacket pocket. Inside she felt a wad of crisp notes and in the trousers some coins. She withdrew two notes and stuffed them inside her bodice and hastily gathered a few coins which she put in her purse.

'Will you let me take the cloak?' she asked, holding it up in one hand as she went into the drawing-room. 'It's too cold for only a shawl.'

He was draped over a chair, one leg over the arm, and reading a newspaper. 'And you're hardly decent anyway.' He grinned lewdly at her. 'Your gown is too tight. Yes, take it.' He flipped over a page of newspaper. 'I shall take the gowns back to the shop. I'll tell them that I am not pleased with the purchase, that they are quite unsuitable.'

'I can't believe that you are doing this to me, Charles,' she said, in one last attempt to placate him. 'Why have you turned against me so?'

'Quite frankly I'm just tired of you, my dear.' He threw the newspaper onto the floor and stretched his arms. 'Apart from you being in the *family way*, as they say, and had I cared to we could have done something about that, you have long outlasted your time.' He smiled patronizingly. 'It's time for us to move along.'

'So you are turning me out! Well, in that case,' she grew bold, 'as I have been nothing more than a whore to you, perhaps I should have payment! I am leaving with less than I came with. I had my self-respect when I met you, now I have lost even that. You can at least pay me for my services, if I can't have the clothes.'

'Hah! The cheek of the bitch. I've fed you and kept you. Why should I give you money?'

'Because if you don't I shall find out where your wife lives and make sure that she knows what you are up to in this fine house. This *whorehouse*.' She stared at him defiantly. She had nothing more to lose.

His eyes narrowed and he leaned forward. 'I've been threatened before,' he scoffed. 'But they've always changed their minds.'

'I shan't,' she challenged. 'And what's more I should take my cousins Gilbert and Billy with me to substantiate my claim that I have been living here; they are gentlemen and would be believed. And,' she glared at him, 'I shall send my brothers to you.'

He swallowed and she saw a tensing of his chin. *He is at best a lily-livered coward,* she thought. *Is he more afraid of his wife than he is of a beating?*

He got to his feet, and in a vain attempt to shame her, he sneered, 'Very well. I'll give you what I think you were worth,' and went out of the room.

She held back her tears, indeed anger was at the forefront of her emotions, and held out her hand for the money he had in his hand when he came back into the room. He counted it out, then counted it again, and she held her breath for fear that he would realize that some of it was missing.

'Take it.' He almost threw it at her. 'Now go, and if I hear one whisper of trouble from you, it will be the worse for you.' His words were empty, he now just wanted rid of her.

'I'm going.' She put her chin up. 'Don't worry, you won't see me again.'

She stepped out of the front door and banging it so hard behind her that the panes rattled in the windows, she turned towards the town and walked away.

44

Autumn had drawn to a close and winter was already tightening its grip on the land. The earth was wet and soggy with the heavy deluge of rain which turned the roads to Holderness into a quagmire, and then hardened into solid ridges which cracked axles and turned carts and carriages over after the biting north east wind dried the surface.

Sammi spent as much time as possible at Tillington, riding over on the back of Boreas and not risking taking the trap. She had told Mrs Bishop that a home had been found for Adam, and the woman had said that she was glad for his sake.

'And for thine, Miss Rayner,' she added, for she had disapproved of Sammi taking him out with her, saying quite bluntly that she was encouraging the rumours which were still circulating. 'Tha'll have some bairns of thine own one day, miss,' she commented. 'When tha finds some rich young gentleman that thy parents approve of.'

But some rich young gentleman would want to take me away from all those I care about, Sammi mused, ignoring the twitch of window curtains as she trotted through the village towards the mill house. *I want to stay near to Mama and Pa and Victoria, and – everyone.*

If only Adam could stay within the family; if only Gilbert was honest, if only we didn't have to keep his secret.

Although she had said that she didn't care what people thought of her, she was conscious of covert glances and whispers behind covered mouths as she came into the village, and she was becoming tense and nervous.

She was apprehensive, too, over Uncle Thomas. He was quite often ill, brought on by worry over Betsy's disappearance, and troubled that Mark had not been in touch with them either, so she spent time with him trying to cheer him when she felt little cheer within herself. The letters from Betsy had stopped coming, and Tom had not found any trace of her, though he had been several times into Hull. Luke Reedbarrow had also searched, but both men were hampered by their lack of knowledge of the town. Gilbert and Billy were both looking out for her, Tom had notified the authorities, and posters for a missing person had been pasted up in the streets of Hull.

Betsy stared dully at the poster on the wall. REWARD GIVEN, it proclaimed, FOR INFORMATION RECEIVED OF THE MISSING PERSON MISS ELIZABETH FOSTER.

They wouldn't want to know; she shivered as much at the thought of her family finding her in these conditions, as from the cold and damp. *I wouldn't want them to know how low I have fallen.*

One of her workmates, Dora, looked over her shoulder. 'I wish I knew her.' She picked her teeth with a dirty finger-nail. 'I'd tell on her. I could do wi' some money. I'm skint. I haven't even got me rent or money for a glass of ale. I don't suppose tha can lend me owt, Mary?'

Betsy shook her head. 'I've nothing left.' She turned away from the poster. 'I owe my rent and I've barely a copper left for food. I've nothing until we get our wages.'

Both girls worked at the Greenland Yards, where they scraped blubber from the whalebone in preparation for it being boiled. It was messy, smelly work, and Betsy felt that she could never get rid of the sickening stench, no matter how she

445

scrubbed under the pump in the court where she lived.

After she had parted company with Craddock, she had at first managed to obtain employment in a grocer's shop, and found cheap but clean lodgings, but after a week she had noticed her employer eyeing her suspiciously, and at the end of the following week he had given her her wages and told her not to come back.

'But why?' she asked. 'What have I done? Isn't my work satisfactory?'

'Oh, aye,' he said. 'Your work is all right, but you're not. You look as if you're about to drop at any time.' He shook his head at her. 'You're not wearing a wedding ring. This is a respectable establishment. I can't keep you on. It just won't do.'

She changed her lodgings, taking something cheaper, and sharing the dingy room with another woman. She sold her yellow gown at a secondhand shop and bought in its place a black skirt and flannel blouse, and also a cheap ring which she wore on the third finger of her left hand, but she kept the cloak to hide her protuberant swelling as she looked for other work. She managed to convince her next employer, a stallholder in the market, that she had been suffering from the dropsy but was otherwise very fit, but she had to give up the work when she could no longer lift the sacks of potatoes and cases of oranges.

Now she felt at least that she was safe. She told the foreman at the yard that her name was Mary Brown and that she was a widow; he was uninterested, simply telling her to hand in the flensing knife every evening before leaving, otherwise the cost of it would be deducted from her wages.

'It says she's dark-haired and pretty and was last seen wearing a yellow gown.' Dora read out the description slowly and haltingly. 'She must've been in trouble for her to run off. Why else would a lass leave a good home?'

446

'I can't imagine.' Betsy stared across the road. There was Gilbert hurrying along on the opposite side, looking as if he had the weight of the world on his shoulders. She only had to call his name and things would be very different for her.

'Here, he's all right, isn't he? I fancy him.' Her companion followed her gaze. 'Shall I whistle of him?' She grinned at Betsy. 'I might be able to earn a shilling!'

'Do as you like,' Betsy snapped and turned away. 'But I've not yet stooped to prostitution.'

'No? Well, how have you got in that state then?' Dora pointed towards Betsy's stomach. She laughed, not reprovingly, but with a lackadaisical indifference. 'You don't expect me to believe that story of dropsy, or of you being a widow? I've heard it all before.'

Betsy didn't answer. How she hated these women with their crude humour and low morals.

'Just don't let 'foreman know tha's pregnant, that's all.' Dora shrugged and walked off in the other direction from Betsy. 'I'm onny warning thee. Tha'll finish up in 'workhouse next, thee and tha bairn.'

Sammi entered the mill house without knocking, debating whether she was making matters worse by coming so often. *Tom seems to be so short-tempered, which is not like him at all; yet I can't stay away.*

Tom was in the kitchen as she entered, about to lift a heavy pan of stew onto the fire, while Jenny stood by. She felt a small pang of annoyance as Jenny smiled at Tom and thanked him, before greeting Sammi and then disappearing with her duster into the parlour.

'Hello, Sammi. It's good of you to call again.' Tom avoided looking at her. 'I, er, I keep meaning to say, don't feel that you must come because Betsy isn't here. We can manage. Jenny is shaping up very well.'

'Oh!' She felt a chill of disappointment. 'Would you rather I didn't?'

'Oh, no. You know I didn't mean that. It's just that I realize you have other things to do.'

'What else do you think I have to do, Tom?'

'Well, I don't know.' He looked perplexed. 'What do ladies do? Shopping? Sewing? Good works?'

'And is that your considered opinion of my life, Tom?' she said sharply. 'Do you think I would prefer to do those things rather than be here with – with you and Uncle Thomas and George, while Betsy is missing?'

He sat down at the kitchen table and put his head in his hands. 'I'm sorry.' His voice was muffled. 'Please try to understand. I'm at my wits' end. It's not knowing that's the worst thing. Wondering if she's dead! Wondering if she's in any kind of trouble that she daren't tell us about; or is she just enjoying herself somewhere and not bothering to get in touch?'

She moved towards him and rested her hand on his shoulder. 'We're all so worried, Tom. And I hate to see you so miserable. I wish there was something I could do or say to make you feel better.'

He gave a short ironic laugh and closed his eyes, pressing his fingers to his brow. 'I'm sure there is, Sammi. I'm sure there is.'

She bent over him and gave him a squeeze. 'Tell me then, what I can do,' and as he looked up at her, about to speak, the door opened and Jenny came back in.

She stood for a moment, open-mouthed. 'Sorry, Miss Sammi – Master Tom. I'll come back in a minute,' and turned to go back out.

'It's all right, Jenny.' Tom pushed back the chair from the table. 'Don't be embarrassed. Miss Sammi and I are old friends. We often give each other a hug, don't we, cousin?' He gave Sammi a peck on her cheek.

'Why, yes,' Sammi said brightly, and unaccountably feeling a constriction in her throat. 'Of course we do.'

'Oh! That's nice.' Jenny gazed at them, her wide eyes bright. 'That's really lovely!'

She didn't visit again for a week, Victoria was in bed with a heavy cold and Sammi spent time reading to her and keeping her company. On the days when the frost was sharp and the wind not too bitter, she walked along the cliff top, taking Sam with her, who was missing his daily walk with Victoria.

On the following week, she visited Mrs Bishop and told her that Adam would be leaving immediately after Christmas.

Mrs Bishop nodded. 'It's for 'best, miss, in 'long run.'

Sammi had mounted Boreas and turned for home. They had had a letter from Aunt Mildred the previous day, saying that she would either come or send for Adam as soon as Christmas was over.

'Anne and I will not be celebrating this year,' she wrote. *'We shall go to church and pray for those who are missing from us, and I will also pray for the child. He will not want for anything material, and I trust that he will have a good life with his new family. I have not yet had a reply from James, but I am sure he will be happy with my decision.'*

She hesitated before turning down the road which led to Monkston, debating whether to visit the Fosters before returning home. Tom's words, though he had denied their meaning, had cast some doubt in her mind. Would he prefer her not to call too often? Was she interfering with the running of the household? Jenny, in spite of being so young, was proving to be a real home-maker. The house was warm and welcoming, and she was becoming a good plain cook.

I'm not needed, she decided. *They can manage without me*, and she turned the horse's head towards home.

She heard her name called before she had gone a

few yards. She reined in and turned in the saddle. Tom was waving to her. She waved back and he set off at a run towards her.

'Hello. Is there any news?'

He shook his head and looked up at her. 'None. Sammi! Why didn't you call? I saw you from the lane and thought you were coming. Da has missed you; he's been asking for you.'

'Has he?' *And what about you*, she wanted to say.

'I thought about what you said, Tom, when I was there last time; and, and I realized that I wasn't helping; in fact that I was probably preventing you ·from getting on with your life, by reminding you by my presence that Betsy was no longer here.'

'I don't understand you, Sammi.' He put up his hand to hers as she clasped the reins. 'Preventing me from getting on with my life?'

'Yes. Betsy and I were – are – such good friends and spent such a lot of time together and now, now that she's not . . .' Her voice trailed away.

'Did you only ever come to visit Betsy?' he asked brusquely. 'Did you not come to visit the rest of us?'

'Oh, you misunderstand me, Tom,' she stammered, unable even to understand her own feelings, let alone explain them to Tom.

'Do you not think that the rest of us might miss seeing you?' His eyes were keen, searching hers.

'But, you said, you said that there was no need for me to call so frequently.' She took a trembling breath. 'You said that I probably had other things to do. I thought that perhaps you were really saying that you didn't want me to call so often.'

'Oh, Sammi, you little idiot.' He put his arms up to grasp her. 'Come down, I can't talk to you when you are up there.'

She slid down into his arms and wound the reins around her hand. 'Am I being silly, Tom? I did want to come.' She was choked with tears. 'I've been to see Adam, he's going away after Christmas, and I miss

Betsy such a lot, and I feel so miserable, and when I thought that you didn't want me either—'

'Don't want you?' He put both arms around her and held her close. 'How could you ever think such a thing. I shall always want you, Sammi,' he whispered. *I love you*, he murmured beneath his breath. He held her away from him and she saw pain etched on his face. He swallowed and said softly, 'You know that we all love you. Da and George and Betsy, and even Mark would say he did.' He gave a twisted grin. 'If he was here and if he dare.'

She gazed at him, her lips parted and a tear trickling down her cheek. 'And you, Tom?'

He kissed the top of her head and then wiped away the tear. 'I just said that we all did, didn't I? We all love you, Sammi, so don't ever forget.'

He won't say it. She rode away and turned back to see him still standing watching her. *He loves me – and he won't say it! And I love him,* she realized with sudden clarity. *I love Tom! But why won't he say? Does he consider me still a child? Surely not! Does he think that I might love someone else? No, he can't. He must know that I would have said if I did. So why?*

The day was drawing on, and the road was dark with overhanging branches. There was a sharpness in the air which tingled her nostrils and sent a chill through her. Then comprehension flooded through her. *He doesn't want to spoil my chances. He wants me to make a good marriage; just as Mama and Pa do!*

She gave a sudden shudder. *It's going to snow.* She clicked her tongue, urging Boreas on. *We shall have a cold, hard winter.*

The lofty wharf buildings around the London Dock appeared to hang suspended in the yellow mist which swirled around them. In the doorway of one of these buildings a huddled figure sat, his knees bent towards him and his arms wrapped around them, absorbed in contemplation.

So what have I achieved? he cogitated. *I've worked as a labourer in 'fields. I've done some prize-fighting. Travelled the length of 'country and seen such poverty as I would never have believed, and for what? For nowt! For a chance to prove my braggardly worth. Nowt else. I left a good home and family to sit here in Port of London and contemplate whether I should go back wi' my tail between my legs or spend 'last of my money on a passage out.*

And so Mark, with his great ambitions shattered, sat through the night in disillusionment, waiting as he had done so often, for the dawn to break and another day to begin. He had tried for work as he travelled, only to find that others were there before him; pale-faced, faded men who had gone without sleep in order to be first in line.

He had never been entirely without money; he had taken all his savings with him when he left Tillington and had subsisted stringently so that he always had enough money for food at least once a day, and he had joined the queues at the soup kitchens when hot soup and bread were given out to the deserving poor.

Deserving poor! He'd sneered so many times when he had heard the expression from the comfort of his home, but now that he was almost ready to join their ranks, he had different views. He had arrived in London during one of the bleakest winters in living memory, and he had been heartened to see great jollity as the crowds skated on the frozen Serpentine, their faces flushed from the exertion and merriment. There was a carnival atmosphere as brass bands played and people danced on the ice; tents and charcoal braziers were set up to provide refreshments of ale and chestnuts, sausages and hot meat pies. It was only when he had joined the thronging mass on the frozen ice that he had realized that, among the warmly dressed, in bright scarves and muffs and skating boots, there were others, gaunt and thin with hollowed cheeks, who were rushing around the ice in a vain attempt to keep warm and forget their desperate hunger.

London during those cold weeks was filled with thousands of people in distress. They queued at the overcrowded workhouses and other charitable societies, begging to be let in or be given relief, and when they were turned away because of their sheer numbers, some, in their anger, stormed the bakeries and butchers, and wantonly emptied the shelves.

Mark saw when he'd walked amongst them that not all were drunken, work-shy or from the criminal classes, as he might once have believed. Most were honest labourers out of work, some were clerks and men with a tradesman's mark. The women were laundrymaids or shopgirls with tattered finery drooping from their thin bones, or widows with a clutch of children hanging around their skirts.

He had decided that he would stay for another month before returning home, and because he was strong, he had found casual work as a porter in a market, shifting barrow-loads of meat, and earning half a crown a day. He found cheap lodgings run by a widow who gave him breakfast and a hot supper, and who was devastated when he gave her notice, when without any reason, he had lost his job.

So what do I do? he considered as he sat. *Do I go home and eat humble pie? Or do I take my chance in another country?* Bleakly he pondered. *I could have sailed for America from Hull, I needn't have travelled over half of England if I'd wanted to do that. And now that Lincoln has been made President they say there'll be civil war, and knowing my luck I'd be embroiled in 'middle of it. Australia! I could afford a ticket – just.* He had enquired of cost, of assisted passages, of when the ships sailed and how long the voyage would take. He had half made up his mind to go, but some homing instinct held him back.

He wouldn't have described himself as being a family man, yet he found increasingly that his thoughts turned to home, to his father, his brothers and specifically to Betsy, whose memory tore at his conscience when he remembered his boorish treatment of her. *I'm lonely,* he admitted. *I miss them all. If there was just one of them here with me, someone that I could relate to, someone that I could care for or grumble at, I would buy the tickets and sail.*

He shifted his position as his legs stiffened, and stretched. He wasn't tired, merely weary; it had been a long day and even longer night. A clock had struck three a short time before; three more hours and then he would have to move from his quarters.

Suddenly he was alert. He wasn't alone; he could hear a whisper, someone else had chosen to spend their waking hours by the waters of the Thames. No. Not a whisper, a song. A soft refrain, like a lullaby with words he couldn't understand. He tensed and strained his ears to listen, but as the soothing melody washed over him he relaxed, it was as if he was a child again at his mother's knee.

It was a woman singing, or a girl, and the music was plaintive, as if she was weeping. He sat up. She *was* weeping. Well, he couldn't help her, there was so much sorrow, and hadn't he troubles enough of his own?

Another sound reached his ears, hoarse whispers and shuffling feet, and he turned his head at the movement to his right. Two figures, shadowy, yet by their outline, broad and thickset, were crossing his path toward the weeping woman. He shifted his position yet again, crouching on his heels and with fingertips touching the floor, hidden from view, he watched the scene.

'Don't scream, my lovely, and we'll not hurt a hair on yer head,' he heard one say. 'Just give us what you've got and we'll be off.'

'Mother of God!' A voice shrieked. 'Give me back me bag! You'll have to kill me first, for I've nothing else left in the world.'

There was a scuffle. 'Come on, lady,' the man

began, but his words choked in his throat as Mark sprang.

His movement was swift, his aim sure. Not for nothing had his miller's biceps developed, and his short career in prize-fighting been successful. One man lay groaning on the ground whilst the other sped as fast as his feet would carry him.

He put his foot on the man's chest. 'Does tha want to run for 'constable?' he asked the girl, for he saw, now that he was closer, that that was all she was.

She got up from her corner, clutching a tattered canvas bag and peered down at her assailant. 'Sure they'd want to know why I was here and why wasn't a daicent girl in her bed at night. Let him go and take his conscience with him; he's a poor specimen of manhood, sure enough, if he's robbing the poor.'

He pulled the man up by his coat collar and thrust his boot into his backside. 'Clear off,' he threatened, 'before I chuck thee in 'river.' He turned to the girl. 'I heard thee singing,' he said. 'It was grand. Then tha started to cry. Afore them varmints struck,' he added.

'And can't a woman cry in peace if she wants to,' she said defiantly. 'I thought I'd found a place to be alone and I find it's as busy as Dublin itself.'

He grinned. She was a spirited creature, sharp-tongued and mutinous. She wouldn't have given up her belongings without a fight, even if he hadn't come along.

'I'll go back to my doorway, then. G'night.'

''Night, mister.' She shrank back into her corner. 'And thank ye kindly.'

'Any time,' he said, as he walked away. 'Tha's welcome.'

As morning broke, he peered out from his doorway; a shower of rain pattered onto the river, but it wasn't so cold. He looked towards the girl's doorway and saw that she was looking towards his.

''Morning,' he called. 'Time to move on. 'Watchman will be round to shift us afore long.'

She came towards him, dragging her bag with her. The rain dampened her hair, spinning a web of raindrops on it and teasing it into dark curls around her neck. 'I was rude last night,' she said. 'I was so scared out of my wits that I didn't thank ye properly.'

He shrugged. 'I didn't expect owt. I wasn't looking for a reward. Will tha sit down a minute?' He shuffled up in his doorway. 'Then I'll have to be off.'

'Where are ye off to?' She gazed at him curiously as she sat next to him, and he thought how pretty she was. Round face, big blue eyes and full petulant mouth.

'I haven't decided. I might go home to Yorkshire or I might book a ticket for Australia.'

'That's where I'm thinking of going too,' she exclaimed. 'But I'm feared of crossing alone,' she added and gazed across the water. 'But to be sure, it can't be worse than staying alone here. I've had more doors shut in my face than I ever did in Dublin. They think the Irish are all tinkers or thieves.'

She told him that her name was Moira and that her parents were dead, her two brothers in Australia. 'I came to look for work in England, but it's as desperate here as in old Ireland, so I thought I'd go look for my brothers. I've just enough money for a ticket.'

'Australia's a big place,' he smiled. 'How will tha find them?'

'Sure won't everybody know them already? The fighting O'Connors, they'll have left a trail. I'll find them right enough.'

He found himself, for the first time ever, opening up from his usual taciturn self, and as the sky lightened into day, confided in her of the family he had left behind. 'My da,' he said, 'he's as strong as an ox, straight as a die and full of humour. Tom, my brother, he's strong too, but more refined, more like a thoroughbred. And young George – why, George goes through life with a smile on his lips, he gambols through life like a, like a—'

'A colt?' she laughed.

'Aye, that's it,' he nodded. 'Like a young colt that's not been broken in.'

'And your sister? How would you describe her?' She seemed eager to know, listening to his every word.

'Betsy!' He shook his head. 'I don't know. She's headstrong and wilful and will only do what she wants. She can't be tamed, can't Betsy.' He thought of their last confrontation. *I only meant it for 'best*, he brooded. *Because I cared.* 'She's pretty,' he said. 'Dark and pretty, rather like thee.'

'It's lucky ye are,' she murmured, 'to have a loving family. To have someone who cares about what happens to ye. I have no-one,' she added. 'If only I had.'

'Your brothers?'

She shrugged her shoulders. 'They left Ireland five years ago. Not a word from them since then. They might be dead for all I know; but that's why I want to go – to find out for sure.'

'I'm going for some breakfast,' he said, rising to his feet. 'Does tha want to come? It's cheap and just 'round 'corner.'

He saw the hesitation on her face. 'I can't spend my ticket money,' she said. 'It's all I've got.'

'Come on,' he persuaded. 'I've enough to feed a sparrow like thee.'

Beneath his shirt in a cloth bag he had money for emergencies, but for some obscure reason he was willing to spend it on this unknown girl. A warmth crept through him in the act of giving, and as she smiled her thanks he felt a sudden sense of elation, of protectiveness and awakening gladness.

'Shall I carry tha bag?' She shook her head and clung to it and he smiled. 'All right, then. Let's go and sup, and then we'll talk about finding tha brothers.'

*   *   *

457

They stood side by side as they waited in the queue of immigrants outside the shipping office. A young married couple stood near, about to spend their savings on a new life. Three brawny fellows with rough hands and eager eyes, bent on finding their fortunes in gold, were shuffling their feet impatiently as they waited their turn. An old widow going to join her son looked so frail as she clutched her bag of belongings that they doubted she would last the voyage.

Moira glanced up at Mark. 'I've something to say before we book our passage, and I don't want ye to take offence. But it has to be said. You've been more than generous to me and I swear to God that one day I'll pay ye back.' Her cheeks flushed. 'But, but I'm a good living girl and – and, well—' She challenged him with a hint of nervousness. 'Ye'll not be tricking me and booking us as married people?'

'We'll be travelling steerage,' he assured her. 'We won't have a choice. But come in front.' He moved her in front of him. 'Book thy 'ticket first and then tha'll be sure.'

A smile lit up her face. 'Ye have a funny way of talking, Mark Foster!'

'It's Holderness way,' he said proudly. 'It's an ancient dialect as strong and forceful as 'folk who live there. No fancy words to hide 'meaning.' His voice softened. 'Not like 'Irish colleens who soften words wi' charm.'

'That sounded almost like a compliment,' she gazed disarmingly at him. 'But don't be forgetting – we travel in friendship!'

The queue shuffled forward, four more people in front and then their turn.

'I won't forget,' he said quietly, and put out his hand. She blinked and swallowed and he saw tears welling in her eyes as she put her hand into his and he closed his fingers over hers.

45

On Boxing Day, Tom rode over to Monkston with gifts for them all. The two families would normally have joined together at Garston Hall for Christmas luncheon, but this year his father said he wanted to stay at home, and so each family dined alone. And at both houses Betsy's disappearance caused an air of gravity, though everyone did their best to be cheerful.

The snow was crisp on the ground and, although it wasn't deep, the weather wasn't conducive to being outdoors as the wind was biting, bringing tears to the eyes and reddening cheeks. Tom's ears and nose tingled when he came inside, and he gratefully accepted a glass of hot toddy and a mince pie. He thanked them for the gifts of goose and ham and Christmas pudding, which the Rayners' cook had prepared and sent over.

'I'm really grateful,' he said. 'Jenny is very good, but she wouldn't have known where to start with preparations. She said she had never seen so much food in her life, and then burst into tears as she remembered the friends she had left behind in the cellars.'

They were all silent for a moment and then Ellen said with a catch in her voice, 'Yes, we must never forget how lucky we are.' Then she added softly, 'There's still no news, Tom?' When he bleakly shook his head, unable to speak, she whispered, 'Then we must think the worst, my dear, for she would surely have been in touch at Christmas.'

Sammi rocked Adam on her knee; he had come to stay until Aunt Mildred came for him. Mrs Bishop had weaned him and he was thriving on cow's milk from a bottle. 'We mustn't give up hope, Mama.' She, too, had a catch in her voice as she spoke. 'We must renew our efforts to find her.'

Tom nodded. 'I intend going into Hull again. I've asked at hotels and lodging houses, and in shops where she might be working.' He sighed deeply. 'Now I will go lower down the scale, for she must surely have little or no money.'

'We must ask Billy again, although he says he keeps looking,' William broke in. 'But the town is full of seamen and navvies and immigrants coming in. It must be difficult for the authorities to know who belongs to the town and who doesn't.'

'Where is Billy?' Tom asked, draining his glass. 'Has he gone back already?'

'He hasn't been with us.' Richard turned from the window where he had been observing the wintry landscape. 'He stayed in Hull to set up soup kitchens for paupers.' He pursed his lips. 'The weather is going to get worse.'

'Don't be such a pessimist, Richard.' Victoria was untying the parcel which Tom had brought.

'Look at that sky,' he insisted. 'There's more snow to come. It's going to be a long winter.'

Tom had brought gloves for Aunt Ellen, cigars for Uncle William, warm scarves for Richard and Billy, ribbons for Victoria and a hair comb for Sammi.

They thanked him and then Sammi gave him their presents: a new pipe for Uncle Thomas, a striped flannel shirt for George, socks for Mark to be kept for him, and a sachet of handkerchiefs for Betsy.

'I embroidered the initial,' Victoria said quietly. 'I know it should have been E, for Elizabeth, but we all know and love her as Betsy, so I put a B on instead.'

'Thank you, Victoria.' Tom gave her a sad smile. 'She'll like that, I know.'

He opened his present there and then, at Sammi's insistence, rather than take it home. It was a silk cravat, made from the same green silk that Sammi's dress for Gilbert's wedding was made from.

'I made it myself, Tom,' she said with a virtuous smile and a keen gleam in her eyes. 'You know how we *ladies* love to sew.'

He glanced up and said softly, 'It's beautiful, Sammi. Thank you.' He bent to kiss her cheek and as she turned her head his lips brushed accidentally against hers. For a fleeting moment he closed his eyes and breathed in her nearness, and as he opened them he saw his aunt and uncle both gazing earnestly at him.

He straightened up. 'I'd better get back,' he murmured, 'I've left George and Reedbarrow working.'

'Wait a moment, Tom, I'll get a wrap and walk down the drive with you.'

'It's so cold, Sammi,' her mother interrupted.

'A brisk walk, that's all, Mama. I've been in all day.'

'Would you like to come, Victoria?' Tom asked. 'This weather would put roses in your cheeks.'

'Certainly not. Out of the question.' Aunt Ellen smilingly reproved him. 'She hasn't got Sammi's constitution.'

'You can look after Adam, Victoria.' Sammi gave the child to her sister. 'It will be our last chance to spoil him.'

The wind whipped against her cloak and tore the hood from her hair as they stepped outside, and she took Tom's arm, whilst he led his horse with his other hand.

'You shouldn't have come, Sammi!' His voice was lost against the wind. 'You'll be blown away coming back.'

She put her head down to break the force and he drew her closer, putting his arm around her.

'Go back,' he urged. 'It's much worse than it was.'

'Just to the end of the drive.' She was breathless. 'It's so exhilarating after being indoors.'

'I'll have to hurry.' Tom mounted his horse as they

461

reached the lane. 'We'll have to shut down if the weather worsens.'

'You'll take care?' she said anxiously. 'You won't go up into the cap?'

He reached down and patted her shoulder. 'I might have to. Don't worry,' he assured. 'I'll be careful.'

'I shall worry, Tom.' She caught hold of his hand.

His face became set. 'Don't.' He released his hand from her grasp. 'I'm a miller, Sammi. Milling is what I do.'

She watched him as he trotted away, the sturdy mount covering the hard ground without effort. She waited for him to turn around but he didn't, she only saw the squareness of his back set resolutely against her.

As she turned reluctantly back into the drive she glanced down the lane towards the sea and saw the heaving mass of grey water and the foaming white wave crests. She swung around again and walked towards it. The end of the lane was pitted and broken, the edge cracked and fissured. Someone had erected a crude wooden fence as a warning, and it leaned drunkenly, as the earth which held it sank precariously before its descent to the bottom of the cliff. Sammi peered cautiously over. The tide was high and breaking great spumes of white, foaming spray against the cliffs, its force dashing so high that she could feel moist droplets against her face.

'Miss Rayner! Miss Sammi!' A thin voice called to her through the gusts of wind and the roaring of the sea.

She turned, and the power of the squall rocked her. An old man was standing in the doorway of one of the cottages, holding on to the edge of the door so that it wasn't torn from his grasp.

'I thought you were moving to Tillington, Mr Geenwood? My father said that you were!' She walked with difficulty towards him. 'Isn't it wild!'

'Aye, it's a bit of a blow.' His leathery face turned

towards the sea. 'Yon fence will go ower afore 'day is out.'

'I thought you were going to Tillington?' she repeated.

'Aye, everybody did. I reckoned on that I was going, till they got all packed up; my lad and his wife and bairns have gone.' He cackled toothlessly at her. 'And then I telled 'em I wasn't shifting. This place'll see me out. I reckon on eighteen months afore it goes ower and I doubt I'll be here then.' He considered thoughtfully for a minute and then chuckled. 'I'll be a grand 'un if I'm still here; I'll be nigh on eighty and past me best.'

She smiled with him and added, 'Well, be careful, won't you? And if you are worried you must come up to the house and someone will take you to your son.'

'It's not me that's to be careful, miss. That's why I was calling thee. Tha was taking a chance leaning ower edge; but then, tha allus was a 'arum-scarum young body, if tha'll pardon me saying.'

'Why, whatever do you mean, Mr Greenwood?' she laughed.

'Why, Miss Sammi, tha allus did take a chance. Allus first to take a risk. I used to watch all 'bairns round here, even thee and thy brothers, and there was allus one who didn't hang back.' He pulled his cap further over his ears. 'I used to say to my missus, that Miss Sammi, she's not afraid to venture. She'll allus take first step.'

She studied this sagacious old man. 'Was I fool-hardy, Mr Greenwood? Is that what you mean?'

'Why bless thee no, miss, I didn't mean that. Tha seemed to weigh up all pros and cons and then determine what must be done. Aye, tha can tell bairn's character right from 'start. Resolute, that's what tha was.'

She turned away and said good-bye. Then she turned back. 'Thank you, Mr Greenwood. I'll remember what you said.'

*   *   *

Betsy walked slowly back to her lodgings. She had arrived as usual at work only to be stopped at the gate by the foreman who told her that there was no more work for her.

'Why not?' Dismay engulfed her. She didn't know where else she could look for employment. 'Was there cause for complaint?'

'No. But I can hire and fire as I please.' Then he'd shaken his head. 'But tha's not cut out for this sort of work. Tha's been used to summat better!'

'I need the work,' she'd pleaded with him.

'Sorry.' He'd turned away. 'Anyway, it's nowt to do with thee; I'm having to lay others off as well. We're waiting on 'whalers coming in. If there's no blubber, then there's no work, and tha can't have wages for sitting around all day.'

She was tired as she walked into the rubbish-strewn court; it was a long walk along the river to the Greenland Yards, and now she'd had to make the return journey, with the additional worry of no wages to pay the landlord.

She opened the door and stepped inside the dank and dark entrance and climbed the stairs to her room. Her door was open and two strangers, a man and a woman were inside.

'What are you doing in my room?' It was a hovel, but it was the only place she could call home.

The man was lying on the bed. He raised his head as she came in but he didn't get up. 'It's ours now,' he said. ''Landlord said we could have it. He said as tha were owing him rent and would have to go. We've paid him two weeks up front.'

The woman was drinking from a bottle, the liquid was clear and Betsy guessed it was gin. She waved it towards her. 'Does tha want a drop?' she asked. 'Tha looks a bit ropey.'

Betsy shook her head. Her mind was numb. What was she to do?

'Tha can kip here with us for a day or two,' the woman said generously, 'till tha finds somewhere else. He won't mind.' She inclined her head to the man lying on the only bed. 'Wilt tha?'

He looked across at Betsy. 'She'll tek up a bit of room, but no I shan't mind, not for a night or two.'

Betsy shuddered. He was lying on the bed with his boots on. One of the toecaps was missing and a large blackened toe protruded. His hair was greasy and unwashed and his head lay on her pillow.

'I couldn't find owt that belonged to thee,' the woman said, conversationally. ''Landlord said tha didn't have much.'

'No. He was right.' Betsy turned towards the door. 'Where can I go?' She stared at them vacantly. 'Who will take me in?'

The woman put down the bottle and putting her elbows on her widespread knees and her chin in her hands, scrutinized Betsy. 'Is tha pregnant?'

Betsy denied it. 'I've got dropsy.'

The man sniggered and nodded knowingly.

'That's a pity.' The woman continued to gaze at her. 'Tha could go to 'workhouse if tha was pregnant. No questions asked. But if tha's onny sick I don't know if they'll take thee.' She picked up the bottle again and, tipping it up, took a long drink. 'If I were thee,' she wiped her mouth with the back of her hand, 'if I were thee, I'd be pregnant. At least tha'll get a bed to lie on.'

Betsy trudged back towards the main streets of the town. The ground underfoot was slushy with wet snow which had thawed with the impact of tramping feet upon it. She passed the squalid court which she had accidentally wandered into all those weeks ago, before Charles Craddock had turned her out.

She stopped and looked down it. People were still standing around in desultory fashion, in spite of the cold; some were swinging their arms or blowing on their hands to warm them. No-one took any notice of her. No-one threw stones as they had done previously. *They don't notice me now*, she thought dully. *I look the same as they do.*

Her feet took her up and down streets which she didn't know, in and out of alleyways which were unfamiliar to her, and she wandered, empty of thought and reasoning, unhindered and unconstrained by the residents who stared at her as apathetically as she stared back at them.

As night fell, so the snow came down, and she took shelter in a doorway. Her back and legs ached and she huddled into her cloak trying to keep warm; her eyes kept closing but she fought to stay awake, and as sleep tried to claim her so she was wracked with hallucinations of food and a warm bed and a loving hand on her cheek. The loving hand was cold and rough and she started up suddenly. A man's face was close to hers and she gave a startled scream.

'I'm not going to hurt thee,' he mumbled. 'I just thought we could sit close and keep warm.'

His clothes were in tatters and his face covered in sores, his eyes a rheumy yellow as they looked distantly at her. 'I'll not hurt thee,' he repeated. 'I haven't 'energy to do owt.'

She scrambled to her feet and rushed away and he cursed her as she ran, calling her dreadful names and wishing her every evil under the sun.

She was so cold that she started to shake and she put her arms beneath her cloak to try to trap what little warmth there was. There were other people wandering the streets, even though it was late; some were very merry, shouting and singing, others were trudging with their heads down and their hands in threadbare pockets. She heard a clamour of voices drifting from the Market Place and a refrain started to run through the progression of people who were heading that way. 'Soup kitchens. Soup kitchens. Come on. Come on.'

Fires had been lit in the street and lamps were

burning on wooden stalls which had been set up in the centre of the Market Place, their glow sending flickering shadows on the golden statue of King William on his horse, which stood nearby. Betsy stared, fascinated. It was almost as if the horse's legs were moving as the shadows quivered and fluttered, bringing the sculpture to life.

'Here you are, miss. Have a bowl of soup and some bread.' A man standing at one of the stalls handed her a bowl of broth.

'I can't pay,' she muttered, and looked with craving at the steaming soup. 'I haven't any money.'

He looked up as she spoke and seemed to appraise her. 'It's free,' he said gently. 'There isn't any charge. The corporation are paying.'

She took it with cold and trembling fingers, and lifted the bowl to her lips. When she looked up the man was still looking at her. *He looks kind,* she thought. He had a calm, tolerant expression and an easy-going smile. Why would such a man be out on a night like this giving out victuals to paupers when he could probably be at home with a nice wife and family?

Although she felt despair and misery pulling her down, she wasn't including herself in this picture of wretchedness; she was simply looking out from within herself at a scene set apart: of vagrants and prostitutes, of children and old people, some with only rags on their backs and no shoes for their feet, a queue of wretches patiently waiting their turn for food.

'Are you not well?' The man spoke again to her as she sipped the soup.

She looked at him with dull eyes. Why did he say that? How could he guess at the pain she felt? The pain of misery in her heart and the ache in her back which was getting worse by the minute.

'I'm all right,' she whispered. 'Thank you.'

Again he appraised her, then he turned back to the

stall and the cauldron of soup which he started to ladle into tin bowls.

'Billy!' She heard him call as she turned away from the stall and walked towards the nearest fire to warm herself. 'Billy. Come here a moment, will you?'

She glanced over her shoulder at the other stall where another man was giving out soup, and a small boy was handing out hunks of bread. A tall slim man with long fair hair. Billy! She thought she would faint as she saw him look up at the other man's summons.

'I won't be a moment,' she heard him say. 'Let me just dish these out. Tim!' he called to the boy. 'Share the bread out, don't let them grab; there's enough for everyone.'

He put down the ladle when he had filled a dozen bowls and crossed to the other stall. She watched, frozen to the spot, as the other man spoke to him and pointed across to where she was standing. There was a sudden shout from the crowd. Someone was pushing in, trying to jump the queue. A ripple of discontent flowed through the line of people waiting and as the two men were distracted, Betsy moved away.

A sudden spasm of pain shot through her as she hastened toward the Church of Holy Trinity, trying to hide herself within its shadows. She stopped and leaned against the walls.

'The soup!' she gasped. 'It must have been too hot. It's burning a hole in me!' She bent double for a few moments, then as the pain eased, she straightened up and walked on. *Where can I go? Where can I hide? I can't let Billy find me. I shall feel such shame. What would he think? He'll tell my da, and Tom and George, and Sammi. Everybody would share the shame of the life I've led, of living with a man, especially a man like Craddock.*

She started to weep. *I'm no better than those women waiting in the Market Place*, she judged. *I'm worse! Those women with their painted faces sell their bodies in order to eat and keep a roof over their heads. I had a good home and I've sacrificed it for my own vanity.*

Another red hot pain ran through her, striking down her belly and out between her thighs, and with it came anger and hatred for Craddock for abandoning her. *I'll have to lie down.* She screwed up her eyes and clenched her lips. *I can't stand. Where can I go?*

Her steps had taken her around the church and as she staggered onwards she heard a cry. 'Betsy!' It was loud and urgent. 'Betsy! It's Billy! Don't be afraid!'

She stood petrified. She didn't want to be found. She wanted to be lost for ever, where no-one that she loved or cared for would find her. Not her father or brothers, not Luke or her cousins. She wanted only oblivion. There was a sound of running feet and Billy's voice still calling and she crouched against the church wall. Then as she looked up she saw the cellar steps of the abandoned and burnt-out warehouse which Billy had once shown her.

She cautiously looked out; his voice was fainter, he had missed her direction, and as swiftly as she could, she scurried across the road and into the entrance, moving aside the cardboard curtain.

It was blacker in the cellar than the night outside, and for a few minutes she felt as if she had walked into a wall of impenetrable darkness, but the denseness lessened as, here and there, the flickering glow from candle stubs lightened the dark.

There were sounds of coughing and whispering and now and again a soft moan, but no-one challenged her as she carefully threaded her way as far as she could from the entrance. Once or twice she trod on someone's hand or foot, but apart from a low curse, no-one impeded her. She put out her hands and searched the walls. There seemed to be some kind of alcove. The wall was damp but it would give ease to her aching back. A candle flame flickered only a few feet away from her and she saw the blank face of a woman. She didn't greet the new arrival but simply stared into space.

Betsy eased herself down onto the floor and stretched her legs out. At last she was safe. Now she could rest and the pain would ease. Tonight she would sleep and tomorrow, tomorrow— Another pain smote her body. *Perhaps*, she silently prayed, *tomorrow won't come*.

46

'Why do you think it was her, Stephen?' Billy rubbed his hand across his eyes. 'She didn't answer to her name.'

'It was the description you gave,' the doctor answered. 'And she wasn't the usual type to be queueing for soup. She sounded different too, more country than town.' He proceeded to stack the empty dishes. The crowd had moved away from the stalls and were gathered around the still burning fires. 'Maybe she doesn't want to be found, Billy. Have you thought of that? She might have reasons not to go home.'

'But there would be no need!' Billy spoke anxiously. 'Whatever has happened, her family want her back. I wish I'd caught a glimpse of her, just so that I knew for certain. I don't know whether to call on Gilbert to help me look further, or send a message for her brothers to come.'

Stephen glanced up at him. 'You look as tired as I feel. I suggest we both go to our beds and have some sleep, otherwise we'll neither of us be fit for anything tomorrow. What a Christmas! I've never had one like it!'

'Thanks, Stephen. I really appreciate your help, and there are a lot of others here tonight – this morning,' Billy added, 'who do, too. Come on, Tim!' he called to the boy. 'Let's get the rubbish moved away and then I'll walk you to your lodgings.'

A youth who had been nearby, collecting up pieces of kindling for the fires, heard him and came over. He was raggedly dressed in a suit that was too short

471

in the arms and legs, and on his unkempt hair he wore a shiny top hat with a curling brim.

''Lads and me'll clear up, Master Billy. We'll take 'carts back to Rayner's yard for thee.'

'Thanks, Joe. I would appreciate that.' Billy was relieved. 'Tell the watchman that I sent you, and if you ask him, I'm sure he'll find you some broken crates to keep the fires going.' He knew that the crowd who were gathered around the embers would be reluctant to leave the warmth for the cold comfort of a draughty doorway.

He walked with Tim to the lodgings he had found for him, when the magistrates had accepted his assurance that he would be responsible for the boy until his case came to court. As they reached the door, the boy pulled out a key on a string from around his neck.

'Mrs Crowle give me this.' He flourished it proudly. 'She said, if we was to live together then we should trust each other. I can come and go as I please,' he added, 'as long as I get me jobs done.'

'And you respect her trust, Tim?' Billy asked. 'You won't let her down?'

'Oh, no,' the boy said eagerly. 'Why 'old lady needs me. I chop wood and bring 'coal in and run errands, and by, Master Billy, tha should taste her meat 'n 'tatie pie, it fair melts in tha mouth.'

'I'm glad it's working out so well, Tim,' Billy said good-naturedly. 'I'm pleased you've found someone who needs you.'

'Oh, she said she doesn't know how she ever managed without me, Master Billy.' Tim's voice was full of conviction, then he lowered it to a whisper. 'She's going to speak for me when my case comes up. She said as she would.'

Billy smiled. 'Good. And I will too, Tim, so everything should work out all right, providing you don't misbehave again.'

He couldn't help but feel a small glow at the way

events were working out for Tim. *Here's another success story*, he thought as he walked away, *first Jenny, now Tim; though no doubt there will be others who will not be as fortunate.*

He felt some satisfaction, too, that he had persuaded the corporation to give two hundred pounds to set up the soup kitchens. His name was already becoming known through his association with the Mayor, Zachariah Pearson, and a public subscription had been organized for the poor.

He walked back through the town, pausing briefly to look up at the towering monument to Wilberforce, the great philanthropist and liberator of slavery, etched high against the night sky, then on impulse he skirted the edges of the lapping waters of the Prince's Dock, and ambled towards the wooden pier which jutted out into the Humber. There were several steam boats moored by the staithes, gently rocking in the swell, with a single lamp glowing on the decks; and out towards the middle of the estuary, sailing ships were silently dipping and plunging at anchor in the dark water as they waited for the morning tide.

He took a deep breath and smelt the salt of the sea and remembered the long walks on the sands at Monkston on Christmas Eve with his brother and sisters. Memories stirred of racing home to help decorate the house with evergreens, and of lighting the Yuletide candles before the wassailers gathered at the door to sing their ancient carols, and who then were invited in for a glass of punch and a slice of Cook's rich and fruity spice cake.

He thought of last year's Christmas Day, so different from the one he was spending now, when everyone ate their fill of roast goose, pork with crisp, salty crackling served with clove-scented apple sauce; of plum pudding black with fruit, and topped with brandy butter. He recalled the singing around the piano and the opening of their gifts on Boxing Day; and he thought now of his family as they slept safe in their beds tonight while he roamed the streets of Hull alongside the destitute whose bellies, like his own, were rumbling from the warm soup of charity.

The sharp air frosted his nostrils and tingled his ears, and as he watched the surging estuary, he felt the consciousness of his sea-going ancestors draw around him, the men who had braved the hostile icy waters of the Arctic in search of the whale. Poor souls, he thought. The men on the two missing whaling ships, the *Polar Star Two* and the *Arctic Star* came to mind: they were causing such anxiety not only to their families and the shipping company, but to the whole town.

News had come in only a week before of a ship from another company which had gone down off Davis Straits, losing all lives on board, and gloom had spread throughout the shipping fraternity and furthered speculation that the missing ships of Masterson and Rayner wouldn't be coming back.

These thoughts turned inevitably to Gilbert, who was so despondent over so many events, and then on to the girl Stephen Sheppard had seen, and decisively he turned from the river and headed towards the home of Gilbert and Harriet. The stars were losing their brilliance and the night sky was starting to lighten as he reached their door and rang the bell. A startled maid in a dressing robe appeared and inched open the door.

'Who's there?' He heard Gilbert's voice from the stairs and saw him through the crack of the door, also in a dressing robe, his hair unbrushed. It was only then that Billy realized that, though it was not still night, it was not yet morning either.

'What on earth! What's happened?' Gilbert shooed the maid off to bed again and brought Billy inside to the sitting-room. 'Do you know what time it is?'

Billy shook his head. 'No. I'm sorry, Gilbert.' He sank into a chair. 'I hardly know what day it is, let alone the time.'

Gilbert looked grimly at the French clock ticking on the mantelpiece. 'It's three thirty, *a.m.*, and it's Boxing Day! The one day in the year when we might possibly have a sleep in. Here.' He reached across to a table and poured Billy a small brandy. 'Drink this while I go and tell Harriet that there isn't more trouble; her nerves are shattered as it is.'

'Sorry,' Billy muttered to Gilbert's back as he went out to reassure Harriet. 'But there might well be more trouble.' He tossed the liquid to the back of his throat, and then coughed and spluttered at its fierceness.

'I think there's news of Betsy,' he said when Gilbert came back. 'That's why I came.' He told him of what Stephen Sheppard had said. 'I just don't know what to do. Whether to go on looking for her or whether to send for Tom. I just – I just wanted to ask your opinion, Gilbert. I gave no thought to the hour. I just came.'

Gilbert gazed at him. 'You know what your trouble is?' he said. 'You're just worn out. You've been working all hours that God sends these last few weeks. You've been working in those stinking cellars, you've been helping with the cholera victims, and now you're serving up soup to the paupers!'

'Somebody has to,' Billy began heatedly but Gilbert silenced his outburst.

'I'm not saying that you shouldn't do it,' he said patiently. 'But you'll help no-one if you fall ill. Have you looked at yourself lately? You look like one of the poor wretches that you're trying to save. You have the aura of penury! I hope in God's name that it isn't catching,' he added bitterly, 'though I feel that it might be.'

'I'm really sorry, Gilbert. I didn't think, I should have realized that you have worries of your own.' Billy was penitent.

'You misunderstand me!' Gilbert burst out. 'I'm not complaining that you came. I'm trying to explain, not very well it seems, that you can't help these unfortunates if you don't take care of yourself. You look like they do, and what they need is someone who appears better than they do, someone they can look up to and yet still trust, and who the people in authority can relate to.'

Billy closed his eyes, he only half understood what Gilbert was saying, and wasn't even sure that he agreed with him, but as the comforting warmth of the room washed over him, all he wanted now was to sleep.

Gilbert hauled him to his feet. 'Go upstairs and have a warm bath and leave those disgusting clothes outside the door. Then go and get into the spare bed. I'll call you in the morning and we'll both go and look for Betsy. Then we'll decide whether or not to send a message to Tillington.'

The woman eased herself from the floor and, holding up the stub of a guttering candle, peered down at the young woman who had been crying and moaning all night long. She grunted and turned away and with the shuffling steps that her ragged slippers would allow, she made her way towards the entrance, leaving a dense pool of darkness behind her.

Two youths were sleeping by the doorway and she kicked one with her foot. He turned over and looked at her with one eye and then turned his back again. 'Clear off, Peg,' he groused. 'Get back to tha corner and let a bloke sleep.'

She kicked him again, in the ribs, and angrily he sat up. 'I just telled thee. Clear off! I'll fetch thee a jug later.'

'I don't want a jug, leastways, onny if tha's offering. A midwife's needed; there's a woman in labour down yonder.' She wiped her sleeve across her nose. 'She's been makin' a hell of a row all night. I've had no sleep for her moaning.'

'And where in blazes do I find a midwife?' He

leaned on one elbow and stared at the woman. 'I wouldn't know where to start looking. Can't tha see to her?'

The woman bridled. 'Me? No, I can't. I can't stand sight o' blood. Anyway,' she said contrarily, 'it's pitch black back there and me candle's nearly snuffed it. Tha can get me another while tha's out.'

Defeated, he got to his feet and reached for his top hat which he carefully placed on his head. 'Give us some money then.' He put out his hand and then ducked as she swiped at him.

'I'll give it thee when tha brings 'candle,' she glowered at him. 'Tha doesn't catch me like that. Now hurry up afore she has 'bairn on her own. There's no joy in that, I can tell thee.'

Joe came out blinking into the brightness of cold day and stood with his hands on his hips. Where would he find a midwife, today of all days? It was Christmas, wasn't it? Or was that yesterday? He shrugged. It made no odds to him, one day was very much like another. He walked down into the Market Place. There were a few people about. Some, sitting cross-legged and their heads bowed onto their chests, were gathered around the still warm dusty ash which were the remains of the previous night's bonfire. But they were all men and vagrants, and wouldn't have known about midwives.

A stallholder had set up with some vegetable produce and was sitting behind a stall with an empty pipe in his mouth.

Joe approached him. 'Does tha know of a midwife hereabouts?'

The man shook his head, then took the pipe from his mouth. 'Has tha got some poor lass into trouble?'

'No! Not me,' Joe protested. 'It's a woman down in 'cellars. She's having a babby.'

'God help her then.' The stallkeeper stuck the pipe back into his mouth. 'They say it's as black as Hell down there. They should fire it.'

477

'Oh, yeh?' Joe glared defiantly. 'It's all right for some folk, but there's others who'd have nowhere to go if it was fired.'

The man sucked on his pipe. 'There's allus work-house for them as can't get an honest job of work.'

Joe turned away, an angry retort on his lips. If the man had said as much to any of the youths who shared the cellars with him, they would have turned his stall over and trampled his produce into the dirt. He was sick, sick to the stomach of complacent folk who, though they hadn't much themselves, assumed that everybody could pull themselves out of the gutter.

But not everybody was like that, he pondered. Billy Rayner, for instance. He'd been here all night giving out soup to those who had nothing, and he even looked the same as them, though you could tell he was different just by hearing him talk. Yes, he was all right. Him, and the doctor that he'd brought to help him.

What was his name? he wondered. Stephen something; he'd heard Billy Rayner say his name. Reluctantly he turned back to the stallholder.

'Does tha know of a doctor called Stephen summat or other?'

'How would I know of a doctor by his first name?' the man countered. 'Who does tha think I am? Prince Consort?'

'A young doctor,' he persisted. 'He's from round here.'

'Sheppard, tha'll mean. He has a place down at 'bottom of Lowgate; he's with Doctor Fleming.' He started to pack up his produce. 'I might as well be at home listening to 'wife blathering as standing here wi' nowt to do but answer questions from 'likes o' thee.'

'Thanks.' Joe set off at a run, then stopped as the man shouted to him.

'Here!' He threw an apple which Joe deftly caught. 'Merry Christmas.'

Doctor Sheppard trod carefully down the cellar steps, following in the footsteps of the youth who had summoned him. He held up a lantern which he had had the forethought to bring, remembering the darkness which he had entered previously when treating the cholera victims.

'I didn't think I'd have to come down here again,' he muttered. 'I thought everybody had gone.'

'No,' Joe said. 'There's still a few of us here, us lads and a few drunks who can't go anywhere else. And then there's old Peg. She's lived down here for years, even before 'fire. Nobody knew she was here. She said she thought she was going to burn to death. As it is, I think 'smoke has addled her brain,' he added cheerfully. 'If she ever had one.'

'Who looks after her?' The doctor stepped over a recumbent form and wrinkled his nose at the smell of spirits which emanated from it.

'Me and 'other lads. We fetch her a bit o' bread or sausage and her ale, and scrounge a candle for her. She's quite happy.'

Doctor Sheppard heaved a sigh. 'That's all right then. As long as she doesn't feel deprived.'

'It was Peg who asked me to fetch help. She said that 'young woman was disturbing her sleep; she thought it was her time or summat.'

'Well, where the deuce is she? I didn't realize that the cellars went so far back.'

'We're nearly there. There's Peg's candle burning up yonder. She's onny one who lives so far in. She says it's more private.'

'She'd be right,' Doctor Sheppard agreed. 'You don't get more private or exclusive than this.'

The old woman came towards him. 'She's in here. Found herself a nice little hidey hole. I might have it meself when she's gone.'

Joe turned and went back, and the doctor wondered how he managed to find his way in the darkness, for it was as black as pitch outside the halo of lamplight.

He bent down into the alcove and caught his breath as he recognized the girl who had queued for soup the night before. He lifted the lantern and spoke to her. 'I'm a doctor. Someone sent for me. They said you were ill.'

She turned her head towards him and he saw pain and suffering. 'Yes,' she whispered. 'I am. But leave me. I don't want your help.'

'Will you let me take you out of here? I can get you a place in the hospital. I can't treat you down here.'

'I don't want you to treat me.' Her voice broke as pain ripped through her. 'It's too late. I'm going to die.'

'Come now, none of that sort of talk.' He put his hand on hers and felt the cold. Then he transferred it to her forehead and felt the heat.

He looked down and saw the swollen abdomen and the thickness of her ankles. 'What do you think is wrong with you?' he asked gently.

'Dropsy,' she said faintly. 'I've got dropsy.'

'You're in labour, Betsy,' he said softly. 'You're going to have a baby.'

'No!' Her voice was harsh. 'I'm not. I've got dropsy. I've got dropsy.' Then she looked at him through narrowed eyelids. 'My name isn't Betsy. It's Mary.'

'I'm a friend of Billy's.' He took hold of her hand and stroked it. 'He's been looking for you. Don't be afraid. We'll take you out of here. We'll make you comfortable and you can have your baby in a proper bed.'

'No,' she interrupted him fiercely. 'You don't understand. I'm not having a baby and I'm not moving from here. Go away. Leave me alone.'

The words were no sooner out than she arched her back and screamed and her hands clutched the air.

480

'Dear God,' she wept. 'What punishment is this? I didn't mean to be wicked. I only wanted something better.'

'You're not wicked, Betsy.' Doctor Sheppard bent over her and whispered. 'You're in labour. I can help you, ease the pain, if only you will let me take you out of here.'

Old Peg came over and bent down over her. 'Tha's not got long to go. Be a good lass and go wi' doctor. Tha'll dee of *pumonia* down here, and thy babby as well. Besides,' she added as she straightened up, 'there's men down here, and it doesn't do for them to be knowing what goes on at a childbed.' She didn't seem to include the doctor in this homily as she sagely shook her head. 'It's not right for them to be there, and it'd frighten 'em to death besides.'

Betsy clutched Doctor Sheppard's hand in an iron grip as another pain wracked her and she gasped. 'All right, I'll see Billy. If he says I should go to hospital, I will. But I'm not having a baby.' Her eyes were wide. 'I've got dropsy, that's all.'

Stephen patted her hand. 'Yes, yes. Rest now between the pains, try to relax, and I'll go and find Billy.'

He asked the old woman to sit beside her, to stay with her until he returned, and with his head and shoulders bent low, he made his way back to the entrance.

The boy who had come for him was sitting by the doorway and got to his feet immediately when the doctor asked if he would go to Billy's lodgings, while he went back to his own lodgings to collect medication to relieve Betsy's pain.

Twenty minutes later, Joe was back, hammering on his door. 'He's not there, sir. Missus says he hasn't been there all night.'

Doctor Sheppard pondered. It was still early, barely eight o'clock, yet time was of the essence as far as Betsy was concerned. Her colour, as far as he could ascertain in the darkness, was poor and when he held her hand her pulse was weak.

'I don't know where else he'll be,' he muttered. 'I'll have to go back without him.'

'I could try at Masterson and Rayner's yard.' Joe was eager to assist. 'They might know, he's a relation, cousin or summat, they give us wood for 'fire last night.'

'Yes.' Doctor Sheppard remembered Billy's words of the night before when he mentioned Gilbert's name. 'Of course.' He spoke quickly. 'Tell them I sent you and that I need to get hold of Master Billy urgently. Ask them if they can send to Mr Gilbert Rayner straight away, or,' he looked at the boy's dishevelled appearance, and fished in his waistcoat pocket for his calling card, 'show them this and tell them that it's a matter of life or death, and that you will go for Mr Rayner yourself if they will give you the address.'

Joe preened and, taking the card, he adjusted his hat at a rakish angle and set off at a run towards the High Street.

Gilbert lay silently in the bed at Harriet's side. Sleep had entirely deserted him since the rude awakening of Billy ringing the doorbell. He brooded that here was another problem for the family. Not, he reasoned, that it concerned him directly, but he had always been fond of Betsy, and of Uncle Thomas, and had had a good relationship with Tom. He hadn't cared much for Mark, he always seemed so boorish, and George was a mere country lad with nothing much to offer in the way of conversation or intellect. *Still*, he sighed, *I wouldn't like anything terrible to happen to any of them, but I'm so beset with my own troubles that I'm inclined to think that if Betsy is foolish enough to run away on a mere whim or because of some foolish family upset, then she should accept the consequences.*

He sighed again, and Harriet turned towards him.

'Gilbert.' Her voice was tremulous. 'Are you still awake?'

'Sorry, my darling.' He moved closer and put his arm around her. 'Did I wake you?'

'I haven't been to sleep,' she whispered. 'I can't remember the last time I slept all the night through.'

'I'm going to ask the doctor to call and give you a sleeping draught,' he said firmly. 'You really mustn't worry so.'

'I can't help it.' She removed his arm and sat up in bed. 'I'm getting up.'

'But you haven't had breakfast yet. I told Tilly not to come up too early.'

Her dark hair fell about her face as she put her head down and her hands across her eyes and he heard the smothered sound of her weeping.

'Harriet! What is it? Tell me. Please don't cry.'

'I can't help it.' Her face was blotched with tears as she turned towards him. 'When I think how hard it is for you. When I think of how my father has brought you down. The money you have lost. Your good name; maybe even to lose your company, yet not once have you censured me.'

'Censured you!' He couldn't believe what she was saying. 'Why should I blame you? You were not to blame for your father's shortcomings.'

'But I am my father's daughter, and fingers have been pointed.' She climbed out of bed away from his entreating hand and stood at the foot of the bed. 'I have heard whispers. People whom I thought were friends have turned their backs on me, yet not one word of reproach has come from your lips. I don't deserve you, Gilbert, and if you should turn away from me, I would understand, even though I should break my heart.'

She must be ill, he worried, *to talk in such a manner.* Her father's violent death must have unhinged her. He groaned. Why else would she think he would blame her for what had happened? It was his own

stupidity, his inexperience and arrogance that had brought him into this terrible situation.

His conscience troubled him. Harriet was so humble, so contrite. If she only knew how often he had been close to confessing his own indiscretion and his dereliction of duty towards his son. His deceit had been furthered when his mother announced that she would take responsibility for the child on James's behalf, and once again he had said nothing. This and the worry over the missing ships and the possible foreclosure of the company, had given him weeks of disturbed sleep and ill-humoured wretchedness.

'Harriet!' He looked at her tear-stained face and was afraid. It was because of Harriet's virtue that he hesitated to confess his lapse, and the pain of deception because he loved her, cut deeper than ever. She was so innocent, unblemished in spite of her father's indiscretions and her mother's constant withering carping; yet this self-same innocence created a transparent barrier between them which he dare not cross, for fear he should shatter her idealized image of him, and turn against him.

'Harriet,' he repeated. 'You must not say, must not even think such things.' His voice broke. 'I am the one, I am the one who is undeserving of you.'

Instantly she was at his side, comforting, reassuring, and the moment for disclosure was gone as the doorbell again rang out in an urgent peal.

47

Billy and Gilbert sped across the town, following Joe who had tracked and sought out Billy and found him at his cousin's house.

Billy had appeared downstairs at Gilbert's summons that he was wanted immediately by some young varmint who wouldn't leave until he had spoken to him in person. He stretched his face muscles in an attempt to waken. He had borrowed a spare robe of Gilbert's and stood shivering in the doorway as he listened to Joe.

'It's that young woman that tha was calling to last night,' Joe explained, and in his haziness, Billy vaguely wondered if there was anything that Joe didn't know about what happened in this town.

''Doctor says to come straight away. She won't leave 'cellar till tha comes, and she might not even then.' He suddenly and respectfully took off his top hat, holding it in front of him like a shield. 'But old Peg says it's no place for having a babby, and if that's what she thinks then it can't be — but I don't know about that o'course,' he added bashfully as if his tongue had run away with him.

Gilbert and Billy had looked at each other in dismay, and had rushed to dress, Billy borrowing a pair of trousers, a clean shirt and a jacket of Gilbert's as his own seemed to have mysteriously vanished.

'But where has she been all this time?' Gilbert heaved, he was unused to running, especially in such an undignified fashion, and was glad that there were few people about. 'She's been missing for weeks.'

'Months,' Billy panted. 'She went to the opening

of the park, apparently. Then I saw her briefly one day, and I feel terrible about the fact that I barely had time to talk to her, though I didn't know then that she was missing, but no-one saw her again after that. Oh, why didn't she tell someone? Sammi or my mother?'

Gilbert slowed down, his heart was racing. 'Shame, perhaps.' His words were low and not just because of his breathlessness. He was confused and miserable; he had briefly told Harriet of Betsy's trouble and she had immediately said that they must bring her back, and had called to the maid to make up a fire in the room where Billy had slept, and to bring up fresh sheets for the bed.

There was a chaise outside the cellar steps and a boy holding the reins of the horse. ''Quack's inside.' He indicated with his thumb and was rewarded with a cuff around his ear by Joe for his insolence towards the doctor.

'You'd better wait here, Gilbert.' Billy bent his head to enter. 'It's dark without a light and you don't know your way like I do.'

Gilbert gratefully conceded that it would be as well to remain above ground, that he would not be of use anyway as it was Billy that Betsy wanted to see.

Billy could hear the sound of crying and the murmur of voices as he approached the furthest reaches of the cellars, and he followed the sound by instinct rather than sight, for he had no light, and trod carefully with arms outstretched until he saw the pinprick of lamplight from Doctor Sheppard's lantern.

He wanted to weep when he saw her. Betsy's hair was matted and her face grey, her eyes creased with pain. He put his arms out to her and held her as he would a child, and she clung to him, sobbing that she was so sorry for the trouble she had brought.

'The doctor says I'm having a baby, Billy.' She took a deep shuddering breath. 'I am, I know. I've not

486

wanted to admit it, not even to myself. I've said all along it was dropsy, hoping that it wasn't true. It wasn't Luke's fault,' she said defiantly. 'It was mine just as much as his.'

'Luke?' he said. 'Luke Reedbarrow?'

She nodded and then grimaced in pain. 'He doesn't know. I never told him. I just kept on hoping that it would go away.'

'He'll have to know, Betsy, you can't hide a baby. He's all right, is Luke,' he added. 'He won't shy from his responsibilities. If you still want him, that is.'

'Want him?' She gave a weak laugh. 'It was wanting him that got me into this trouble! There, I've shocked you now, haven't I, Billy? You didn't know how sinful and immoral your cousin Betsy was?'

'Let's have no talk of morals,' Stephen Sheppard interrupted. 'We must get you to a hospital bed straight away, otherwise you'll give birth down here, and that would be scandalous.'

'Will you attend her at Gilbert's house?' Billy murmured as together they lifted Betsy and followed old Peg who held the lamp up high. 'He lives only ten minutes away and a bed will be ready; it will be quicker than the hospital.'

The doctor agreed, and with some difficulty they eased themselves and Betsy up the cellar steps out into the street, and felt fresh flakes of snow on their faces.

Betsy screwed up her eyes against the light and they saw now how ill she looked, how pain-wracked her face, how gaunt her cheeks and her dark-ringed, sunken eyes. Her clothes were dirty with soot from the cellars, and her swollen feet were bare.

Gilbert's eyes filled with tears as he helped them lift her into the carriage, and he offered to ride with her and the doctor to show them the way to his home. He was beset with grief as he thought of another girl who had given birth to a child not so very long ago, and perhaps in similar impoverished surroundings as the ones from which Betsy had been rescued.

She was lying quietly now as they drove along; Doctor Sheppard took hold of her hand, his fingers on her wrist. 'Ask the driver to hurry,' he said softly.

'We're here,' Gilbert said and called to the driver to pull up.

'It wasn't Luke's fault,' Betsy murmured as she was lifted out. 'He would have married me, if I'd wanted.' She turned her head towards Gilbert. 'Billy? Where's Billy? Tell him. Tell him that he must say to my da and to Tom that it wasn't only Luke that was to blame.' She clutched Gilbert's hand. 'You'll tell him?'

'Yes, yes. Don't upset yourself, Betsy. You'll be able to tell them yourself.'

Gilbert didn't know what to say. He had no words of comfort to offer, and was glad to see Harriet at the door, her expression anxious as she ushered them in.

They got her onto the bed where she lay very still and Doctor Sheppard urged Harriet to send the maid for a midwife to come in all haste. 'She's very ill,' he whispered to her. 'She hasn't been eating and she has no strength in her to deliver the child.'

She gazed wide-eyed at him. 'But she's going to be all right, isn't she?'

He didn't answer and she hurried down the stairs to call the maid, then went into the kitchen herself to fill the kettle for boiling water as the doctor directed.

Billy had run all the way from the cellars; his hair was tangled with the wind and wet with the snow which was gusting down in a bitter white flurry. He stood outside the bedroom door, not wanting to enter, until the doctor came to him from the side of the bed where Betsy lay.

'You must send for her family, Billy.' He spoke in an undertone so that Betsy couldn't hear. 'It doesn't look good. The baby is alive, but Betsy – she has poisons in her body. Her feet and hands are swollen and she appears anaemic; if she loses much blood then I can't save her.' He hesitated for a moment. 'Besides which, from what she has told me, I don't think she has the will or the want to live.'

Shocked to the core, Billy went to Betsy's side. She opened her eyes and gave a small smile when she saw him. 'Hello, Billy. Did I ever tell you that you were always my favourite?' A tear trickled from the corner of her eye. 'Except for Sammi. I loved Sammi best of all, but of all my male cousins, you were the best.'

He knelt down and took her hand. 'No, I never guessed. Why didn't you tell me?'

'I don't know,' she murmured. 'Why don't we tell people we care for them?' She screwed up her eyes and bit her lips as a spasm wracked her and she squeezed his hand in a painful grip.

She began to breathe heavily and Stephen Sheppard came back to the bed. 'I think you'd better leave now, Billy. It won't be long.'

'No. No. Please don't leave me, Billy.' Panic showed on her face. 'Not yet, not until the last minute. I must have someone here, someone who cares a little for me.'

'I'm going to send for Tom,' Billy said gently. 'He'll come to fetch you home; home where everyone cares for you. They've all missed you, Betsy, they've worried about you.'

The tears coursed down her cheeks. 'I know. I shouldn't have treated them so. My poor da.' She gave a sob. 'He deserved a better daughter than me. But I couldn't tell them, Billy. I couldn't tell them where I'd been.'

She suddenly arched her back and screamed. Billy cast an alarmed glance at Stephen Sheppard. 'Can't you give her something? How can they stand it?'

Stephen poured a few drops of liquid onto a spoon and tipped it into Betsy's half-open mouth. He shook his head. 'I don't know, but they do, and then they go on and have more. Men have a lot to answer for,' he said, grim-faced. 'There should be more men at their wives' bedsides at a time like this.'

Billy hurried downstairs and spoke to Gilbert and then came back again, following the midwife who had just arrived, unbuttoning her coat as she climbed the stairs and handing it to him without a word. 'Gilbert will go to Tillington,' he whispered to Stephen, 'but if you think the birth won't be long, then we decided that he should wait so that he can tell them – tell them about the baby. What it is, I mean,' he faltered, 'and how Betsy is.' He looked appealingly at his friend for encouragement, but Doctor Sheppard had donned his professional demeanour and wouldn't be drawn.

'Billy!' Betsy's voice was low but the appeal reached him and he glanced at the midwife who was drawing the curtains and turning up a lamp.

She nodded and he went to the bed. 'Tell Luke I'm sorry.' Betsy was calm now from the result of opium. 'Tell him I know he would have stood by me, only – only I didn't want to get married and stay for ever in Tillington. Like Mark, I wanted to see something of life.' She gave a hint of a grimace. 'I hope he fares better than me, but at least he won't be having a baby. He warned me, you know,' she muttered, and Billy thought that her mind was wandering. 'But he needn't have warned me about poor Luke. He should have warned me about the other sort of man. Luke wouldn't have abandoned me the way he did.'

'Who, Betsy? Who are you talking about?' Billy bent his head towards her. 'Where did you go after you left home?'

'Craddock!' Her hair and face were wet with pain. She closed her eyes and moaned. 'Dear God, I can't stand this. Billy, tell him to do something.'

The midwife motioned him away. 'You'll have to go, sir. Your wife is about to deliver.'

Betsy half screamed, half laughed. 'I'm not his wife! I'm nobody's wife. Never wanted to be.'

'Betsy!' Billy hesitated at the foot of the bed. 'What has Craddock to do with this?'

She took deep shuddering breaths and drew her legs up beneath the sheets. 'I went to live with him,' she gasped. 'He promised me so many things. Then when he saw I was pregnant he turned me out. I daren't go home. Daren't tell anybody.' She fell back weeping. 'I kept hoping it would go away.'

The midwife's mouth set in a thin line. 'Babbies don't go away,' she muttered. 'And there's no changing tha mind once they've started,' and she ushered Billy out of the room and firmly closed the door behind him.

Billy, Gilbert and Harriet all sat silently in the sitting-room. From time to time, first Billy and then Gilbert shivered, even though a fire was lit.

'She's been living with Craddock,' Billy said in a low voice. 'She's just told me. He turned her out when he realized she was pregnant.'

Gilbert gaped. 'It's not his child?'

Billy shook his head. 'No. She said that it's Luke Reedbarrow's. She must have known even before she – she joined up with Craddock. She said she didn't want to admit that she was pregnant.'

'Poor Betsy,' Harriet murmured. 'How troubled she must have been to have carried the secret all alone for so long.'

Gilbert glanced up at her. His face was ashen. 'A troubled conscience is a terrible thing, Harriet.'

'Yes.' She took hold of his hand. 'It is. We all know that now.'

'No, Harriet, you don't know. How could you?' Gilbert got up from his chair and started pacing the room. 'You couldn't possibly know.'

'Ssh.' Billy held up his hand. 'I thought I heard something.' His ears had caught the sound of a door opening and closing, and some other sound which

491

he couldn't define. Then there was the measured tread of footsteps on the stair.

They all stood up as Stephen Sheppard entered the room.

'Is it over, Doctor?' Harriet whispered. 'Is she delivered?'

He spoke gravely. 'She is. Betsy has given birth to a girl.'

They all gave a half smile and breath of relief at his words, yet were hesitant of joy as he looked so solemn. 'I'm afraid there have been complications,' he said. 'A very difficult birth, made worse by the mother's lack of strength; she was debilitated because of lack of food. Seemingly she has been wandering the streets of Hull for some weeks and has had little nourish- ment.'

'The child?' Harriet whispered. 'Will she live?'

'I think so. She's small and probably premature, but with care she should pull through.' He glanced at Gilbert and then towards Billy. 'I'm sorry, Billy,' he said quietly. 'But Betsy is very ill. You must prepare yourself for the worst. Would you like to come up to see her?'

Billy felt the colour drain from his face, his legs were weak and felt as if they didn't belong to him and he put his hand out to a chair to steady himself. 'Her father,' he stammered. 'And her brothers. We must fetch them.'

Stephen put his hand on his shoulder. 'There is no time, my friend. You must come now. You too, Mr Rayner,' he said to Gilbert who had slumped into a chair, whilst Harriet clung to his hand. 'If you wish to see her.'

Billy hauled himself up the stairs. He couldn't be-lieve what was happening. His mind couldn't accept what had been said. Everything had happened too fast. He wanted to wind the clock back and take each moment more slowly so that he could recognize and endure what was to come.

How could the happy laughing girl from their youth be taken from them? It wasn't right. What would he say to her father? Her brothers? To his mother? To Sammi? He started to shake as he entered the dimly lit room, the curtains drawn against the brightness of the cold day. How could he take on the responsibility of breaking the news?

'Hello, Billy.' Betsy lay perfectly still. The midwife had washed her bloodless face and tidied her hair which lay black against the starched white pillowcase. She saw Gilbert behind him and gave him a tired smile. 'It's all over. It's a little girl. Such a tiny baby, and she didn't want to come into this big bad world.' She put out a weak hand towards Billy. 'Hold my hand, Billy.'

He clasped hers and said in a choked voice, 'I never realized how beautiful you were, Betsy. Motherhood – motherhood suits you.' He put his head down to hide his weeping.

'Don't cry.' She patted his hand. 'It's all right. It has to be this way. I wasn't meant to be a wife or mother. I wouldn't have been any good at either.' She glanced across at the midwife who was standing at the other side of the room with the infant in her arms. 'Though I would have loved her.'

With a sudden strangled sob, Gilbert knelt down at the side of the bed and, clutching Betsy's other hand, kissed it, then got up and rushed out of the room.

Her eyes were half closed. 'Gilbert never was as brave as you, Billy,' she said softly. 'Though he means well.'

Billy wiped his eyes. 'He has a lot of troubles. And I'm not brave, defiant perhaps, but never brave.'

'I'm going to die, Billy,' she whispered. 'You must be brave for my sake, for I'm afraid. And you must be brave for my da and everybody else, and for my poor babby and Luke.' Her voice dropped low and he put his head close to hers to hear her words. 'You'll have to help them as well as those poor souls in the cellars.'

He knelt, cramped, at the side of the bed as her eyes closed in sleep or from the effect of the opium which the doctor had given her, then the nurse brought him a chair to sit on and, taking the baby with her, went out of the room.

Doctor Sheppard touched him gently on his shoulder and he sat up with a start. *I can't have been asleep! Did my eyes close for a moment? I didn't hear him come into the room.*

He looked at Betsy sleeping. She looked so peaceful, as if her pain had gone. Surely, surely Stephen must be wrong? She would recover once she had got over the trauma. *We'll all help her, even if she doesn't want to marry Luke.*

Stephen tapped him again on the shoulder. 'Come on, old fellow. No sense in lingering.'

'What? What do you . . . ?' He looked again at Betsy. Her eyes were closed, her hands folded in front of her, her breathing so faint you could hardly—

'She's gone, Billy,' the doctor spoke softly. 'Her last breath taken, the long sleep begun.'

Gilbert was sitting at the top of the stairs, his head bowed to his knees when Billy finally came out of the bedroom. He looked up and, seeing Billy's grief, he rose and preceded him down the stairs. 'Billy. Will you go to Tillington or will I?'

Billy swallowed and took a deep breath. 'I think that perhaps I should, Gilbert. Unless we go together.'

Gilbert hesitated at the door of the sitting-room. 'If you don't mind, I'd rather not. Doctor Sheppard has told Harriet. She is very upset, I'd best stay with her. Besides,' he clenched his trembling lips together, 'the Fosters are fond of you. I'm sure they would prefer it if you broke the news.'

'Yes,' Billy murmured. 'You're probably right. Can I borrow a coat, Gilbert? I seem to have lost my clothes.'

Gilbert silently pointed to the coat-stand in the hall,

and Billy unhooked a warm overcoat and a scarf. 'Stephen said he would see to everything,' he began.

'It's all right,' Gilbert interrupted. 'She – Betsy can stay here. We'll take care of her until her brothers come for her.' His voice broke. He was having great difficulty in forming his words. 'Take care on the road, Billy.' He was going to hire a chaise. 'Don't break your neck or turn the carriage over.'

'I won't.' Billy turned and went out of the front door, leaving Gilbert hesitating outside the sitting-room door.

He waited a moment, then, straightening his shoulders, he took a deep breath and turned the door-knob to enter the room where Harriet was sitting, a handkerchief to her eyes.

She looked up at him and put out her arms. 'I'm so sorry, Gilbert. So very sorry. I hardly knew Betsy, but I liked her such a lot. She was so pretty, and jolly and good-natured; and that poor baby, who will take care of her?'

Her face was pale and as he looked at her, his vision blurred with tears, she became almost ethereal. It was as if the faces of his dark-haired wife, and Betsy, the girl Sylvi, whom once he had loved, merged and dissolved, co-existed and became one and the same.

He sat down besides her and she put her arms about him. 'My poor darling, you are so sad.'

Gilbert started to weep; he put his head onto Harriet's shoulder, wetting her gown with his tears. 'Harriet. Please forgive me! There is something I must tell you.'

48

The early evening sky of Boxing Day was dark and low and threatening as Billy drove up the snow-covered drive of his home at Garston Hall. He had decided, during the seemingly endless road to Holderness, that he would enlist his family to help with breaking the news to Betsy's family. And someone would have to stay with Uncle Thomas while he drove back to Hull with Tom and George. He was dreadfully tired. The day had taken its toll of him, and his mind was dull and lethargic. He felt drowned in sorrow for Betsy and was barely able to think about what he should say.

But somehow he did find the words to tell his family of the tragedy, and to ask his parents to come back with him to Tillington. Sammi was shocked and speechless, unable to comprehend or believe what he was saying. Then she blurted out, 'But Tom was here, only a few hours ago. I said we mustn't give up hope. And now you're saying – you're saying . . . !'

Her father came to her side. 'We must be brave, Sammi. All of us, for the sake of Thomas and Tom and George. They'll need our help and fortitude.' His words were shaky but under control. 'Go and get your cloak and your mother's; we'll all go together.'

The action of doing something helped, and when she came back with her mother's outdoor things and already dressed in her own warm bonnet and cloak, she was more composed, though she trembled.

'We'll take the carriage, and Johnson can drive you and Tom and George back to Hull.' Their father had taken charge and was busy organizing, planning for subsequent action. 'You look ill, Billy. You must come back home with them and stay to recover. This has been a terrible shock for you. Ellen, you and I will stay with Thomas until they bring Betsy home.'

'May I stay too, Pa?' Sammi whispered. 'I'd like to prepare Betsy's room for her.' She glanced at Victoria who was sitting in a corner of the room, white-faced and breathless. 'Victoria isn't well, Mama will have to come back.'

Martha packed crisp white lavender-scented sheets and lace pillowslips into the carriage for them to take with them, and had said that she would walk to Tillington the next day. 'For that young maid won't know what to do,' she said softly.

Sammi wanted to put her arms around Tom to comfort him as he stood straight as a ramrod when Billy told them what had happened. Then he spoke. 'Reedbarrow's child!' His voice was bitter. 'Mark warned me she was being led astray. He'll answer for this!'

'Betsy said, she said that you were not to blame Luke.' Billy didn't want to tell all of what happened to Betsy, he felt that somehow he would be betraying her, yet he couldn't let Luke take all of the blame. 'She said that it was her fault as much as his. He doesn't know about the child. She never told him.'

'No? Well, I shall tell him. I shall tell him that he's sent a young girl to her death.' Tom reached for his coat which was hanging over the back of a chair.

'Tha'll go nowhere.' His father's voice was firm. 'Not until I say so. I'm still master here, even though I'm tied to this chair. There's more to this than we've been told. George! Is Reedbarrow still in 'mill?'

George nodded, he looked with frightened glances from one to another.

'Then fetch him inside,' his father demanded, his grief superseded by impotent anger. 'And let's get to 'bottom of this.'

Sammi pressed Tom's arm as she and her mother

went into the kitchen to organize Jenny to make tea for everyone, but there was no response, it was as if he didn't see her or know she was there. They heard a cry of anguish from Luke as he was told of Betsy. There were sounds of raised voices, of anger and weeping, recriminations and apologies.

Presently they went back into the parlour and Jenny handed round a tray of tea. She had put a teaspoonful of whisky in Thomas's cup and extra sugar in George's, and gave him a look of sympathy as she handed it to him.

Luke sat, his big body bowed. 'I would have done 'decent thing,' he mumbled. 'But she never said! She said she didn't want to get wed. Nor did I. Not yet any road, but I would have! And I onny ever wanted Betsy. 'Other lasses meant nowt to me.'

'Aye, lad, all right,' Thomas said wearily. 'We'll believe thee. She was fond on thee I don't doubt. Sup tha tea, Tom, and then get off to Hull with Billy. I'll not rest till she's brought home. Spare no expense,' he said abruptly. 'In spite of what's happened, she'll have 'best that money can buy, even though she'll not be here to see it.'

Luke raised his head and looked at Billy. 'But where's she been?' It was as if comprehension was only just filtering through. 'Tha said she was found in a cellar, but she can't have been there since August when she left home. She'd have lost babby if she had been!'

Billy flushed and swallowed. 'She, she was staying with a friend.'

'Aye, she told us that in her letter,' Thomas said. 'We knew that.'

'But who was the friend?' Tom's voice was harsh. 'What kind of a friend would let a pregnant woman wander alone in the streets?'

Billy looked pleadingly at Tom, silently beseeching him not to ask the question.

'Who was it, Billy? You know, don't you?' Tom's

eyes, cold as steel pierced into Billy's. 'Who was it? Was it a man?'

Billy looked down at his feet. 'Yes,' he said nervously. 'It was Charles Craddock.'

Johnson was waiting for them, his manner stoical. He had lived all of his life in Holderness and most of his working years had been with the Rayners. He had known all of the young people at Garston Hall and their cousins since they were children, and he was as upset as anyone over Miss Betsy, and would have waited all night if necessary. But he didn't have to wait long as Tom charged out of the house, followed more slowly by Billy and George.

Luke opened the big wooden gate for the carriage to pass through and as the team picked up their heels in the lane, he suddenly flung himself on board and climbed up beside Johnson.

Tom saw him through the window and put his head out, calling to Johnson to stop. 'Where do you think you're going, Reedbarrow?' he yelled. 'There's no need for you to come.'

Luke put his head down towards him. 'Need or not, I'm coming. I've a babby to collect and a score to settle.'

Tom considered. The same thoughts were going through his head. He, too, had a score to settle. He remembered that braggart Craddock from Gilbert's wedding. Betsy may well have gone willingly to him, but it would give him infinite pleasure to crack his jaw. 'You'd better go back, George,' he said. 'There's no sense in all of us going.'

George climbed down, relief showing on his face. 'I think tha's right, Tom.'

Tom called up again to Luke. 'You can come inside if you want.'

'No thanks. I'll stop on top. I know my place,' he muttered and Johnson raised his eyebrows and cracked the whip.

Billy stayed downstairs with Gilbert and Harriet while first Tom and then Luke went upstairs to sit by Betsy. Tom came down looking white and shaken, but Luke's face was flushed with anger, his eyes wild and wet with tears, and he demanded to know if Gilbert knew where this Craddock bloke lived.

'He might be at his club at this time of night.' Gilbert spoke quietly. His face was drawn but he was composed and calmer than he had been.

'Can tha tell me where it is?' Luke's manner was not impolite but neither was it complaisant.

'Do you not want to see the infant?' Harriet spoke up softly. 'She's sleeping, but I'll take you up.'

'Not yet, ma-am.' His brusque attitude changed deferentially as he spoke to Harriet. 'Thank you. I've a bit o' business to attend to first. Then I'll see her.'

Gilbert went to the door. 'Come on then, I'll take you.'

Harriet opened her mouth to protest, but he quickly said, 'We won't be long, Harriet. They can't get in without me. You have to be a member.'

The snow was coming down thick and fast as they went outside, and the four men piled once more into the carriage to be driven to the gaming club in the heart of the town.

'You'd better wait outside, Gilbert,' Tom said as they arrived at the lamplit door in the dark side street. 'You might be banned from coming again if there's trouble.'

'It's all right.' Gilbert nodded to the doorman and ushered the others in. 'I'm resigning anyway.'

They all stood in the doorway of the gaming room, looking round at the tables through a blue haze of cigar smoke. Gilbert, tall and broad, Billy, long and slim as a reed but with his patient face set and determined; Tom even taller, his frame strong and muscular, and Luke towering over them all, his shoulders and large head filling the doorway.

They were mostly men who were gathered around the card tables, though there were a few women, women garishly overdressed and beribboned, some smoking cigars and with wine glasses in their hands; Tom shuddered and wondered if Betsy had ever been brought here.

'There he is,' Gilbert murmured. 'At the table over in the corner. The fellow with the red braces and smoking a cigar.'

'Right!' Tom muttered to Gilbert. 'I want you to take Billy and leave. This isn't your concern and you have your name to think of. You've both done enough. Now go.'

His words were cut short as Luke barged past them and through the milling crowd towards Craddock's table. He dashed after him as Luke was saying, 'Is thy name Charlie Craddock?'

Craddock looked up in amusement, his eyes narrowing as he blew out a circle of smoke. 'Depends who wants to know,' he drawled. 'If I owe you money or have seduced your lady friend, then no.' He glanced round at the table anticipating general laughter, but as he discerned none he turned around, only to have a large hand clutch his shirt collar.

'Wait. This is my business.' Tom placed his hand on Luke's arm and felt the iron strength beneath it as he was pushed away.

'Ah! Don't I know you from somewhere?' Craddock's eyes lit on Tom as he tried to pull away from Luke's grip. He blustered. 'Little Betsy's brother, aren't you? How is the little dumpling? Been delivered of her bastard yet?'

His feet didn't touch the floor as Luke hauled him out of his chair and his face reddened as his grip tightened about his throat.

Tom pulled back his fist and aimed it fairly and squarely on Craddock's nose. He felt no satisfaction in the blow. He would have preferred to be outside in the open and without the help of Luke

Reedbarrow, who was holding Craddock up with one hand like a rag doll.

Luke dropped him and Craddock scrabbled to his feet, his nose bleeding and hatred etched in his eyes. 'You'll pay for this,' he glared at Tom. 'You and your whore of a sister.'

'She's already paid!' Tom spat out. 'She's dead. And you killed her, you dunghill rat.'

He drew his fist back once more but was stopped by Luke who pushed him to one side and with a mighty thrust of his fist punched Craddock in his stomach.

'That's for my Betsy,' he snarled. He lifted Craddock's doubled-up body by his chin and aimed again between his eyes. 'And that's for my babby who'll never know her ma.'

He turned round and, pushing Tom ahead of him, he elbowed his way through the watching crowd and marched out of the club into the darkness of the night.

'Spare no expense,' Betsy's father had said, and so they didn't. Betsy was put to rest in the churchyard next to her mother, the polished hearse pulled by a team of glossy black horses with black plumes nodding as they carried her on the short journey from her home.

The York Rayners' absence was barely missed, and though Mildred came with Gilbert and Harriet, Anne didn't, and some of the villagers stayed away to show their disapproval of the miller's fallen daughter; but most came for the final departure of the young girl they all had known, whilst others came out of curiosity to observe the united gathering of the Fosters and Rayners.

Tom, George, Luke and Billy carried the coffin on their shoulders down the churchyard path into the church, the soft black crêpe around their top hats floating behind them in diaphanous veils.

Sammi, shrouded in black as she sat in the pew with her family, watched Tom's straight, relentless back in front of her and wished that she could comfort him. She thought of that night when he had gone to bring Betsy home. Uncle Thomas had insisted that her mother return to Garston Hall. 'Tek 'trap and get her back home, William,' he'd said. 'That bairn, Victoria, needs her more than me. Sammi will stay, won't you, lass? She'll give me comfort.'

She'd said she would, and later had climbed the stairs and looked into Betsy's room. She had turned away in grief and couldn't sleep alone in the room which she had so often shared with her cousin and friend.

'Why don't you sleep in Master Tom's room, Miss Sammi?' Jenny had detected her reluctance. 'Sheets are all clean,' she added. 'I changed them all just afore Christmas.'

'Yes,' Sammi had said. 'I will. Tom won't mind.' And she had slept in his bed and guiltily felt his presence; felt the hollow of the mattress where he had lain and the pillow where he had put his head, and, conscience-stricken, she wept as she realized that hc was in her thoughts as much as Betsy was.

In the morning she had lifted his working jacket from the hook behind the door and pressed it to her face, smelling the grain, the grease from the mill, the very essence of him, knowing for sure that she loved him.

She had gathered evergreens, the white and purple Christmas rose, golden winter jasmine and early snowdrops, their green sheaths not yet unfurled, but which showed tips of white as they opened in the warmth of the house, and had made a garden within Betsy's room to await her.

As the relatives took their leave of Uncle Thomas after the funeral feast, Gilbert took her to one side. 'Harriet and Mother and I are going back to Garston

Hall with your mother and father. Will you come with us?'

She was going home anyway, to leave the Fosters to their sorrow, for it seemed to her that she could do nothing more to help them. Uncle Thomas was coping in the manner of one who had contended with grief before, George seemed to be totally bewildered by events, and Tom was barely speaking to anyone, and as she took her leave, he said good-bye as if she was a stranger leaving his house.

She glanced up at Gilbert. He looked so solemn. 'What is it? Nothing else is wrong?' she began.

'No. On the contrary. I think you will be pleased.'

He's confessed! He's told Harriet! But what about Aunt Mildred? Thoughts tumbled through her mind, but Gilbert refused to be drawn as she hesitatingly questioned, mindful that Harriet was within hearing distance.

The family were already gathered in the drawing-room when they entered. Her father's face was flushed and angry, though her mother looked composed and relieved. Aunt Mildred sipped nervously on a glass of sherry, Victoria had been sent upstairs and Richard and Billy sat together talking quietly.

'I have been told, at last, that *you* are Adam's father.' Sammi's father spoke directly to Gilbert without any preamble. 'No-one thought fit to inform me previously,' he said, with a meaningful glance at his wife and Sammi. 'Had anyone done so, the matter might have been resolved earlier.'

Sammi's mother folded her hands together, but said nothing as he continued, 'I will not give my opinions on how I regard your past behaviour towards your mother, your wife and particularly to your brother, let alone your aunt and Sammi,' he went on, 'because it will not alter the situation as it now stands.' He then proceeded to air his estimation of Gilbert's conduct, his foolishness that was past comprehension, his letting down of the family name and his late father's standing in the community. 'However,' he drew breath and softened, 'as my wife constantly reminds me, the young do make mistakes – and I might add not only the young; and as your father's brother, I take it upon myself to support you in your commitment now, for you will need all the strength we can offer. It will not be easy for either of you.'

Commitment? What commitment? Sammi grew tense with apprehension as she waited for a subdued Gilbert to speak.

'I accept all that you say, sir. I have no excuse to offer. None but that of not wanting Harriet to discover my lapse. I was so afraid that she would hate me for it; she in her innocence,' he reached out and held Harriet's hand, 'thought I was as flawless as she undoubtedly is.'

Sammi felt her eyes prickle as Harriet drew close to Gilbert and spoke in defence of him. 'He was afraid that I would cancel our wedding,' she said softly. 'I wouldn't have, but my parents would have made me. I wouldn't have had a choice in the matter and, and I would rather have Gilbert as he is than be without him.'

'You will write to James? I must insist on that,' William said sternly. 'This cloud must be removed from his shoulders, then if he wants to return—'

'I was the one who sent James away,' Mildred broke in. 'I will write to him again and explain, but – but—' her cheeks became pink, '—Gilbert's actions cannot be excused, nor mine either, but the effect of James leaving home has contributed to proving his worth. He has found his own kind amongst the arts. He has become whole. He knows himself at last.'

They all looked at her, only partly understanding, then Gilbert spoke. 'No. I will write, Mother. I can't shirk my responsibilities any longer. I have caused enough havoc.' He squeezed Harriet's hand. 'With Harriet by me, I can do anything.'

Sammi went to fetch Adam from the nurse and dressed him in his outdoor clothes, pressing his plump little body close to her and murmuring in his ear, 'You are going home, Adam, to where you belong. But don't forget me, will you? I was the first to love you and I always will. I'm your Godmother so I will always have a special claim on you.'

She carried him downstairs and handed him to Harriet. 'Will you come with us, Sammi?' Harriet asked. 'I would like to meet the woman who nursed him.'

Sammi blinked away her tears and nodded.

'I want to thank her,' Harriet said softly.

They returned again to Tillington. Mildred, Gilbert and Harriet with Adam on her knee, in their carriage, and Sammi in front driving the trap pulled by Boreas.

'Mrs Bishop,' Sammi began diffidently, 'Adam is to leave us at last to go to his home in Hull.'

Mrs Bishop looked from Sammi to Harriet and then to Gilbert. 'Why – can I see 'likeness of his da?' she beamed. 'That's a Rayner head o' hair if I'm not mistaken, sir.' Then she shook her head and commiserated. 'And now there's another poor babby come into 'world, and I'm right sorry that I can't nurse her like I did this one. Folks' tongues 'll have summat else to chew over now, Miss Rayner.' She smiled at Sammi. ''Reckon tha'll be forgotten.'

Harriet stepped forward, holding Adam in her arms. 'I wanted to thank you, Mrs Bishop,' she said, interrupting her flow. 'Miss Rayner has said how kind you have been to our son.' Mrs Bishop's brows shot up in her rosy face. 'I wanted to thank you in person for taking care of him.' Harriet lifted her chin. 'Things haven't been easy for my husband and myself, but now we are able to take him back home where he belongs.'

Gilbert gazed humbly at Harriet. How strong she had become since he had confessed. No censure of his behaviour, only regret that he hadn't trusted her enough to tell her before, and demanding assurance that he did indeed love her. And now, by tokenly admitting motherhood to Mrs Bishop, she was freeing Sammi from any misinterpretation which might have arisen over Adam's parentage.

Sammi waved them good-bye and turned for home. She felt empty, part of her torn away as the carriage carrying Adam bowled away down the road towards Hull. She glanced back at the mill. The skies were darkening above it, the white canvas sails at rest. No milling today while the miller and his kinsfolk mourned.

She flicked the reins. Fortunately Boreas instinctively knew the way and didn't need her directive, for she could no longer see the road for her tears.

49

Doctor Sheppard had arranged a wet nurse for Betsy's baby, and she thrived under the supervision of the doctor; but three weeks after Betsy's funeral, Jenny answered a knock at the door and found Luke and his mother standing there.

'My ma wants to speak to 'Master,' he said brusquely. 'Mr Foster, not Master Tom.'

'I'll speak for myself.' Luke's mother was quietly determined. 'Get back to thy work now.'

She addressed Jenny. 'If Mr Foster is well enough, I'd like a word.'

Jenny went inside and then came back. 'Please come in, Mrs Reedbarrow.' She invited her in and closed the parlour door behind her.

'How do, Dolly? Haven't seen thee for a long while.'

Mrs Reedbarrow looked at him. 'No,' she said quietly. 'Well, I didn't know if I'd be welcome. Folks were saying tha wouldn't see anybody, that tha was sick. But tha looks healthy enough to me – 'cept for tha legs.'

He gave a snort. 'Aye, well, without use of my legs, I might as well be dead and buried alongside my wife and daughter, for all 'good I am to anybody. I can do nowt!'

'It's no use feeling sorry for thyself.' She sat down uninvited. 'There must be plenty tha can do – accounts and that for one thing. And tha can allus count tha money for another!'

He gave a terse grin. 'Tha allus was a comic, Dolly. Though I don't know how tha keeps tha humour, married to yon fella. Tha should have had me when I asked thee.'

'What and finish up married to a cripple who can't work?' Her flippancy died and her pale face creased. 'I don't mean that, Thomas. I'm right sorry about thy accident. I should have come afore.'

He dismissed the remark. 'But tha's come for a reason?' he asked. 'This isn't a social call?'

She shook her head. 'I was at Betsy's funeral with our Luke. He's really cut up about her. He said he would have married her if he'd known about 'babby.'

'Aye,' he sighed. 'I know, he said as much, and I believe him. There'd have been no scandal nor misery if they'd wed.'

'But, what we want to know is what's happened to 'bairn? Luke said she was onny a little scrap and a woman in Hull has been found to nurse her; but he knows no more 'n that and doesn't like to ask. He says Tom hardly speaks to him.'

Thomas rubbed his hand over his beard. 'He's taken it badly, has Tom. Blames himself for not watching over her better; so he takes it out on everybody, not just Luke. As for babby, well, I haven't seen her. I don't know what we shall do. A houseful of men and one young maid!'

He was silent for a moment, then spoke softly, 'It'll be like when their ma died and left me alone with 'bairns. I had to hire a woman to look after us all.'

'Aye, tha's had some misfortune in thy time, Thomas,' she commiserated. Then she drew herself up and folded her hands in the lap of her grey skirt. 'We'd like to have her.'

Thomas gazed at her, his thoughts elsewhere. 'Have her? Have who?'

'Luke's babby. Thy granddaughter, and mine,' she added. 'It might not have come to thine ears, but I've just had another bairn. Please God it'll be 'last, but I'm willing to have her. I can't nurse them both for long, I'm getting too old, but I can supplement them wi' bottle, and if I can have some help from thee wi' finance for her, I'll bring her up. It's what Luke wants,' she said firmly.

'Would I be able to see her?' There was a brightness in his face, a look of hope. 'Would tha bring her here?'

'Aye. That was 'idea. We'd both have a share in her. But I can't do it alone, Thomas.' She looked down at her careworn hands. 'We all work hard, and Luke more than anybody, but no matter how I scrimp and save we've never any money left over.'

She glanced appealingly at him. 'I wouldn't ask for owt, tha knows that, not if I could help it; but I thought tha'd rather have her with 'family than with strangers.'

He closed his eyes wearily. When he opened them they were moist with tears. ''Reedbarrows and Fosters allus used to be close,' he said. 'So my da used to say. 'Two families used to be like that.' He put his middle and forefingers together.

'Maybe this bairn'll unite them again,' she smiled, her eyes gentle. 'What name wilt tha give her?'

He put out his hand and she put hers into it. 'I don't know,' he said, giving a gentle squeeze. 'Her da will have to choose.'

So the baby Elizabeth was brought home to Tillington to be petted and spoiled by her father and maternal grandfather and George, though Tom kept his distance from the tiny infant, unable and unwilling to accept that this was his dead sister's child.

In the weeks following her arrival, the weather worsened and the snow fell, covering the land with mountainous drifts and making the deep drains of Holderness perilous pitfalls for human and animal alike. The road between Tillington and Monkston was blocked, no horse or vehicle could get through, and the Fosters and the Rayners knew nothing of the others' activities for a month, for after the snow ceased to fall, the wind blew, hardening the snow's surface to a treacherous, leg-breaking ice-rink, and the children of the Holderness villages cheerfully risked their limbs as they skated on the frozen fields.

As the thaw began, the overflowing streams and ditches flooded the banks, the low-lying fields lay under water, and the farmers despaired of ever being able to sow their crops; while on the top of the cliffs, great cracks appeared as the sea hungrily licked the foot, devouring the crumbling boulder clay and washing it down towards the peninsula of Spurn.

Sammi watched the swollen sea and the shrieking, whirling gulls from her window, unable to venture out into the hostile landscape; but as the weather gradually improved she started to walk across the sodden fields and through the battered copses, or trudged on the sands beside the boisterous waves and came back home revitalized, her cheeks rosy from the constant wind which dried up the flooded fields, and started to plan.

The church bells of Holy Trinity and St John's could be heard from the house in Charlotte Street, and Gilbert, after finishing his breakfast of bacon, kidneys and omelette, peered into the almost empty coffee jug and poured the remaining drops into his cup.

'Would you like more, dear?' Harriet sat across from him, eating buttered toast. 'Shall I ring?'

Gilbert pushed his chair back from the table and shook his head. 'No thank you, Harriet, I have had sufficient.' He glanced towards the window. 'Could you face taking a walk? The weather isn't quite so cold, and if you wrap up warm, I think it might do you good to get out.'

'And take Adam, of course?'

They exchanged an implicit glance. As Uncle William had predicted, it hadn't been easy bringing the child home. Harriet had been given many a pitying glance by young matrons, and Gilbert had put up with sly winks and jibes about being a roistering blade from his acquaintances, and a brash cavalier by his elders. Harriet's strength had sustained him. She had cancelled all their social engagements to save anyone from the embarrassment of having to do the same, and had appeared to be unmoved by the snubs of society; she was, as she said, thankful to know now who were her true friends. They were few, but faithful and understanding.

He had been grateful that she had taken to Adam. It would have been so natural if she had spurned the child of another woman, but she was so loving towards him that no-one would suspect, if they didn't already know, that he wasn't hers.

'All right.' She rose from the table. 'I'll tell Nurse to get him ready.'

They had hired a nursemaid to look after Adam, though they had to live more frugally in order to pay her wages. The failed bank's affairs had not yet been settled, but Gilbert was heartened to learn that shares in the Dock Company, in his father's name, which had been held by an independent broker, had soared to double their value of five years before.

Of the two ships belonging to the company, nothing was heard, and they were now presumed lost. The steam whaler *Chase* from the Hull Whale and Seal Fishing Company had been wrecked in Ponds Bay; the *Kingston* was lost and also the *Wesley* and *Bothnia*, and the town had been in mourning all the winter.

Gilbert had taken advice from other shipping merchants who were also being hard hit, not only by the loss of vessels, but by the declining whaling trade, and he had now made up his mind that they would diversify. Fish was plentiful, and the industry was expanding, and he heard from Hardwick, who was not only a very capable working partner, but also a great source of information, that many former seamen and those who had served their apprentice-ship in the whaling industry were joining forces to buy sailing smacks and setting up in business for themselves.

'What I might suggest,' Hardwick had said during one of their many discussions, 'is, that once we know what finances are available, we adapt one of our ships to carry ice from Norway, and then trawl from the North Sea. The fish can be gutted and iced on board, transferred to a fast cutter and sent home in less than a week.'

Gilbert had approached his uncle, Arthur Rayner, to ask for comparative prices for transporting the boxed fish by rail to London, which was where the best prices could be obtained, against carrying it direct by cutter, which could reach the Thames from the Hull docks in three to four days.

'Come along, Gilbert. Are you not ready yet?' Harriet interrupted his reverie and he rose from the table where he had been quietly meditating.

He gathered up his coat and hat and helped Harriet on with her wool cloak. Taking the baby carriage by the handle, he eased it down the steps from the front door into the street. They took a roundabout route from Charlotte Street into the wider Albion Street, with its elegant Doric buildings, and glanced at the row of houses where Harriet had formerly lived with her parents. They noted the freshly painted front door and new lace curtains, and Gilbert thought grimly of Harriet's father who had ruined so many lives, and of her mother who had left Hull to live with a relative and who, having heard the news of Adam, wrote to say that it came as no surprise to her, as all men were blackened with the same brush, and to expect no sympathy or support from her.

They walked on into Prospect Street where the Infirmary stood behind its low walls, and into Savile Street which led towards the Queen's Dock, where Gilbert pointed out the ships to a wide-eyed Adam, then turning back, they walked across the Monument Bridge and into the old area of Hull.

A flower seller had set up her stall near the old workhouse in Whitefriargate. The fresh flowers which were brought in by boat from Holland, or sent by train from the London markets, spilled over onto the footpath in a riotous profusion of colour. Harriet gave a small gasp and bit her lip. Her father had bought a flower for his buttonhole from this same flower seller every morning before going in to the bank.

Gilbert took her arm and steered her towards the stall. Ghosts had to be laid, fears had to be faced up to; he knew that now, better than most. 'What would you like, Harriet? Lilies for the drawing-room? The perfume is so lovely. Narcissi? How early they are!'

The flower seller picked up each of the flowers as Gilbert mentioned them by name and artistically displayed them into a bouquet for Harriet's approval. She was a leathery old crone with gnarled hands, but she had a flair for presenting the blooms to perfection. 'What about these yellow daffydillys, Mr Rayner, sir? Tha won't find a lovelier colour anywhere. Colour of sunshine which'll be just round 'corner for thee and thy good lady.' She nodded sagely. 'Mark my words, sir. Winter is over.'

'I hope you're right.' Gilbert smiled as he put his hand into his pocket to pay her, and extended his smile to a woman who was also standing by the stall, apparently waiting for the sale to be concluded so that she and the stallholder could continue their conversation.

They moved off to continue their walk, and he saw the second woman bend her head in enquiry to the flower seller. She was a poor thing, he thought. Overweight with dropsy, her swollen feet almost bare in her torn shoes and her clothes little more than rags.

He put his fingers into his waistcoat pocket. Like his father, he had started to keep a few coins there to give to beggars. But the woman hadn't asked for anything, though she had kept her tired eyes on his face as the flower seller had spoken to him; she was not like some who regularly begged from the same spot, catching business people as they left their premises, or laid in wait for ladies to come out of shops with their purchases and small change in their hands.

He turned round, with the uneasy feeling that they were being discussed, and saw that the woman was staring. He hesitated and as he did, she moved towards him.

'Mr Rayner, sir?' Her voice was breathless as if she had no energy.

'Yes!' He answered brusquely, he knew not why, for he felt no animosity towards her.

'Mr Rayner from 'shipping company? Thy father died last year?' The eyes which stared at him from her pasty face were large, though heavily shadowed, and of the deepest blue.

'What of it? What can I do for you?' *That was a mistake*, he thought. *I shouldn't have asked. She probably wants a job for her husband or sons.*

'Oh, nothing, sir. It's just – it's just . . .' She looked down at Adam in his baby carriage and Harriet instinctively moved nearer.

'Yes?' Gilbert asked guardedly; he was getting a curious prickle down the back of his neck.

Her mouth trembled as if she was trying to smile but she failed as her eyes filled with tears. 'It's just that Masterson and Rayner have been in this town for a long time, and I heard that things had been going wrong for thee, sir.'

She took a deep breath and continued, 'I just wanted to say that I hope that thy fortunes turn, Mr Rayner.'

'That's kind of you.' Gilbert fingered the coins in his pocket but the woman saw the gesture and waved it away.

'I don't want thy money, sir.' She looked at Adam

again and the child gurgled at her. 'I heard that there was a Rayner babby brought home and I onny wanted to take a look at him.' She clenched her lips and swallowed. 'He'll bring thee love, I'm sure.' She looked at the dark-haired Harriet, who was gazing at her with compassion. 'He's like his ma, I can see that. Same eyes and pretty nose. But he's got his da's hair!'

She gave a little laugh which was more like a sob. 'Aye, anybody can see who he belongs to.'

She had a bunch of rosemary in her hand and she leaned towards the baby carriage. 'Could I – I've just bought this from old Mary, could I give it to little fella, sir? It'll bring him luck.'

'Rosemary is for remembrance!' Harriet said softly.

'Aye, so it is, ma-am.' She laid it on the satin-frilled coverlet and Adam reached out to grab it. 'God bless thee, sir, and thee, ma-am, and 'little babby. May he allus know love and have good fortune.'

They watched her as she hurried away; she didn't stop by the flower seller but scuttled past her, turning into a gloomy narrow passageway and out of their sight.

'How very strange,' Harriet murmured, rescuing the rosemary from Adam's mouth. 'Who do you think she was?'

'I don't know.' Gilbert stared back at the empty passageway. He felt humbled by the woman's dignity in refusing his money, though she was surely in a desperate plight, and bewildered to think that a stranger would care what happened to the company of Masterson and Rayner if their livelihood didn't depend on it.

He felt again a tingle or sensation of touch on the back of his neck which spread meltingly down his spine. It wasn't something he could define, but as he remembered the woman's fine eyes looking into his, it was as if a hand had brushed against his skin in a warm remembrance of love.

50

The golden flowers of winter jasmine gave a splash of colour to the corner tower wall of Garston Hall and caught Sammi's eye as she stepped into the trap. The sight of the flowering cascade was always such a bright reminder during the long dark days of winter that spring was only a promise away. But this winter had seemed longer and darker than most, not least because Betsy wasn't here to share companionship with her as she had done since childhood. The days of gathering wild flowers for posies, of apple-bobbing at Christmas, of sharing secrets in their childhood innocence, had gone for ever.

She heard regularly from Harriet that Adam was making good progress, and so although there was yet another gap in her life, she was glad for all their sakes that he had settled.

But now there was a breath of spring in the air and she had started to ride once again to Tillington, calling on Uncle Thomas who was always glad to see her, and hoping to catch a glimpse of Tom who, however, whenever he saw her, had very little to say to her.

'He's very morose, that lad,' her uncle had remarked one day when Tom had made his excuses to her and gone back into the mill. 'He doesn't have to do so much.' He chewed his lip. 'It's as if he keeps on working so that he doesn't have to do any thinking.' He sighed. 'I remember having 'same feeling when their ma died. But it's different with Tom. I reckon he feels 'shame ower Betsy more'n anybody. And he misses Mark.'

As she rattled out of the drive, Sammi felt elation rising within her. She had made a decision; and though she felt apprehensive, she was determined to be bold. Her disposition wasn't normally nervous, but her intention today would not be considered either normal or proper for a young woman of her station, and in spite of her determination, social convention still held her in its grasp, and she had therefore some slight doubts as to how her plans would be received.

Though there was a slight breeze blowing, the sails of the mill were at rest when she turned in at the gate. She heard a shout and saw George sitting astride the ridge of the barn roof. He waved a hand which was holding a tile, and she held her breath, hoping that he wouldn't over-balance.

The door was open and she walked in. Jenny was sitting by the fire mending a pair of socks and Sammi warmed to the sight of the girl in such a domestic scene, giving silent thanks that Billy had rescued her from the cellars before the cholera had struck and taken so many young people.

'G'morning, Miss Sammi.' Jenny put down her mending and stood up. 'Would you like a cup of tea? Mr Foster is having a nap. He's had a bad night; he had terrible pain in his back and legs. Master George and me had to get him up to try to ease it.'

'Where was Tom? Couldn't he have helped?'

'We didn't wake him, he was fast on. He doesn't sleep so well either, he's often up during 'night. I hear him moving around or sometimes he sits up with his da and reads to him to pass 'night away.'

Sammi refused the tea and sat opposite Jenny by the fire. 'Is Tom in the mill now? I saw George up on the barn roof.'

Jenny nodded and picked up the socks again. 'Aye, he is, though they're not grinding till this afternoon. Luke Reedbarrow's gone to deliver animal feed to a farmer somewhere and George is fixing 'roof while 'weather holds.'

Sammi stood up and took off her coat. 'I need to talk to Tom,' she said. 'I'll go now while Uncle Thomas is asleep.'

Jenny looked up at her. 'He might be up at 'top, Miss Sammi. I doubt he'll hear you.'

Sammi delayed for a second only. 'Then I'll have to go up to him.' She lifted up her skirts and petticoats. 'Jenny, will you unfasten my hoop?'

Jenny blinked and gazed open-mouthed, but without a word got up from her chair and unfastened the whalebone hoop, holding on to Sammi as she stepped out of it.

'Thank you.' Sammi stood it in a corner of the kitchen. 'I won't be long, and – and I'll probably have a cup of tea when I come down.'

'I'll put 'kettle on then, miss, and it'll be on 'boil when you're ready.'

As Sammi went out of the door, Jenny moved a pan from the fire and replaced it with the kettle, and then stood looking at the hoop in the corner. She hesitated before skipping to the window where she could still see George up on the barn roof. She picked up the hoop, and, holding on to the table, put first one leg and then the other into the hoop. Her skirts were too short and the hoop showed below her hem, but she twirled around the kitchen floor, her skirts swaying, and singing softly to herself.

Her back was to the door and she didn't hear it open but as she was just rising from a deep mock curtsey, she heard a chuckle, swung around and there was George in the doorway.

He gave a bow and joked. 'May I have this dance, ma-am?' and took hold of her hand.

She snatched it away, blushing crimson. 'I didn't mean no harm, Master George. I haven't damaged it. Don't tell Miss Sammi, will you?'

'Sammi wouldn't mind,' he protested. 'She'd see it was just a bit o' fun. Come here.' He grabbed her hand again and whirled her round the table. 'I'm no dancer,' he said. 'Me feet are too big.'

She laughed, her fears disappearing, but once more around the table and she stopped. 'I'd better take it off before she comes back, she's gone up to see Master Tom, that's why she took 'hoop off.'

'Gone up into 'mill?' His face showed alarm. 'What for? I'd better go up in case she tummels.'

'No.' Jenny hopped first on one foot, then the other to remove the hoop. 'No, don't, Master George. Don't.'

'Why not?' he asked, grabbing her arm so that she didn't fall. 'What's up?'

'I don't know why not.' She gave him an impish grin. 'Only don't.'

Sammi stepped into the bagging room and called Tom's name. The mill appeared to be empty. The floor was swept clean of the previous day's milling, no loose grain left lying around that would attract vermin, and the rope and chains neatly coiled or hung so that no-one could trip and fall. Sacks of grain were stacked ready for the afternoon milling, but above her head on the stone floor, the stones were still, and above them the great spur wheel, the wallower and brake wheel were silent.

'Tom!' she called again, but her voice echoed around the room and didn't reach any higher up the battered walls. She lifted her skirts to climb the access ladder and put her head through the hatch into the stone room. Stone dressing tools were laid out neatly in a wooden box and the hoppers had their covers in place. Tom wasn't there either, but she heard a sound above and awkwardly she climbed up, putting her feet cautiously on to the wooden boarding and up the next ladder to the bin floor where the grain bins were clean and empty.

She looked out of the small window and saw below her the mill yard and the hay cart, and shuddered as she remembered Uncle Thomas's fall, then continued up again until she reached the cap, where she could hear Tom's footsteps. She tiptoed precariously on the rungs and peered through the hatch into the cap; the chocks were firmly lodged in the brake wheel and the two access doors set into the walls were open to the sky; one led to the fantail, and through the other, the storm hatch, which led to the sails, she could see Tom's legs. She dare not call in case of startling him, nor could she climb up unaided as the gap between the ladder and staging was too great. So she waited, perched on the narrow ladder, until he finally put his head through the storm door and re-entered the cap.

He gave a startled exclamation as he saw her head sticking up through the floor, and the thought flitted through her mind that the sight of her disembodied head wasn't quite the effect she had planned for him.

'Sammi! Whatever are you doing up here?' He crouched down to speak to her.

'I came to talk to you.' She suddenly felt foolish.

'Why didn't you shout? I would have come down.'

'I did! You didn't hear.'

He said nothing but she saw an impulsive twist to his mouth as if he was hiding a grin.

'Well, I can't talk to you like this,' she said impatiently. 'Can you help me up?'

'Are you sure you want to come up? Will you feel safe?' He stood up and towered above her and this time he did grin and then started to laugh.

She gave him her hand. 'I'm glad you find something funny,' she said, and with her other hand, hitched up her skirt. 'I haven't heard you laugh in a long time.'

He heaved and pulled and she half jumped, half fell onto the floor where he hauled her to her feet, and because there was so little room between the open doors and the hatch below, he kept a firm hold of her.

'There hasn't been much to laugh about.' He was serious again and she regretted her pettish words.

'No.' She looked up at him and saw grease on his cheek and a look of wretchedness returned to his eyes. 'I'm sorry.'

'Don't be.' He dropped her hand and bent to pick up an oily rag. 'It's not your fault.' When he straightened up it was as if a shutter had dropped; his face was expressionless.

'Don't shut me out, Tom,' she whispered. 'I need to talk to you.'

'I'm not shutting you out,' he said abruptly. 'You know you can talk to me any time.'

'But I never see you now. You don't call.'

He turned away. 'No. I'm sorry. The weather was too bad before and I've just been so busy since. There's little time for a miller to socialize.' He had a note of bitterness in his voice. 'And you forget we are two men short.'

'I haven't forgotten, Tom. I realize how hard it must be for you.'

He turned back at her quiet words and gave her a slight smile. 'I'm sorry, Sammi. I'm an old grouch these days. Forgive me?'

'Of course,' she said lightly.

'What was it you wanted to talk to me about? It's something important or you wouldn't have climbed up here.'

Sammi looked up into the dome of the cap. The wind was rushing in through the doors and the timbers were creaking. 'It's like being on a ship,' she murmured. 'I can feel the movement.'

'Yes.' His eyes roved her face. 'It is; especially when the sails are turning and the mill shakes; and more so at night when you can see the stars.'

She looked towards him and caught him off-guard as he was gazing at her; for a second they neither of them spoke. Then he repeated, 'What was it that was so important?'

'I wanted to tell you something. I wanted you to be the first to know.'

It was as if a shadow fell across his face. 'The first to know?' His eyes were anxious. 'To know what, Sammi?'

She moved across to the access door and looked out. The morning was clear; a kestrel was hovering, suspending its flight with buoyant wings, and across the meadowland and hedgerows as she gazed towards Monkston, she saw the white surging crests of the sea.

'You know how everyone thinks that it's time I was contemplating marriage?' She had her back to him, but heard a sharp intake of his breath and smiled in satisfaction. 'Oh, I know that Mama and Pa don't want to rush me, but even you—' she turned back to confront him and was taken aback by his anguished expression '—even you have said, "soon you'll be thinking of marrying".' She gave a deep sigh as if in resignation. 'So I have decided that as it is expected of me, then that is what I shall do.'

'But – but, have you met someone? I mean, you mustn't rush into an unsuitable – someone you don't care for,' he finished miserably.

She wanted to put her arms around him, to comfort him, but resisted the urge and continued. 'Oh, but Tom! Times are changing, women have more control over their lives nowadays, and although men can dictate to their wives, I shall make sure that the man I choose – have chosen – will eat out of my hand.'

He was, she felt sure, barely listening to her. 'So you have met someone?' he asked quietly. 'Someone you care for? He's a lucky man, Sammi.'

'Yes. Well! That's just the trouble. You see, he doesn't know it yet!'

'Doesn't know it?' A frown wrinkled his dark eyebrows. 'You mean he hasn't asked? Has he not spoken to your father?'

She shook her head and lowered her eyes. 'No,'

she whispered. 'I don't know why he hasn't, for I'm almost sure that he loves me.'

'Then the man is a fool! He doesn't deserve you, Sammi.' He took hold of her hand and, looking down, he gently stroked her fingers.

'He has his reasons, I think, why he won't ask. He is such a principled, honourable man.' She took another deep breath. 'So I have decided to take matters into my own hands. If he won't ask for me, then I shall have to ask him.' She kept her eyes on his face and as he quickly glanced up, she pressed the hand that was holding hers to her lips and kissed it. 'So will you, Tom?' she whispered. 'Will you marry me?'

He gathered her into his arms and held her close. 'I can't marry you, Sammi.' His voice was low and bitter. 'Our family has lost its good name, your father would never agree to it. You must marry someone else. Someone with prestige and power; someone from a grand house who'll take you to parties and balls, not a man like me who works with his hands.' He released her and turned his hands over. 'Look,' he said. 'That's a miller's thumb.' His right thumb was flattened where he tested the grain.

She took hold of his hand again and stroked his thumb. 'It's the sign of a good miller,' she smiled. 'Like the sight of a miller's fat pigs is a sign of a cheating one.'

She rested her face against the roughness of his coat. 'You can't teach me anything about country customs, Tom. You forget that I am a farmer's daughter.'

'A rich farmer,' he objected. 'A land owner!'

'Your father owns land,' she persisted. 'I've heard my father say so.'

He stroked her hair. 'Sammi,' he murmured. 'Be sensible. How could you join your name to ours? It's for the best. I'm only thinking of you.'

She looked up at him, tears were beginning to well

in her eyes and his expression changed to one of anxiety. 'Our names have been joined for generations,' she said, 'and besides, I'm only thinking of me, too. I don't want to marry someone who will take me away from everyone and everything I care about. I only know that I love you and want to be your wife. A miller's wife.' She let the tears fall. 'Are you telling me that I have been mistaken? That you don't love me after all?'

He groaned and took her in his arms once more. 'Love you? Of course I love you. I've always loved you, only I didn't know it until Mark told me I did!'

'Mark told you?'

He kissed her on each cheek and on her forehead, pushing aside the wisp of curls. 'He told me that I had always been sweet on you, and I realized then that I had.'

'So will you marry me, Tom?' She held up her face to his and tenderly he bent to kiss her lips. 'For better, for worse?'

'Yes,' he breathed. 'I give in. I'll marry you, Sammi.'

She felt a great surge of emotion pass between them as she put her arms around his neck and his tender kisses turned to passion.

'I've missed you, Sammi. I love you so much,' he whispered. 'I have wanted to tell you so often. I've wanted to shout it from the roof tops.'

'Then do!' She laughed with happiness. 'Go on. I dare you.'

He held her at arm's length. 'You think I dare not?'

She nodded. She was so happy she felt as if she could fly. 'You dare not,' she challenged.

He moved away from her and she held her breath as he bent his head and stepped outside the door onto the narrow ledge.

'Sammi!' he bellowed into the air. 'I love you!' and the breeze gathered his words and scattered them like seed.

As he stepped back inside, she held out her arms to him to hold him close. Then she looked down at the wooden ladder below her feet. 'Tom!' she said uneasily, clinging to him. 'How am I going to get down?'

51

'There's going to be a wedding! There's going to be a wedding!' Victoria skipped and danced when told of Sammi and Tom's declaration. 'And I'm to be a maid of honour.'

There was a flurry of excitement in the air as the two families prepared for the marriage, and Tom and Sammi walked in the sweet meadow grass and crushed the newly growing clover and dandelions beneath their feet and ran their fingers through the soft hairy stem of Yorkshire fog and the rolled leaves of marram grass which grew on the cliff top, as together they made their plans.

'A simple wedding, Tom,' Sammi said. 'It's too soon after Betsy's death for anything lavish.'

Tom demurred. 'Betsy wouldn't begrudge you a grand wedding on her account, if that's what you want, Sammi.' He had become forgiving of his sister as he had allowed his own passion and love for Sammi to flower.

She shook her head and smiled. 'But it isn't what I want. I want a country wedding; a May day with the sun shining, the scent of blossom and everyone to share our happiness.'

He took her into his arms and kissed her. The breeze blew her fiery hair into his face and he breathed in the sharp sea air and heard the call of gulls as they wheeled over the sands. 'Then that is what you shall have, my darling. I shall order it specially.'

*   *   *

And as Sammi awoke on that May day to the repeating refrain of the song thrush, and of Martha drawing back the curtains to reveal a sweeping blue sky dotted with chasing white clouds and the sun already climbing high, she knew that Tom had ordered well.

Martha placed a breakfast tray on the counterpane and snuffled. 'There you are, Miss Sammi. I wanted to bring it meself, seeing as it'll be 'last time I get 'chance.'

'Oh, Martha.' Sammi clutched the housekeeper's hand. 'It isn't as if I'm going away. You will see just as much of me as you do now.'

Martha shook her head and reached into her apron pocket for a handkerchief. 'It won't be 'same, Miss Sammi. You'll be mistress of your own house. Mrs Foster you'll be, after today.' She looked shrewdly at her young mistress. 'I allus thought it'd come to this. I knew Master Tom cared for you.'

'How?' Sammi smiled and sipped her tea. 'How could you know?'

'Never you mind, Miss Sammi,' she replied significantly. 'Sufficient to know that I did!'

Her mother and Victoria and two of the maids came to help her dress in her gown of pale cream silk, its heart-shaped neckline and leg o' mutton sleeves edged with lace. Beneath the gown, tiers of crisp petticoats gave the gown fullness, and rustled and whispered like young aspen leaves as she walked.

Her long red hair they coiled and dressed with a garland of myrtle and cream rosebuds, and caught with a short mist of a veil of Brussels lace which merely touched her forehead and fell about her shoulders. She carried a posy of honeysuckle, ladies mantle and roses, and around her throat she wore Tom's gift, a single strand of pearls.

Victoria and Anne, who were her attendants, wore gowns of deep gold satin with overskirts of soft cream silk, with pointed bodices and a ribboned band around the hem and neckline; short satin fichus

edged with lace sat around their shoulders and a
circlet of fresh flowers intertwined with pearls were
dressed in their hair.

Johnson waited outside Garston Hall in his new
outfit of green and black. He doffed his topper as
Sammi and her father, he dressed in a pale grey tailcoat and dark pin-striped trousers, appeared at the
door, and murmured approvingly as he helped her
into the carriage for their drive to the church at
Tillington.

The organ resounded and everyone stood as she
smilingly came down the aisle on her father's arm.
Everyone is here, she thought, *except for three: James and
Mark and Betsy*. She felt a lump in her throat as she
thought of Betsy and saw Luke standing alone with
baby Elizabeth in his arms. He hadn't wanted to come
to the wedding or reception, saying that he would
come to the dance which was being held later in the
day for the farm hands and villagers of Monkston and
Tillington.

But both Sammi and Tom had insisted. 'Please
come, Luke,' Sammi had pleaded. 'Come for Betsy's
sake if not your own; and bring her daughter, your
daughter, to see her uncle wed.'

Tom's relatives, his uncle, the miller from Beverley,
stood in a pew at the back with his wife and three of
his six children, the York Rayners, neighbouring
farmers, her mother's cousins from the Wolds, and
other guests, all crowded the pews. And Tom's father,
with Jenny in attendance, was given a special smile as
she passed him.

Adam was gurgling and chanting in Gilbert's arms
and she reached out to him as she passed, catching
hold of him by his chubby fingers.

Her brothers, Richard and Billy, handsome in tail-
coats of grey, with red waistcoats and grey striped
trousers, and attending as ushers, had greeted the
guests as they filed into church.

She raised her eyes towards the altar steps and saw

three figures standing there. Mr Collinson, the vicar, with a welcoming smile as he waited to greet her, and George as his brother's best man, nervously fingering his high white collar, his face wreathed in a bashful grin.

But her eyes were drawn to the third figure, who held out his hand towards her. Tom, tall and handsome in a dark blue frock coat with a velvet collar, doeskin trousers and a pale cream rose in his buttonhole; his dark hair brushed and gleaming curled on his collar, his mouth serious and tender, and with love in his eyes.

The tables in the dining-room were decorated with the first summer roses, cream and gold, to complement Sammi's gown and flowers; they were garlanded with ropes of sweet-smelling herbs and foliage, lime blossom, golden marjoram, white daisies and buttercups, and bound together with wild grasses.

The wedding breakfast of consommé, lemon sole, asparagus, hare roasted with mustard and thyme, with an array of vegetables, was consumed before glazed salmon stuffed with dill, honey and lemon, was brought on to the table, followed by duck and roast goose; and before the desserts of syllabub and burnt cream, apple and plum tart were brought in, a sorbet to freshen the palate was served.

The guests settled back, replete after the feast, to listen to the speeches. George spoke first, bashful in his unaccustomed finery of claret-coloured tailcoat, and blushing and stumbling over his first public speech as he thanked everyone for being there, and then sat down in relief as Sammi's father rose to give his loving praise of Sammi and her fine choice of a husband.

'The Fosters and the Rayners,' he began, 'have once again joined their hands in matrimony. My mother and father – Sammi's grandparents – who were also Tom's great aunt and uncle, were a Foster and a Rayner who defied convention by marrying one another, in the same church in Tillington as these young people did today. Their marriage was a long and happy one. They were forever united and,' he paused emotionally, 'I like to think that somewhere they still are.' He raised his glass. 'Let us drink a toast to two more pairs of hands, as strong and steadfast as those others, who have joined together today.'

They raised their glasses and as Sammi and Tom linked arms and drank from each other's glass, they gave the tribute. 'To the Fosters and the Rayners. May they always be united.'

As they sat down again and waited for Tom to reply, Gilbert rose to his feet. 'If I might intrude into the proceedings,' he said. 'I have a message from James which I would like to give. He tells us that he is very happy in Italy, but now that he is away from us all, he finds that he misses us and would welcome a visit if anyone could undertake the journey. The message is sent with special regard to Sammi, whom he describes as the best friend he ever had, and ends by saying that he hopes that Tom realizes what a lucky fellow he is.'

Tom smiled and kissed Sammi's cheek, which brought a round of applause from the assembled guests.

As the laughter died down, George rose to his feet again. He fished an envelope from out of his pocket. 'I have a letter too,' he said, 'it came a week or two back, and Da asked me to read it to you. It's from Mark.' There was a murmur from his attentive listeners and anxious eyes watched as he opened up the letter.

' "*Dear Da,*" ' he began, hesitatingly. ' "*I am about to begin a new life. After being so long away from home, I have at last come to realize that all I left behind was good and true, and was all that any man could wish for. However, Da, as you have always known, and which I have only just come to know, I am an obstinate, mule-headed sort* of fellow who never recognized a good thing when he saw it." ' George blinked his eyes and continued. ' "I do know now, as I wait here for my passage to Australia, and I can tell thee by letter what I could never tell in speech, how much I care for all of thee. For thee, Da, who will always be in my thoughts; for my brother Tom who should break down 'barriers and set out to capture 'girl we both know he loves." '

Tom held Sammi's hand as he listened.

' "For my cheery brother George, who finds such merriment in life. If I could only find half of his cheerfulness I would think me a lucky fellow. And for Betsy." ' There was a stunned silence as George paused, swallowing hard, knowing what Mark did not.

' "For Betsy, I ask for her forgiveness for my harsh words before I left, but tell her that I only uttered those words because I cared. God bless and keep thee all. I don't know if or when I will see any of thee again, but I will write when I am settled. Think of me sometimes and know always that I am thy everloving son. Mark Foster." '

George turned over the page. 'He put a postscript. He says, "I ought to tell thee that I'm not travelling alone, so don't fret on that account. I have a companion with me. She asks that we travel in friendship only and I respect her wishes, but one day I hope for more. Mark." '

Some of the guests who had a long way to travel departed after the wedding breakfast, and others rested or walked around the garden while the servants prepared for the jollifications which were to be held in one of the meadows. A marquee had been erected and a fire lit in a brick oven to cook sausages and pies, and two spits had been fixed over open fires to roast a pig and a side of beef, which were already crackling and spitting and sending mouthwatering smells floating across the fields, urging the villagers who were tramping along the lane between Tillington and Monkston to make haste.

Lamps were placed in readiness in strategic places;

at the gate to the meadow, around the square of mown grass where dancing would begin, and a low wooden staging was pronounced safe for the musicians; an accordionist, a fiddler, a drummer and a penny whistler.

'This will be the best of all,' Sammi said, as she and Tom walked arm in arm to see if all was in place.

'No, the best of all will be when we are alone, Mrs Foster,' Tom murmured in her ear. 'When I can tell you, and show you, how much I love you.'

'I know it already, Tom,' she whispered. 'And I love you too, so very much.'

He shook his head and smiled. 'No, you don't know, Sammi, and it will take a lifetime to tell.'

The meadow started to fill with crowds of laughing, merry people. Sammi and Tom stood by the gate and greeted everyone, inviting them to partake of the food and wine and the ale, which was stacked in barrels beside the trestle tables, which were groaning with meat and pastries, sweet cakes and trembling jellies.

'Who's this?' Tom looked across the meadow to the house, where a hired chaise was rolling into the drive.

They watched and then saw Doctor Sheppard descend and look about him.

'Stephen!' Billy hurried across the grass. 'You came after all!' Stephen Sheppard was greeted warmly by Billy who shook him by the hand. 'I'm so glad you could come. Your patients could be left after all?'

'My uncle took over for me.' The doctor beamed at Billy. 'He felt that it was most important that I come.'

'Important?' Billy said, puzzled. 'We wanted you to come, yes, after your kindness to Betsy; Sammi would have been disappointed if you hadn't come.'

Stephen nodded sombrely, then unable to conceal his information any longer gleefully said, 'I've seen Pearson! He's looking for you. He has news!'

'Yes? Tell me!'

'He wouldn't say. But he's setting up a meeting with the two benefactors, and he needs you there to finalize everything! That's what he told me to say. Billy, it means that everything is in place! Your children's home is about to become a reality!'

Billy gaped, unable to comprehend, that at last what he had set out to achieve was about to come to fruition. 'I'll travel back with you tonight! There's not a minute to lose. We must find a site. Find builders – and tell the children.'

'Oh, Billy!' Sammi and Tom had come up to welcome Stephen Sheppard and overheard. 'What wonderful news, and today of all days!'

He was filled with enthusiasm. 'I will be faithful to these children, Sammi. They will have food and clean water without begging for it, a warm bed at night. They will have training for a trade. I will see that they do! On my life, I will promise them!'

She put her arms around her brother and hugged him. 'How good you are, Billy. But you will give them more than those things. You will give them hope. You Knight of the Poor!'

He flushed at her praise. 'If this succeeds, Sammi, just think how much more can be achieved.' He glanced at Tom, not wanting to darken his wedding day. 'Perhaps a home for young women who are in trouble? A place for abandoned children.' He clenched his fists. 'So much to be done!'

Billy took Stephen to meet his parents and tell them the news, and to say that he would be leaving for Hull that evening in order to attend the meeting.

They chatted for a while and then Billy excused himself to go and tell Gilbert who had first arranged the introduction with Zachariah Pearson.

'Don't tire yourself, Victoria!' Ellen called to Victoria, who was running across the grass.

'Mrs Rayner. Forgive me for saying this.' Stephen Sheppard hesitated, and then continued, 'You may

534

think me impertinent, but Billy has told me how anxious you are over Victoria's health.'

'Yes,' she said. 'I worry constantly.'

'Then if I might make so bold, I suggest that you don't. Your anxieties, no matter how you try to hide them, will affect her.'

'But I don't tell her,' she began.

'There will be no need. She may well be sensitive and if so, she will know when you are anxious and that anxiety will be transferred to her. She has been ill, I know,' he said sympathetically, 'but I suggest that she tries to lead a normal life, meet other young people, so that she forgets about her illness. She is almost a young woman.' He turned to watch her. 'Could I offer the suggestion that you take her away somewhere warm for a few months? Perhaps to Italy. Take her in the autumn – give her a good start before winter.'

'Why, Doctor Sheppard, what a wise young man you are.' Ellen looked at him and, with a gleam in her eye, said, 'You wouldn't care to come and live in Holderness, would you?'

He laughed at her implication and said, 'I fear not. From what I gather, Holdernessians rarely need the services of a physician, but I am sorely needed in town.'

'You are right,' she agreed. 'On the whole, they are a hardy breed.'

Doctor Sheppard left her and she looked across to where Thomas was being made comfortable by Jenny amongst a crowd of other men, and who was then shooed away by him, followed closely like a gambolling puppy, by George. *I think perhaps I might bring Jenny to us*, she mused discerningly, *if Thomas will part with her; and I'll find an older housekeeper for Sammi.*

She lifted the hem of her figured blue silk gown from the ground, and walked across to where Mildred was sitting on a blanket- covered bench, with another blanket tucked around her. 'Whatever is wrong with Anne?' she asked. 'Are you not enjoying yourself, dear?'

Anne was kneeling on the grass with her head buried in her mother's lap. 'She says that everyone is getting married but her,' Mildred said resignedly.

'Oh?' Ellen waved to her husband who appeared to be looking for her. 'But I thought she had an understanding with a young man?'

'She had, unofficially, but he seems to have faded away since the business with the bank.'

'Then he's not worth crying over, my dear,' Ellen said cheerfully. 'Mildred! I've had an idea. How would you and Anne like to accompany Victoria and me to Italy in the autumn? We could visit Florence and you could see James.'

Anne sat up and wiped her eyes; Mildred gazed at Ellen in astonishment. 'Would you, would you like me to come?'

'Why not?' Ellen asked quietly. 'We used to be friends.'

'Planning without me?' William caught the conversation as he approached. 'Ellen! How could you?'

'Would you come?' she asked eagerly. 'After harvest?'

'To Italy!' Mildred breathed, and her face flushed with animation. 'I never thought – never ever thought!'

'Shall we then, Mildred?' Ellen sparkled with enthusiasm. 'It is a beautiful country, I believe. It would suit us very well!'

'Yes.' Mildred looked up and her warm smile encompassed them all. 'I think it would.'

George, Richard and Luke had carried Thomas in his chair across the meadow towards a group of other men who were in earnest conversation. 'Leave me now,' he said to Jenny who was hovering over him. 'Go off and enjoy thaself. George!' he commanded, 'Look after that wench. Make sure none of these

536

ne'er-do-wells bother her.' He nodded towards a group of village lads who were eyeing the retreating Jenny.

George grinned as he caught up with her. 'Da says I've got to look after thee. I'd better do as he says. He's scared tha'll go off back to Hull and leave him.'

'I'll not do that, Master George,' she declared. 'I like it out here.' She put her head up. 'What's that lovely smell?'

George put his nose in the air and sniffed. 'Roast pork and beef, and woodsmoke.'

'No. Behind that. Can't tha smell something sweet?' she asked fervently.

'Onny May blossom. Is that what tha means, Jenny?' He looked down at her eager young face, a rosy glow cast upon it by the fires.

'That's it!' she laughed. 'I'd forgotten 'name.'

'How old ist tha now, Jenny?' he asked in his slow manner.

'Fourteen,' she said. 'I've just had a birthday.'

'Tha's had a bothday and tha didn't tell us?'

She grinned cheekily. 'Why? Would tha have given me a present?'

'Aye.' He shuffled, embarrassed. 'I reckon I would have.' He stood for a moment, gently nodding his head, looking away from her and at the fires burning and the crowd milling around, as if they were of the utmost interest. 'Fourteen, eh?'

'Yes,' she said softly. 'So can tha wait for me, Master George?'

A flush touched his cheeks and he lowered his eyes, then he turned towards her and diffidently fingered the shawl around her shoulder. 'Aye,' he murmured. 'I'm in no hurry. I reckon I can.'

Victoria dashed across to where Richard was talking to Luke. 'I'm going to Italy,' she declared and then flew off again.

'As I was saying,' Richard thrust his hands into his trouser pockets, 'why don't you come and work for us? Our foreman is ready for retiring; he could ease off a bit if we had an extra pair of hands, and if things work out between us you could take over when he goes. It can't be easy for you working at the mill – not now.'

'No, it's not,' Luke said bluntly. 'It's not easy having my babby's granfer and uncle as employers. They don't know how to treat me and I don't know how to treat them.'

'Well then, if you worked for us, you could visit them as family, or almost,' Richard persuaded. 'You'd maybe have married Betsy if things hadn't gone so wrong?'

'Aye.' Luke warmed to this member of the Rayner clan. Richard Rayner was like Miss Sammi, or Mrs Foster as she now was, without frills or affectations. 'I would have stood by her. I was right fond on Betsy.'

'So you'll come then?' Richard was glad that he'd had the conversation with Tom earlier, when he'd confided his embarrassment over Luke; it would work out well for all of them. 'Shall I tell Tom? Or will you?'

'No, I'll tell him, and his da. It's onny right and fair. I like to do things right, and I'll work my notice out, they'll be short-handed otherwise, seeing as Master Tom, seeing as Tom will be away on honeymoon with his wife.'

Dusk was just starting to fall, and the musicians started to tune up into a merry jig, when the clop of hooves was heard and carriage lamps were seen swinging up the drive.

'More late arrivals!' William said cheerfully to Gilbert as they stood chatting. 'We shall have to open up another meadow to accommodate them all.'

'It's Hardwick!' Gilbert stiffened. 'Oh, God! Something must have happened.' William followed more slowly as Gilbert ran towards the carriage, where Hardwick, his features lit by the lamp, peered with his hand to his forehead as he tried to make out who was who in the gathering darkness.

'What's happened, Hardwick? Something's wrong?'

'No, sir. Nothing's wrong.' Hardwick's normally serious features were wreathed in a trembling smile. 'But I had to come and tell you myself. I knew that you'd want to know!'

'What? In God's name, man! Spit it out. What's happened?' Gilbert wanted to shake him.

Hardwick put his hand to his face to control himself. 'It's *Polar Star Two*, Gilbert – and *Arctic Star*. They're safe! Damaged, but safe! They're heading towards 'Humber and home.'

Gilbert sat down on the nearest bench, put his head in his hands and wept. *I don't deserve this*, he repeated again and again. *I don't deserve this reprieve*. Then he thought of the women who would be scurrying down to the Old Harbour to wait through the night hours to greet the ship and their menfolk, who, God willing, would be on board; and he gathered himself together to tell Harriet the news and tell her that he would return at once with Hardwick to Hull.

'I must be there,' he said. 'I must be there this time. I can't let them down again.'

'I shall come with you.' She grasped his hand. 'We'll both be there, and Adam too,' she added valiantly. 'We'll all three be there to greet the ships and the men as they come in to harbour.'

A rousing cheer went up as the news circulated, and the health of the returning Hull seamen was drunk by the countryfolk as the carriage pulled away in the darkness towards Hull.

'What a perfect ending to a wonderful day.' Sammi held Tom's hand. Soon they, too, would be changing into travelling clothes and leaving for their destination. They were to stay overnight in Bridlington and then the next day were going to drive wherever their fancy took them. They both wanted to go to Whitby, and to the North Yorkshire moors, where

539

they would walk or ride in the landau which Tom's father had bought for them.

'The old devil,' Tom had said when he'd told Sammi of his father's gift. 'He has a fortune tucked away and told nobody of it!'

'What a lovely day.' Ellen linked arms with William. They watched the guests milling in the meadow and in the garden of the house.

'Look.' He pointed to the moon which had risen above the sea, appearing from behind a cloud which it edged with silver. The cloud moved on, leaving the bright orb shining alone in the night sky, casting its light down on the glinting foaming ocean, touching the hedges of the paddock, and lighting the rose walk and gardens.

They watched in silence as the house was illuminated by its brilliance, the castellated turrets and towers lit like a romantic illustration from a fairy tale. They cast their eyes around the meadow and saw Sammi on Tom's arm, flitting wraith-like in her cream gown amongst their guests.

'It's as if we are looking at a memory,' William murmured. 'We have to catch it while we can.' He glanced up again at their well-loved home and saw the windows with the moon's reflection, like dark eyes gleaming as they surveyed the scene.

Ellen squeezed his arm. 'Don't feel sad,' she whispered. 'We have had some happy times here.'

'Yes,' he answered. 'But soon it will all be gone. The house, the land; we haven't so much longer.'

'But we shall have our memories,' she urged, 'and the children will have theirs.' She smiled. 'And we will have grandchildren too, who will perhaps remember. It won't be lost for ever; the memory will be passed on.'

The fiddler began to play; he closed his eyes and, with the bow poised, he began a waltz melody. There came from within the mellowed wood a haunting sound of crying gulls, the call of an owl and the soft sighing of the sea as it broke against the cliffs below them, the whoosh of a breeze filling a canvas sail, and those who were listening, really listening, didn't know if the sound was music from the supple plying of the fiddler's fingers, or from within their hearts.

'Come! Dance with thy lady, Master Miller!' Mrs Bishop beamed at them as she sat with a glass of ale in her hand and her brood of children playing around her, in the company of Mrs Reedbarrow who had two sleeping babies on her knee.

Tom took Sammi's hand and bowed low to her and she, in smiling reply, gave him a deep, old-fashioned curtsey. He led her to the square of grass and as everyone stood back and began to clap their hands, he held her in his arms and they began to dance.

THE END

ANNIE
Val Wood

Annie Swinburn is harbouring a terrible secret. She has killed a man. The man was evil in every possible way, but she knows that her only fate if she stays in the slums of Hull is a hanging.

And so she runs. As fast as she can, and as far as she can – up the river, along hidden paths of the Humber and into a new and unfamiliar territory where she can start a new life.

There she meets Toby Linton – a man born into a good life but now estranged from his family. He and his brother Matt earn a dangerous living as smugglers, but Annie soon realizes they have more in common than she thought. And this new way of life might just offer her the chance of love, in spite of all the tragedy that has gone before . . .

HIS BROTHER'S WIFE
Val Wood

When Harriet Miles is fired from her job at the hostelry while struggling to take care of her seriously ill mother, it seems things can't get worse.

The last thing she expects after her mother dies is a marriage proposal from a man she barely knows, but her only alternative is the workhouse.

But instead of marital bliss with Noah Tuke, Harriet finds herself in a cramped, angry household where she is met with bitterness and hostility – from all except Noah's brother, Fletcher.

Gradually she learns the true reasons behind Noah's desire to marry her – and realizes that the only person she finds real companionship with is the person she can't possibly be with…

THE INNKEEPER'S DAUGHTER
Val Wood

Holderness, 1846.

Life isn't turning out quite as hoped for thirteen-year-old Bella. She lives at the Woodman Inn – an ancient hostelry run by her family in the Yorkshire countryside – surrounded by her unreliable siblings. When Bella learns not only that her father is seriously ill, but that her mother is expecting a fifth child, her dreams of becoming a schoolteacher are quickly dashed.

Times are hard, and when their father dies Bella must also take on responsibility for her baby brother. Her days are brightened by the occasional visit from Jamie Lucan – the son of a wealthy landowner in a neighbouring coastal village. But then her mother announces that she wants to move the family to Hull, where the public house they are now committed to buying is run-down and dilapidated. Could things get any worse? Or could this move turn out to be a blessing in disguise for Bella?